The Assassin and Her Knight

Minstrel Knights
Book 3

Cara Hogarth

ARE YOU SIGNED UP FOR DRAGONBLADE'S BLOG?

You'll get the latest news and information on exclusive giveaways, exclusive excerpts, coming releases, sales, free books, cover reveals and more.

Check out our complete list of authors, too!

No spam, no junk. That's a promise!

Sign Up Here

www.dragonbladepublishing.com

Dearest Reader;

Thank you for your support of a small press. At Dragonblade Publishing, we strive to bring you the highest quality Historical Romance from some of the best authors in the business. Without your support, there is no 'us', so we sincerely hope you adore these stories and find some new favorite authors along the way.

Happy Reading!

CEO, Dragonblade Publishing

Additional Dragonblade books by Author Cara Hogarth

The Minstrel Knights Series
The Minstrel and Her Knight (Book 1)
The Rose and Her Knight (Book 2)
The Assassin and Her Knight (Book 3)

Historical Note

The Assassin and Her Knight is set during the Hundred Years' War (the name we now give to the span of 116 years the English spent trying to conquer France). In 1367, the war temporarily shifted into northern Spain when Castilian King Pedro "the Cruel" persuaded the English under Prince Edward to help defeat his usurping half-brother. Pedro promised the English great rewards, but even after the resounding English victory at Nájera, he never paid up. *The Assassin and Her Knight* opens in the aftermath of this battle.

The Hundred Years' War prompted innovations in medieval warfare, some of which appear in my story. For example, I was surprised to learn that gunpowder first came into general use in Europe in the 1300s. This was an era of experimentation, in which gunpowder could be unpredictable and positively hazardous to those using it.

Fighting forces too underwent changes. England had no standing national army; instead, units of fighting men were raised by individual lords and leaders. The feudal obligation to fight for forty days a year was insufficient for an overseas war, so soldiers were increasingly hired under contract. Some joined the notorious "free companies" that ravaged France, seizing castles, land, and booty in the 1350s and '60s. My fictional Company of the Ruin is a compact company of fighters contracted to Sir Garit and operating primarily in Southern France.

The history behind my heroine, too, warrants explanation. Zhila's family are Nestorian Christians from Persia (roughly modern-day Iran). In the 1300s, Christians were finding Persia increasingly difficult to live in, partly due to persecution by

Muslims. Thus Zhila's family flee to Europe, hoping for acceptance and safety among fellow Christians. They are disappointed.

Zhila herself is a minstrel who both dances and plays the *daf*. The *daf* is a traditional Persian percussion instrument, a bit like a tambourine. (You can see what it looks like on the book cover.) A skilled *daf* player can create very complex and intense rhythms, even inducing ecstatic trances.

Finally, a word on the word "assassin." The term came from medieval Persia and initially referred to a sect of Muslims who were notorious for murdering their political and religious adversaries. From this early meaning, the English word gradually took on its modern sense of a hired killer. Zhila Kurian is both kinds of assassin…and neither.

Chapter One

Northern Spain, 3rd April 1367

H E ROUNDED THE corner and found a damn woman on the street.

Sir Garit of the Ruin did not swear. Cursing would be a waste of nonexistent breath. His chest was still heaving from sprinting from the battlefield to these cramped stone streets. He did not even slow his strides. He had Spanish noblemen to seize and loot to locate. The rewards of war lay within his grasp, and his men were hungry for it. Droolingly ravenous, more like. They had slogged across mountains and Castilian plains for this. The English had just beaten the rebel army of a pretender king. Now, finally, they might gain a little hard-won compensation for all that sweat and blood.

And there was a damn woman in the middle of the street.

Oh, there were men as well—a couple of them, closing in on the woman like rabid curs scenting a kill. And two human forms, slumped like piles of discarded clothing on the cobbles.

Worse even than the woman, there was a child.

A girl about the same age as Marie.

God in heaven, what were they doing out here? Hadn't they noticed the flood of fleeing Spaniards inundating the town? Or perhaps they thought it was safe to wander the alleys of Nájera when a battle had just been lost on its doorstep?

The two before him looked nothing like his mother and sister. *They* had both been blonde, fair as angels. These two were dark—darker than Spaniards, for, even at a glance, they seemed quite distinctively un-Spanish. Still, the similarities in age and situation struck him.

Like a fist driven into his gut.

Women had no place in war. This needed fixing, immediately. Then Garit and company could get on with the program of capturing and looting.

All the same, Garit hesitated. The woman—probably younger than his mother had been, now he came to think of it—was not cowering before the closing men. Then, like sunlight glancing between clouds, a gleam of amazement lit his soul. The woman who did *not* remind him of his mother was preparing to fight. She held a short, wickedly curved dagger in each hand and had planted herself protectively before the young girl. Even as Garit watched, she flashed a backhanded blow at a lunging soldier. More surprisingly still, the dagger struck home, sinking into the fellow's neck just above his mail collar.

The blade sank practically its entire length into the man's flesh. The man went rigid. Then the woman raised her right leg and shoved the body backward off her blade.

No, she definitely did not remind Garit of his mother.

For one thing, his mother never wore long, loose leg coverings beneath her gown. Not that he had been in the habit of looking under his mother's dress, but he *had* explored beneath plenty of other women's gowns. These were strange undergarments indeed, but very practical garb for kicking dead men off one's dagger. It was almost as if she was prepared for such eventualities.

All the same, Garit had prisoners to capture. He couldn't stand here gawking at a strange woman on the street.

Nor, unfortunately, could he simply stride off and leave her. One woman with two tiny, if evil, daggers against the whole

English army? Oh, he knew where that would end, and he couldn't stomach it. Not again.

"Edmond," he snapped. "You grab the little girl. I'll take the woman."

His second-in-command cast him a glance. Edmond's visor was thrown up, so his expression was evident. Surprise writ large upon it, yes, but also a flash of anger, mixed with...lust.

Garit's stomach contracted, but he simply added, "Quickly. No time to waste."

A second man was approaching the woman, an English man-at-arms, curse him. This one was acting more warily. After all, the woman's dagger was slick with blood.

"Stand down!" Garit barked at him.

The fellow hesitated and glanced at Garit, doubtless making a quick assessment of his armor and insignia. Apparently it did not impress, for the fellow snarled, "I found 'em first. Get your own, knight."

"Aye," Edmond added. "Time for this later, Garit. We loot first."

It was true enough that the mass of English army would shortly swarm over Nájera. The Company of the Ruin had pelted here to be among the first on the scene—first come, first served, so far as captives and loot went.

"We do it quickly, then," retorted Garit, and strode toward the woman.

A pair of large, dark eyes blazed at him from a flushed olive face. She spat something at him in a foreign language. No dialect of northern Spain—he'd have recognized one of those. But it was likely just as well he didn't understand her, given the venom in her gaze. Doubtless it wasn't complimentary.

Then the damned stupid English man-at-arms stepped between them. The fellow turned on Garit and snarled, "Bugger off and find your own bit of skirt, you—"

Garit never discovered precisely how he was going to be slandered, for the man-at-arms ended his sentence on a half yelp, half gurgle.

Never turn your back on a dagger-wielding woman. Of course the dark-eyed creature had sunk her blood-slicked blade deep into the soldier's armpit. Garit had to admire her choice of target. No bouncing a blade off bone or armor for this woman. She knew where best to steal the lifeblood from a man.

The man stiffened and arched, his eyes bulging.

This time the woman had no opportunity to casually kick her victim off her blade. For, in the frozen moment in which her dagger stayed buried in human flesh, Garit took advantage. He stepped around behind her and clamped his arms about her torso.

And, dear God, was he grateful for his hideously expensive plate armor in the moments that followed.

The woman transformed into a writhing, stabbing fury. She couldn't maneuver or raise her arm properly because he held her tight against him—which was for the best, given her proven deftness of aim—but she was going to cause him a good few dents in his precious steel.

"Be still, woman," he growled. "I'm not going to hurt you."

She likely didn't understand English, because there was no cessation in her writhing. By God, it was like trying to restrain an eel fresh from the trap. His layers of steel and padded cloth did nothing to enhance his grip. Much more of this, and she might squirm out altogether, weaker sex though she was.

"I've got the girl." Edmond entered his field of vision, a field dominated by a thrashing woman. His second-in-command had one hand clapped over the young girl's mouth, the other around her waist. "So, do we fuck them here or take them inside?"

Garit nearly lost his grip on the eel.

"*No.*" One syllable, uttered in a tone to slice through plate armor. "We take them to a church. Now."

"Reckon that's sacrilege," muttered Edmond, but Garit did not deign to reply. He and Edmond would have words. But later. No time now.

Garit flung a look over his shoulder. "Follow me!" he ordered his men. "But keep an eye out for Spanish nobles."

Not that he needed to tell them that. Everyone knew that was where the money was: capture a nobleman and then beggar his family with an exorbitant ransom.

Garit glanced up and around, raking his surrounds for a bell tower or some other indication of a church. A landscape of reddish stone walls rose around him, dwarfed by the terracotta bluffs of Nájera. Oh, and a bell tower.

He began to move toward it, hauling the woman with him.

She froze for a moment—just long enough for Garit to hope she was finally going to stay still.

Then, "No!" the being in his arms shouted. "I slit your nether-purse and squeeze out the cods! I cut off your yard and shove it up your arse! Release me, you—"

It seemed she could speak English, after all. But apparently her own language offered her more scope for genital abuse.

Garit overrode the flow of foreign invective. "Be silent, woman. I'm taking you to a church."

"No! My mother! My father! I do not leave them—I die here!"

And she recommenced writhing with more ferocity than ever before. Garit set his teeth and held on.

"What do you mean, mother and father?" he gritted.

She nearly lunged out of his arms—in the direction of the huddles of cloth on the cobbles. "There!"

Oh hell. Time was slipping away. More English were entering Nájera by the moment, but Garit jerked his chin at one of his men.

"Walt, check the bodies. Do they live?"

The man pulled a face but crouched by the fallen forms. The woman stilled in Garit's arms. Watching Walt.

But Garit already knew. The flop of the limbs, the wide-open eyes. He didn't need Walt's silent shake to tell him.

The woman sagged. He almost lost her then. The sudden weight of despair almost had her trickling out of his grip to puddle on the street. Like her parents.

She no longer reminded Garit of his mother. She reminded him of him. A hollow, aching gulf cracked open inside.

Loss, guilt, emptiness.

Garit swore. He blasphemed between his teeth and felt the startled looks of him men upon him. Sir Garit of the Ruin was all implacable composure. He did not give vent to his emotions. He had no emotions.

And he had wasted enough time. He scooped up the damnable woman and stalked off in the direction of the church.

THE MAN STRODE into the dim interior of the church, and Zhila sagged like a cloth doll in his arms. *My parents. Maryam.* The horror washed over her like a flood tide, sapping all strength. She knew full well what would happen now. She had heard tales, her father had warned her. This was the usual aftermath of war. But in a church, of all places? It was a horror to cap all. An insult to God. But at least if she lived long enough afterward, perhaps a priest would give her absolution. Maryam too.

No, not Maryam! This must not happen.

A final dose of desperate energy shot through her limbs, and Zhila twisted. She still had one dagger. True, it was immobilized against her side. The arrogant ogre who'd seized her obviously assumed she could not possibly do him any damage with it, but she'd prove him wrong yet.

But his arms were made of iron. They held her in a pitiless grasp. All the writhing in the world would not move them. Which left her with only one option.

"Let my sister go!" she cried. "Do what you want to me. Me only, not her!"

The plea had the opposite effect. The arms about her turned to stone.

Then her captor spoke.

"Edmond, drop the girl."

Hope flamed in Zhila's chest. It was a tiny flame, battered by a fierce draft. She stared at the creature who held her sister, willing the fiend to obey. Promising him a fate worse than hellfire if he did not.

But whatever was meant by "drop the girl," Edmond did not seem inclined to do it. His eyes were narrowed upon Zhila's captor. He wore a strange expression. His arms still held Maryam.

And her sister was looking at her, dark eyes huge, pleading with Zhila to do something. Anything.

For some reason, her captor had ordered the remaining soldiers to stay outside. Perhaps he wanted his privacy for what was to follow.

"Drop her, Edmond," her captor repeated, his voice hard and even. "We leave now."

Edmond did not release his prey. "What do you mean, *leave?*" he growled. "We drag them all this way, wasting our time when we could be looting, and you say just leave?"

"Yes, you know the rules."

"Rules be damned." But then the fellow's voice turned oddly cajoling. "Aye, you hold to your rules like a true and noble knight, Sir Garit, and I honor you for it. But the rules don't apply right now, do they? Look at them—a couple of Saracens, heathens, whatever they are. They warrant no knightly protection. You and I, Garit. Won't take but a few moments. By God, we deserve it. Got our blood up from the battle, and I've never yet seen you—"

"I am ashamed to call you kin."

The words were uttered with no evident emotion, but the man who held Maryam rocked back as if he'd been slapped.

"It's what a man does," he managed. "They're just heathen scum. They've got nothing else worth looting. So take your reward, Garit."

"*Drop her and get out of my sight.*"

Edmond stared. His gaze flicked between Zhila and the man

who held her. There was something vulnerable in his expression.

Vulnerable? By the Holy Mother, she would turn him more vulnerable than a tadpole if he didn't release Maryam immediately. Just as soon as she got free of these arms of iron.

But Edmond hadn't given up yet. "You want 'em all to yourself, eh? Fine, then. Just let me watch."

The grip on Zhila tightened. She gasped. The grip loosened somewhat.

"Let the girl go, Edmond. I am about to release her companion. You may have noted she holds a dagger. Believe me, you will want your hands free."

Had she misunderstood? Zhila thought she comprehended the barbaric English tongue well enough, but there were strange undercurrents at play here.

"Devil dight you, Ruin. You want her, I can see. Be a man and take her."

Zhila was released so abruptly her legs buckled. An instant later, she had transferred her one remaining dagger to her right hand and was stalking toward the filth named Edmond.

Said filth bared his teeth and flung Maryam from him. He fumbled at his belt.

Zhila sprang. She grabbed her little sister and pulled her against her, further into the church. She crouched, one hand about Maryam's waist, the other holding the dagger. Not daring to hope. Ready to sink her blade into the first man who approached, however much iron he was wearing.

The man who had seized her looked straight at her. He still wore his helm, but its visor was thrown back. In the dim of the church, it was hard to make out much of his face, but what she could see sent a chill down her spine. Eyes like winter, blue and cold, fixed their implacable gaze on her.

"You will stay here, woman. Claim sanctuary. Do not leave and you should be safe."

Then he turned his back and flung the door open, and in poured his men. Englishmen, all wearing the tabard of a black, half-ruined tower. Soldiers fresh from battle, doubtless hungry for loot…or worse.

"Search the building for Spanish nobles. Quickly."

So much for sanctuary.

Zhila backed against a wall, still holding Maryam. Her little sister was trembling like a storm-tossed leaf. Now Zhila's eyes had adjusted to the muted light in the church, she could see other people too. Townsfolk, priests, disheveled Spanish soldiers trying to sink into the shadows.

The English soldiers shoved through the crowd. Searching. Apparently not finding. Doors were flung open, a few people were hauled out, but no one was made captive. And despite the shoving and evident weaponry, no blood was shed.

On the other hand, all the silverware promptly disappeared from altars into English sacks. Evidently, church property was not sacrosanct to these invaders. Just how much could she trust to her own safety here?

At long last, with one more icy look at her, the English knight left. Taking his men with him.

ZHILA SANK TO the floor, taking Maryam with her. Her legs could no longer hold her up. She wrapped both arms about her sister and held her tight, absorbing Maryam's trembling, not sure where her sister's ended and her own began.

Footsteps. A shadow fell over them. Zhila glanced up to see a priest looming over her.

"You are not welcome here." Spoken in deep Spanish.

She had expected this. It was why they'd been caught on the street in the first place. The Kurians had been thrown out of their cellar refuge by the first fugitives from the battlefield. They'd tried to enter a church after that, but the door had been slammed in their heathenish faces. No other doors would even open to her father's frantic knocking.

Then the first English soldiers had arrived, naked blades in hand.

They had seen her father was armed, ready to defend his womenfolk, and that was all the excuse they had needed.

She closed her eyes.

"Get out," the priest said.

She shook her head. She was not moving. She and Maryam would stay here in this unwelcoming sanctuary unless they were tossed out bodily.

Or those English soldiers came back for them.

She shuddered. Ugh, maybe the man who'd grabbed her would return after he'd finished his looting and murdering. Those hard blue eyes had not shown any compassion. He'd probably just stowed her here for later, when he had more time at his disposal. She was sure the man Edmond intended something of the sort. His final glance had been plain to read. It spoke of unfinished business.

A foot prodded her, none too gently. "Leave, woman. I will not have heathens in my church."

Zhila released Maryam just enough to dip a hand into her bodice and draw out an object.

The priest squinted, obviously not believing the evidence of his eyes. Zhila held out a small wooden cross. It was attached to a leather thong about her neck.

Her father had carved it. Was this all she had left of him now?

"I am a Christian and I claim sanctuary." Her own voice sounded foreign in her ears—choked, speaking halting Spanish.

The man snorted, but he withdrew his foot and retreated from her contaminating presence. For now.

Zhila was left huddled to Maryam, weak-limbed and wobbly, wondering what the future could possibly hold for them with her parents lifeless refuse on a foreign street. Questioning how safe they really were inside this church.

And considering the intentions of a man with icy eyes.

Chapter Two

GARIT STRODE OUT of the church and surveyed his surrounds. Where to now? Where would a Spanish nobleman secrete his quivering hide? The urge was strong on him simply to charge through Nájera, flinging open doors. But there were more English soldiers in the street now. Every last one of them would be pursuing the same goal, and there were definitely not enough Spanish dons to go around. He had to be clever about this.

"What in hell are you waiting for?" came a voice from behind him. "You dally around with a couple of filthy heathens when we could be looting, *and* you do nothing with them, I note—now here you are, dithering on the steps."

Garit swung around. Sir Edmond Ingram stepped back. The man was the only other knight in the Company of the Ruin, not to mention his distant kin, thus by right of rank his second-in-command. But now…

"You knew my rules when you entered the company. No molesting women."

Edmond's eyes narrowed. "Devil take your rules. You're a damned hypocrite. I saw how you looked at her. You wanted her. I reckon you'll come back and help yourself later without me."

Garit stood statue-still. Yes, now she was out of his sight, he could admit the woman had appealed to him. There was something wild and elemental about her, as if she would defy all rules. And the way she writhed against him…

He would never see her again. She was a brief interlude in his savage war. She was an ounce of atonement in the midst of death.

"No, I will not. And nor will you. Be silent, Edmond. I am thinking."

"Thinking be damned! You're wasting time and losing us loot. I joined your company because you've a reputation. You're the Ruin, curse you! I didn't join you to beggar myself being nice to little girls. This is war. They are heathens. All they're good for is—"

"No," Garit said, flat and hard. "The Company of the Ruin is an effective fighting machine because it is bound by rules. But ever since I took you into the company, you have contested them. No more. You do not like my rules, so leave. Now."

Garit reached out and grabbed Edmond's tabard, the sleeveless tunic emblazoned with a black tower. He jerked his fists apart and the fabric tore. A ruin divided.

Edmond did not resist. Nor did he speak until Sir Garit of the Ruin had yanked the tabard from his shoulders and cast it on the ground.

"You cannot do this," he said, voice hollow. "I am your kin. We signed a contract. You owe me a portion of the loot. You cannot simply say go."

"I can," Garit said calmly. There was something distinctly un-calm at his core, but he sealed it away. "The contract shall be treated in the same manner as your tabard. Your words and actions have rendered it void. Go, before I forget we share the same blood."

Edmond stared at him. Something about his expression reminded Garit of a kicked hound. Almost wounded.

Wounded, a knight who had just proposed the hideous abuse of two women?

"Burn the contract," Edmond snarled. "And shove your company up your impotent arse. Think all you like, Ruin. I'm going to act. And when I catch myself a brace of Spaniards, I'll share the spoils with no man."

With that, Sir Edmond Ingram turned on his heel and vanished into the hordes filling Nájera.

Garit breathed out. At least now he could think.

And, as if Edmond's absence was all it took, an idea elbowed its way into his head. *Ah.*

"Grab me a local," Garit ordered his nearest man. "I need inside information on Nájera."

ZHILA HUDDLED ON the church floor, her arms about Maryam. Her shaking had subsided, thank goodness, and now she simply felt weak and drained. Helpless.

And she didn't like it.

Yet more Englishmen had barged into the church. Like the first, they had shoved through the people, searching. Not finding. Some of the English had got frustrated with the lack of loot and nobles. The priests were still muttering prayers over stone slabs freshly cleansed of blood. A church defiled.

But no one had touched Zhila and Maryam. Yet. That was probably because the invaders were intent on enriching themselves while they could. The sisters were evidently destitute. Everything they had had was spilled on the street, along with their parents' blood.

Something stirred inside her at that. Zhila welcomed it. A spark of an idea. Anything was better than feeling weak and helpless—and utterly bereft.

Her family had been thrown onto the street with all their meager belongings. They were travelers, so they had little enough. But Zhila had discarded her bags in favor of daggers when the first soldiers approached. Just as well. But she'd lost one of those daggers when that English lump had grabbed her. And then she'd been dragged from her parents and all that they owned.

Zhila drew Maryam close. She dropped a kiss on the girl's midnight hair. Her little sister. All she had left.

Maryam shifted. "Are they dead, Zhila?"

Zhila squeezed her eyes shut. They were the first words Maryam had spoken since they'd entered the church. What was she to reply?

There was only the raw truth.

She bent her head and whispered in Persian, "Yes, sweet one. They are with God."

Maryam whimpered and burrowed her head into Zhila's shoulder. Zhila could do nothing but stroke the disordered curls...and wonder.

Were they with God? Death had descended without warning. A few swift sword strokes. Her parents were unshriven. No one had even said a prayer over them. They lay on the street like discarded rags while she, Zhila, cowered in the corner of a church.

Zhila leaned her head back against the stony wall and gazed up at the painted ceiling. In the low light, the images seemed almost real—demons and angels, souls in torment, saints being martyred in horrendous and inventive ways. Wild, intense scenes, in which none of the participants were cowering. No, they were living—or dying—to the very fullest. Those saints knew what they were in for when they refused to conform. They embraced the pain.

The ceiling told her that death was inevitable—it was how you *lived* that mattered.

And Zhila could sit still no longer.

"Pull out your cross," she told Maryam. "Wear it on the outside of your dress. Come, we will talk to these people and see if they can spare you anything to eat."

Food. That did it. It was midafternoon now, and they'd had nothing to eat since dawn. Maryam got to her feet, wormed her hand into Zhila's, and followed her sister to the nearest group of women.

Zhila steeled herself. She was doing this for Maryam. Her family had been in Spain for years now. Her father, Kurian, had reasoned that the mishmash of races in this part of Europe would mean his family was more easily accepted. The Spanish didn't agree. Somehow, despite black hair and olive skin not dissimilar to many Spaniards, the Kurians were always identified as different. Foreigners. Worse—heathens. Hence her father had whittled them conspicuous wooden crosses. He'd done a beautiful job, too, but to no avail. Cross or no cross, the Kurians continued to be treated with suspicion verging on hostility.

It didn't help that they were also wandering performers. Oh, the Spanish liked their music and dance well enough, but that did not mean they were nice to the people who so entertained them. After all, everyone knew itinerant musicians had no morals. They had even fewer if they were foreign.

But Maryam was pretty. She chose to wear Spanish clothing, unlike Zhila. In such garb, and with her black curls and big, dark eyes, she might pass for a little Spaniard, at least in the dim of the church. Zhila hoped.

"Go talk to them," she whispered to Maryam. "They'll like you better than me. They look like nice ladies. Go on."

Her sister was a true Kurian. She had been raised to charm an audience. Maryam hesitated only a moment, and then she pattered to the huddle of ladies and began distributing sweet smiles and innocent questions until the black-clad *doñas* softened like butter in the sun.

Zhila hung back, watching with a flicker of pride as Maryam charmed a woman out of a portion of *jamón* and bread. Doubtless these women were terrified. They likely didn't know what had become of their menfolk or whether they themselves would survive the day. But in such a situation, Maryam offered a welcome distraction. She was a pretty little thing to pet and comfort—and in so doing, the women would feel comforted as well.

They would keep Maryam safe, as far as they were able. Maryam was in a church. She wore a cross. It was all the protection Zhila could provide for the moment.

For she had other things to do.

Zhila approached and spoke a few words to one of the older women. She begged a favor, and, strangely enough, she got it.

She did not speak to Maryam. Her sister would only cling to her, terrified she was about to lose the only remaining member of her family, but Zhila had to do this. Carefully, she edged away from the group.

Moments later, Zhila Kurian slipped out of the church and entered hell.

THANK CHRIST FOR kindly old Spanish women. Zhila only had to traverse two streets, but she doubted she would have made it two steps if it wasn't for the dull black shawl she'd wrapped around her head and torso, courtesy of an aged *doña*. She complemented the outfit with a bent back and a hobbling gait, and prayed no battle-maddened soldier's tastes ran to old widows.

The streets were seething with the English prince's men now. Practically every door she hobbled past was smashed open. Screams echoed from some of those gaping holes. Feminine screams. Zhila gripped her dagger beneath the shawl. Not that one little curved knife would protect her for long.

But her caution evaporated when she reached her parents.

They were still lying there, sprawled upon the stained cobbles of Nájera. Zhila ceased to hobble. She ran to them. She threw herself down beside her mother and tenderly turned her over.

No!

Staring eyes, a frozen mouth.

She scrabbled for her father. He was harder to roll onto his back. Kurian had been a strong man, solidly built.

Had been, but no longer.

One glance at his face, and Zhila raised her face to the uncaring sky and keened. No words could express this feeling—only a screeching, unearthly sound would do. So she knelt between her parents, one hand on each of them, and gave herself up to inhuman wails.

It wasn't exactly a sensible choice for passing unnoticed, yet it worked. No soldiers approached her. They gave the keening, black-clad figure as wide a berth as if she were covered in plague pustules.

She didn't know how long she knelt there. Her throat grew scratchy and the sky darkened. Eventually Zhila ceased, panting, emptied, and simply gazed at her parents. No more. Gently, she ran her fingers over her mother's eyelids, closing them forever, then lay a lingering kiss on her cold forehead. The same for her father.

Then she raked her memory for a prayer.

It had been so long since they left their homeland. Zhila had only been a little girl. Maryam hadn't even been born. Zhila knew there must be proper prayers in the rites of their church to speak over the dead, to ease their path to heaven, but she had no idea what they might be. They had left in part because the Nestorian church was crumbling in Persia. It certainly didn't exist here in Spain. And now her strongest links to Persia were gone and she had no idea how to farewell them properly.

All she could do was presume to speak to God directly, and explain the matter to Him. A most improper prayer.

By the time she finished, the street was growing dark. She gazed at her mother and father, eyes desert-dry. She had no more tears left to shed. Did they look a little more peaceful now, or was that only the effect of the closed lids? But she could do no more tonight. She slipped their crosses out from under their clothes and laid them in plain sight. She would go back to the church and speak to the curmudgeonly priest about burial.

The church. Maryam.

She had been here too long.

Zhila scrambled up. She tugged her shawl about her and cast a wary glance about the street. There were fewer English ruffians about now, thank heaven. They had likely exhausted themselves with all that killing and looting and now were seeking a well-earned bed for the night. All the same, she had no intention of warming any of those beds.

Her family's belongings were still here, oddly enough. Probably no one had ransacked them because they were already strewn all over the street. She crouched over her own bag. She shoved things back in, leaving everything that was not vital. Her *daf*, for example, that was vital. The instrument was part of her Persian past and, she was determined, her future. Then she dug into the other bags. Maryam would need clothes. Finally, there were her parents themselves—the leather pouch of coins at her father's belt, her mother's jewelry. She hesitated over Kurian's sword. The sword that hadn't saved him.

No, she preferred her daggers.

That reminded her. Zhila glanced around.

Her parents weren't the only bodies that littered the street. Zhila felt a most un-Christian flare of pride. *She* had avenged them, in part. The two soldiers who had presumed she was a helpless female thing ripe for the plucking also decorated the cobbles. One of the bastards still sported her dagger.

She kicked the man over.

Perhaps she should have kicked him more circumspectly, in part because the force of it sent a spike of pain through her toe. But more so because, of all the things she had done this evening, kicking a dead Englishman seemed to attract attention.

Two men stopped in the street.

Zhila bent, seized the dagger handle, and pulled. It did not budge.

The men were striding toward her.

She pulled harder. No wonder she'd had to abandon it earlier. The thing seemed attached as firmly as an extra limb in the man's torso.

She wiggled it. The footsteps drew nearer.

"What are you doing, woman?" Spoken in English.

The blade came free. Its curved tip had evidently tangled with some part of the man's innards. It came out an evil, dark red.

Zhila sprang up, dagger out, and snarled back in the man's own uncouth language, "I kill this bastard, now I kill you."

Two pairs of eyebrows rose. The second man tweaked his fellow's arm. "Locals are friendly, eh? Come on, Dick, don't reckon you'll get any joy out of that one tonight. Leave her to it."

"We won. We can do what we damn well please."

"Aye, and get ourselves knifed in the process. I've fought enough battles for one day. I'm for food and bed." At which the second Englishman turned and stumped off down the street.

Leaving Dick glowering at Zhila, eyeing her bloody dagger.

Slowly, she drew the second dagger from her belt. This one had been cleaned. Perhaps it was time to dirty it again.

Dick's eyes flicked over her, assessing. Zhila took a step forward. Suddenly she wanted to thrust this blade into the ugly fellow's throat. She wanted to dance in his blood. He and his kind had torn her world apart. Worse, he was keeping her from hurrying back to Maryam.

Perhaps brave Dick read the bloodlust in her eyes, for he took a miniscule step back and summoned up a fine look of disdain.

"Evil hag. I wouldn't dirty my hands on you."

After which he backed away carefully, and then strode down the street after his friend.

Zhila lowered her daggers, her heart thumping a battle tattoo in her ears. She was almost disappointed.

Almost.

No, she had tarried here far too long. She had done what she could for her dead, but now she had to think of the living. With one more silent farewell to her parents, she grabbed her bag, pulled her old-woman scarf close, and hobble-hurried back to the church.

And Maryam.

Chapter Three

THERE WAS SOMETHING different about the church. Zhila felt it as soon as she burst in the door. But whatever it was didn't matter. She was only here for Maryam.

She paused to sign the cross—in the western fashion rather than the eastern, so as not to completely alienate the locals present. Then she stripped off her borrowed shawl, all the time scanning the interior for Maryam.

She found her.

And Zhila went cold.

Her sister was not alone, but it wasn't a group of Spanish women who so thoughtfully kept Maryam company. It was a man.

Worse, she recognized that man. He was looking straight at her. The recognition was mutual.

In part, she remembered him because of his unusual coloring. Unusual to her, anyway. He'd been wearing a helm the last time she saw him, but his eyebrows and facial hair had been evident, and they were the color of rust. The skin around them had peeled in patches, doubtless burnt by the Spanish sun. It made the fellow look leprous.

Now he had discarded his helm, she saw that his hair was also strangely rusty. Foxlike. And this blotchy English soldier was holding her sister.

He was smiling at Zhila.

Zhila let her bag slither to the floor. She slipped both daggers from their sheaths, one in each fist. She heard an outraged splutter from a nearby priest, but ignored him. Now was not the moment to consider the sanctity of holy ground. Blood *would* be spilt.

She stalked toward the man who leaned so casually against a pillar, the crook of his arm about Maryam's throat. She saw now that her sister was gagged, and her hands tied.

"Let her go, and maybe I not kill you," Zhila informed the man from between her teeth. Edmond, she remembered this scum had been called—the man who'd grabbed Maryam earlier that afternoon. Couldn't keep his filthy hands off her, evidently.

"Well, who'd have thought it," the man replied. "The slut speaks English. If badly."

Zhila was tempted to demand how well the turd knew Persian, but that was not the point.

She flicked a look around the dim church. Ugh, the fellow had friends—a handful of scruffy-looking, tabard-less soldiers—but the Englishman who had grabbed her earlier was not among them. *He* had not been scruffy, and he'd worn the tabard of a ruined tower. But he had been frightening—Zhila could admit it now. Something about that implacable chill.

"Where is your master?" she snapped.

It was foolish, perhaps, but the Englishman with icy eyes had inspired a faint flicker of confidence. He had ordered Edmond to leave them in the safety of the church.

An illusion. Edmond had returned.

All the same, it seemed she had hit a nerve. The rusty fellow straightened abruptly, and his pale-lashed eyes flared.

"Sir Edmond Ingram has no master. But know that you look upon *your* master, heathen whore. Drop your weapons unless you want your sister gutted before your eyes. You will come with me, and willingly."

Zhila did not drop her weapons. She gripped them tighter.

Perhaps the icy knight was off looting and killing elsewhere. Perhaps he'd delegated this rusted man to seize her and drag her before him. His evening's entertainment.

Despair washed over her. And guilt. She should never have left Maryam alone. Prayers for her dead parents should never have taken precedence over her live sister.

"Let her go. What do you want—money? I give. Just let her go. And me? You not want a *heathen slut*."

"Oh yes, I want money. But I want a sight more than that. Cease your gab, woman. Drop your silly knives or I try a bit of bloodletting on this little thing." The knight ran his dagger tip down the column of Maryam's neck. No blood was drawn, but Maryam's eyes widened. And Zhila's heart lurched.

Edmond glanced at his men. "Barto, David, take her."

Zhila flashed her blades into position, one high, one low, and narrowed her eyes at her targets. Barto and David hesitated.

Her parents were gone, her sister was captured, Nájera seethed with hostile men. Zhila knew what would happen.

"I think we die anyway. Better now," she said, looking into Maryam's eyes. Begging her to understand.

"Goddamned heathen! Listen, I'll not touch you, nor your sister. I won't let anyone dirty his cock in you just so long as you cooperate. You have my oath. Now drop your cursed blades or I get inventive with mine."

Zhila could not think straight. The man's dagger caressed Maryam's cheek now. One twitch, and her sister would be scarred for life—or worse.

"You do not hurt Maryam? Oath of a knight? You swear?"

Sir Edmond Ingram shrugged. "I swear I will not permit her to be molested in any way. So long as you do as I say."

He stroked the flat of his blade over Maryam's wayward hair. The tip tangled with a curl. A tiny flick, and a dark lock skittered to the floor.

Edmond smiled at the blade. "Sharp, eh?" Then he looked at Zhila. "Well, woman? I grow impatient."

These knights tended to take their oaths seriously, she knew. Most of them. But an oath to a supposed heathen—would he feel obliged to keep that?

She tapped the wooden cross on her chest with her dagger tip. "I am Christian. Swear your oath on this. No harm to my sister—you *swear?*"

With his free hand, her sister's captor made a cursory sign of the cross.

"Yes, yes. I swear. Now—"

Zhila gave him no more chance to order her about. She thrust her daggers back into her belt and grabbed her bag.

Then she glared at Sir Edmond.

"Take me. I cut out your eyes if you lie."

GARIT WAS EXHAUSTED. Nevertheless, there was one more thing he must do before he barricaded himself into a chamber and sank into sleep.

Torch in hand, he descended the narrow, debris-strewn streets from the Jewry to the lower town. Half a dozen of his men followed behind. Darkness had fallen over Nájera, and it wasn't only an absence of light. Looting was still going on, and some dedicated drinking too. There were memories of battle to drown in Spanish wine. Englishmen were celebrating having made it through the day. Garit would take no further risk in the madness.

This journey in the dark was risk enough, but it was one he must take if he was to sleep. He was as tired as a decades-old dog, but that was no warrant against memory-stalked dreams.

He paced toward the church on unsteady legs. He hadn't drunk anything to speak of yet, but his head whirled as if he were already half under the table. It was the result of an overly full and fruitful day. His men had been awake in the predawn, preparing for battle—bundles of nervous energy, each needing to piss a half-dozen times, check their weapons even more, mutter a quick confession to a priest in case they died in the fray. And Garit had moved among them, a steady rock in the torrent, unflappable and unfearing for their sakes. And perhaps for his own. What good was fear? He had seen the worst already.

Then there had been the clash against the Spanish. Enrique of Trastámara's rebel mob. No time for fear then, only action. Garit had held his men together with an iron hand, as ever. They were the Company of the Ruin, small as companies went but renowned for cohesion and swift, strategic action.

That strategy had sent them flying toward Nájera as soon as the battle was won, practically on the heels of the fleeing Spanish. But Garit wasn't bent on scything down Spaniards and making the Najerilla flow red. They could all scuttle back to their families so far as he was concerned. He did not hate the Spanish, only the fiendish French. No, Garit and company were focused upon ransom and booty. The spoils of war, hard-earned. And when one considered it, ransom really was the best outcome for all concerned—the ransomed nobleman lived, and the ransomer was recompensed for his mercy.

Assuming the nobleman paid up, which, sadly, was not always the case.

But today, fortune—and a spot of strategy—had been good to them, despite the delay over a couple of girls. A quick interview with a local had revealed the existence of a second, walled-off part of Nájera. It was the old Jewish quarter on the slopes above the town, deserted because Enrique of Trastámara had killed most of the Jews some years back. Where better for a canny nobleman to secrete himself? After all, it was a place the invading English were unlikely to be aware of.

And a spot of digging in the Jewry had turned up gold—of the noble, non-Jewish persuasion. The Company of the Ruin had bagged itself a trio of Spanish dons. A windfall beyond all expectations.

Yes, it had been a good day. None of his men had died, and

there would be rich ransoms to share between them—of which the largest share would naturally go to Garit.

As an added benefit, Edmond bloody Ingram had revealed himself to be a carrion-eating worm who must be evicted from the company. The man was a trained knight and knew his stuff, but he'd been a burr in Garit's hose from the start, casting him strange glances and questioning his rules. The man thought himself a law apart from the company, definitely a class above, and Garit required cohesion amongst his warriors above all. Men would die if they did not act together. The company would fall apart.

No, Garit would not miss Sir Edmond Ingram.

He mounted the steps of the church. The door was still in one piece. In a town full of shattered entranceways, that was a good sign. Garit's misgivings were all for naught. What conscience was left to him could rest easy.

He nudged the heavy wooden door. It creaked open. There was light inside, but not much. He stepped inside, cautiously. Every sense was jittery, over-strained. He half expected some maddened Spaniard to throw themselves at him.

He wouldn't blame them.

He stepped further inside and held up his torch. He heard the steps of his men behind him. The door closed.

The infernal light of the flame bathed an array of faces, some coifed, some still helmeted, all wary. Spanish faces without exception.

He couldn't see her, or the little girl who reminded him against all probability of Marie.

"Where is she?" he demanded in a rough approximation of Spanish.

Uncomprehending expressions. What, had he mixed his words and asked for the location of the nearest donkey?

"She?" echoed a priest. "What woman do you seek, sir?"

Ah, not a donkey.

"A woman and a girl. Not Spanish. Not English. They were

here earlier." A breath. "I brought them here."

The priest was giving him a level stare. It didn't look in the least Christian and forgiving.

"I do not keep your *puta* here."

"She is not a *puta*." Well, maybe she was, but she certainly wasn't his. More to the point, Garit wasn't in the mood to argue semantics with a priest. "Where is she?"

He looked around more generally. Violence didn't appear to have been committed in here—he saw no prone bodies, no dark smears soaking into the stone, no smashed church furniture. At least, not much. So where were they?

Perhaps the locals were hiding them. Perhaps they thought he was back for nefarious purposes. Not an unreasonable assumption, given the circumstances.

But would they have had the time to stow them away? He'd only just entered the church.

Garit took a slow step toward the huddled people. His gaze raked over each and every face.

"Where—is—she?"

He got an answer. In fact, he got a lot more answer than he was equipped to receive. It burst from one of the coifed faces before him.

"You know full well, English murderer! Your man took her. He snatched that sweet little girl from my arms and put a knife to her throat. He gagged and bound her, then he waited for the older one. You are filth, all of you—filth and murderers! Heaven will curse you. Devils will feast on your innards. This is holy ground!"

Well, he *thought* that was what the old woman said. Garit's Spanish really wasn't up to such a deluge, delivered in tones verging on a screech.

"My man took them? Is that what you said? What man?"

"The one with Judas coloring. Flame-red hair, curse him. He threatened me with a knife—in a church!"

Garit's brain scrambled for purchase. It took some deciphering, not to mention the filtering of Spanish predictions for his afterlife, but he got to the bottom of the matter eventually.

Edmond had returned to the church. He had seized the little girl while her sister was absent, then grabbed the sister when she reappeared, although apparently the latter took some doing. Garit wasn't surprised. The memory of grabbing her himself was still written into his arms and somewhat-dented armor. Then both girls and knight had gone, the old woman knew not where.

Garit closed his eyes and leaned against a pillar. *Think, damn it.*

His head roiled. Past and present were blurring. It was only because he was tired. The little girl was nothing like Marie. The woman was her sister, for God's sake, not her mother. Not *his* mother. He owed them nothing. They were just another couple of unfortunate casualties of war. This sort of thing happened all the time. Women and war should never mix. It was her fault for being here, whoever she was.

But why Edmond? His kinsman didn't have much of an appetite for skirt, as Garit recalled, but battle wrought strange effects on men. Yet in a town filled with vulnerable women, Edmond had come back for these two. Why?

The answer was obvious.

It was his fault. He, Garit of the Ruin, had brought this fate upon the two females in Nájera he most wished to protect. It was his damned fault, just like last time.

Edmond was smarting over Garit's treatment of him, so he'd lashed out. But not directly. The sneaking coward knew he had no chance of attacking Garit directly, so he'd taken his ire out on the very thing Garit had denied him. Two helpless women.

Garit thunked his head against the pillar.

It was unthinkable. He could *not* think about it.

That woman—that vibrant spitfire of a woman—and her frightened little sister were…

No.

He could do nothing. Darkness had fallen over Nájera. War

madness. To hunt for two girls in a city full of drunken, half-crazed soldiers would be worse than searching for the proverbial needle.

Part of him demanded that he storm through the streets this very minute, forcing his way into every house, raking all Nájera for Edmond and his victims.

But his more rational self knew it was impossible. They could be anywhere by now. Edmond could have returned to the army camp or fled further afield in anticipation of Garit's wrath.

Or worse, Garit would find them—two girls beyond repair, a hideous reminder of past and present failures.

For they were almost certainly dead already.

And he wasn't sure he could face the evidence of his failure again.

So Garit ceased to prop up the pillar. He squared his shoulders and looked at his men.

"Come. That is all. Let us return to our quarters." Then he paused, and narrowed his eyes at each and every man before him. "If any one of you lays eyes on Edmond Ingram, you will inform me directly. But do not kill him. I wish to talk to him first, at length. And I do not believe he will enjoy the conversation."

Chapter Four

I T WAS A ghost. Sir Garit was back in Nájera and he was seeing specters.

It had been two long weeks since he was in this accursed city. The day after the battle, the captured Spanish nobles had been duly paraded before their reinstated king—the king they had deposed. Garit was all set to parade his own captive trio, and hope to hell they were worth a good ransom, when good King Pedro flew at a prisoner and stabbed him to death.

That threw the whole procedure into unholy turmoil. A knight gave his word that his captive would remain unharmed. For this act of courtesy, the knight demanded a hefty ransom in return. Pedro of Castile had just undermined the financial workings of war.

Meanwhile, the ghost was dancing.

Garit blinked. When that didn't work, he rubbed his eyes.

Actually, Pedro's fit of pique had turned out to be a good thing, at least for the Company of the Ruin. Their three prisoners had immediately upped their own ransoms *and* promised prompt payment, if only Garit kept them out of Pedro's clutches. Naturally, it was a knight's duty to honor his word. Sir Garit undertook to keep his captives safe, and Pedro never laid eyes on the trio. The upshot was all three ransoms were paid within a week of Edward's army's shifting to Burgos. It was a minor miracle, and the company was substantially enriched as a result.

As ghosts went, this one was quite attractive.

Garit shook his head. The same could not be said of Prince Edward.

Enriched, that was. The man was attractive enough. King Pedro had promised the English all manner of land and gold in return for their assistance. Now the Castilian king was casting up an inventive array of obstacles to that payment. So Edward dug his heels in in Burgos, determined to extract payment from slippery Pedro. The English army faced a long, hot summer in ungrateful Spain.

But not the Company of the Ruin. Garit was under no obligation to stay, and he had pressing matters to attend to north of the Pyrenees. Thus the moment the last ransom was paid up, the company left Burgos. Now it was heading for the Pass at Roncesvalles, and back into France.

The ghost possessed inhuman grace. Its skirts belled out on ethereal air. Red skirts.

It had been unfortunate but necessary that the Company of the Ruin pass Nájera on its way north. Garit definitely hadn't wanted to stop here, but the timing had been all wrong. Dusk had been falling just as the red cliffs hove into sight. At their feet lay an accursed city, red in stone and soaked in blood. Red in sunset, too, as he'd approached. The place had lured his unwilling soul like a ghoul, but Garit would only stay one night and then the company would move on, leaving the ghosts behind.

He hoped.

His men had taken over a tavern. They were determined to have their fill of Spanish wine before they left this benighted country. Now it seemed they were to be entertained as well.

By a ghost.

But at least the music was real. It had begun innocuously enough—a vielle accompanied by some kind of drum. Two musicians playing in a dark corner. It wasn't every night the company got music. His men had been pleased. Some of them had even done a bit of dancing themselves, once they'd got wine enough in them.

But they had deserted the floor when the ghost-woman began to dance.

She had risen from the corner—the musician with the drum. She strutted to the center of the taproom, still keeping time with her fingers on her strange, flat drum. The instrument rattled with each beat, an eerie shiver of metal.

A shiver to trickle down his spine.

It was her. The woman with the curved daggers. She of the heavy, lustrous black hair, olive skin, and trousers beneath her strangely cut gown.

The woman who was dead because of him.

He glanced about for her younger sister. He'd abandoned both of them—it stood to reason they'd both come back to haunt him, here in this red city.

But no, he saw no girl who looked nothing like Marie.

Good. Dead or not, he wouldn't want little not-Marie in a tavern full of soldiers.

His gaze slipped back to the dancer. The ghost.

Having sashayed a slow circle in the center of the taproom, tapping a shivering beat, she raised the flat drum high and began to whirl. Her bright skirts flared out, shimmering and rippling. The woman whirled on and the skirts floated higher.

They rippled scandalously above her knees…then they rose still higher, hovering mid-thigh.

Once Garit had levered his jaw shut, he cast a glance around—just to see if anyone else saw what he saw. Was this a mass hallucination, or had it appeared just for him?

No, it seemed she *was* a mass hallucination. The Company of the Ruin had conjured itself a communal ghost with blood-red skirts and loose leg coverings beneath. And every last man of them was gawking.

But did they see what he saw? A woman who should be dead. A ghost from the past—yet another shade to haunt Sir Garit of the Ruin.

And then she looked at him.

After long, long moments of spinning, she had floated to a halt. Like a leaf twirled by the wind coming to rest on the ground.

She should be dizzy, but the dark, shining gaze that held his was absolutely firm. It held a depth of purpose.

He was her purpose.

OH, GARIT KNEW she wasn't strictly one of the restless dead. Her chest was rising and falling in eye-catching splendor. Ghosts didn't need to breathe.

But her eyes told him clearly enough—she was here to haunt him.

She had ceased her percussion when she began to whirl, but now she began it again. A slow, persistent beat. He saw now that the flat drum was rimmed with chains. They created the eerie metallic accompaniment. The slightest tap upon the membrane set the chains shivering.

She stalked closer to him, her drum the slow beat of an impending storm, her gaze never leaving his. In the background, the vielle scraped on unseen, unnoticed. The whole tavern had eyes only for his ghost—and she, it seemed, had eyes only for him.

Garit was seated at one of the trestles, on one end of a wooden bench. The Ruin never allowed himself to be cooped up in the middle of a bench. That were no defensible position. But now his seating choice permitted the ghost to approach so close that her skirts feathered his hose and the air about him breathed essence of woman.

It was not the scent of rotting flesh, but of warm skin and spice. Cloves, maybe. An unsettling scent. It tangled with the tightness within him, a tension so habitual he wasn't aware it was there. Until it unknotted, just slightly.

The drum tapped on, a heartbeat rhythm that permeated his ribs and messed with his pulse. And the woman danced before him, not actually touching, but with a gaze so intimate and meaningful she may as well be.

Garit of the Ruin was no monk. He could appreciate a beautiful woman. Sometimes he even appreciated a beautiful woman without her clothes. Not that a female ever remained with the company, and such a being certainly did not linger in Garit's bed. The Ruin had encounters, not relationships. His bed was his alone.

But an encounter with a ghost? That was breaking new ground.

The woman swayed before him. The drum tempo increased, growing more urgent. The vielle kept time in the background.

Very much in the background. Garit's foreground was entirely filled with apparition—the hypnotic sway of her lithe frame, the flick and tap of her fingers, the dark luster of her hair. He remembered how she had writhed in his arms. He wanted her to do it again.

But that was all wrong.

He closed his eyes, tried to block out the insistent percussion.

This ghost had suffered. He didn't know what had happened after he left her, but it couldn't have been good. Only hours before that, her parents had been slaughtered in front of her.

And all Garit could think of was making her writhe? He was as despicable as Edmond.

IT WAS HIM. The man with the icy eyes.

Now his helm was off, she discovered he also possessed cropped wheat-blond hair and a jaw chiseled from stone. Indeed, the man might be attractive if he ever smiled.

Perhaps Zhila would unfreeze those lips.

Slowly, incrementally, she increased the beat of the *daf*. The vielle player followed her lead. Zhila had promised him all the takings from the performance in the tavern, if only he play second fiddle to her. This was her chance, perhaps her only chance. She had trailed the Company of the Ruin all the way from Burgos, barely keeping pace, and now—back where it had all begun—she had to convince him.

Whatever it took.

But he was not cooperating. He had closed those icy eyes against her.

She was being too obvious.

So she expanded the focus of her dance. She circled the tap-room, tapping the *daf* to an ever-increasing tempo, her body catching its wild rhythm, setting her afire. She danced faster and faster, hectic and impassioned, and the vielle scrambled to keep up.

Until Zhila could bear no more. She beat the *daf* to a mad crescendo, her fingers buzzing to the repeated blows, and then she cast the instrument into the Ruin's lap.

That startled his eyes open. Big hands automatically closed around the drum, keeping it safe, praise God.

But Zhila had no room for thought left. She must dance.

She whirled for a few moments, her arms lifted, feeling her skirts take flight, letting the airiness enter her head.

Then she floated free. Nothing but untrammeled move-ment—the airy joy of leaping to catch a ceiling beam, swinging and releasing, hair flying free, skirts taking wing. And then again. She vaguely noticed the circle of men about her, but more as obstacles to avoid with aerial legs and swooping arms.

But she did notice the Ruin.

His was a face carved from stone, giving nothing away. But at least he was watching her now.

Like a bird of prey.

That was all she had room to consider. The music had taken over her soul. She danced as she had never done before—more passionately. For her parents, and for Maryam. Transcending the pain. Transforming it.

But of course it had to end. The movement was intoxication, it was a distillation of wine in her veins, but all inebriation must wear off eventually.

The minstrel's fingers were tiring, stumbling. Her own body was nearing exhaustion. Almost mindless now, she let the vielle lead her to a whirling conclusion.

The music ended. Zhila's arms floated out. All was still, save the heaving of her chest and her final intricate, flicking finger gestures.

Her mother had taught her these. They were one of the few elements in her dance that she was sure were Persian. Zhila had been so young when she had left her homeland, and they had passed through so many lands since, absorbed so many new ways, yet she retained this. An element of her mother.

Zhila lifted her eyes to heaven (actually, to the soot-blackened ceiling) and twisted her fingers, hand and wrist in the shapes her mother had taught her. In remembrance. *You will always be with me.*

A tear rolled down her cheek. Others gathered beneath her eyelids.

And the spell dissolved.

The room was suddenly unsteady about her. She reached out. Her palm contacted something solid.

Skin, slightly rough, and a grip like rock. The hand steadied her.

It led her to a bench. She plunked down, grateful for the solidity of wood and wine-stained bulk of the table before it.

The man with the icy eyes evicted the remaining bench occupants unceremoniously. Naturally, he was the owner of the hand. The Ruin, as Sir Edmond Ingram called him. She had focused her *daf* beat and her dance on him, and he answered her call. He'd had no choice in the matter. That was simply how men reacted to Zhila's performances. Her mother had taught her well.

How Sir Garit of the Ruin acted afterward was more uncertain.

"WHAT DO YOU want from me?"

His voice was low and calm, but her musician's ear caught it—there was an edge to his tone that spoke of something more. Some deep-buried feeling.

There. That was what she must target.

"I want…"

But he was too blunt. What was she to say—her sister's life? Impossible. She would never get what she needed that way. Besides, an English killer would not care. Zhila had to target *his* needs. His desires.

"I want to travel with you, Englishman."

But the way she said the words spoke a different sentence. It said, *I want* you, *Englishman. The travel is incidental.*

"The Company of the Ruin takes no women." A hard, flat tone.

Zhila's fingers gripped the wood of the trestle, smoothed by hundreds of hands and steeped in years of wine.

"You will take me."

She met his gaze. In the low light, his eyes caught the flicker of the fire and flare of torches. The glow turned his eyes violet and bathed his pale hair a shade that recalled the fox. Sir Edmond Ingram.

Her reason for being here.

"You will take me. My parents are dead. My sister…" Zhila shook her head. "You leave Spain, yes? You go to France? So take me. I must leave."

Two weeks with Edmond Ingram had improved her English. It was just as well. Her imperfect grasp of the language must not undermine her at this crucial moment.

"Women do not travel with the company," he said, never changing expression. "Camp followers hinder us. They slow us and cause problems among the men."

"I am no camp follower," Zhila declared. "I am a—how do you say in your language—a minstrel? Yes, a minstrel. I entertain, I perform. I do not warm beds."

I do not warm beds in the plural, her tone said. *Only one bed.*

For it would not do to say such things aloud. She would lure him into accepting her. She would hint at pleasures to come. But if she were too direct—if he took his pleasure now—he might simply discard her afterward. Leave her here.

No. The Ruin must take her with him. She must worm her way beneath that stony exterior and pierce his heart.

Chapter Five

THE DAMN WOMAN stirred him, and Garit of the Ruin did not like to be stirred.

More precisely, he was unaccustomed to feeling the flat mill-pond of his mind rippled, let alone churned. It did not happen. He had campaigned in France and further afield for a decade or more. One did not keep command of a company of warriors by becoming easily agitated.

Her dancing, that drum thing, it was probably designed to delve into the guts of a man and wreak havoc with his innards. Or maybe parts of him that lay a trifle lower. It made Garit want to dance…intimately, and with her.

Preferably with no clothing on.

Come to that, it probably did the same to all the rest of the men in the taproom. Christ, the woman had just made love to a whole tavern full of men.

But it was her plight that truly stirred him. Her parents dead, and her sister—what in hell had happened to her sister? Or to the woman herself, for that matter? Whatever the case, he could understand why she wanted out of Spain.

To get far away from memories.

Nevertheless, women did not travel with the Company of the Ruin. They were only trouble. Endless, company-dissolving trouble.

This one in particular.

"Do you think my men understand the distinction, woman?" he said flatly. "Minstrel, bed warmer—the one does not preclude the other. Indeed, they generally go together."

It occurred to him the instant after the words left his mouth that, foreigner that she was, she might not understand his meaning.

The notion was dispelled an instant later—when she sprang to her feet and leaned halfway over the trestle, hands on the boards, offering him an unparalleled view of lush cleavage and a pair of furious, dark eyes.

"Devil dight you, Englishman. I am no *puta*. See this?" One of those small, wickedly curved daggers appeared in her hand. "A man shows me his lance? *Voilà!* I slice it off. I give you an army of eunuchs, yes?"

Oh, she had an English vocabulary, all right. A grin threatened his lips.

He controlled them and settled for a simple statement. "My point exactly. You would cause problems amongst the men." He raised a brow. "Injuries, even."

"Ah! You do not understand. I *must* go. You take me. You *will* take me."

She was already on her feet. Now her hands left the wooden boards and, sadly, the V of her bodice ceased to hover in his line of sight. She stood, shoved the bench back with a disdainful flick of her leg, and strode around the trestle to confront the Ruin.

No, she didn't confront him. She sat herself on his damn lap.

It seemed there were advantages to shorter skirts. They not only facilitated self-defense (witness her action on the street) and her wild dancing, but also let her slip a leg over his thigh and settle herself a mere hand's breadth from his groin.

The latter responded immediately. Garit set his teeth and raised his hands to remove the woman posthaste.

He was not quick enough. Her palms cupped his jaw, and in the next instant her mouth descended on his.

The taproom exploded with cheers. Garit barely noticed.

The woman took him by storm. It was a swift attack, no time for defense—soft buttocks upon his thighs, two surprisingly strong hands clasping his face, a curtain of curls descending about him, and a mouth that knew no quarter upon his.

In front of all his men.

Her lips slanted over his, warm, generous, and softly open. They sent his brain a-slumbering and woke up other parts of his body. They demanded he open to her in return.

He had no time to consider his reactions. Garit's lips obeyed before he could order them otherwise. His mouth opened, and she snaked her tongue between his teeth.

Her damnable tongue. It was utterly brazen. It just slipped in and challenged his to a duel, and what could a knight do but accept? Next thing he knew, their two mouths were as one, and she was taking possession of his very soul by means of her tongue. And Garit was responding. Stroke for stroke, his tongue twining with hers, his hands in her hair.

The woman smelled maddening, entirely edible, and he had never, ever been kissed like this before. Garit was no blushing virgin. He had charted the terrain of a woman's lips many times before now. But this was different. This woman held nothing back. She was possessing him with a passionate intensity that demanded no less from him—that he lose himself in her, tangle his tongue with this wild thing's, and ravage her lips in return.

It was a complete loss of control before his men.

Not that they cared, by the sound of it. There was a dull roaring in his ears. Perhaps it was their shouting, or was it the beat of his blood, demanding that this insane kiss go ever further, deeper? *Now.*

Then she squirmed a little closer on his lap. Far too close. She brushed up against a groin that was entirely too eager to be noticed—and, at that contact, it nearly burst out of his braies of its own accord.

Which was definitely a step too far before his men.

Garit jolted back. He seized the woman around the waist and wrenched her away. He lifted her from his lap and plunked her too-delicious buttocks on the trestle. At the same time he rose from the bench himself, the better to hold her at arm's length.

Which meant he still had to look at her.

Her eyes were huge and dark, awash with need. Her lips were parted and so very inviting. They lured him with near-demonic force.

Dear God, he wanted to pull her back against him. Damn the watching men to hell. Damn the fact that she was a woman alone, bereft of family and friends, perhaps recently abused herself, and that he had been all too willing to…

"Is this supposed to convince me to take you?" he rasped. His voice was not up to normal speech. Rasping was the extent of his vocal capacity right now.

And then he realized what he'd said.

Yes please, said his groin.

"No, I will not take you," he clarified, at least partly for his own benefit. *Not to France, not to my bed, not even against this trestle here and now.*

Then the witch smiled at him. A smile without restraint, as wide as the dawn and just as breathtaking.

"Do you fear for your lance, Englishman?" Her fingers stroked her dagger hilt.

Actually, no. That had been the thought furthest from his mind. Not that any thoughts had much disturbed him with their presence.

But it was certainly a consideration he ought to bear in mind. After all, would his men respect a eunuch leader?

Her eyes dropped to the region below his belt. Her smile widened, if that were possible.

"Take me to France, Sir Garit of the Ruin," she addressed his groin. "You have declared me yours before all your men. They will not touch me now. No trouble, see?"

Oh yes, said the item so addressed.

Christ, didn't it realize the danger it was in?

"I am no exception to the rule," he said. "No women in the company."

She leaned toward him. His hands were still about her waist. Her gaze snared his. It no longer smiled.

Then she squirmed. One lithe undulation, and the woman freed herself from his grip, sprang down from the table, and, rather than fleeing his grasp, slid her delicious frame up against his.

He should have remembered her ability to wriggle. But Garit was not in the way of remembering anything right now, for her breasts were pressed soft against his torso and her hips nudged his thighs—and the insistent hardness between them. His thoughts were all for taking a holiday.

"Come with me," the woman whispered, winding her arms about him. "Somewhere private, yes?"

She was fire in his veins; she was madness in his soul. Garit found himself obeying against every better instinct. He *wanted* this wild creature. She had crashed through his every barrier and the freedom of it was intoxicating. No thought, no caution.

His feet were moving.

He grabbed her hand and led her toward the taproom door, the one that led to the staircase that wound up, up to the chambers above. Which included his sleeping quarters. Vaguely, he registered the thumping of fists on trestle tables, the yells of his men. Oh, this woman was a performer, all right. She had dragged him onto her stage too, and his men were a very appreciative audience.

But he was damned if he was going to perform before them.

Garit slammed the wooden door behind them.

A dark passageway. Torchlight leaked through the cracks in the door, but otherwise all was night. And the night was filled with *her*.

He did not attempt the stairs. He could not wait that long. She was in his arms, sinuous as a serpent, and his hands were in her hair—glorious, thick, waving hair. She wrapped one leg about his thigh, drawing him ever closer. One hand snaked about his nape. She hadn't kissed him again yet. That had to be rectified.

He bent his head, seeking her lips, craving the abandon with which she kissed him. She wriggled yet again, brushing up against his rearing nether regions, sending a jolt of madness through him.

He didn't even know her name.

Did it matter? After tonight, he would never see her again.

But right now, he *needed* her lips.

He bent to claim them. And then he froze. A length of icy steel was caressing his throat.

"Take me with you. Take me to France."

Garit blinked. It made no difference in the near darkness. At least she hadn't laid her knife against his lower regions. In its current overexcited state, his member was an unmissable target. Just one twitch of the blade…

"No women in the company."

He said it flatly. An automatic reaction. His thoughts were a little scattered at the moment.

The blade slid over his skin. A close shave in the dark.

"You are the leader, yes? So change the rules, just for you."

Her leg was still hooked about his. She was still draped against him, warm and pliant against his larger frame.

It was an illusion. She was not pliant at all. Certainly, her dagger was not.

Yet his body still cried out for her. Her presence, her scent, even her low-accented tones stirred madness within him.

A madness that shouted, *Change the rules. Make an exception.*
Make her yours.

"The men—" he began.

She cut him off. "I am yours. That is what *the men* think." She undulated against him. It sent a shudder of longing through him. "You know what they think we do right now."

He saw a flash of white teeth in the dim, and she cried out—half groan, half shriek. It was the sound of pure pleasure, deep-throated and very audible. It set every inch of his skin prickling.

Doubtless, it prickled the skin of every man on the other side of that door.

Oh, they *knew* what he was doing.

She cried out again, even louder. He felt the sound shiver her chest. His own body thrummed in reply. Dear God, it was enough to drive him moon-howlingly mad.

His men knew what he was doing, and they were wrong.

"Take me to France. The men think I am yours," she murmured. Another undulation. "I cause no trouble, see? And I dance and play my *daf* for them. They are happy, I am happy."

Yes, everyone would be deliriously happy—except for him. She didn't want him. Her knife spelled that out. She just saw him as her passage north.

Of course he could overpower her. She was good with her knives—he had witnessed her skill—but she wasn't currently lunging at him in a surprise attack. As things stood now, he could simply flick her hand away, disarm her, and get on with what his men already assumed he was doing.

But Sir Garit of the Ruin had sworn a knight's oath to protect women, not to take fiendish advantage of them. Some knights took their vows lightly, but not Garit. He had good reason not to.

Besides, that wasn't what he wanted from her. It wasn't just her body he craved, it was her unfettered passion.

At least he'd *thought* it was passion, but now he wasn't so sure. The woman had been performing, and he was her stage. A very convincing act. She was simply passionate about getting what she wanted.

What else could he expect? She had just lost her family to the violence of men like him.

There was a sobering thought. A wilting thought, even.

Perhaps she read his mind, or at least his diminution in urgency.

"You owe me, Garit of the Ruin. I lose my sister. Because of you. Take me to France."

Her sister. His sister.

Garit's arms sagged. He no longer clasped this maddening woman to him, yet she didn't back away. Her leg was still hooked about his thigh, her hand about his nape. The other still held a cutting edge to his jugular.

"Take me," she whispered. "Say yes."

His groin tightened. A clear *yes* there, delusional organ that it was. But there was another part of him whispering an insistent yes. A part long buried.

This was ridiculous. Sir Garit of the Ruin commanded a tight-knit company of warriors—of *men*. They were a fast-moving, disciplined force. They had a hard-won reputation and had reaped significant rewards as a result. A woman threatened all of that. The Ruin did not let an inclination of the cock and an echo of the past imperil all he'd achieved.

"No," he said.

The dagger pressed a little harder. He felt his skin part.

Ghosts rose before him. A little girl and a woman. Two ghosts who might still be alive now, if only he'd acted differently.

They were why he'd thrown himself into this life. They were the reason he'd achieved everything he had. Yet they would remain ghosts. This woman was real. She could still be saved, even if her sister couldn't.

"No," he repeated. "I will not take you in the sense my men believe me to be doing."

A drop of blood slid down his throat.

"But I will let them believe so if it will keep you safe. I will keep you safe," he murmured almost to himself, or perhaps to the listening ghosts.

The body against his stilled. Even her breath seemed to cease.

"You take me with you? To France?"

This was a terrible idea. But he had already regained so much over the last decade in a material sense. It was time to atone in a different way.

"Yes, now take that knife from my throat. Dead men don't

travel."

Although perhaps dead women did.

The blade lifted. A slight shift of the body against him informed Garit that she had sheathed it.

But before she stepped away, Garit had to know one more thing.

"Do you have a name, woman?"

She laughed, a soft, throaty sound, and leaned a little closer.

"I am Zhila. Kurian was my father, so I am named Zhila Kurian."

Then something warm touched his throat. Her tongue. She lapped the trickle of blood from his jugular in one long, slow lick and then stepped back.

"There, you are clean. Now let us tell the men."

Chapter Six

H E HAD PUT her on a horse that did not go.

Zhila had never ridden a horse before, but she wasn't sure if this one counted. Was a horse still a horse if it crawled like a snail? She banged her heels against the beast's flanks one more time. No noticeable effect. The animal's neck sagged toward the dirt.

Then, worse, it spied a tuft of grass and came to an absolute halt, the better to lip it up.

"Go, you fiend of hell!" Spoken in Persian. Another thump at the beast's sides. No reaction. Maybe she should have addressed it in English.

Another rider approached. Zhila paused in her heel banging. It wasn't the Ruin. He hadn't spoken to her or even looked her way since he'd allocated her a horse. It probably didn't help that he rode at the front of the cavalcade while she lagged further and further behind its tail.

This man *should* have been named the Ruin, though. He was one. She wasn't sure she'd ever seen an uglier human being. The question was—what part of that ruined physique did Zhila fix her gaze upon? There didn't seem to be any safe territory. The fellow sat his horse like an under-stuffed sack, his form lopsided, and his face was a scrunched parchment of ill-knit scars.

So she fixed upon his eyes. There had been a couple of near

misses, to judge by the scars about them, but his eyes were still present and apparently working. Even better, they wore a benign expression. He wasn't looking at her as if he'd like to eat her, like some of the men did.

Best of all, her horse perked up. Its ears had flattened at the ugly man's approach. Now it abandoned its grass and began plodding at a slightly faster pace than before.

"Horses don't like me, see?" the fellow said, steering his horse alongside hers. "Reckon it's the way I smell."

He grinned at her, revealing a wreck of teeth. One front tooth was missing, and the other was chipped in a jagged line. Actually, quite a few teeth were chipped. Zhila couldn't help but stare. Rotten or missing teeth she was used to, but snapped off?

"Nah, it's probably the noises I make," the man went on. "And the smells. Touchy beasts, horses."

Zhila savored the air, cautiously. "Smell? You don't wash? I smell…nothing."

It wasn't quite true. There was a hint of rotten eggs at the edge of her nostrils. Not a terrible smell, though. No reek of ancient sweat. Obviously horses were touchy beasts.

The ugly man shrugged. One shoulder rose higher than the other. "Like I say, the noises."

She wasn't going to inquire. Did the fellow have digestive issues as well? Maybe that was what he meant about the smell. Still, flatulence was preferable to lewd looks. Marginally.

"I do not smell," she informed him. "I do not make noise—and this horse does not *move*. Your leader breaks his oath. He tries to get rid of me!"

A look of alarm entered the brown eyes. "Shh, little lady. That one's touchy about his oath."

"Touchy?" Zhila did not lower her voice. "Horses are touchy; that man is touchy. I do not understand this touchy thing."

The fellow's grin renewed itself in all its glory. "Reckon you did last night. Never seen him act like that before."

Ah, that focused her attention. After all, the Ruin was the

whole reason she was here, astride an uncooperative hairy beast and plodding ever further away from Maryam. She turned to the fellow directly and made herself smile. It felt like a betrayal of her parents, to smile so soon after their deaths.

Smile for Maryam.

But the smile seemed to work. What was left of the man's brows lifted.

"You have been with him a long time?" She angled her head toward the front of the cavalcade, where a figure in half-armor led his men northward out of Spain.

"Aye. Years. Since the company began. See, I'd made myself unpopular blowing the wrong thing up for some fancy lord. Accident, of course. Can't say I benefited from it neither." He tapped one long, puckered scar. "But old Garit said I ought to come and work with him, seeing as I hadn't made friends where I was. Not that he was old then, course. Bare youngster. But he'd had enough of fighting for other half-baked bastards. He was all for setting up on his own."

Zhila comprehended perhaps half of that speech, but the *yes* part was straightforward enough.

"So you know him well," she said, more to herself than her audience. This noisy, smelly man might prove useful.

The fellow grunted. "Well enough. As much as any kaynard knows him well. He don't give much of himself away, that one." He seemed to consider the matter. "But you get to know a man by what he does, and the Ruin's a good 'un to work with. He thinks clever, he does. Strategic, he says. Rakes in the silver too. *And* he lets me have my fun."

Zhila's lips tightened. She didn't care to inquire what this man did for fun. Some mercenaries indulged in peculiar tastes, she knew. She had avoided catering to those tastes in the past.

Yet her horse was moving now, edging ahead of her strange-smelling companion. It was jigging a little, but its pace had stepped up. This man equaled information *and* speed. Yes, she would cultivate this human horse goad.

She turned her smile on him again. "I am Zhila. I do not think you smell bad, but my horse doesn't like you, so you can keep riding with me."

Another glimpse of broken-off teeth. "The priest named me John when he splashed water on my head," the fellow returned. "But there's too many Johns in the world, so this lot call me the Wreck, affectionate-like."

Zhila glanced toward her target at the front of the cavalcade, then back at her companion. She lifted a brow. "So, he is the Ruin and you are the Wreck. They are the same thing, yes?"

They didn't look like the same thing at all. This man was maybe her father's age—a thought to twist her gut—while the Ruin had seen, what, thirty years?

But beyond age, there were greater differences. Sir Garit was not misshapen. Not in the least. Come to think of it, he had a rather nice shape. And this Wreck's brown eyes were warm and seemingly candid. The Ruin's eyes froze you out.

Except when he was kissing you.

The display of broken teeth grew wider. "Nah, not the same thing at all when you get down to it. He's Sir Garit of the Ruin. He's a real *sir* and he's got a castle to prove it, 'cept it's a ruin. Still a castle, though. Me, I'm just a wreck. No sir about me. And I like wrecking stuff…or stuff gets wrecked around me." He cocked his head. "But it sounds good, eh? We're a right pair: the Wreck and the Ruin."

"He has a ruined castle?" This explanation of his name was a little disappointing, somehow. She'd assumed he was so named as the bringer of other men's ruins. What was more, he couldn't be that wealthy if his home was a pile of rubble. Did Edmond the Fox know this? "Where is the Ruin's ruin?"

"Long way off. South coast of England, near Portsmouth. Not that I've seen it. They say that's why he's so set on squeezing the French of silver. He wants to rebuild his ruin."

"Oh."

She only had the vaguest notion where England was, but she

knew there was considerable water between it and France. The English had to sail across that sea in order to fight the French.

"He has no ruins in France?" she tried.

"Ha!" The Wreck's cheeks developed new furrows as he guffawed. Strange, though—Zhila found herself less aware of his monumental ugliness the longer she spoke to him. His appearance just made him more intriguing. "I've wrecked a few for him, times past. But you've hit upon something there, girl. He says he's after a castle now, a *whole* castle, more's the pity. He wants to get us a secure base, he says. He reckons the situation in France is getting more slippery. We need ourselves some solid walls. That's the plan as soon as we get over them mountains."

So the Ruin wanted a castle.

This Wreck was an excellent source of information. She treated him to another smile. One more smile closer to Maryam.

But it was the Ruin she really needed to get close to. This secondhand information was useful, but Sir Garit was the key.

"I need another horse," she announced. "This one doesn't go. We must cross mountains? The ground is flat here, but *still* this thing doesn't go."

She poked it with her heels experimentally, just to see if it had changed its mind.

No more reaction than prodding a rock.

It was her companion's presence that was giving the beast any energy at all, and, intriguing bundle of ugly and amiable that he was, she couldn't ride by the Wreck all the way to France. She needed to cozy up to Sir Garit.

The Wreck gave her a skeptical look. At least, that was how she interpreted the shift of his scars.

"That's as may be, but I'm not the one to give it to you. Speak to yon Ruin." Then he grinned. "Maybe give him a smooch or two to soften him up."

"How? He is up there, and I am back here." A bang of the heels. "And this thing doesn't go!"

The grin grew wider. Dear God, did he have a whole tooth in

his mouth?

"How? Oh, I don't reckon you need no lessons from me in tongue-work. Never seen our Ruin get so enthusiastic about the matter in me life."

"No, not that. Can I shout at him from here?"

"Don't reckon you can kiss him from here, neither," her helpful companion added.

"Argh!"

"Simmer down, girl. You'll get your chance soon enough. We'll stop for a break round noon. Food, drink, a kiss or two even—"

GARIT PUSHED ON to Logroño before he halted for the midday meal. It wasn't just that the city was the most logical place to stop—taverns, markets, a blacksmith to reshoe a couple of horses—he'd also needed a long ride to think, and to think those thoughts well away from a certain woman.

She had the knack of stirring his thoughts to mud.

It had been a mistake to bring her along. He'd known that even at the time, but she'd churned up thoughts…emotions…in him to such a degree that he made a decision based on feeling. Sheer stupidity.

Once he was safely separated from her by the length of a column of men, Garit could think more clearly. He could mull over the company's future, and his own. So he'd spent the morning riding through Spanish countryside, thinking.

He knew he was right to leave Spain and Prince Edward now. There was nothing more to fight for south of the Pyrenees. Garit had no argument with the Spanish. They hadn't killed his family. He'd come south to fight for prince and profit, and now all the fighting and profiting was done. Garit had a greater plan for his men—for himself too—and to achieve it he needed to get back to

Southern France before the bulk of the English. As for the woman, she was a stone in his boot. An unnecessary complication to that plan.

Yet something had driven him to give her his oath.

He resolutely shut his mind to exploring that something. It was irrelevant to his plan. It would only obstruct it.

He located a tavern on one of the central plazas and informed the company they would travel on when the bells rang for nones. What they did with themselves in the meantime was up to them. He had horses to shoe and a woman to avoid. She would be safe enough with the Wreck. He'd had a word with his engineer before they left Nájera. The Wreck reserved all his lust for gunpowder. By contrast, he was quite the gentleman around women.

A quick discussion with his horse-master narrowed Garit's task down to two animals. Perfect. He could handle two on his own and leave the rest of the company to take their ease. Normally, he'd allocate the task to an underling, but today a visit to the blacksmith was downright appealing. He'd find something to eat while he was waiting.

Garit choked up sufficient words in the local dialect to locate a smithy that specialized in warhorses. The route took him down a street ringing with hammers, its air hell-scented and smoky. The two horses he led were not impressed by the general atmosphere, but they had recently passed through battle and did no more than snort and snuff.

Then there was the smithy and the ensuing discussion bellowed in fractured Spanish above the general din.

The smith grasped the need to shoe the horses—all that took was a lift of a horsey leg or two and some pointing. What was trickier to convince him of was the need to do it *now*. Before nones. The smith kept patting the substantial stomach beneath the leather apron and then indicating his mouth. Garit suspected the fellow understood him well enough but had a case of hunger-induced incomprehension. The racket in the background didn't help.

Garit was just explaining for the third time that the horses required shoeing, and they required it now, food and siesta be damned, when a stream of fluent Spanish interrupted him.

"*Burro! Babosa!* Do you know who you're talking to, *idiota?* This man is *La Ruina*. He's just put your King Pedro back on his throne. He ruined Enrique's army to do it. You? Your smithy? Pah! A flick of his finger, and it is a ruin too. Shoe his cursed horses and be done."

Garit was inclined to sink his head into his hands. But a lead rope already occupied each palm, and besides, the Ruin did not indulge in public displays of emotion.

Especially in front of this woman. Not again.

His unwelcome fellow traveler flounced in front of the smith, hands on hips, and the fellow's eyes widened. Then his mouth sagged. Garit felt a grin threatening. He clamped his lips tight.

Unfortunately, that also meant he wasn't able to insert a soothing word or two—or clap his hand over the woman's own mouth—before she began again.

She jabbed a finger at the smith, then she jabbed it at each horse in turn.

"*Ahora!* It will not take long. A few whacks of your hammer and it is done!"

Christ, he definitely should have secured her far-too-talented mouth. The smith had ceased goggling at Zhila now and was eyeing her instead with appreciation. Next thing you knew, the lout would suggest an alternative use for his hammer, and he wouldn't be referring to iron.

Garit didn't need his horses shod at that sort of cost.

The smith was grinning at Zhila now. It was a grin with meaning.

"*Bueno, bueno,* I'll sort your nags out right now, little *bonita.* But in—"

Garit had to act. There was no time for any subtler means. One quick step up to the infernal woman, and he took her face between his palms and dipped his head to hers.

It was just meant to be a statement—just like a dog cocking its leg on a tree trunk so the next dog knew whose tree it was. Garit only needed to put as much feeling into it as was sufficient to convince the smith.

That was not the way it worked out.

There was an instant of frozen shock as he touched his lips to hers.

This woman, shocked? That sent a spark of triumph skittering through him. But he was only allowed to enjoy it for the briefest instant.

Then she reacted.

It was like setting a flame to one of the Wreck's powdery concoctions.

The only touch he'd intended was his hands upon her face, his lips against hers. And just possibly a brush of the tongue. She had other plans.

Her lips parted beneath his, her arms looped around his neck, and her hips were suddenly all too aligned with his. And she was kissing him back, lips generous and open. Holding nothing back. Definitely not holding her tongue back.

Garit couldn't help but respond in kind. He retained a vague notion that this kiss was all part of some plan, but beyond that, her lips were a madness that turned his brain to mush. Such a sweet, seductive madness, to lose himself in this woman's touch, set afire by her unchecked passion. He drew her to him, slipping one hand down to her buttocks, pressing her closer. He no longer needed to capture her face—his hands could roam where they pleased. And they wanted to roam *everywhere.*

A significant clearing of a throat registered in his ears. Come to think of it, it was probably the second time said throat had been cleared. Garit had been too busy to attend to the first.

Sentences in Spanish followed. "I *said* I'll sort your nags out, man. *Sí, sí,* I'll do 'em now, since you're so desperate. I warrant you've got plenty to keep you busy while you wait, but for God's sake, take it elsewhere. I'll shoe your beasts crooked for watching if you hang around here."

That gave him pause.

And in that brief pause, the world came rushing back in. Hard reality. His hands dropped and he stepped away abruptly. She swayed slightly, but recovered herself with the ease of a true performer. Which did not prevent her lips appearing a delicious, bruised burgundy, soft and inviting. His own lips parted at the sight. Oh, he wanted her with a force that was frightening.

The Ruin was never frightened.

He straightened. He beckoned Zhila. An abrupt command. "Come, we must eat. Let us find food while this good smith sees to the horses. Doubtless he will not take long."

At least, that was what he hoped he'd said in Spanish, primarily for the benefit of the smith.

It didn't seem to be the message the aproned man got, for as Garit turned, he heard a snort. "Eat? Ha! Just see that you don't take too long. Some of us *do* have to eat."

Chapter Seven

Z HILA LET HIM seize her by the arm and steer her back onto the street of smiths. She seemed to be floating just above the level of the cobbles, drunk on a single, heady kiss. She half expected he would begin again once they had rounded the corner, found an alley, some nook or anything that passed for privacy.

And if he did, what then?

She knew what he wanted. The evidence between his thighs had spoken loud and clear. It nudged hard against her stomach as she draped herself to him.

But she couldn't. Not here, not now. If he got what he wanted so soon, she would lose whatever hold she had over him. One woman, used up. And this was the wrong place.

Sir Garit kept a firm grip on her upper arm. He towed her along first one street and then another. Perhaps he was heading to an inn he knew of—and a private bedchamber. He'd already passed by a number of alleys and potential nooks without a glance.

And then? What should she do?

They stepped into a plaza. Garit paused, looked about him, and then towed her onward again.

Toward a tavern.

Zhila's heart had been replaced by a frog in her chest. A very active frog. They drew closer. People took one glance at Garit and melted out of his way. He was a man with a purpose. A tall, strong man with a sword at his thigh.

That frog was still leaping about. *What to do?* Oh, she knew what she wanted. It was a raging hunger in her belly, and it had nothing to do with food.

This big man, this blond, impassive Englishman with eyes of sky, was what she craved. She wanted to melt the ice in him and feel him blaze. She wanted *him.*

Selfish wantonness. What would her parents think, for heaven's sake?

The tavern door stood open, welcoming customers in. Garit tugged Zhila through. He glanced about the interior. It was dim after the spring sunshine, even though the shutters were thrown open. The Ruin evidently spied what he was looking for—a woman to serve him. The woman had an air of matronly authority—modestly covered hair, a snowy apron, and a set of keys at her girdle. What would she make of an incoherent Englishman's demands for a private room upon the instant?

Zhila would shortly find out.

They halted before the matron.

"Señora," the Ruin said. "We need a private table and some food. Without delay."

ZHILA SANK DOWN on the bench. She thought she'd misunderstood or that he'd mangled the word for *chamber* with his bad Spanish. But no, here they were at a table in a secluded corner of the tavern—but not *that* secluded—and he'd made no demur. In fact, he was sitting down opposite her, and no part of his body was in contact with hers.

Maybe he was serious about eating. But was she on the menu or not?

He ordered two of whatever pottage the tavern was serving, and wine to go with it. He paid for it, too, which was just as well. Zhila had the coins she'd taken from her father's body, but it was no fortune. She could earn more, given the right circumstances, but she had other things to attend to. She'd worry about earning a living afterward.

He said nothing as a maid bustled about them, laying down slabs of stale bread as trenchers, then setting a bowl of stew between them. His face had resumed its usual impassive lines. She could not tell what he was thinking.

Except he was not considering the delights of the bedchamber. He wouldn't be looking so utterly unmoved if he was, would he?

The frog in Zhila's chest subsided. It slumped into a puddle.

He didn't want her. He had, he definitely had, but evidently the urge was easily put aside.

She was easily put aside.

It was for the best. No need to feel disappointment. She would *make* him want her again, but only when every single condition was aligned.

The Ruin took a long draft of wine. Just as well the woman had left a full pitcher on the table. Whatever had been in Sir Garit's cup was mostly not there anymore.

Then he began to spoon stew onto her trencher.

"No." She stilled his hand.

"Aren't you hungry?"

She looked at him—the watchful blue eyes, the strong, still lines of his face, tanned by the Spanish sun but so very un-Spanish.

She kept her hand over his. "I serve myself."

He moved not a muscle. "It is courtesy for a knight to serve the lady who shares his bowl first."

"Courtesy?" Zhila knew the word. It existed in French and Spanish, and was apparently used by the English too. But it was not applied to women like her. It was a knightly word.

Did it imply respect? Probably not. It was more likely just habit—a habit of overbearing behavior toward others. All the same, Zhila removed her hand, by means of a lingering stroke, and let him have his way.

The stale bread was loaded with stew, and then he turned to pile his own trencher.

"Eat," he commanded. "The smith will be finished soon, and we leave by nones."

No time for bed sports, then. The man was on a schedule. Was that the explanation?

She ate. The stew was surprisingly good. It contained genuine chunks of meat—goat?—alongside onions and a wine-rich sauce. Zhila discovered an appetite for more than an Englishman, and her meal was soon reduced to shreds of soggy bread. The Fox had not fed her so well—mostly a pottage of beans with just a hint of bacon. And before that, her parents had not splashed their hard-earned coin about on plentiful servings of meat.

Her parents. What would they think of her plan? All the Kurians had ever had were each other. Family was all. They were viewed by everyone else as amoral entertainers, suspicious foreigners, even though they'd been in Spain for years and spoke the language like natives.

Of course her parents would approve of her plan.

"Your mother and father died in Nájera, didn't they? Your sister too."

His hands were wrapped around the wine cup. His voice was as passionless as if he were discussing the contents of that cup.

She stared at him. "Yes."

She did not clarify which part of the question she was answering. Let him assume what he would.

"Do you not mourn them, woman? They are barely in their grave and—"

The Ruin broke off. Zhila had the feeling he didn't often sever his sentences, but she knew why this was the exception.

They probably weren't in their grave, and he knew it. At best, they had been shoveled into a pit, with a priest muttering prayers over them and a hundred others at once.

At least she had offered her prayers first—and many times since.

She lifted her chin. "I mourn them."

"You do not show it."

Zhila shoved aside the trencher, the better to lean over the trestle. "I mourn them, knight. They live in my heart. I pray for them. What should I do? Wear black like the crow and caw all day? No! I do not die. I *live* for them."

How to express what she felt? More importantly, how should she convince him? She leaned further across the table and seized his hands.

"I nearly died. Who knows how long I live now? Life, it is short. I do not dwell on death. I *live*."

She ran her fingers over the backs of his hands, the tanned skin crisscrossed with innumerable small scars. Big hands, strong and capable. Accustomed to killing people. He was a warrior and an Englishman, just like the men who'd killed her parents.

She gazed at him, willing him to reveal something of himself in return. "I dance for them, I play for them. I *live* for them, but I also live for me."

Still no expression. *Dios mío*, what did it take?

So she wrapped her fingers around his much larger hand. She lifted it and drew it to her lips. She took his forefinger into her mouth, her lips caressing its length. He tasted of stew and horse leather.

A flicker of feeling in those winter-sky eyes.

Then he removed his hand from her grasp. He laid it on his lap and sat back, out of her reach.

"You do not have to play the temptress, Zhila Kurian. I will take you to France. Dance, sing, entertain the men if you will. I ask no further payment."

Ah. A man of principle. That could prove troublesome.

"*You* kissed *me* back there." Zhila flicked a hand in what she thought was the direction of the smithy.

"That was…necessary."

She smiled then, and angled her head at him. "I kiss you, you kiss me—we are even, yes? No more needed?"

His gaze dropped to her lips. "Indeed. No more needed."

"But your men think we do more. Much, much more. You say it keeps me safe if they think I am yours. I must, how you say…*play the temptress*. To you, in front of them." She smiled at him, a slow, wide smile. "It entertains them too, yes?"

Perhaps it even entertained her, this campaign to melt a man of ice. Which was definitely not the reason she must pursue it.

"You are safe enough with the Wreck," he said. "It will not take long to return to France. Then you can find your safety elsewhere."

Ah. It was as she'd suspected. He'd sent the Wreck to her. He left her well alone himself, but got the ugliest man in his company to keep her company.

"I thank you for the Wreck. He is a nice man."

Garit's brows rose.

"But he cannot protect me all the time. So you must help. Continue to pretend, Sir Garit. *Pretend* I am yours, and your men leave me alone. Then I am not a problem." She smiled at him then. "That is why you kiss me back there, yes?" Another flap toward the street of smiths.

He inclined his head, slowly. What did it mean? Yes, that was why he'd kissed her, or yes, he would continue to claim her so in public?

She had a feeling she would squeeze no more certain answer out of him now. Better not press it.

Zhila would press a different *yes* out of him instead.

"And I want a horse that goes. That thing you put me on— pah, it is a donkey. No, it is a *tortuga*. How do you say…?"

"You said you'd never ridden before. That is why I put you on a tortoise."

"Tortoise—*tortuga*—donkey? No! Give me a horse! I will stay on. You will see."

Chapter Eight

G ARIT DEMOTED THE animal the woman had been riding back to pack animal and put her—with reservations—on a horse that wasn't a tortoise.

Naturally, it was a mistake.

The Company of the Ruin had gathered at nones, just as arranged. His men knew better than to be tardy. Garit would simply leave without them. Either you obeyed orders or you parted company with the company. For the most part, his men complied. They saw the benefits of fighting as part of a coherent, disciplined force. They were less convinced of his orders concerning women—no abuse, no taking advantage of women in the course of war. Where was the benefit in forgoing a warrior's rightful spoils?

The rule extended to camp followers too. Women did not belong in the Company of the Ruin. His men might have liaisons of a consensual nature, but they couldn't bring those liaisons along with them. Some men grumbled about women being useful for laundry and cooking as well as more recreational purposes, but no, Garit had been firm. Do your own damn laundry.

Now, to all appearances, Garit had broken his own rule. Not that Zhila would wash his undergarments, but his men were convinced she was riding him—perhaps much in the manner she was currently riding his horse. Legs wrapped tight, buttocks glued to the saddle, while the rest of her jolted up and down wildly to her mount's reaction to her touch.

Garit swallowed a smile.

"Don't hold the reins so tight, woman," he said.

She cast him a sideways glance.

The Ruin kept his gaze trained on the road in front—offering her a model of imperturbable horsemanship, his stallion under perfect control.

His thoughts were not.

If one of his woman rules were broken, perhaps his men would see fit to break others. And Zhila drew men like moths to a flame. At least, that was the unfortunate effect she was having on him. She burned hot and bright, and Garit was all set to singe himself. He had to keep his men's hands off her. She had suffered enough.

Garit of the Ruin would atone. Not only for his mother and Marie, but also for this woman's sister. He would see Zhila to safety for the sake of all those he hadn't.

And she would be safer if everyone thought her his woman. Or so his base desires whispered.

"If I don't hold tight, the animal will go. It will run," the flame said.

"You mean gallop. Or canter. Horses don't run."

"This one will," she retorted, but she eased back on the reins just a little. The animal immediately increased its pace. Zhila let out a squeak and hauled back on the reins again. "See?"

"You're giving it mixed messages," Garit said. Oh yes, mixed messages were the order of the day. "Your legs are telling it to go while your hands are holding it back. When you squeeze a horse's flanks, you're urging it on. Understand?"

"I squeeze the last horse. I squeeze it hard and, *voilà*—nothing."

"There was a reason I gave you a tortoise." He was tempted to reach out and loosen her legs. But no, he'd be an idiot to put his hand to the flame.

He was already an idiot for giving her a horse that wasn't a tortoise. A plodding horse had kept her safely at the back of the cavalcade. In the dubious safety of the Wreck's company, anyway. Now she had a horse that reacted to her clinging legs, she was prancing at the head of the procession. Inconveniently next to him.

Nor would it do to ask the Wreck to ride beside her while she rode this horse. The Wreck's scent of sulfur was a constant reminder of the bangs, judders, and rain of rocks that were known to occur around the man. Horses objected to his presence. The French often did too.

"Yes." She narrowed her eyes at him. "The reason is you not want me. My tortoise stops to eat grass. *Good!* you think—you leave me behind."

"Horses follow other horses. It would have caught up."

As for the *not wanting*, that was not a subject he was going to discuss here in full view of the company. It was a subject best not discussed at all.

So he changed the subject to a brief dissertation on how to ride a horse. Not a tortoise, not a man, and most certainly not himself. Unfortunately, it was necessary to demonstrate by means of his own body.

Garit was not bashful about his form. He had all the usual physical attributes. They served him well as a warrior and, when the mood took him, as a lover. But now he felt her gaze warm upon him, lingering and assessing. And it made him grow warm too, very aware of this strange woman who rode beside him.

What did she perceive as her gaze raked him over?

A knight who controlled his horse with effortless ease? A man inopportunely inclined to kiss her? The sort of soldier who had killed her family?

Whatever it was she perceived, it had a beneficial effect on her riding. She eased her grip on the horse's flanks and rein. She ceased to lean forward in the saddle. Garit caught all this by brief glances. It was an effort to keep his eyes from her, but it was an effort he must make.

He attempted to take in the countryside instead. They were traveling an ancient pilgrim route, after all. He ought to pay it some attention. A dose of the holy was just the antidote he needed.

Her heathen accents broke into his thoughts. "Where are we going?"

Not to Santiago de Compostela, his brain supplied. They were traveling in the opposite direction—no salvation lay this way.

"We stop in Los Arcos tonight," his mouth answered. "Then we cross the mountains to France. This you know. You asked to go to France, did you not?"

"France, yes. But it is a big place, true? Where do you go in France? Why?"

Garit didn't particularly like being interrogated, but he supposed she needed to know. She wanted to get out of Spain, but for all she knew, France would be just as hostile to her. He frowned. What would she do there? How would she survive, a lovely, foreign woman alone?

An obvious solution presented itself. It left a bad taste in his mouth.

But her future wasn't his problem. He had promised to take her away from war-ravaged Spain, a land crawling with soldiers. That was all.

He ought to take her to Bordeaux, the English capital in the south. Zhila would have opportunities for income there, with her looks and her skills. He would arrange an introduction into a high-class whorehouse. They would look after her there. Mostly.

"You do not say. It is a secret, yes?"

He shook his head, as much to clear it as in negation. The idea of Zhila in a whorehouse, however safe it might keep her, did murky things to his thoughts.

"No, no secret."

"Where, then?"

"Bordeaux is where Prince Edward will return to, once he's finished in Spain. Most of his force will be concentrated thereabouts. I will not return to Bordeaux."

Zhila was looking impatient. Her horse began to jig again. Garit realized he hadn't answered the question, only said what he wouldn't do. Anyone would think he had something to hide.

Every man in the company knew their current purpose. The one woman accompanying them may as well know too.

"We go inland, to the edge of English territory. That is where the opportunities lie." He looked at her directly now. "I will acquire a castle. The company needs a secure base. We have gained much from these wars, too much to lose. It is time to consolidate."

He was speaking as much to himself as her, explaining his decision in ways that were probably beyond her comprehension. It helped to voice the matter aloud.

"You acquire a castle—how? You buy it? You have gained much, you say. Now you spend it?"

He almost laughed at that. One did not buy a castle as one bought a loaf of bread. He had thought she wouldn't understand his musings, but of course both *acquire* and *consolidate* sounded almost the same in Spanish as English.

Garit looked at her calmly and laid out the facts.

"No, I will not buy it. I wish to consolidate, not throw away all I have gained. I will marry a castle."

He saw her expressive brows lift, and he clarified.

"That is, I will marry the woman who holds it."

LOS ARCOS WAS more of a village than a town. They reached it well before the sun sank—not a moment too soon for Zhila. This business of sitting on a horse was straightforward enough—once one had a horse that moved and the Ruin had explained the basics—but her buttocks and thighs were not used to clamping around a hairy body all day. She wanted off this animal, and the animal probably felt the same way about her.

They clattered to a halt before an inn. Zhila was all for parting her posterior from the saddle that instant, but Garit warned her they may not be able to stay. The Company of the Ruin wasn't large, as companies went, but it contained far more men than an inn was usually equipped to deal with.

Zhila stayed put. Her lower body was one big, aching complaint, but once off this horse, she really couldn't face clambering back on again. At least not today.

"Where will we go?"

The Kurians had sometimes struggled to find a roof for the night, but that was more because of their heathen looks and dubious trade. She had slept under the stars before, but she didn't fancy doing it surrounded by strange men. She could defend herself while awake—but asleep? Besides, her buttocks demanded a softish surface to rest upon for the night, not a stony field.

The Ruin shrugged infinitesimally. "We'll find somewhere. Cow byres, a barn. Failing that, the night looks to be fine."

But it turned out Los Arcos was used to catering to floods of pilgrims. Or more recently, soldiers. They would stay, and the inn floor would be lined with male bodies that night. Zhila caught the comments of the harassed innkeeper as he snapped at staff and soldiers alike.

But where would she sleep? Or would she sleep at all?

Last night in Nájera, she had tucked herself away in a half-ruined house. The building was a casualty of the recent battle. No one had bothered her there, and she had emerged at dawn to ensure the company did not leave without her.

This was a smaller settlement, and there were no handy ruins. Perhaps she could sleep alongside some of the local women? Or perhaps…

Perhaps it was time to act.

Zhila sighed, leaned forward, and swung her right leg back

over the horse's rump. This seemed the proper way to dismount. Thank heaven for split skirts and trousers beneath. They meant she could sit astride a horse as easily as a man did. Some women had taken to sitting sideways on a horse, Garit had told her. Lunacy. It was bad enough trying to control the beast with two legs, but with effectively one?

When her feet hit the cobbles, the attached legs were disinclined to stay straight. They buckled. They were used to a horse holding her up. She grabbed hold of the stirrup. The horse snorted and pulled away, obviously worried she would get back on.

"Come," the Ruin said. "Lead your horse this way. You must care for your mount so it will bear you tomorrow."

Zhila looped the reins over the animal's head, willing her legs to behave. Then she followed the Ruin on wobbly legs.

"It will bear me?" she muttered, eyeing the creature. "Yes, but can I bear it?"

But of course she would. She would bear aching thighs and abraded skin and much, much more to get Maryam back. And that process would continue tonight.

For the Ruin had declared he would marry soon. Once he was in a castle and bedding its mistress, he would be inaccessible to her. Zhila had to act now.

Chapter Nine

S HE DANCED. THAT was a given. She danced in the central hall of the inn, on the floor that would double as a bed for most of the company that night. This was how she would pay her way to France. Dance was her skill, along with the *daf*. Her mother had trained her to catch men's eyes—to catch women's too, if they had silver and patronage to give, but men usually had more silver. Zhila was a performer. It was how the Kurians had always made their money.

But she was not a whore, so tonight she danced with her daggers. Her two small, beautifully weighted daggers that curved like eagle's talons. They were daggers that could and had taken a man's life, and the watching men knew it.

But there was another reason for the dagger dance tonight. Zhila's legs were not up to their usual acrobatics. The successful management of airborne daggers required restrained leg movements. Besides, the torchlight flashed most deliciously on the surface of the polished blades.

The expressions of the watching men were quite delicious too.

They'd likely never seen a woman scythe the air with intricate, twisting blade gestures, then flip the small weapons up, glinting in the red light, to catch them neatly again. Thank goodness she managed not to embed either into the ceiling beams above.

Yes, it made a nice statement. *Do not mess with Zhila. She has knives and knows how to use them.*

But it was not the only statement she wished to make tonight.

The Ruin was watching. Unlike the rest of the company, his features remained devoid of emotion. Whenever she observed him, he seemed merely…polite.

Zhila needed a stronger reaction from Sir Garit of the Ruin.

She moved closer to where he sat on a bench, his back against the wall. She held his gaze, then sent first one dagger up arcing up before her, then the second. She caught both without shifting her attention from those wintery eyes. His expression changed not one mote. He didn't seem worried that she would cut herself—or perforate him.

She smiled at him. He didn't smile back. Not that she'd expected him to. Her smile was simply a promise of things to come.

She lifted both daggers high above her head, eyes never leaving his. Then she slid them down, looping them in slow, serpentine curves about her form. Holding his gaze.

Still no alteration in expression.

She held the left-hand dagger wide, motionless, and focused on its mate. She lifted the blade to her cheek. Slowly, she stroked the flat of the blade down. The chill steel slipped over her cheek, neck, and then traced her bodice. It traveled lower. When it reached the line of her waist, she dipped a bow—first to the Ruin, and then she turned to offer another to his company.

It was a clear message: the show was over.

A thumping of hands on trestles followed. Some men called suggestions. They included some rather explicit warnings aimed at Sir Garit.

Zhila needed to sit. All day on a horse, and her legs would take no more. So she turned back to the Ruin and availed herself of his lap.

He jolted as she settled her buttocks on his thighs. No one

else would have noticed a thing, but Zhila felt it, and it was like honey on her tongue. She wriggled a bit, making herself comfortable.

His wine cup sat on the trestle before her, so Zhila lifted it to her lips and drank. Then she sighed and sank back against her man-seat. It was so wonderfully solid and strong. Quite immoveable, in fact.

"I am tired," she told him. "Take me to bed."

THE WHOLE COMPANY was watching him. The entertainment hadn't ended with the dance. They were waiting for him, Sir Garit of the Ruin, to react.

Devil damn them all, they knew their commander didn't do reactions. Doubtless that was part of the fun. They were probably hoping for a repeat of last night's kiss.

Garit was not going to oblige.

But a certain mutinous part of him was already reacting. Her buttocks on his lap were not helping.

The solution was to scoop her up. It was easily done. She was already sitting sideways across his legs, her shoulder resting against his chest. So he dipped one hand under her knees, secured the other about her back, and got to his feet.

She didn't wriggle as he'd expected she would. She simply lay in his arms, a deliciously warm weight nestled against him.

And predictably, the men cheered. More accurately, they bellowed a din to shake the dust from the beams. Garit set his teeth and walked to the door, careful not to trip with his burden.

What sort of an example was he setting, that this was what one did with a woman? Would they now think Zhila was available for all?

Just pick the woman up and cart her off.

He kicked the door open with one foot and exited into the

courtyard.

Damn it, there was no privacy here either. A couple of his men were ambling back inn-ward, probably after visiting the privy. Or one of Los Arcos's more enterprising women. It was dim out here in the starlight, but they saw him immediately. How could they not, outlined with a most interesting burden in the doorway?

Jos and Walt stopped dead, and the moonlight illuminated two sets of teeth.

Garit muttered an abrupt goodnight and strode past them with his burden.

"Oh aye, a good night to you too," floated back to him. "Very good, by the looks."

His burden laughed softly.

Garit did not deign to respond to either. He strode to the stairs leading to the upper level of the inn and its handful of private chambers. One of which was his.

He paused, heart banging against his ribs—not because he'd just taken the stairs two at a time with his arms full of woman, but because...well, because he was considering breaking his own rule.

She was still lying quiet in his arms, breathing softly. His arms about her, Zhila's seeming trust in him, the need to keep her safe from every last man in that inn—it all added up to a dangerous urge to do the unprecedented.

She was looking up at him. Garit stared stolidly at the door before him.

"Why you wait?" she said in her imperfect English. That mellow, slightly husky voice colored with Spanish and something far more foreign. A siren's call.

"What do you want?" he said flatly.

"Want?" He could feel her gaze upon him. It burned. "I want to sleep. I sit on a horse all day. I dance. No more."

Garit's jaw loosened. Just a little.

"Just sleep," she repeated, and then added the unthinkable. "With you."

"No." One harsh, very definite syllable.

But he didn't put her down.

"I sleep on the floor, if you like," she said, and he caught a flash of teeth. "I not steal your blanket, I promise."

"No. No one sleeps with me."

Even as he stated the fact, he knew why she was asking this thing. Safety. Any man might enjoy a single assignation with a woman—as he'd apparently done last night—but if he then left her alone, she would be considered available. In fact, one very audible encounter in a stairwell was probably the most dangerous signal of all. It was practically an advert for business.

Well, on the positive side, his men probably thought him engaged in round two at this very moment. Maybe he should get Zhila to utter a few cries, just for verisimilitude.

But for true verisimilitude, she should share his chamber.

Absolutely not. He stared at the door as if it would give him answers.

Her hand lifted—her free hand, the one not snugged up against his chest. Fingers trailed softly over his brow. They traced his cheekbone, stirred his stubble, and ran along his jaw.

"Why not? You will sleep with your wife. In her castle."

"No. Not with her, and not with you."

Yet he still held her.

Of course he did. He judged by the languor of her limbs that, should he deposit her on the boards, she would simply slump to the floor.

"You will not..." She paused, probably searching for words. "You will not do what husbands do? With your wife? What about babies?"

Garit tensed. He hadn't got that far in his plans. Besides, it was hard to imagine the exercise of his husbandly rights on a person he'd only seen once.

It was all too easy to imagine indulging in the same act with this warm bundle in his arms.

"Rest assured, I will be an adequate husband. But I do not have to sleep in the same chamber as the woman."

She regarded him. He could feel her curiosity, but she could think what she liked. He didn't need to explain his sleeping arrangements to this thorn in his side.

Zhila moved then. She'd been lying quiescent in his arms, so he wasn't holding her tight. She slipped her legs from his grasp and slid them down his body. His other arm remained about her shoulders. She stood within his embrace.

Ah, the feel of her—the lithe form, her impetuous movements, the promise of nothing held back. Dear God, how he wanted that. He craved her lips upon his, her legs wrapping about him, the passionate breaking down of all barriers.

She rose on tiptoes and kissed him then, but she did it with her lips closed. She kissed him like a sister and slipped from his arms.

Then she opened the chamber door and stepped inside.

For the space of two heartbeats, Garit didn't move. His lips craved more. Did she know whose room she'd entered? More to the point, what did he want to do about it?

He dug a hand into his pocket. His fingers closed about cast iron and his lips twitched. Decision made, and it was the right decision at that.

He yanked the door to and fitted the heavy iron key into the lock. Clunk, and it was done.

Then he leaned against the door and called softly, "You are safe, Zhila. This is your chamber—yours alone, and only I have the key. Rest well."

Garit lingered there a few moments, listening for some reply. A squeak of outrage, perhaps, or gratitude for his splashing out coin for her own private chamber. But perhaps the door was too thick, for there was nothing.

Now for his own room and its empty, spacious bed.

Yes, he had done the right thing. Sir Garit of the Ruin strode down the gallery to his private chamber, and shoved the flicker of regret to the dark corner of his mind where all unnecessary emotions belonged.

Chapter Ten

HE UNLOCKED HER before dawn. A simple *snick* of the key in the lumping great lock, and a low "We leave at prime. Be ready or be left behind."

Zhila did not burst out to confront him. What would it achieve? One approach had been attempted. It had failed. But there was always tonight…and the night after. She would simply try another means to her end.

One night she would succeed. Soon. She had to.

So she exited her chamber with all the nonchalance her sore thighs would allow, and hobbled down the stairs in search of breakfast.

It could have been worse. She'd slept alone in a chamber Sir Garit had hired exclusively for her, and no one had got overfamiliar with her in the night. The Ruinous Garit could have saved his silver if she'd simply slept on the taproom floor.

Zhila located some bread and well-watered wine. She bit into the former.

Why was the noble lump of ice so averse to someone sleeping in his room? It seemed Ingram was right—Sir Garit of the Ruin always slept alone. He had even declared he didn't want to sleep with his future wife. So strange.

Zhila's lips tightened. The bread lay like a rock in her mouth. How could you not want to sleep with others warm about you?

The intimacy and safety of her mother and father nearby. Maryam, curled like a kitten up beside her. She would do anything to have that again.

Anything Edmond Ingram demanded.

Time to go. She swallowed the rock, and washed it down with blood-red wine. Outside, Sir Garit of the Ruin was watching his company assemble from atop his big bay destrier. Mail draped his torso in iron, an effect barely softened by the tabard of the Ruin belted atop. A helm shadowed his features.

Zhila stowed her things on a pack mule and clambered aboard her mare on legs stiffened to well-seasoned planks. Then she nudged it toward her goal.

He turned to her, gaze expressionless as a frozen lake.

"Ride with the Wreck," he said. "You'll be safe with him."

Which was to say, ride at the back of the company, practically in the baggage train. *As far away as possible.* The Wreck, she had observed, liked to keep a particular light wagon close at hand. Had the fellow stowed his battle loot in there?

She smiled up at him. "John is a nice man, but you are nicer to look at. I talk to the Wreck yesterday. Today I talk to you." She filled that smile with promise.

It was like smiling at a stone.

"I lead this company," the stone said. "Those who ride in it obey my rules. Ride with the Wreck, or don't ride with us at all."

Her smile wanted to run away. She wouldn't let it.

She turned it sultry instead.

"Whatever Sir Ruin wants."

There must be some way to breach his defenses, but outright defiance did not seem the best choice right now. So she sought out the Wreck and persuaded her horse to keep him company instead. It was a good opportunity to assert her mastery over the animal—it wasn't keen on keeping pace with her battered-looking friend. It was also a good opportunity to squeeze the Wreck for information.

But she mustn't be too obvious in her interrogation.

As they rode out of Los Arcos, Zhila made her first mistake. She asked John the Wreck what his role in the Company of the Ruin was.

"Engineer," the ugliest man in the world told her.

Zhila frowned. "What is *engineer?*"

A wide grin with not enough teeth to fill it. "The Ruin fights clever, and I help him do it. I mine walls, make holes in an enemy's defenses, even build the odd siege engine. But"—and here the Wreck's eyes gleamed with the fervor of true devotion—"I like gunpowder best."

"Gun…what?"

That was her second mistake. There was no halting the Wreck then. He explained in doting detail the mixing of gunpowder from sulfur, charcoal, and saltpeter, tales of his mishaps and triumphs with the tricky stuff, and generally sketched its fickle nature as fondly as a lover. Various aspects of his physique were pointed out—puckered burns, a missing finger, an eyebrow that wouldn't grow back. Yes, it seemed his sweetheart was a jealous mistress. She had left her marks all over him. Truly, Madam Gunpowder had wrecked him for any other.

By the time they neared Pamplona, Zhila was something of an expert in powder. It didn't contribute much to untangling the mystery that was Sir Garit, but it did give her an idea of his activities over the last ten years.

War. Endless campaigning. Ransoms, sieges, and battles. A rootless life that appeared to have been quite lucrative.

Not that the Wreck cared much about money, she gathered. So long as he could play with gunpowder, John the Wreck was a happy man.

But the Ruin—what drove him? Perhaps it was just the money. Or maybe, like some men she'd met and then made a point of avoiding, he'd acquired a taste for killing. His engineer shed no light on the matter. The Wreck tended to skirt the topic of Sir Garit—probably because his leader didn't explode.

Subtlety be hanged, they were nearing their destination for

the day, and she needed a chink in the Ruin's armor. He must *not* hold her at a distance for another night. It was time for a more direct approach.

She turned to the Wreck plodding alongside her with an abstracted look in his eyes. He was probably planning more fun with gunpowder in the not-too-distant future. "Sir Garit of the Ruin," she murmured. "If his home is a ruin, where is his family? They live in a ruin?"

The Wreck focused. His eyes lost their soft look and saddened instead.

"No. They don't live at all. And the place weren't always a ruin. A pack of Frenchies ruined it for him. His family too. Killed them all. A raid when he was nobbut a child. Don't know how they didn't get him too."

Zhila stared at her horse's mane. Here was information with a vengeance.

The Ruin knew what it was to lose one's parents to sudden violence.

She clenched fists upon her reins. The feelings threatened to rise again, to overwhelm her with grief and rage. She was tired after a long day of riding, vulnerable to the rising emotion. If she let it, it would crash over her like a wave, rendering her helpless.

Unable to help Maryam.

And the realization flashed upon her—this was how *he* felt too, this tight-lipped pain. Endless control and holding it together.

"Don't tell him I told you, though. He don't like to talk about it," the Wreck went on, glancing at her in concern.

Oh yes, that would be a fine topic for seduction. *How did your parents die?* She snorted. It was partly a release for her own feelings, but the Wreck's wrecked eyebrows rose.

"Don't worry, I won't tell him," she said, wrenching her focus onto the now—on what she *could* do. "So, he has no family but he will fix that soon, yes? He will get a wife."

The Wreck gave her a long look. The scars and puckers on his face assumed new alignments. She wasn't sure what they implied. She wasn't used to reading a face so radically altered.

"Aye, he's said he will marry."

Zhila pressed on. "This wife—what is she like?"

What is his taste in women? Where are his vulnerabilities in that respect? Give me something to work with.

The Wreck took some time to consider that.

Eventually he muttered, "Lords gotta marry. They gotta get an heir to pass their lordliness on to. Don't much matter what the wife is like, so long as she's a lady and can breed a brood of little 'uns."

"Yes, and this wife has a castle, not a ruin. Very good. A wife does not want to live in a ruin. But what is she *like*?"

The Wreck heaved his shoulders. "Don't know. He only clapped eyes on her the once. Never actually spoke to her, so he couldn't tell you neither."

"He's never *talked* to her?"

That was not helpful in the least.

The Wreck clearly misunderstood her reaction, for the brown eyes were looking kind again. "Never swapped so much as a *bonjour*. He don't give a dried fig for her. But he *does* like you, little dancer."

Zhila's mouth fell open, ready to declare that was not her point at all.

But the engineer hadn't finished yet. "See, he's never taken a woman along with the company before. Never. And the way he kissed you…" Parts of the wrecked cheeks actually blotched pink. He shook his head. "Wives don't matter. Lords gotta wed ladies. It's not a love thing, and, after a bit, both of them can dally with whoever they really fancy on the side. That's the way it works, I hear. Not that I'm a lord, mind you. Ha!"

Yes, John the Wreck was a nice man, even though he liked to destroy things. He was trying to make her feel better.

But she had to correct him: "The Ruin doesn't like me much."

It was the unfortunate truth. Any man could get hard in his

braies, but that didn't mean he *liked* the object of his urges. Sir Garit seemed determined to hold her at a distance, whatever she tried.

The Wreck leaned toward her, listing like a ship on a reef. Zhila was briefly alarmed that he was falling off his long-suffering nag, but no, it turned out the Wreck felt the need for a conspiratorial whisper.

"I've known the man for years, little dancer. He likes you, aye, better than you know. Don't you worry about wives."

GARIT WATCHED HER swing down from her horse. A grimace flickered over her face at the motion, but his unwanted minstrel still moved with fluid grace despite the long, hard day in the saddle.

When her feet hit the cobbles of the inn yard, her legs buckled, and Garit had to restrain himself from striding to her side. She didn't need him. She had grasped at her stirrup for support.

And he definitely didn't need her.

The Ruin was about to turn his attention to more fitting subjects—such as stabling for his horse and generally herding his company—when he caught a movement behind said pestilent camp follower.

A man stepped up behind Zhila. Not a member of his company. All of his men wore the tabard of the Ruin. It helped hold them together in battle. What was more, the image of a black and crumbling tower was a none-too-subtle statement to those he fought. *Look, I will ruin you too.*

This man wore no tabard. He walked up behind Zhila and laid a hand on her shoulder.

Garit stiffened. The damnable fellow hadn't even seen her face. What, was a rear view of waving hair and a lithe figure enough to prompt a proposition? His legs were definitely inclined to stride across the cobbles now.

Still Garit held back, staring across the courtyard and cursing whatever obscured his view. He would not leap to her side unnecessarily. So he watched, fingers flexing. If the fellow gave her any trouble, he would intervene. Just as he would for any of his men.

But no trouble ensued. It was almost a disappointment. A few sentences, a gesture or two, and the man turned and exited the yard without a backward glance. Zhila stared after the fellow for a long moment—and then one of Garit's men had the temerity to lead a horse across his line of sight.

When the view cleared, his minstrel was leading her horse to the stables as if nothing untoward had happened.

It probably hadn't.

Garit rolled his shoulders in an attempt to loosen them, then he too plodded toward the stables. The company had been forced to divide between hostelries in Pamplona. The city had no shortage of pilgrim accommodations, but none of them had sufficient room for fifty-odd arrivals so close to nightfall.

He had selected this inn because it not only boasted a roomy dormitory but also a number of secure—and available— bedchambers. Cost be damned, he'd dished out for two chambers. One for him, and quite another for Zhila. Just like last night. She would be safe, and he would sleep well.

So long as she stayed away from random, tabard-less men and didn't go sitting on anyone's lap.

THAT EVENING IN the taproom, his minstrel didn't dance. She didn't play her strange instrument either, but sat on a bench beside the Wreck and ate her repast with a distracted air.

She didn't even attempt to sit beside Garit.

Which was a good thing. Maybe his message had finally sunk

in—*You do not have to pay me for passage to France with your body.*

Yet it niggled him that she preferred the Wreck's company to his. It made it all too evident she'd only ever paid him attention to attain her own ends. And he—knowing this—had still reacted with frightening force. Christ, was he such a gullible fool?

Garit seized his cup. A draft of good red wine and a lowered cup later, Zhila still dominated his view. Only now she was rising from the bench and apparently bidding her companions good-night.

Not a bad idea, even though it was barely past dusk. Garit was more than ready for bed himself.

He waited until Zhila had exited the room. Every other man's gaze seemed to track her passage across the taproom, damn them all. The attention did not appear to affect her, but then, she *was* a performer. She was used to eyes upon her. Why, she probably encouraged them. Of course Garit's gaze followed her too—he was no better than the rest of the mangy curs. But he also scanned the taproom's contents for any undue reactions to her exit.

If any mongrel here had the cheek to follow her out into the dark, the Ruin would be pleased to show him the error of his ways.

But no one moved, save to lift mug to mouth or shovel in more food.

After the shortest possible decent period, Garit rose abruptly and bade his fellows sleep well. They would leave the inn directly after prime, he informed them, and then he turned for the door.

"Aye, and I'm sure *you'll* have a good night, captain," came an indistinct answer.

That prompted a few guffaws.

Other kindly wishes for his not-rest floated to his ears. Garit ignored them all and strode from the taproom, definitely not following hot upon his minstrel's heels.

It was only when he discovered she hadn't mounted the courtyard stairs to slip into her allotted chamber—nor was she anywhere else in the inn's vicinity—that it dawned on him.

He'd left it too long. He hadn't fooled a single fellow in the taproom with his delaying tactics, and, worse still, he'd lost her.

Where in hell had Zhila disappeared to in the nighttime shadows of Pamplona?

※

Chapter Eleven

Z HILA NEGOTIATED THE inn yard on unsteady legs. It didn't help that the courtyard was lit by a solitary guttering torch, or that the night was clouded, or the cobbled surface of the yard was treacherous. Perhaps the wine had seeped into her muscles, yet there was a deeper reason for their wobbliness too.

She was being called to account.

But Zhila couldn't wait for her eyes to adjust to the darkness. She had to go, now. Before anyone else emerged from the inn.

She slipped under the arched gateway and into the street beyond, then leaned against the wall for a moment, trying to recall. She hadn't been paying much attention to directions when they'd arrived. She'd been too tired, and there were too many things to gawk at in Pamplona. It was an impressive city, surrounded and divided by towering fortress walls, stuffed with narrow streets and teaming inhabitants. They even spoke differently here. It was nothing like the Spanish she was used to.

Zhila had simply trailed her mount behind the Wreck's as the company wound their way through overly full and under-wide streets. One of the men doubled as a billeting officer, she knew. It was his job to work out where the company would eat and sleep, their horses likewise. She didn't envy him the task in this warren of a place.

As for Zhila, she hadn't needed to consider geography—until

someone tapped her on the shoulder in the inn yard and murmured those words in her ear.

The remembrance firmed her limbs. No more dallying here, so close to the inn. Zhila Kurian pushed off the wall and stole down the ill-lit street.

THE CHURCH WAS fronted by heavy arches, great mouths of darkness dividing the street from church itself. The space within contained not one single flame. Zhila's eyes had adjusted to the grays of the street, but where she must go now was beyond gray.

It was idiocy to enter. She was alone, in a strange city where even the language was strange, and nobody knew where she'd gone. Anything could lie within those arches.

Zhila was not averse to the odd moment of idiocy, but this?

She called out quietly in Spanish, "Are you there?"

There was no answer.

Perhaps no one was there. Perhaps it was perfectly safe.

Perhaps gargoyles could fly.

No matter—she had her instructions. She had to do this thing. So Zhila drew a breath and stepped under the nearest arch.

Nothing happened. She heard no noise, save her own over-loud heartbeat. She blinked, straining to adjust to the blackness. Perhaps then she would be able to discern a figure if it came toward her.

One cautious step further, fingers tight about a dagger. But she must take care how she reacted. It would not do to kill him outright. He—

She heard the footstep too late. Arms seized her from behind. They pinned her own arms to her sides.

All the same, Zhila fought. She writhed and kicked and stamped down with her heels, trying to free a dagger hand.

Until her captor snarled in her ear, "Be still, whore. You damage me and, by God, I'll more than damage your little sister."

Zhila sagged abruptly in the man's arms. It nearly worked. She started to slither free, but he tightened his grip in time.

"Let me go!" she hissed back in his language—in English—stamping down on his foot for emphasis. A pity it seemed sturdily covered.

"Like hell," he growled. "I know what's in your hand. It's not my skin you must puncture, recall?"

Zhila stamped down again. "What do you want? Why am I here?"

She didn't need to ask *who* he was.

She recognized the man's voice. The Fox himself. Sir Edmond Ingram was deigning to wrap his arms about a mere Persian minstrel. The touch of him made her feel lice-ridden.

"Why am I here, whore? It seems you need reminding of your task."

"I do not forget! How can I forget, you—"

Only Persian curses would suffice at this juncture, but what was the point in detailing his descent from pigs if he didn't comprehend?

So she settled for: "Where is Maryam? Let me see her!"

"I think not. You have my word as a knight she is well. But she will not stay so if you continue to delay in your task."

"I am close! I join the company, as you ask. I seduce the Ruin, just as you ask."

"Ha! If you did do so, it was but a quick fuck in a stairwell. It hardly counts. You haven't stuck a single toe into his chamber."

A sensation like a spider walking down her spine. Zhila did not like spiders.

"How—?"

"You are being watched, woman. Did you think I would trust the word of a heathen whore?"

"I'm not—"

Zhila broke off. *I'm not either,* she wanted to yell. But that would be admitting she was lying. The bastard *wanted* her to be a whore. The payment she would receive for her services was her sister's life. But she could do what he required without lowering herself so far. The stupid Fox simply thought sex was the only way to get what he wanted.

"You should have done it by now," the man murmured. "I fear you are forgetful. Repeat your instructions. Reassure me."

"I remember," she whispered.

How could she forget? Maryam's absence was a gaping rent in her very being. Whenever she looked at the Ruin, she remembered what she had to do to get her little sister back.

"Prove it. Tell me what you must do."

Zhila drew a slow, tainted breath. "I must join the Company of the Ruin. I must make its leader break his rules. See, I do these things! The Ruin says no women, but here I am!"

"That is but the first step. What else must you do?"

"Sleep with him," she whispered. Her mouth felt wiped with dung.

"Yes, make him *sleep* with you. Not just fuck, but sleep. In his damned chamber. Make him break that cursed rule. Aye, ride him to exhaustion in his very own bed, then listen to him snore. Drag his mightiness so low that he breaks his rules for you, a heathen minstrel slut."

The man holding her was breathing hard. His words grated like a blacksmith's file. It was almost as well he was gripping her tight—Zhila's head felt unmoored.

"Be assured I will know if you succeed," Ingram went on. "I have friends in the company still."

So that was how he knew the seemingly unknowable. *You are being watched.* He hadn't told her this in Burgos. After Nájera, he'd dragged the sisters to Burgos in the wake of the prince's army. Then he had freed Zhila and demanded she do this despicable thing—in swap for Maryam's freedom.

"Well? Have you forgotten the rest?" the Fox snapped in her ear. "What else?"

Speak the foul words aloud? It would make it too real.

Ingram shook her. "Say it!"

"I am to…to wait till he's asleep—"

Again she stopped.

"Asleep or awake, it doesn't matter," Ingram corrected her. "Just so long as you do it in his chamber. Well? What then?"

"I kill him."

There. She had said it. Zhila stared ahead into the darkness. A life for a life. The Ruin for Maryam, that was what Edmond Ingram required. But Sir Garit's death was not enough. She also had to ruin his life.

"Yes, and…?"

"I steal from him. I unlock his strongbox and take his parchments. I bring them to you."

Thief, murderer, whore. It wasn't only the Ruin that Ingram wanted to bring low. Zhila must do all of this to a man who'd tried to protect her.

A man she wouldn't mind kissing for his own sake.

Perhaps it was foolish to argue with a rabid Fox, but she had to try.

"And if I can't do it all? Maybe I just steal from him. I—"

"You *can* do it all," Ingram fairly snarled into her ear. "Remember, he rescued *you*. He tossed me out of the company because of *you*. He did it because he wants you. I saw it. Sir noble Garit lusts after you because he has the tastes of a midden rat, and I will damn well grind it in his face. You will fuck him and kill him—you, a mere woman—and then bring all his parchments to me. *Do you understand?*"

Zhila's stomach was threatening revolt.

"But he doesn't share his chamber with anyone," she managed. "You know this. He sleeps with his valuables, all by himself. He bolts the door. His parchments and silver are locked in a chest. You told me all this, and it's true."

"Aye, he thinks he's too high and mighty to share his chamber with anyone, man or woman. Always has. But you can do it. You *must* do it. Bring him low, whore. Drag him through your heathen dirt."

Of a certainty, the red-haired knight had spent too much time in the Spanish sun. It had boiled his brains dry. Back in Burgos, when she'd been bound hand and foot in a goat shed, she had shouted at him, "Why me? If you want him dead, kill him yourself, you coward!"

But Ingram didn't want anything so simple as a Ruin's death. He demanded far more. And he had Maryam. The only way Zhila was going to get her back in one piece was by complying with a madman—or seeming to.

"My sister. How is she?" Zhila whispered.

"As I said—well enough. Alive and gabbling. Pretty little thing, she is. My men quite like her."

"No! Take me to her! Show me Maryam!"

"Keep your voice down, whore," he snarled in her ear. "I thought you might kick up, so I got the little girl to talk. She sent you a message in your cursed heathen tongue—proof she's still alive and jabbering—so be still and listen."

It worked. Zhila promptly turned into a statue.

"Yes?" she said after some moments. Her captor seemed to have been struck mute.

"Devilish tongue. Language from the pit of hell," he muttered.

He cleared his throat. It took a couple of tries, but eventually the words came out—mangled, mispronounced, but indisputably Persian. And Maryam's.

"I don't like the Fox. Take me away."

ZHILA SAGGED AGAINST the inner arch. Having delivered his message, Sir Edmond Ingram had left her with the parting words:

"Go back to the Ruin and get on with it. You follow me and I'll take that as a no. I'll cut my losses along with your throat, and as for your sister… Well, I'll let you imagine her fate."

Now the fiend was striding off down the street, confident that she did *not* wish to say no.

He was right, but Zhila would still follow him.

He would lead her to Maryam. She still had her daggers. Ingram hadn't deprived her of weapons. After all, he thought she needed them to put an end to the Ruin.

She would prefer to bury them in one rust-headed knight. Hilt deep, and with a vicious twist at the end. But better to let him lead her to her little sister first.

Enough sagging. The Englishman was turning a corner.

Zhila slipped out of the archway and ran softly down the street.

AN UNKNOWN CITY at night. Houses leaned drunkenly over the streets, shadowing the littered cobbles, and nightwatchmen appeared without notice, requiring Zhila to melt against a wall or dart into the nearest alley upon the instant. Then there were less savory customers about—slinking shadows, both two- and four-legged. Zhila must avoid them all.

It meant multiple stops and starts, twists and turns, and the result was inevitable.

She lost the rabid Englishman.

But Zhila kept on going. She might stumble upon him again. She had to keep going. He was in this midnight maze of a city somewhere, as was Maryam. She *would* find them.

She nearly stumbled over someone else entirely. Two someones, it turned out, although they were so closely entangled that they may as well have been one. They were occupying the far end of an alley Zhila was forced to leap into.

She paused, waiting for the danger in front to pass—and trying not to hear the sounds emanating from behind.

She had encountered such transactions before, plenty of times. It was one of the hazards of earning one's living as an entertainer in streets and inns. She knew exactly what was going on back there in the alley. It was an unnecessarily stark reminder of what she must do to free Maryam.

Zhila exited the lane the moment the street was clear. She would most definitely leave the lady and her customer to it. Of course, it wasn't necessarily a prostitute down there. Maybe it was an overly amorous couple, gone for a midnight stroll and overcome by the erotic charms of a dark alley.

Oh, very likely.

She walked on, slowly and carefully. Keeping to the shadows, stopping frequently to listen and look, under bombardment by jagged thoughts.

Sir Edmond Ingram was demanding she become a whore. Just like that woman in the alley. She must seduce a man who'd been good to her. Yes, in his own chilly way, Sir Garit of the Ruin was attempting to do the right thing. And how would Zhila repay him? Seduce him, pierce his heart, and then steal from her dead lover.

She must do it all to save Maryam.

How would she ever live with herself if she succeeded?

Or if she did not?

Zhila stumbled to a halt in the narrow street. It looked almost the same as the last street, and the one before that...except that this one boasted a small shrine built against a larger building. The shrine itself was barely more than an alcove. Even in the dark, she could make out the glint and flutter of innumerable votive offerings.

She had no idea which saint presided over this small dark space. Footsteps sounded on the street behind, and the nearest alley was too far away. Zhila's limbs were drained—of energy and of hope. She slipped inside the tiny building and sank down on the floor.

Any man finding her on the street, alone and at this hour of the night, would immediately assume she was exactly what Ingram wanted her to be. A whore. Perhaps her daggers might persuade him otherwise, but right now, she wasn't sure she cared.

Zhila was lost. She had lost the man who could lead her to Maryam, and she no longer knew her way back to the inn. To the Ruin.

She couldn't seduce him if she couldn't find him.

Zhila wrapped her arms around her knees and hugged them tight, keeping herself warm. Or just holding herself together.

The footsteps drew nearer. Firm, male footsteps.

Heavenly saint protect me, whoever you are. Show me some way out of this.

The owner of the footsteps wasn't necessarily malign. Perhaps she could ask her way back to the inn. If she could make herself understood—and understand in return, that was. He might not simply assume she was a prostitute or a beggar.

Or a heathen.

Or likely all three.

The footsteps drew closer. Zhila slipped a dagger from her belt. Ah yes, she was about to shed blood in a shrine. She was surely destined for hell.

The footsteps halted right in front of her. She could see the shoes that made them now. Travel-stained boots. They looked vaguely familiar.

"Well? Do you intend to sleep here? What's wrong with the chamber I hired?"

Chapter Twelve

"Y OU!"

There was a scuffling within the shrine. Its sole occupant rose in a flurry and launched herself at him.

Garit braced himself. This woman came equipped with daggers, and she knew how to use them.

But no blades darted at him this time. Only an armful of woman.

Garit found his arms wrapping round her, holding her tight—but not for his own safety this time. Not even for hers.

Simply because she needed it.

For Zhila didn't fight him. She melted against him. She buried her head into his chest. Nor was her full-frontal attack a new form of seduction.

She was shivering like a hunted animal.

So he just held her against him, offering what comfort he could because it simply felt right.

Gradually her shivering subsided, but still she nestled against him, apparently disinclined to move. Garit didn't have any objection to continuing to hold her, although it began to occur to him their surroundings could be improved.

"What are you doing out here?" he said at last. His voice sounded unnecessarily gruff to his own ears.

Zhila simply shook her head against his chest.

"If you wish to leave the company, I will not stop you," he began, but then remembered his glimpse of her room. He'd checked it before leaving the inn. Her bag, all her meager belongings, still lay on the bed.

She wasn't leaving him.

Which shouldn't make his heart feel suddenly buoyant.

"No, I not leave. I… My sister…" Another shake of her head. Worse, it was followed by a muffled sound that was almost certainly a sob.

It twisted Garit's heart sharper than any laundress's hands. She'd been so fiercely resilient so far. He'd even doubted she felt much sorrow at the loss of her family.

Oh, Garit understood the need to build defenses. Sorrow did the departed no good at all. It didn't do the living any favors either. But he didn't expect such resilience from women. They were the weaker vessels. They wept while men acted.

So, because she didn't weep, he had assumed she didn't mourn. His lovely dancer wasn't wailing now, but that one sob had said everything.

Even Zhila's resilience had its limits.

He stroked her hair back. He only did it because stray strands were tickling his neck. Her hair was so thick. It slipped like richest sarcenet under his fingers. It was like stroking a sleek, semi-wild cat.

"I take it you don't want to sleep in the shrine of Saint"—he peered at the crude image over the alcove—"Saint Fermin's for the night? Is the Bull Inn an acceptable alternative?" He paused. "Or were you trying to turn Christian?"

Ah, he thought that would do the trick.

The head he was stroking lifted abruptly. He felt rather than saw dark eyes glaring up at him.

"I *am* Christian. No need to turn." She straightened a little. "I lose myself. That is all. Pamplona is big. I lose the inn. Take me back."

THEY WALKED IN silence. He seemed watchful, disinclined to talk. Which was good. Zhila's thoughts were quite noisy enough.

She had nearly succumbed. He was still a rock, but she needed that rocklike solidity. He was an unshakeable boulder Zhila could throw herself against, knowing he would remain firm.

She wanted to rely on that firmness, in the hand that stroked her hair with seeming tenderness. She wanted so badly to tell him about Maryam. He had come to find her, hadn't he? He would know how to deal with the Fox.

But that jibe about turning Christian—it was a timely reminder. Too much divided them—culture, rank, even the state of her soul. Sir Garit of the Ruin thought her a lowly minstrel, an inferior heathen. He would never, ever take her side against one of his own. For all Garit had thrown him out of his company, Sir Edmond was still a fellow knight. There was honor amongst knights, she knew. A strange Christian code. That code did not extend to foreign minstrels, and especially not to heathens.

Worse, Ingram had informants within the Company of the Ruin. That was the point of this meeting tonight. A warning—*You are watched. Get on with it.*

She could not murmur a word about her dilemma in case Ingram found out. Maryam would suffer, and that wound a gag tight about her mouth.

The Ruin had hold of her arm. He was leading her through the shadowed streets of Pamplona as if he feared she would slip away again, but she didn't mind. His hand was strong and warm where it closed over her forearm.

And there was the Bull Inn, the placard of the horned animal just visible above the gate. Sir Garit wasn't lost. But then, Sir Garit hadn't trailed an enemy through unknown streets in the dark.

He led her under the archway just as the bells began to chime matins. The dead of night. Only monks and nightwatchmen were up at this hour.

"You, woman, are not good for my rest," the owner of the hand said as the bells died to echoes.

He seemed to be leading her toward the stairs that ascended to the bedchambers. Zhila halted.

"You came to look for me, yes?" She twisted and tried to look up into her companion's face. It was shadowed, unreadable. "You could have slept instead. So why look? Why not rest?"

"True," came the flat reply. "I could have left you to nap on a shrine floor for the night. Why ruin my own sleep?" A sigh. "I lead this company, woman. I have a responsibility for those within it."

She cocked her head at him, wondering if he could see her smile in the dark. "You tuck all your men into bed?"

This was her chance. He did not seem angry at her, even though he'd raked the streets of Pamplona when he'd prefer to be asleep. The Fox demanded a seduction. Here was her opportunity to thank the Ruin properly for coming to find her.

The knight was looking down at her, his features shadowed.

Zhila could step into his arms now. Just one pace would close the gap between them. She would wind her arms about his neck. She would coax him into kissing her as he'd done before...in the smithy, with enough fire to melt iron. It really wouldn't be so bad.

Not at all objectionable, actually. She was leaning toward him even now. Yes, she'd felt that mouth against hers before, and she wanted more.

No. The thought of kissing him—more than kissing him—simply because the Fox dictated it was abhorrent.

Yet she had to. For Maryam.

And she wanted to, for herself.

"God help me," she whispered in Persian.

Her voice broke on the last word.

"You are right, Zhila. I do not tuck all my men into bed. Not even one of them. But you…" He reached out and brushed her cheek. Then withdrew. "Something is wrong. Something has frightened you. Tell me."

⟫⟫⟫⟪⟪⟪

IT WAS TRUE enough. His dagger-wielding dancer seemed strangely vulnerable. In need of his arms about her.

No, that was the last thing he needed at this time of night, with his chamber so close by.

But something was going on. She had walked out of the inn deliberately, in the dark. He could think of no good reason for such a hazardous action.

Zhila shivered. Cold? He could fix that.

No. Garit held himself immobile.

"I… Nothing. No, I lose myself. That is all."

Oh, very convincing.

She made a convulsive movement as if to reach for him, only to rein herself back.

It was too much. He closed the distance between them. He scooped her up into his arms, promising himself that this was absolutely the last time he would ever do so.

After a moment of startled stiffness, Zhila softened against him. A delicious weight in his arms.

"You are ready for bed, are you not?" he murmured down at her.

She shifted her head to look at him, an unreadable gaze in the darkness.

"Yes," she said. "Take me."

He ascended the stairs, slowly. He halted before the door. Sadly, Garit had to put his burden down to open it—he had ensured it was locked when he left.

He released her legs, and Zhila slipped down his length. Then he fumbled for the lumpish iron key and handed it to her.

He had to close her fingers about the object. Even then, she didn't appear to comprehend its use.

"The key to your door," he said. "Turn it once you're inside. It will keep you safe."

She looked up at him, the starlight catching her eyes. "No, not my room. I want *your* room."

"No."

Said automatically. Absolutely. It was an article of faith. No one shared his chamber, although Garit was struggling to remember why right now.

She leaned against him.

"Please," she said. "I am… Yes, I am frightened."

Even in the midst of his own struggle, he registered the oddness of her tone.

Odd? She had lost her family, her protection against the world, he'd just found her lost on the streets of a strange city, and she was asking him for—what? Shelter? Or comfort of a more physical kind?

"You not have to…to take me if you not want," she whispered.

Garit nearly snorted. *Not want,* saints forgive him. That was certainly not the problem.

Gently he tilted her chin, trying to read her expression in the low light. "What do you want?"

His gaze lingered on her lips. He waited for them to move in reply. Beautiful lips, sweetly curved and inviting. Too inviting.

"I sleep in your room…in your bed." She paused. The words that followed were almost too quiet to hear. "Then I feel safe."

Garit stared down at her. Not that he could see much. She was all dark hair and warm woman against him.

He had slept alone for so long, so very long. It was an iron fact of life. But this woman was temporary. She only wanted to be taken to France—safely.

"I not used to sleeping alone," she explained. "My family…"

She broke off, but Garit understood. *He* was the strange one.

It was downright peculiar to sleep solus, especially if one fought for a living. Beds were scarce and soldiers had to share. Even when safely at home, lords slept with servants and family in their chambers. As for the lower orders, they didn't get a choice. It was all together for warmth and want of room. And human comfort.

For Zhila to sleep alone only emphasized all she'd lost.

It was the same reason Garit slept alone. Almost.

"I don't take up much room," she added. He saw her lips curve. He could not pull his gaze away. "I not snore. Promise."

Oh yes, she sensed his resolve crumbling like the ruin it was. Garit struggled for clarity. The thought of this untamed creature in his bed, her vibrant presence, her odd ways… Well, it wasn't as objectionable as it should have been.

She *was* strictly temporary. And a woman in need. Perhaps there was no harm in breaking his rule for so short a period. A knight was sworn to protect women, was he not?

Garit knew he'd regret this. He just couldn't remember why right now.

"All right," he muttered. "You asked for it."

Chapter Thirteen

S HE HAD DONE it.

The Ruin ushered her into the dark of his room. The door closed with wooden finality behind him. Then came the scrape of a bolt, followed by the iron clunk of a key. She was encompassed by blackness.

She had done as the Fox demanded and inveigled herself into the enemy's room, but would Sir Edmond even know of his triumph? Who would be watching at this godforsaken hour?

And what happened now?

There came the chink of iron on flint followed by a tiny shower of sparks. A wisp of tow caught fire and illuminated the shadow of a man. Bending over a candle.

The candle flame wavered and grew. The Ruin used it to light another. There was no hiding in the darkness anymore.

Rather than look at him, she eyed the bed. It was a sizable piece of furniture. It would likely accommodate three grown men at a pinch. Travelers were accustomed to share. Zhila's family had. It provided warmth and security. Closeness.

"Well, will it do? Climb in, woman."

The soft words raised gooseflesh on her arms. She'd asked for this, he had said. So best get on with it.

Her fingers fumbled at the buttons and ties that secured her clothing. First the belt about her hips. It held her daggers. But how would she kill him if she didn't have her daggers near? The belt dangled from her hand a moment, then she cast it to the floor. She would deal with that problem when she came to it. There was more than one way to kill a knight. Smother him with a pillow, maybe.

Then there were the buttons that secured her thigh-length dress. It was an unusual garment, hugging her torso, casting a deep V at her cleavage, and fashioned of true Persian brocade. Unusual for women of Spain, but not in the least unusual for her people.

It was just pooling at her feet when the Ruin spoke again.

"Leave the rest on."

She still wore her under-gown and trousers. She glanced at him for clarification, but the Ruin wasn't even looking at her. He had turned away to place the candle on a ledge. As she watched, he began to unbuckle his own, much heavier belt.

A shiver rippled through her. It wasn't due to the cold. All the same, she flicked back the coverlet and clambered into bed. She tugged the musty coverings up to her neck and watched him.

He laid his belt and weapons on a small wooden trunk. His strongbox. Then he bent to unlace the greaves protecting his legs with calm efficiency. He'd been armed when he stalked the streets of Pamplona looking for her, not for full battle but certainly in anticipation of a fight.

Zhila's heart was beating in her ears. Her body did not feel her own. Would he like it? Her body, that was. Doubtless he would make short work of her under-dress and trousers, and then…

It didn't matter if he liked it. He would be dead. Fox's orders.

He would be dead and she would be dishonored, but Maryam would be free. Just as soon as Zhila gave Ingram his precious parchments.

The Ruin knelt to tug off his boots and then straightened to draw down the hose that wrapped about his legs so snugly.

He laid the discarded hose on the trunk and turned to the

bed. Zhila stared at bare legs in the candlelight. Long, strong legs, dusted with golden hair that caught the light. Nicely muscled legs, actually. Her gaze wandered up their length, and she noted the odd scar and wheal, only to snag on a line of linen mid-thigh.

The hem of his tunic. She would lift her gaze no higher.

Wordlessly, he walked to the bed. He drew back the coverlet, and Zhila tensed. The candles still burned. He had not snuffed them out, as any sensible person did before sleeping. He wanted to see all, did he? So be it. Hopefully the flames would remain burning long enough for her to aim a dagger or a pillow afterward.

The mattress dipped beneath his weight, and Zhila's entire body became one sensory organ—watching, feeling, waiting.

Heartbeats passed—quite a few of them, at the rate Zhila's heart was going. She peeked sideways. The Ruin was sitting, seemingly at his ease amidst the pillows. She could not see his face, curled up in the bed as she was. But she knew he was gazing down at her.

"Comfortable?" came the deep voice above her.

At any other time, she might have laughed. He, inquiring after her comfort when he was about to seriously discomfit her? What was he waiting for?

"No," she retorted.

The bed was undeniably comfortable, but she was not.

Did he require a signal of some sort?

This was her first, perhaps only, chance. She was finally inside his chamber. She would steel herself to do this thing. All of it. The Fox was nearby. She could get Maryam back tomorrow. Family. Duty. Love. Maryam was all that mattered.

She reached out. Found a leg. Felt muscle, warmth, tension.

"What are you doing, Zhila?"

She didn't answer. She did move her palm slowly up his leg.

"Stop."

She hesitated. Her fingers had been about to slip under his tunic. Had she done something wrong?

"Sleep, Zhila. Know that you are safe. I will watch over you. Your safety does not come at a price."

Price? The price of prostitution. That was what the Fox demanded.

Her fingers seemed to burn where they caressed his skin. Super-sensitive, craving, *move just a little further and he won't be able to resist.*

His hand encompassed hers. It lifted hers from his leg.

The message was clear.

She was meant to be seducing him, damn him! That was the point of her being in his chamber, but a certain Ruin did not seem to comprehend the rules. Surely he knew he needn't act the chivalrous knight with a low-as-mud minstrel?

"Sleep, Zhila," he repeated, and smoothed her hair back from her forehead.

What was she—a child?

The very fact that he was refusing her settled the matter. Zhila rolled over. She slipped her upper leg over the Ruin's and slid neatly into place, right where she belonged. In his lap. There were considerably fewer layers between her skin and his than at any time she'd sat there before. She could feel almost everything.

She took him by his tunic collar and gazed into his face.

It was not expressionless.

How could it be when his manhood was a solid pole between them?

She stared into his eyes and felt the dreadful realization sink in. She wanted this. She longed to tug off his tunic and make a minute inventory of the naked man that lay below. She wouldn't mind the favor being returned.

Then she wanted to sink herself onto that pole and watch the ice in his eyes turn to fire.

She craved all that, but she must still rob him and kill him.

"Don't you want me?" she said.

Silly question. His eyes burned in the affirmative. His manhood was a lance against her belly.

"I promised you safety. You have my word," he said.

"I see no contradiction."

She shifted slowly against him. He closed his eyes.

"No, Zhila. You are vulnerable. I will not take advantage. Sleep, now," he said. "I will remain awake. I will…keep watch."

Two big hands clamped about her waist. They hoisted her off him. They were quivering a little.

Zhila let herself be replaced on the mattress. *He wants me, but he will not take me.* It was a puzzle to play a wild push and pull with her heart. *He will not sleep. He will keep watch like a good and faithful knight. So how do I kill him?*

He doesn't trust you. You are in his chamber, therefore he will not sleep.

But he does *want me.* Her body tingled with delicious warmth. Frustrated warmth.

"Lie down, Zhila. Sleep."

Were his words strained, as if Sir Garit was holding on to knightly resolution by a thread? Or was it simply impatience with a recalcitrant bedmate?

Zhila couldn't think straight. The day had been too long and too full of strain. How could you argue a man into an audible bout of lovemaking? And it must be audible, just in case Ingram or one of his cronies was hovering near. Proof.

So she subsided on the mattress, just as ordered. But she didn't give up.

Perhaps she could tell His Foxiness she had done his foul bidding and bedded the Ruin, but the man hadn't made more squeak than a mouse in the process. Quiet in love and quiet in life, that was Sir Garit. How could Ingram know otherwise?

Zhila snuggled up against a long, strong leg.

The leg tensed, but it didn't move away.

But the Ruin *must* sleep. There was no way she could kill him while he was awake. Not without her daggers. Perhaps not even *with* her daggers. Garit was a consummate warrior.

Maybe that was why Ingram demanded copulation. Men

were notorious for pounding away with no thought for the one pounded upon, and then snoring immediately afterward. She could kill him easily then.

No. There was more to it than that. Ingram wanted to undermine the Ruin's rules. No women in the company; no company in his bedchamber. The Fox likely desired revenge against Zhila, too. He blamed her for his eviction from the company.

But there was something else as well. Something that Zhila couldn't put her finger on.

No matter. With a bit of luck, the Ruin would doze off anyway.

She nestled her brow against a motionless shoulder. She tucked herself up against a big, warm, unmoving male. It did not appease the yearning in her own limbs one iota. Such a strange tension, her whole body intensely aware of his, as if he were a lodestone drawing her irresistibly near.

Now she must pretend slumber. If she was drowsing, surely he would doze off too? Zhila forced herself to relax, to soften in trustful repose against an immoveable Ruin. It wasn't so hard, really. She was curled against the warm bulk of someone she knew with absolute certainty would protect her. Who refused to take advantage, damn him.

She listened to a Ruin breathing, waiting for the rhythm to slow into sleep.

Zhila never heard it happen. She slept herself.

BIRDS TWITTERED IN the eaves. The candles had long since burned out, but now the ink of the chamber lightened to gray. And Sir Garit of the Ruin stirred not a muscle.

Actually, Garit *needed* to move—his bladder was asserting the matter with some insistence—but there was a woman beside him, her body tucked against his, her breath warming his shoulder. He didn't want to wake her, and certainly not to the sweet sound of Garit availing himself of the chamber pot but a pace from her bed. But the only alternative was to step outside into the chill dawn and locate a patch of grass.

Damn it, this was just one of the reasons why he never shared his chamber with anyone. Practically all the company's valuables lay within it. Garit was its guarantor.

But he would only be gone a moment, and the key to the chest hung about his neck. What could happen in so short a span?

He glanced down at Zhila. She was merely a shape in the gray predawn—a slumbering warmth beside him.

But even that much was a mistake. Something within him contracted. A fist clenched around his heart, or perhaps about a region lower down. Pain, craving, or a seething stew of both? Ah, he had to get out of bed.

He slipped out with as little disturbance as possible and padded to the door. Success. She didn't stir.

Once outside, he hesitated on the gallery, key to the chamber in hand. Locking Zhila up again seemed wrong, as if she was his property as much as the strongbox. But she was asleep, and Garit would be gone only a few moments. He was doing this for her safety too.

He turned the key in the lock.

THE MOMENT SHE heard the key clunk, Zhila rolled out of bed. She sank on her knees by the chest. Yanked it open.

And failed.

The lumping great lid wouldn't open.

She peered in the half-light, observing heavy iron banding wrapping around the chest, and a blocky-looking affair midway that must be a lock. A locked lock.

Perhaps she should just climb back into bed. Stop risking everything for nothing. After all, the Fox demanded more than parchments from her.

But the thought would not be banished.

If only she could get the parchments, she might convince the Fox she'd done as much as she could. *I tried to murder him. Really, I did. I did everything else you asked. Just give me my sister back.*

No matter—the horrible thing was locked.

Zhila was sorely tempted to kick the strongbox, but her feet were bare and she knew which party would come off worse. She had minimal experience of locks. Her parents had never owned anything valuable enough to lock up, or anything permanent enough to lock it to. Besides, locks were expensive, heavy things, requiring considerable blacksmithing skill.

But she knew they required a key, or something approximating one.

Zhila began to scrabble through the Ruin's things.

GARIT HAD TO descend the stairs outside to locate the desired patch of greenery, with grass not thriving on balconies. Then he hauled a bucket from the well in order to splash his face and hands. On second thoughts, he gave his nether regions a wetting too. He had to stifle a yelp at the chill water, but it was for a good cause. With his bladder relieved, his groin had begun to contemplate other activities. Garit needed to cool that impulse down before returning to his room.

Time to rejoin Zhila. Garit ascended the stairs slowly, frowning. A woman awaited him in his chamber, in his bed. Not just any woman, but one who had lost everything and yet somehow remained vividly alive. A woman he felt the most inconvenient urge to protect.

It felt both deeply right and quite wrong.

This human contact, the simple trust implicit in sharing a bed with another person, left one feeling so exposed. It was a breach in defenses. And with it came the temptation to let it continue.

He paused at the door and patted about for his key. The chest key was about his neck, but the chamber key…

Curse it, yet another consequence of sharing a room with another—one must wander outside half undressed to relieve oneself, and consequently without a pocket in which to stow one's key. So where had he put the devilish thing?

He glanced about. Heaven help him, had he locked his dancer in and tossed the key down the well? Oh, she would be pleased.

A movement below. Down in the inn yard, a figure leaned against the well rim. Garit wasn't the only member of the company to be up before dawn. The fellow had been looking at him, Garit was almost certain. He raised a hand in greeting, but the man did not seem to see it. He began to haul water from the well.

Garit was just considering calling down to the fellow—what was his name? Jack? Joe?—to ask if there was a stray key lying about, when his gaze snagged on an object nearer at hand. Praise heaven. He must have laid the thing on the gallery railing in his befuddled state. Thank Christ no one had happened along in the meantime. He might even now be availing himself of Garit's silver…or his Zhila.

The mere thought had him snatching up the key and shoving it at the lock with more energy than finesse. The key fell to the wooden floor. Garit stooped for the recalcitrant piece of iron, and, in that moment of crouching, he heard a noise. *Inside* his chamber. Hasty noises.

His bed companion was up and about, evidently. Pity. Garit wouldn't have minded slipping back under that prewarmed coverlet and—

No, something about the scuffling didn't sound right.

This time, Garit inserted the key successfully and made short work of the door.

There was no one inside but Zhila, and—

Garit turned his back and slammed the door shut.

"For God's sake, woman, get some clothes on," he said to the door.

Zhila was quite naked.

"I thought you'd gone. I change my clothes, you see."

Yes, he had seen, and by God he wanted to see more. But if he turned around right now, certain parts of him might forget they'd just received a dousing in cold water.

She was vulnerable. She just wanted safe passage to France. He had rules for a reason. What reason? *She reminded you of your mother, dammit.* Once.

"Well, I've come back. Clothe yourself, Zhila."

He stared at the door, listened to her rustling just feet away, and thought celibate thoughts. Damn it all to hell. This was just another reason why the Ruin did not share his sleeping quarters with anyone. Especially not a woman like this one.

Oh, Zhila *would* sleep with him, Garit knew. She would do far more than sleep. She had made that plain last night. Perhaps she was doing so again. He was her safety, her passage to France. She was willing to swap all sorts of interesting favors for those two things.

But only if she had to.

No, this was his atonement, long overdue and gathering ruinous interest. He would see Zhila to safety for the sake of everyone he had ever failed. For Marie and his mother. Why, those two were probably looking down from heaven right now, praying Garit would pass the test.

So Sir Garit of the Ruin took a deep breath, thought heavenly thoughts, and passed the test.

By a weasel's whisker.

Chapter Fourteen

FOUR AND A half days later, Donal strode up to Zhila's seat in the inn. She'd just topped a long day off in the saddle with a bout of energetic *daf* playing. Now she needed a rest, and Donal looked all set to disturb it.

All the same, Zhila grinned up at the approaching horse-master. She'd talked to Donal and plenty of others in the company too over the last few days. Luckily, the men appeared to find her curiosity about their reserved leader entirely natural. As the Ruin's acknowledged lap warmer, she was entitled to a little context.

"Got word of a certain knight," Donal said. "Seems he's been asking about—"

"Wait." Her seat flung up an imperious hand, and Donal's mouth instantly stopped producing sound. "Outside," said the Ruin.

Zhila's seat rose, and she slid off.

The two men promptly stepped out of the inn, closing the door behind them. Zhila frowned. *A certain knight.* But whatever Donal had to announce, his master did not want her hearing it. And there was no way she could listen in, not without being obvious.

She'd had no further opportunity to carry out her Foxy orders since said animal had made them so horribly clear. The company had left Pamplona and wound up the pilgrim way into the mountains. Over the pass of Roncesvalles and toward France. And Zhila either slept beside John the Wreck or in a lonely chamber of her own. The night in Pamplona was an anomaly. The Ruin continued to let her cozy up to him in public, just for show, but that was as far as it went.

The Ruin slept alone. It seemed a rule cast in rock. He hadn't even broken it in Pamplona, for he had not slept while she was in his chamber. Apparently one such night of sleep loss was enough. His superfluous minstrel could sleep elsewhere after that.

Whoever Ingram had set to watch her would know this. Ingram himself would be growing impatient. But how was she to enter his chamber?

The inn door was flung open. The Ruin re-entered, minus his horse-master. He strode back to Zhila with purpose in his eyes.

"Come with me."

His hand closed on her arm. Strong fingers, gently but irresistibly urging her up.

She followed. He led her out the door, through the dark, and right to his chamber.

There was a guard at the door. Zhila couldn't make out much, but she was certain the fellow's eyebrows rose.

The Ruin paused. "Go, Piers. I'll see you in the stables. Donal will explain."

Then the Ruin opened the door and steered her in.

A small oil lamp burned in a niche. It showed her a plain room furnished only with a bed. It was the sole private room this isolated inn had to offer, and the Ruin had taken it. She was supposed to sleep on the taproom floor tonight, moored alongside a Wreck for safety.

Had her luck suddenly changed?

But why? She'd been sitting on his lap a short while ago, true, and as usual she'd been aware that her presence stirred him. Not that his expression gave the least clue. But now he wasn't even looking at her.

He led her to the bed and pushed her gently down, and her heart skittered. But then he turned on his heel and stared at the door instead.

Zhila eyed the door too. It was a plain, sturdy affair, designed to be secured with a simple bolt rather than a more expensive lock.

"I didn't ask you before because I feared the answer would be too painful for you," he said to the door. Then, more quietly, "And because I didn't want to know."

Given that the door didn't answer, Zhila did.

"What?"

Her fingers dug into the mattress. He had noticed her attempt to access his strongbox in Pamplona after all. She had rifled through his things for a key that wouldn't be found. She had been trying to twist her dagger in the lock when she'd heard him at the door. So she'd done the only thing she could think of to distract him—stripped off her clothes and tossed them over the mess she'd made, in the hope a naked woman in his bedchamber would claim a Ruin's attention above jumbled belongings.

How convenient that he'd turned his back. Under the guise of dressing, she'd been able to set his things to rights.

It was almost a disappointment.

But now...

He turned and faced her. "What happened in Nájera after I left you in the church?"

Zhila gripped the mattress edge for a whole new set of reasons.

"I...I go to my parents. I check... I see that they—"

"Were truly dead?"

"Yes," she whispered. "I pray for them. *Christian* prayers," she added with a flash of fire. "Why do you ask this? Why now?"

"What happened after that? I came to look for you later. You weren't there. A Spanish woman said that... Well, you tell me."

"You *looked* for me—why?"

It was a delaying tactic. Something *had* aroused his suspicions.

He wanted to know about Ingram.

"I felt a responsibility." His face was like hewn rock in the lamplight. "Do you remember the man who helped me rescue your sister in Nájera? A knight. Red hair. He wore the tabard of the Ruin then. He does so no more. Did he come back?"

Zhila's heart was pounding in her ears. She couldn't think. Much more of this, and he would find out all. Maryam would be lost.

"Yes, he came back. He waited in the church—for me."

"He wrested you from holy sanctuary, you and your sister. What then? What did he do?"

His blue eyes burned. What did he know?

She gave an inarticulate cry and drew her knees against her chest. Her daggers were sheathed on her belt, but she didn't like her chances even if she got them out. She noticed now that the Ruin was armored. He hadn't been so in the taproom, back when he was her comfortable seat.

He approached. A hand landed, heavy on her shoulder.

"Zhila." His voice was soft. "I am sorry, but I—"

A thudding on the door. "Sir Garit? Ready, sir?"

The hand on her shoulder tensed.

"One moment, Donal," he called, then, more quietly: "I will not pain you with further recollection, Zhila. Not tonight. But know this—you will be avenged. Now I must leave you for some hours. Stay here. This is the safest location in the inn. Bar the door. Do not unbolt for any but me."

Zhila lifted her head, barely daring to hope, but the Ruin was a flurry of action, throwing on the remainder of his weapons and armor, pinning his cloak. He paused a moment, hand on the door, to look at her. A long, expressionless look that somehow contained a sea of expression just beneath. If only she could understand what it was.

"Bolt the door after me," he said, and left.

GARIT TOOK LESS than half the company. He left most of the archers sleeping or doing whatever they saw fit to do with their evening (dice, drink, dubious women). They were not adapted for swift horseback maneuvers in the dark. Garit needed men who could ride like the Horsemen of the Apocalypse and handle a sword at the end of it too. Archers couldn't aim in the dark. Besides, Edmond Ingram reportedly had but a handful of men.

It was drizzling, which also meant the night was damnably dark. They rode back the way they had traveled. Even at a trot, it was dangerous riding. Rain and leaves whipped at his face. Truly, Garit could think of more pleasant ways to spend an evening. Stretched out in bed with a sinuous dancer, for example.

"Why the hell didn't you tell me this in daylight?" He raised his voice so Donal could hear him over the rain and hoofbeats.

"Only had word after dusk," his horse-master called back. "Group of travelers. Said they had to push on here 'cause some red-headed bastard had taken all the beds in the last village."

Garit frowned. That didn't sound quite right. "You said Ingram doesn't have many men. What's he doing occupying all the beds, then?"

Hooves thudded on, and Garit awaited a reply.

"Dunno. Didn't ask."

Garit's frown didn't lift. It was probably for the best—lowered brows were good protection against spitting rain.

"What *did* you ask?"

"I told you."

"Well, tell me again."

"You said you wanted word of Ingram's whereabouts if ever we got to hear of it. So I checked that it *was* Ingram. Other knights have rusted hair, you know."

"And? What convinced you?"

"He was asking after you. Wanted to know the whereabouts

of the Company of the Ruin."

"That doesn't mean he's Ingram," Garit called back. "Maybe some other red bastard is after my hide."

"And your woman? Why'd he ask about her, then?"

"What?" Garit barked. His stallion flung his head up at his tone.

"The heathen dancer who's riding the Ruin. Ingram's very words, apparently."

The words floated to Garit in the dark. Like bat wings.

"She's not a heathen," he muttered, but didn't bother to repeat the sentence at Donal's request.

For lights flickered through the trees ahead. A village. *The* village, with any luck. A small settlement containing an inn, which in turn contained a certain red-headed knight who would find himself answering a goodly number of questions this very night. Whether he felt inclined to do so or not.

Garit's frown lifted. He found himself hoping Edmond Ingram was disinclined to talk. The Ruin was in the mood to encourage a bit of chat.

ZHILA WENT TO the strongbox the moment she was sure Garit was gone. She could hardly believe her luck. Whatever Donal had called him away for would evidently take some time. Even better, this chamber had no lock. It was equipped with a bolt only—a sturdy, iron-enforced bolt that was drawn across from the inside. Thus, only Zhila could open it. The Ruin could not burst back in again and surprise her into taking all her clothes off again.

Not that she could try that trick a second time. He might find it coincidental—or just plain desperate.

No, if he came knocking too soon, she could unbolt in her own good time. Any suspicion over delay could be attributed to her being asleep.

She settled the oil lamp just above the chest and took a moment to observe the precise layout of the Ruin's belongings on and around the wooden strongbox. The man had a penchant for neatness, which was convenient for Zhila. She simply removed the items from the lid and placed them in an identical row on the floor—a leather roll she knew contained toiletries, a linen towel, a spare tunic, and braies.

Then she took a deep breath and raised the lid.

Of course it didn't budge. She couldn't expect that much luck in one night.

A quick search for the key. She had a horrible suspicion the Ruin kept it on his person, but she had to look. Alternatively, she was willing to shove any bit of metal she came across into the keyhole. She'd met characters who'd boasted that no lock could keep them out. Not the sort of characters she'd want to call friend, admittedly, but it showed that one did not need a key to open a lock.

No key, so she looted his toiletries roll for *faux* keys and came across a narrow, wickedly sharp dagger she guessed he used for shaving. Jammed it into the lock. Wiggled it. Likely blunted it in the process, but achieved no more. Oh well, what did Zhila care if the Ruin cut himself while shaving?

Perhaps she could wallop the chest with a sword? No, he might wonder why his box looked like a woodcutter had been at it.

Oh, for God's sake, why was this so hard? Here was the perfect opportunity to steal the parchments without having to seduce or kill their owner, and the Ruin had wrecked it by taking his key with him. There must be some other solution.

Zhila was searching the room with exhaustive intensity, tossing each item that proved useless or keyless onto the bed, when the door rattled.

She froze. He was back. So soon? And just look at this mess.

Two raps on the door.

"Let me in."

Chapter Fifteen

Z HILA TURNED INTO a whirlwind, returning items in what she hoped was their approximate position, if occasionally upside down.

"I'm back, Zhila. Open the door," came the muffled voice outside.

"One moment!" she called, and lined up the little row on top of the chest. At least that looked immaculate.

"Hurry up, woman. It's cold out here."

She gave the room one final, frazzled scrutiny.

"By God, woman, I'll give you such a kissing as—"

Zhila flung back the bolt just as the words sank in. Off key. Too late.

It wasn't Sir Garit of the Ruin who inserted his leg into the doorway and followed it up with the rest of his frame. Once inside, he slammed said door shut, bolted it, and turned to her.

She recognized him. One of the company. An archer. Zhila drew breath to scream, but the man lunged at her. She evaded him, but at the cost of letting out a mere squeak.

"Shut your trap, woman."

Which meant she must do exactly the opposite. Yell loud enough, and someone would hear.

"What do you want?" she screeched at him, ducking away from his reaching arm. "This is the Ruin's room! Leave! You won't like what he'll do to you."

"Oh, I know whose chamber it is, and he's not here to do anything to me, is he? Or you. No matter how you like it."

He was closing in on her. The room was too small. It would take too long to unbolt the door to flee, so she slipped out her daggers.

The man drew his sword.

She sprang at him with a bellow that would do a bull proud, but he was ready for her. The sword lashed out. It walloped her across her ear. Zhila fell sideways.

Her ear was ringing, but somehow she was still alive. He must have hit her with the flat of his sword.

The tip of said blade was leveled at her throat. That part was not blunt.

"Drop them." He glanced at her daggers. "I don't want to kill you, but I will if I must."

Zhila hesitated, then let the lovely things drop.

"Good. Now stand."

Zhila rose to a crouch. She looked at her daggers, but the sword hovered. He did not want to kill her—that gave her a chance—but what did he want?

She rose to her feet. The world swayed.

The intruder grabbed her. His mistake—he had approached her from the front. Her knee shot up with unerring aim.

Unfortunately, he'd dressed for such exigencies. A plate-lined brigandine prevented the fellow from joining a boys' choir. But he felt her intent, and he snarled.

"Damned whore. Be still or I'll break your teeth."

He wrenched her around. One hand seized her throat while the other clamped her torso against his.

She tried to yell, but his hand was squeezing her throat. She could only emit a strangled croak.

She squirmed wildly. She stamped, but his hand was tightening.

"What you want?" Her voice was a whispering rasp.

She'd thought he wanted her body. She thought perhaps he was Ingram's man. But now?

She couldn't breathe. Dark spots swirled, grew bigger.

"A share of the loot," he murmured in Zhila's ear.

Her knees buckled.

THE RUIN RETURNED to the inn well past midnight. To *his* inn, and his bedchamber—which contained his dancer. Not the inn that had contained Sir Edmond Ingram.

Had being the operative word. The fellow had been there last night, or so the innkeeper he'd hauled out of bed claimed. Yes, a rust-headed English knight with a ragtag band of followers. Slept here last night. Left just after dawn. Probably miles away by now.

All the same, Garit had searched the inn. He'd picked the place apart. It had taken some time, and he'd made no friends in the process, but the innkeeper's words were confirmed—not a single redhead on the premises. No likely ragtags, either.

Donal's informants had got their days muddled.

Which left nothing for it but to plod back through the drizzle to the inn and Zhila. At the thought of *his* minstrel in *his* bed, a smile besieged his lips.

"Zhila," he called through the door. "Are you awake?"

No answer. Silly question—of course she'd be asleep by now.

He rapped on the door.

Well, that was the intention. Actually, he only got one rap in before the planks of wood opened on their own accord. There'd been no footsteps, no drawing of bolts—the door just creaked into darkness.

Garit's sword slithered from its sheath. He flattened himself against the wall by the doorway, and waited. And listened.

No sound but his own overloud heart.

"Zhila?"

He didn't expect an answer this time, and he didn't get it.

A movement down in the courtyard distracted him. A man's shadowy shape. Garit recognized it, mostly because it had walked out of the stables.

Garit risked raising his voice. "Donal, bring a light!"

The shape paused, then hurried off.

It seemed to take his horse-master an age to locate a torch. In the interim, there was still no noise from within. Garit remained where he was, one with the wall and prey to a procession of images in his mind. None were pleasant.

But at least when he snatched the torch from Donal and marched in, it wasn't to discover Zhila's mangled body sprawled over his bed. That had been the predominant image.

There was no body in his bed at all, alive or dead. Things were strewn all over the chamber, but they were *his* things, not Zhila's.

Her bag was gone. She was gone.

The strongbox was gone.

"What in deepest hell…?" Donal said behind him.

"I told her to bolt the door. I told her to open to no one but me." Garit's voice was flat.

"It's not been forced," Donal said from the doorway.

"I know."

A moment later—a long, blank moment—Garit spoke again. "The horses. Are any missing?"

"Maybe." Donal drew the word out. "Don't reckon I saw the mare your dancer's been riding, come to think of it."

Garit swept the flame slowly around the room. It only confirmed his first impressions. When he spoke, his voice seemed to come from some distance away.

"It won't be there. She's taken it, Donal. Look, the strongbox is gone."

And you, Garit of the Ruin, are a trusting fool. What did you expect? You took a minstrel into your company—an amoral, heathenish, beautiful minstrel—and she played you.

SHE WOKE TO find herself upside down, her cheek pressed against a rough surface that reeked of horse. Her whole body jolted rhythmically. Chill damp dusted her neck and her hands, and the world was dark.

It took some moments of nightmarish panic before she worked it out—the upside-downness, the jolting. The smell was a clue. She was gagged and tied and slung over a horse. It wasn't a particularly soothing revelation, but at least now Zhila knew what sort of nightmare she was inhabiting.

It wasn't Hell—it was too cold to be the infernal realm. Therefore she wasn't dead.

Zhila wriggled her hands. Yes, they were definitely bound, but perhaps with some concerted tugging she could loose them.

A whack startled her. A stinging impact against the exposed skin of her hands.

"Stop that."

Zhila froze. A man—she must be slung in front of him on the same horse. Could she slide off without him noticing? True, she'd probably land on her arse. She'd risk a trampling and still be tied, but what option did she have?

As surreptitiously as possible, Zhila tried to slide. It should have been easy—just jolt back at each pace until her momentum downward was irresistible—but it didn't happen. The hideous creature must have strapped her against the horse itself. Like some kind of a saddlebag.

Another whack, this time on her backside.

"Be still, woman. We'll halt soon enough. God knows I've got to. Won't get anywhere at this rate."

Well, that was something to look forward to. Zhila set her teeth and jolted on. In fact, she set her teeth on the cloth that gagged her. Surely the worm couldn't see her gnaw it?

By the time the horse ceased its interminable jolting, her

teeth were squeaky from sawing at whatever rough cloth he'd jammed in her mouth. But she had it down to a few threads.

She felt him dismount, then hands were fiddling with whatever bound her to the horse. She was hauled off the beast like a sack of corn and barely managed to keep her feet when they hit the ground. Numb feet, hands unavailable for balance, head spinning, she staggered against her captor.

He chuckled. "Aye, now you're all over me, eh? The Ruin's a right greedy bastard to keep you to himself. Fair shares, the man says."

Zhila wriggled her toes and tried to stand. The blackness of night had grayed, and she could see something of her surroundings at last. Dripping trees, a mere track of a road, and a second horse, loaded with baggage. She made out her bag on it—and the Ruin's strongbox.

"Damn me, ground's all wet." A hand hooked about her waist, and she was half steered, half hauled backward. "Plan was to do this in the open, but—"

Zhila spat the remains of the gag out of her mouth. "What plan? What are you doing?"

She ceased even trying to support herself. He wanted to move her? Well, she'd be a leaden weight in his arms.

He twisted her around and peered at her face, ran his free fingers over her cheek, and grinned.

"Chewed it through, eh? No matter. No one to hear you yell out here."

Which gave her a good view, in turn, of his face. Not a particularly interesting or memorable face, but she'd seen him around. He was one of the few company members she actively avoided—because of the way he watched her.

She tried a different tack. "You stole the Ruin's chest." She jerked her chin at the loaded horse. "He will follow. You won't get far."

He heaved her upright. "Nah, you've got it wrong, bawd. *You* stole the Ruin's chest. He'll follow *you*." He grinned again. "But you're right—you won't get far."

"I didn't steal it! There's no point—the Ruin has the key." She glared at him. "No point in you stealing it either. You work for Ingram, yes?"

He tucked her to him with one arm and began to move again.

"Key doesn't matter. Why bother with a key when you can take the whole box? Gimme a handy axe and I'll make short work of any lock. And Ingram—pah! Ingram don't matter either."

Zhila twisted sharply against him. Jos—that was the man's name, she recalled. And this Jos was unsurprised at her mention of Ingram's name. Which almost certainly meant Jos was the Fox's source of information within the company.

But it made no sense. This was not Edmond Ingram's plan, not as Zhila knew it.

Jos engaged both arms and clamped her against his chest.

"Just you keep it up, dancing woman. Saints, I like it when you wiggle."

Which was quite enough to make her cease, if temporarily. "Ingram doesn't *want* the whole chest," she cried. "Just the parchment. Take it back! Take me back and I'll do what Ingram wants!"

"Oh aye," the fellow growled in her ear. "Ingram wants you to fuck the Ruin and lighten the company chest. Edmond bloody Ingram gets his box and the Ruin gets a bawd. Can't see much for me in all that. Oh, Ingram says he'll give me a share, but I've had it with shares. And rules. Ruin and his damned rules. No helping yourself to women in the field, he says? Well what's the two-faced bastard doing with you, then? You took the chest—so I'll take you and then I'll take the chest."

All the energy leaked out of her. Zhila sagged. This man was betraying two masters in one blow. He thought himself entitled to women and loot, so he had simply grabbed both and run. In the process, he had destroyed her hope of saving Maryam.

Unless…

Jos knew where the Fox was to be found. He could lead her *to*

Maryam. Certain half-heard phrases fell into place. She straightened.

"You told the Ruin where to find Ingram, yes? That's why he rode off tonight."

Jos was towing her backward again. A roof materialized over their heads, cutting off the misting rain, and Jos leaned against something.

"Aye, I told the stupid sir where he might happen upon Ingram. Didn't tell him directly, of course. That'd look strange. Didn't tell him the whole truth, neither. Ingram was there a day past. He's shuffled on since. Wouldn't want the noble sirs swapping news about me, see? *You're* the thief, not me." One of her captor's hands began to move. It commenced a wandering exploration of her bound body. "The Ruin'll hunt you down, not me."

She tensed against the roving hand.

"Yes, he will hunt me down, and find you!" she snapped.

It was meant to be a threat. It was meant to make the man desist, but instead the implications washed over Zhila in an icy flood.

The Ruin would hunt her down. He would want his strongbox back, and he would take revenge upon whomever he believed stole it—which was, at the moment, almost certainly her. But if he seized Jos in the process, her captor would reveal all. The Ruin would discover she intended to thieve so much more from him, and Maryam would be lost. For Ingram would do his worst.

The last thing Zhila wanted was for the Ruin to rescue her.

A chuckle behind her. "Oh, he'll hunt you down and he *will* find you, bawd. But you'll not be saying nothing about me, save the tale your sweet body does tell."

The disgusting worm ground his groin against her.

"See, you fled with yon chest and ran afoul of some lawless types in your haste. A pretty girl and a box full of loot? Oh, the Ruin'll read the story well enough. One ravaged body and the smithereens of one chest. Can't trust outlaws these days."

"What?" Zhila managed.

It was hard to think straight when one was tied hand and foot, and a lout was pawing at you. Not to mention the threat to Maryam.

In answer, Jos actually stopped his pawing. He let go of her entirely and stepped back a pace. Zhila twisted around. Her captor had brought her to some kind of barn or animal shed. There was a scattering of old straw and animal droppings on the earth floor. The roof was low, its beams hung with dusty cobwebs. Luxurious it was not, but it was dry. And she could see the use Jos intended to put it to.

The man was tugging at his brigandine. He was evidently in a hurry. A couple more impatient tugs, and the iron-plated coat fell to the floor. The man's breathing was heavy, and when he looked up—looked straight at her with eyes dark as the depths of hell—Zhila knew.

"Didn't want to kill you," the fellow said. "Nothing against you, for all you're a heathen whore. I like your dancing, and that drum thing. But needs must. You thieved, you got thieved from, then you got fucked and died. Sad story, but that's what the Ruin'll read. Speaking of which…" Jos dipped a hand beneath his tunic. "We've not got all day. Best get on with it, eh?"

✦

Chapter Sixteen

Z HILA STARED AT the man's groin. At least, that was what she assumed his hands were busy with.

"You want to, how you say, fuck me?" she said in a voice she barely recognized as her own. "So untie my legs. You cannot do it otherwise, yes?"

Jos's answer was to draw a long dagger from his belt. He stepped toward her.

She didn't have time to react. He kicked her ankles out from under her, and she tumbled to the dirt floor. She squirmed to right herself, but Jos was kneeling over her, dagger at the ready.

Dear God, it couldn't end this way. Who would help Maryam? And the Ruin would believe her a thief who betrayed him. Which she fully intended to be, but *not this way*.

She drew back her legs. One chance. That was all she had left.

"Oi, hold your legs still, else you'll get yourself cut."

But did he mean to cut her bonds or her throat? Zhila took the chance and prayed Jos was thinking cock-first. She held still.

He was. The rope at her ankles was sawed through.

Jos sat back to shove his dagger back into its sheath, and Zhila could wait not a moment longer. She lashed out and caught him under the chin with both heels.

He tumbled backward. Zhila rolled and sprang to her feet. Should she kick a man when he was down? Absolutely. As hard as she could. Her hands were still bound behind her back, so feet were all she had. She stamped down hard on his groin. Twice. Ah, it was a beautiful feeling. She hoped she broke something.

Her would-be ravager curled up like a centipede and made a noise like a cow. But what to do now? Zhila was tied—Jos had a dagger in his belt, but how was she to get hold of it?

Oh. The dagger *had* been in his belt, but now it was in his fist. Jos had uncurled and was driving it toward her with a rictus of rage on his face.

Zhila leapt. She avoided the blade and stamped down on the arm that held it. He yowled but did not drop the weapon. She stamped again, but he jerked his hand away—then lashed out at her leg with the blade. Hot pain streaked over her calf.

"First cut, bitch," the man snarled. "Saints be my witness, I'll cut you so bad afore I'm done, the Ruin'll barely recognize you."

His words were slurred. She'd done him some damage with that kick to the chin.

Zhila limped out of reach, yanking furiously at her wrist bonds. No result but rope burn. He had the dagger, and now he was struggling to get up. The cut on her leg didn't seem that bad, her blow to his arm had likely weakened him, but what was she to do—kick the bastard unconscious somehow?

No more thinking. Jos had rolled to his hands and knees.

She took aim and kicked him in the face, full on the nose. While he was occupied with those sensations, she followed up with a stamp on his dagger hand. Obediently, he let go of his blade. She kicked it away—which didn't assist in cutting her bonds in any noticeable way.

Her leg was wet with blood, her hands were numb, and Jos still wasn't going down. God in heaven, what ought she to do— run? She couldn't mount a horse without hands. But if she simply ran, Jos would ride her down.

He tried to rise. She kicked at his face again, sickening at the crunching sensation, the pain she must be causing him.

"No more!" she cried. "Listen, you don't hurt me, I won't

hurt you. We stop, yes?"

She just wanted an end to this. She wanted to bury her face in the Ruin's shoulder and forget everything.

"Aye. Stop," Jos mumbled. He spat blood.

"You'll leave me alone?" Zhila demanded. "Truce?"

Jos didn't answer. He rose slowly, gripping the wall for support. He was a bloodied mess. Surely he would alter his infernal plans now?

"Truce? Ha!" He spat again, and a tooth landed on the dirt floor. "Stupid whore. I let you live and Ruin'll kill me."

He gave her no chance to consider his words. He simply launched himself at her. Jos thudded into her, a sticky, panting mass. They both crashed to the earth, Zhila squashed beneath a bulky, bloodied man. He was fumbling at her, and she couldn't move. Her arms were trapped painfully behind her. Fumbling, yes, but Zhila knew there'd be no rape now, just outright murder.

Somehow, she dragged her bound arms up behind her, enough to prop herself on her elbows. He was reaching for her throat. She let her head drop back, then jerked it forward with all the force she could muster. Her forehead slammed into his bloodied nose. The same portion of his face she'd kicked earlier.

Yes, that worked. Quite disgusting, but wonderful, too. One good head-butt, and Jos transformed into a leaden weight on top of her, an unconscious slab of bloodied meat. Zhila heaved at him. Now was her chance…just as soon as she could dislodge the foul creature, locate his knife, and somehow cut her own bonds.

As it turned out, she didn't have to do any of those things.

GARIT PLUCKED THE mess of a man off his errant minstrel, tossed him aside, and stared down at Zhila. Her hair was full of musty straw, there was blood and dirt all over her lovely face, and her expression was inexpressibly wild.

He looked down at her and uttered one word.

"Thief."

He'd intended the word to be flat and hard, not loaded with the tangle of emotions that surged up in him at the sight of her. For she was victorious, furious, bloodied beneath an unconscious man. And so burningly beautiful, despite the dirt.

His accusation came out like a caress.

Garit watched as the fact of his presence sank in. Her expression ran the full gamut between joy and horror.

"Not a thief," she managed, and levered herself into a sitting position.

That was when he saw her arms were tied. He frowned. He glanced toward the man he'd tossed off her, and his frown deepened.

"Jos?"

"Aye, that's our Jos all right," came Donal's voice behind him. "Christ, he was never pretty before, but now…"

"What did you do to him?" Garit crouched down by his bound thief. He ran a finger over the abraded skin of her wrists. Should he leave her tied?

"Me?" she squeaked. "*He* tried to rape me and kill me so you think me a thief."

"She lies." The words were slurred. They emerged from Jos's bloodied lips. "She attacked me. But you won't believe me. She's your leman."

Garit felt the harsh truth of it. He didn't want to believe she'd done it, but only Zhila could have unbolted the chamber door. He should never have left her alone with the company valuables. He should never have let her travel with them in the first place. It was Garit's fault, his weakness, and all because of a lovely face.

A face that reminded him of the past.

"What are you doing here, then?" he snapped at Jos.

"Followed her, didn't I? She rides off in the middle of the night with your strongbox, so I followed."

"No! He took me! He…he is…" At which Zhila ran out of

words. Doubtless because she had run out of truth.

Garit got to his feet. He did not untie his thief. He walked to the shed entrance and stared out. He would not look at her reddened, roughened wrists, the blood soaking her trouser leg, the plea in her traitorous, dark eyes. He had been a fool. He would be so no longer.

"No more talk," he said. "We return to the inn. I will hear what you have to say there. Donal, check their horses."

His horse-master gave him an odd look, but obeyed. Donal walked out to inspect the mounts that had brought Jos and Zhila here, one of which was still conveniently loaded with his strongbox. Garit observed two mounts, one fully loaded. His sleep-deprived brain wrestled with that contradiction for a moment, before—

A cry interrupted him.

He whirled. Jos was on his knees. He had a dagger in his hand, and he was driving it at Zhila.

Who had rolled out of the way and lashed out with her feet.

Jos didn't even register her blow. He threw himself at the bound woman, dagger-first. Garit didn't think. He simply intervened by throwing his own frame into Jos's.

It worked, primarily because Garit was the heavier man. It nearly worked too well—there were consequences in throwing oneself at men clutching daggers. Jos stabbed a wild blow at his leader. Garit batted his arm away.

But when the bloodied madman drove his dagger at Zhila again, something in Garit snapped. Blame the tiredness, blame the fact that a man was attacking a woman *under his protection*, blame the searing guilt over his misjudgment—the result was the same. Garit struck out with all the force bottled up within him. His fist smashed into Jos's jaw, the man's head snapped back, and the rest of him toppled after.

Garit sprang on the man, fist raised, ready to repeat the blow, again and again if necessary.

"I think you kill him, Ruin."

Her voice was wobbly. Croaky too. The sound raked claws over his heart.

He peered at Jos. This rough shed was damnably dim. But the staring eyes and peculiar angle of the neck were solid clues.

"I think you are right."

Sir Garit of the Ruin waited for the man's chest to rise and fall. It did not. Garit rose slowly. He ceased to crouch over the man he'd just killed—the man who'd nearly killed his dancer. He inserted himself between Zhila and her would-be assassin and said the most inane thing in the world.

"Are you all right?"

Zhila couldn't help it. She laughed. The laugh ended in a cough. He was quite priceless—her icy Ruin, so pushed and pulled about by his own emotions. After the furnace of fury he'd released at Jos, he seemed to be struggling to regain his customary calm. Oh, he was trying, but the moment she wriggled to a sitting position with a squeak of pain, that equilibrium evaporated. Then he was stroking back her disordered hair, examining her grubby face, and, when his fingers reached her neck, he emitted a growl.

"He throttled you."

"Yes. I told you—he wanted to rape me and kill me."

But you didn't believe me. The words hung silent between them.

He must trust her again. If that meant she played upon his guilt, so be it.

"My wrists hurt. You untie me now?"

He muttered some choice blasphemy and slipped a dagger from his belt. Zhila flinched. It was a thing of bodily reaction. She knew he wouldn't hurt her.

But he didn't know that.

He froze. Then he laid the weapon carefully on the dirt floor.

"You say you did not steal the chest, Zhila. I believe you. I am not about to decorate the floor with a second body." A pause, in which blue eyes gazed into her own. "Will you come back with me? Continue with the company until you reach a place of safety?"

He'd regained control of his intonation. The delivery was as flat and emotionless as ever. But the words... It was almost as if he wanted her—all of her, not just her body. Those words did strange things to her insides.

But she would still rescue Maryam. She would do what the Fox demanded.

"Pick up your knife, Ruin. I trust you. I will come back...with you." Just the lightest emphasis on those last two words.

He didn't answer. He simply took the knife and sliced through the rope at her wrists. The steel slid cold against her skin, but she didn't flinch this time.

"Are you hurt? Did he..."

He was still at her back. Her wrists were free now, but he did not move around to look her in the face.

Zhila smiled at nothing. "Yes, Ruin, I am hurt. I am sore and tired and he cut my leg. It bleeds. But no, he did not rape me. He tried. I disagreed."

A muttered expletive behind her.

"Your leg. Is it...?"

"The horses are rea... Devil damn me, what'd you do?" Donal strode into the shelter. "Jos?" He poked the man with the toe of his boot, then he turned to the Ruin.

"He came within a feather's breadth of killing my minstrel," said the Ruin at her back. "So I hit him. Throw him over the back of a horse. We'll see he's buried." In a lower tone: "The consecrated ground's optional."

"Ah." Donal eyed the two of them. "He's the traitor, then—not her?"

The Ruin's arms were about her. He scooped Zhila up and

rose to his feet. Ah, this again. His eternal need to pick her up.

"She is the wronged party. I promised her safety, and *this* happens."

Zhila's leg was all hot pain. The rest of her was cold and shivery, and she was dog tired. But she smiled.

◆

Chapter Seventeen

GARIT RODE BACK to the village with a sleeping minstrel in his arms.

She trusted him, she said. Foolish woman. And she was proving her words this very moment. Zhila had protested that she was fit to ride a horse, but Garit wasn't having it. He had failed her enough already. The least he could do was see she returned to the inn in one piece.

And he'd been right. The rough hut was barely out of sight before her head was sagging on his chest and she was soft and limp in his arms.

The rain had eased with the daylight, thank heaven, but the trees still dripped. They aimed their fat, cold droplets for any part of Garit's exposed anatomy. Or Zhila's, which was worse. Fresh blood was still soaking her trouser leg and reddening her skirt. He needed to get her wound tended, not have her catch cold. Naturally, his motives were purely selfish. The sooner her leg was seen to, the sooner she could entertain the company again.

Finally, the inn—where he found half his men sleeping (those who had ridden with him in the night) and the other half absent, scattered over the countryside, seeking a scent of either Zhila or Edmond Ingram. And, damn it, Tommo was among the absent.

Tommo had been a barber back in Southampton until he'd accidentally employed his razor-sharp knives in a manner contrary to the law. Then he'd made a strategic career change and taken a fast ship over the Channel. Whatever the morality of the matter, a barber-surgeon was a wonderful addition to the company. But the barbarous Tommo was currently useless to Garit—or Zhila—now. He was miles away, hunting a rogue knight.

Garit carried a sleepy Zhila to his chamber, and Donal helpfully shoved the debris littering the bed onto the floor.

"Tell the innkeeper we'll be staying another night," Garit ordered his horse-master. "And ask for hot water." He looked down at his bloodied minstrel. "I've seen Tommo bind enough wounds. I'll see to this one myself."

Donal snorted. "You just don't want the barber playing with her legs," he said, then made a swift exit at Garit's flat look.

Garit frowned. It was just possible Donal was onto something. He turned back to Zhila and asked abruptly, "Do you want to wait for the barber-surgeon? He knows his business."

"No. I want you, Ruin."

Evidently, he was getting bad at remaining expressionless, for a smile lit his dancer's face at Garit's reaction to that particular statement.

She carried on, her voice liltingly strange, winding a spell around his tired brain. "I think it is not bad, my cut. It just bleeds…and hurts. You wash and bind it. Please. I too do not want the barber at my legs."

He grunted assent. It made sense that after one too-close encounter with one unwelcome man, she would not fancy another.

But even the smallest cuts could fester if not treated properly. He'd seen it many times before. At least the barber would know what to do.

Damn it all, he was mixing emotions with rational decisions, and it was making a mess of his thoughts.

A servant appeared with a bowl of steaming water before Garit could change his mind, and Zhila immediately reached under her skirts to loosen her trousers. Dear God, would she get undressed before just anyone?

She is a minstrel. You thought to offer her employment in a good whorehouse. Just look at her—she's beautiful. She's likely lain with dozens of men.

Garit had no time to sort out that tangle of logic. He simply propelled the servant out of the door with hasty thanks and bolted it behind him.

Zhila chuckled. He ignored that, just as he attempted to ignore her subsequent wriggling out of her loose trousers, punctuated by a gasp or two of pain. He set his teeth and sought out a strip of clean linen that would serve as a binding.

"There. It is not so bad. I clean it myself, if you like."

Her words made him glance up—and then he couldn't glance away. Zhila Kurian was half reclined on the big bed, her skirts pulled up to mid-thigh, and her legs bare. Defined dancer's legs—all curves and creamy skin. But she was having to twist to get a good look at her wound.

"No, I do not like," he said.

He strode over to the bed and stared down at her leg. There was blood smeared everywhere—mostly dried, but some still seeping. It made a mutiny of his stomach, and Garit had seen oceans of blood before.

"Lie back. Let me wash it." He looked into her eyes. "Tell me if it pains you too much."

Beautiful, dark eyes gazed back at him. *She* did not shield her emotions. They crowded across her face this very moment—pain, a glint of humor, deep-flowing purpose, tiredness, trust...in him. Of course, he probably read them all wrong. Feelings were most definitely not his forte.

"Thank you, Sir Ruin."

She wriggled onto her stomach, for the wound was mostly at the back of her calf. Blood smeared the sheets, and she gave another little gasp of pain to rip at Garit's nerves.

He dipped a square of linen into the water, clenched it overly hard to squeeze the water out, and began.

THE WARM CLOTH lapped at Zhila's skin. He was working from the outside in, so, to begin with, there was almost no pain. Just warmth and gentleness. Zhila angled her head toward him, but she could see little more than his profile bending over her. Intent on his work.

The pain grew. His gentle strokes tweaked the wound's edges. Little, jagged spikes shot through her. But flinching would do no good, so she tried to focus her thoughts instead. To plan. Anything to distract from the notion that she might be maimed.

And never dance again.

No, her situation was unexpectedly good. She had nearly lost all hope of Maryam last night. Incidentally, she'd also nearly been raped and murdered. She'd definitely been strangled, although not terminally. And she'd nearly forfeited the Ruin's trust forever.

But here she was, and here he was. He was tending to her wound with exquisite gentleness, and she had another chance.

This time she wouldn't waste it.

"There." He'd just finished patting her skin dry, and now his hands left her entirely. "Do you want to look before I bind it?"

"Yes…sss." The word ended in a hiss as she tried to turn.

"No. Don't move. I'll do it."

His arms slipped around her, and he eased her onto her back. Ah yes, this Ruin liked to wrap his arms about her, whatever his mouth might declare. It was all to the good.

But she had a leg to inspect. She steeled herself and craned to look. It was a long cut, evidently made with a wickedly sharp knife. Fresh blood welled within, despite the cleaning. Zhila closed her eyes. It was a clean cut, and thankfully not deep.

"Do you want the barber to look at it?"

"No." She opened her eyes and looked into his face. Why had

she ever thought his eyes icy? "Just pour clean water over, then bind."

"I've already washed it."

"Yes. Rinse again with *clean* water, not dirty with blood. My mother..." Her throat tightened and the words refused to emerge. She swallowed. "My mother said you Westerns don't know how to care for cuts. No dirty poultices, she said—just clean water. We Persians know better."

He looked at her a long moment. "And your mother treated many wounds?"

"Many," Zhila whispered.

Was that a hint of compassion or respect in his voice? So much the better. She needed every bit of leverage she could get for what she was about to do.

He obeyed. He dribbled boiled, cooled water over to the tune of her gasp, patted it dry, then bound it up with linen.

"Not too tight. Just enough to stop the blood," she instructed, and watched him handle her lower leg as if it were made of eggshells.

A smile crept over her mouth.

He tied the linen off and glanced up. "There. Everything to your satisfaction, my lady?"

"Not yet."

A slight frown creased his brow. Zhila held his gaze.

"You must kiss better me now."

FOR ONCE SHE wasn't laughing, but he wanted to. It was the exhaustion infecting his brain. The Ruin was not prone to laughing, and certainly not over matters like this.

And while he was fighting off crazed laughter, she reached for him. She tugged him unresisting toward her and took her required kiss.

It began softly, a simple brushing of her lips against his. But something akin to laughter—or madness—was still simmering within him, and it needed no greater invitation than this. Before he knew what he was about, he was drawing her to him, wrapping his arms about her, and his lips had a mind of their own.

She opened instantly to him, and that blaze of passion so distinctively Zhila flared over him, setting him aflame. She wound her arms about him, her fingers were in his hair, and her tongue lapped his.

Garit was in no state to refuse. Not only did this foolish woman trust him, but she *wanted* him. After everything. The knowledge ran through his blood like strong wine. He was too tired to think straight. No one else should have his dancer. Only him.

Her hands slipped beneath his neckline. Cool fingers gripped his bare shoulders. He responded by deepening the kiss, and her nails curled into his flesh. Sweet pain to send a bolt straight to his braies.

He pushed her back against the pillows, the better to kiss her, explore her—and she gasped.

Garit froze.

Zhila had gasped in pain. Devil damn him, his dancer was wounded, exhausted, and horribly shaken by the night's events, and all Garit could think of was the contents of his own underwear.

He was no better than Jos or Ingram or all those other soldiers who treated women as spoils of war.

No better than those Frenchmen all those years ago. His mother. *Marie.* He was a despicable animal.

"More," she murmured against his lips.

"What?" He broke free.

She lay back on the bed, hair splayed over the pillows, sleek black against white. Her chest rose and fell noticeably. Garit tried not to notice.

"More," she repeated. "You must kiss me better. I am not better yet."

"No more," he growled. "Or I'll do a damned sight more than kiss you, woman, and that won't make you better at all."

She regarded him with great, dark eyes. Eyes that burned black fire and drew him irresistibly.

Garit clenched his fingers and resisted.

"Why not? Listen, Ruin—your man nearly took all I have. *All*. Nájera too, it nearly took all. I will not wait to be taken any longer. I will take what I want. *Now*. I take you." She reached for him. "So kiss me."

She pulled herself up by two fistfuls of his tunic. A spasm of pain flickered over her face.

Garit swore. "Woman, has it escaped your notice you are injured?"

She smiled at him. "Yes, I am injured. In other places too. You haven't looked at those. You must check, yes?"

She angled her neck for his inspection. Garit swore again. The lamplight played over creamy olive skin—and livid bruises. It was only a pity Jos was already dead. Garit would like to kill him all over again.

"You must kiss me better here too—and other places. Many other places."

"Kiss you better, by God," he muttered. "You do not know what you are asking."

She was a minstrel. Of course she knew what she was asking.

And she had a point. Jos had nearly stolen what she now wished to give. Zhila wished to reclaim her power. Her own body.

Who was he to stand in her way?

SHE WOULD NEVER have a better chance. She was in his chamber, on his bed, and, if Zhila was any judge of a Ruin, her target was vulnerable—remorseful, tired, uniquely prone to emotion. No, Sir Garit of the Ruin would not throw her out of his chamber tonight. Nor would he spend the night sitting wakeful in bed.

She had her orders, but her orders could join Jos in hell. Zhila had come within a dagger's breadth of death tonight, and now it was time to *live*.

This was for her.

But if it happened to coincide with a Fox's demands, so be it.

She began to unbutton her dress.

She'd only managed two buttons before a hand covered her fingers, stilling them.

"Let me."

She did.

But his fingers did not immediately tackle the buttons. They lingered at the apex of her bodice for some moments. They traced a slow line over the exposed skin above.

Zhila shivered.

The hand paused. The Ruin's gaze flicked to her face. Expressionless. Intensely so.

"Do I continue?"

"You do," she said.

His big fingers were surprisingly nimble about her buttons. One after the other opened under his silent assault. She lay back on the bed and watched him bend over her in the lamplight, her breath shallow.

When all the buttons were undone, he ran his fingers down the line of her bodice, over the linen of her underdress. The outer dress fell open, but it was going nowhere—not with her lying on it.

Zhila began to sit up, then winced.

"This is a bad idea," the Ruin's voice said. His eyes said something else entirely.

She raised her arms to him. "Lift me up, Ruin."

He did. Her big blond knight scooped her up and set her on

her feet, as she directed. Zhila felt the care in his every movement. He was trying not to hurt her, but she felt the shivering need in those movements too. Barely constrained desire. Ah, it was delicious. Her reserved Ruin on the brink of passion.

She shrugged off her brocade outer dress. She stood before him, her armored knight, in her simple linen shift. He wasn't touching her now.

She must make him do so.

"Take this off me, Ruin." Zhila tweaked the pale linen. "If I bend, I hurt."

She would use her injury to gain what leverage she could.

Sir Garit of the Ruin sank on one knee before her. He grasped her hem, and a sensation of dizzying triumph washed over her. Leavened with just a dash of terror. Carefully, the Ruin drew her shift up over her buttocks, over her torso, and then her head. Let the shift flutter to the floor. And there was nothing left to shield her.

Zhila sank back on the bed. Her legs would not support her. She lay back, quite naked, and felt gooseflesh prickle over her bare skin.

She was not in the least cold. Impossible to feel cold under such a burning gaze. There was no ice in those eyes left now.

The Ruin bent over her. His fingers skimmed her throat.

"Does it hurt?" His voice was rough; his fingers were not.

"A bit." She smiled. "But you will make better, yes?"

In answer, he dipped his head to her throat. But he didn't kiss as commanded. Instead, a tongue trailed over her bruised skin.

Her gooseflesh broke out afresh. For some reason, it saw fit to center on her breasts. Ah yes, she wanted this. She wanted to break this Ruin down. She wanted him to break in her.

Orders coinciding with inclination.

She shivered.

He drew back immediately. "I am hurting you."

"No." She smiled. "You are making me better."

Her smile grew as he gazed at her. Ah yes, this implacable

block of muscle was human flesh after all.

Speaking of which…

"Your tunic—it scratches my skin. Take it off."

It was a lie, but it had the desired effect. The Ruin divested himself of his tunic with gratifying speed.

Zhila did not gasp, but that was only because she knew he would take it the wrong way. Ah, this Ruin was no ruin at all. He was a marble sculpture dusted with golden hair. Muscled perfection carved from rock.

Perfection with a key about his neck, hanging by a simple chain.

But then she could admire no longer, for all that breathtaking man was descending on her, and he felt not in the least like marble.

Again, she must not gasp, but the sensation of all that warm, heavy skin against her own demanded a reaction. Zhila arched her back and rubbed herself against him. Slowly. Glorying in the incredible feeling of his skin against hers.

He growled and pushed her back down.

"Christ, Zhila, do you want this over with in two thrusts? Lie down and let me look at you."

She sank back down and grinned at his expression. No implacability now. His gaze roamed over her with the hunger of a winter wolf. Doubtless, he was looking for further scrapes and bruises. She could only hope he would pay them proper heed when he found them.

She hadn't thought her breasts were bruised, but evidently she was wrong. That hungry gaze lingered on them, and his hands slid slowly down from her shoulders to trace a lazy circle about each. Zhila shivered. Yes, one could shiver from heat. Of course, the Ruin took that the wrong way too and perceived she needed warming. He dipped down and warmed her right breast with his tongue.

She nearly cried out at the sensation. It was like pain, but so achingly sweet as well.

He raked his tongue over her nipple again, then startled her anew by closing his mouth about it. She arched against him with a little cry.

Damn him, he took that the wrong way too. He released her nipple and sat back.

Before he could inquire, she cried, "No—more!" And he actually smiled and dipped his head back down obligingly. Her left nipple needed equal attention, and got it.

She slid her hands over his shoulders, over his back, reveling in the texture of him, digging her nails in when his attentions would otherwise make her gasp or cry out. Ah, he liked that. Every time she did it, a ricochet of reaction rippled through him. That power was the sweetest of all. *She* made the Ruin react.

Eons later, he sat back, observing his patient with intent.

"Do we continue?"

She reached for him, but he caught her arms. Laying one down, he inspected the left one by the lamplight. Yes, it was bruised. He kissed each and every dark smudge—and when he got to the abrasions at her wrist, his eyes seemed to catch fire.

"The bastard. I will find salve to rub on these. Tommo will have something."

"Not now. Later," she murmured.

He obeyed, thank heaven. Her man was uniquely open to her manipulations right now. She *would* do this.

He picked up her right arm. That left her free to trail her other hand over his chest. To feel heated skin, the thud of a heart beneath, an expanse of muscle and need. Her hand wandered down, tracing the ridges of his abdomen, encountering little scars. Some not so little. And then fabric. Linen.

She had forgotten—he still had some clothes on. That did not suit her purpose at all.

"Stand up," she said.

"My lady?"

That stung. "I am not *my lady*. You mock me."

He rose slowly from the bed. The warmth of his body left

her.

"I do not mock you, my lady. Today, you are exactly that. I am yours to command. I have failed you before—more than once. I will not do so again."

Zhila frowned at the big, semi-naked knight standing over her. Was he mocking her still? No matter. She would have her way.

"I command you, then. Your clothes are strange. Take them off."

"Strange?" He glanced down. "How so?"

"My leg coverings are of one piece. They make sense. Yours are in three parts—they make no sense. See?" She reached out and touched the linen over his nether regions. She trailed her fingers over the interesting contours beneath. He closed his eyes. "One garment here, two more on your legs. Too many clothes, so take them off!"

"With pleasure, my lady."

He tugged at the ties that held his hose to his braies belt. He bent and stripped both leg coverings off with the efficiency of a soldier. Then his hands were at his linen braies. They too dropped to the floor.

A naked Ruin. Dear me, the man was quite ready for campaign. Zhila had seen the male equipment before, although not at such close quarters. But the sight had never inspired such reactions in her previously. He was big, damned big, but that was only to be expected. He was a big man in general. She reached out, tentatively, and touched.

Hot, smooth skin. So hard. She slid her fingers around it to feel its breadth. No, he was not small.

He watched her.

"Well, will it make you better, my lady—or worse?" His voice was rough-edged but the meaning was not. Even now, he offered her a way out.

She still had her hand around his shaft. She used it to tug him toward her.

"Back on the bed, Ruin. I have more bruises."

"Aye, that you do," he murmured, but before he obeyed, he snatched a pillow up and carefully slid it under her wounded leg, elevating the thigh. "To keep the pressure off," he said.

Ah, his fingers on her thigh—gentle, purposeful, yet sending little bolts of heat up her leg. Then his hands were upon her opposite leg, examining her ankle. It too had been tied, she remembered. He must kiss it better. He did. Then he was lifting that leg—not raising it like the other, but angling it out. Nudging her legs wide open.

Zhila tensed. She knew what happened next. He would climb on top of her and push that thickness inside of her. His knightly lance. A few ferocious thrusts later, and that would be that. He would make a strange face and groan and roll off her. She'd seen the performance plenty of times before, and as a performer, she'd thought the whole act a bit, well, uninspired.

Ah well, if that was what it took. She let him push her legs wide.

He did indeed climb onto the bed, between her legs, just as expected.

She hadn't realized her eyes were closed until he touched her. But it wasn't his manhood between her legs. It was something larger than that.

Her lids flew open, and she pushed herself up onto her elbows to see what on earth he was doing.

His face was between her legs. His *face*. His lips had just grazed her inner thigh.

He glanced up. A smile flickered in his eyes. A genuine smile.

"I found a bruise," he said. Then he bent and licked the soft skin of her leg.

She mewed. It was exactly the sort of noise a cat would have made, and not at all in Zhila's usual vocabulary.

His answering chuckle was a purr.

He looked up again, and all amusement fled his eyes. "You say Jos did not harm you here?"

At which his fingers brushed over the curls between her legs.

Zhila gasped. Then, immediately realizing her mistake, said, "No. He did not... I kicked him. Many times. He did not touch me there."

"That is good. Nevertheless—"

The Ruin's fingers returned. This time they brushed a little deeper. Zhila cried out.

The warmth returned to the Ruin's eyes. "Yes, I will make you better."

And he dipped his head down and kissed her.

He did not kiss her on the mouth. He spread her inner thighs with his hands. He laid his lips between them and kissed her full on her womanhood.

Zhila shrieked.

The Ruin ceased kissing her just long enough to chuckle and say, "Not so loud. You'll have Donal breaking down the door if you do that again."

His breath feathered over her very core. Zhila squirmed. He held her down the firmer. And before she could beg him to kiss her better again, he was doing just that. His tongue, so smooth and hot and knowing, snaked between her folds and flickered over the very nub of her pleasure. Remorselessly. His hands pinned her thighs open, the stubble of his jaw scraped over her skin, and his tongue... Ah, his tongue drove her to delirium. She didn't care if Donal broke down the door; she must shriek and writhe. She needed...she needed *more*.

His lips left her. He was moving. The muscled bulk of his torso slid over hers, so wonderfully heavy. She stirred beneath him restlessly, still craving, still unbearably tense. His hips were between her legs.

Ah, this was it, then.

She wrapped her arms around him, looked into his eyes, and commanded, "Take me, Sir Ruin."

The need in his eyes flared. The head of his shaft nudged between her folds. Ah, he was so big. How was this ever going to work? Just like dancing, this must be something one got better at with practice. But he was advancing too slowly. He might…

Zhila grabbed the Ruin's buttocks. They took a deal of grabbing, being essentially pure muscle and currently engaged in an infinitely slow, controlled assault. So she dug her nails into his flesh and pulled him forward with all her strength.

It had the desired effect. His hips jolted forward. He drove into her in one deep, powerful thrust.

Zhila screamed. Silently, for Donal's sake. And because the feeling was beyond the realm of sound.

But the Ruin took the point.

He began to withdraw, but she hauled him back with her clinging, piercing nails.

"No! You stay there," she ordered him.

He obeyed, eyes wide. Fixed on her.

The feeling. There had been a white-hot flash of pain, followed immediately by the sensation of incredible fullness. Almost too much. But the pain had vanished and the fullness was…indescribable.

"Again," she told him. "More."

He said nothing. She could not read his expression. She would worry about that later. The important thing was that he did obey.

He leaned his considerable weight on his elbows and drew his shaft back so far she feared he would withdraw entirely. Then, watching her face with the intensity of a hawk, he pushed deep within her again.

This time there was no pain, just absolute rightness.

"More," she commanded.

"It shall be my pleasure," he said, and dipped to kiss her on the lips. A gentle, lingering kiss.

Then he drew back his hips and sank inside her again. And again. He seemed determined to be slow and controlled, but she dug her fingers into his buttocks and drove him on. She did not want slowness. No restraint, not from the Ruin. Not when she had him precisely as she needed him.

She did it, or her nails did it. His control crumbled. His eyes went wild. Zhila smiled a beatific smile. She arched her back and clenched about him, just to feel the divine thickness within her. *Yes, my Ruin. Lose yourself in me. Melt. Burn.*

He thrust wildly, so very deeply. He rose from his elbows in order to grip her hips and angle himself ever deeper. His gaze locked on hers, and she ignored the visual feast of that magnificent torso hovering over her, claiming her, and simply held his blue, blue gaze.

Until the moment it happened. Combustion. He made no sound at all, but his expression transformed. A blaze of endless wonder, as if he stared into eternity itself.

And that eternity was her.

But Zhila could spare no thought for such trifles. For she too was arching against him as indescribable sensations racked her body. As if whatever he was feeling could not help but transmit itself to her.

And in all of that, her gaze never left his.

This was the key. A Ruin stripped bare. He was hers.

Chapter Eighteen

GARIT STIRRED. DELICIOUS lassitude fogged his brain. There was something unusual about the circumstances, the time of day, a part of him knew, but he didn't want to shake this feeling in order to figure it out.

He kept his eyes closed and curled his arm closer around the warm body it was draped over.

That was wrong.

Bright remembrance pervaded Garit's brain. Zhila. His arm was draped over Zhila. She was lying flat on her back, her leg propped by a pillow *because she was injured*, and he, Garit of the Ruin, was on his side, snug up against her, stark naked and suddenly recollecting why.

His groin remembered it too. In fact, it had woken up quicker than the rest of him and was now entirely ready to refresh his memory.

Garit wrenched his arm away and rolled onto his back. She was still a warm presence by his side, but at least now he wasn't pressing his naked barbarity against her vulnerable, silky skin.

He stared at the ceiling. What hour was it? Daylight filtered through the shutters and danced with the dust motes. They had returned in the early morning. He had slept through much of the day. He had been exhausted after a night of chasing an imaginary knight through the damp darkness, and then pursuing a thief.

Thief.

He had wronged her. She had nearly died, and he had called her a thief. She had nearly been raped, and he…

"Fiend take me!" he cried. "Animal! Dastard! Call yourself a knight? Christ!"

"What?"

The figure beside him sat up abruptly, then let out a squeak of pain. Garit cursed himself anew. He turned to her, to ease her back onto the sheets, only to see his dancer's naked torso rising from the covers. Satiny skin, a tumble of dark hair over unclad shoulders, and breasts that simply begged to be worshipped.

He swore again, and wrenched his gaze away.

"What is the matter? You shout. Is there danger?" She began to get up.

"No!" He turned and pressed her back against the sheets, palms on her shoulders. He would not look lower. He kept his gaze fixed on her face.

"Lie still. You are injured, recall? There is no danger." *Except for me.*

"Ah." She sank back. "You have a bad dream?"

Quite the opposite. The best of dreams; a reality that should never have happened.

"No. No matter."

He too lay back on the bed. He tried to create a little distance between the naked body that occupied it and his. As a plan, it was a failure. She simply wriggled closer to him.

So much for subtlety. Garit glared at the ceiling. Best to have it out in the open, then.

"There is blood on the sheets, yes?" he said.

"I am sorry. My leg still bleeds."

"But that is not all," he said flatly. "If I were to inspect my yard, I believe I'd find blood on it too. Yes?"

A stirring on the bed beside him. "Let me inspect."

"No!" Christ help him, his shaft was as stiff as a tree trunk. It did not care whether it was bloodied or not.

She subsided.

He took a deep breath and tried again. "Zhila, what I did… Forgive me. I assumed… Well, you are a minstrel, a dancer. I thought… Perhaps I did not think."

She laughed. Of course she laughed. She laughed at the most inappropriate things. Mostly him. "You mean you thought me a *puta*, a whore, yes?"

Words with all the force of a battering ram. "Yes," he muttered. One syllable was all he could force between his teeth.

"And now you think I am not?"

"Yes…no." Damn it, what was the right response?

Her hand found his. She snaked her fingers between his.

"I am Persian, but I am Christian. I am a minstrel and a dancer, but I am not a whore."

It did not make him feel one whit better.

"I did not ask you for money, and you did not force me," she went on. "Jos tried; other men have tried. You—no. I gave what other men tried to take. I wanted this, Ruin." Her hand slipped from his and found his shaft. Not that it was currently hard to locate. Dear God, it wanted to be found.

He snatched her hand away and held it tight.

It *was* payment. She had given herself to him out of gratitude, in swap for safety.

The Ruin was no celibate. He indulged when the mood took him—with professionals or willing women. But he was also a knight. *He did not abuse damsels.* He actively ensured his men obeyed that rule too.

He had taken this woman into the company for the sake of the past. Atonement. He had thought to keep her safe.

Devil damn him into the deepest pit of hell, he had failed. He had believed the very worst of her, and then he'd fucked her. A maiden.

HER KNIGHT'S FACE was quite fascinating. The stubbled jaw was clenched, the lips were a bloodless line, and his brow had turned ferocious. Zhila feasted her eyes upon the Ruin. The man was in turmoil, and it was delicious. *She* had done this to him. If it wasn't for her leg and his grip on her hand, she'd be doing a lot more right now.

No, if it wasn't for her leg, she would have killed him by now. Then slipped the key from his neck and stolen from her dead lover.

In truth, it wasn't just her leg that had stopped her. The sun was high in the sky when the Ruin fell asleep. Wounded Zhila couldn't just hobble out of his chamber, parchments in hand, and hope to steal a horse in daylight.

Thus her target still lived. No matter. Ingram would understand. He *must*. After all, she had just fulfilled another one of his conditions. One step closer to his foul goal.

Zhila frowned. With Jos gone, maybe Ingram would know nothing at all. What did that mean for Maryam?

A fist closed about her heart—a panicky feeling of time running out, of her sister wondering when she would breathe her last. Wondering whether Zhila had forgotten her.

No, Ingram *would* understand. She was so close now. She hadn't been able to kill the Ruin yet, but…

Zhila must consolidate her advantage now.

She rolled to her side, careful not to bump her leg. She laid a hand on his bare chest. Her fingers luxuriated in its warmth, breadth, the jolt that rippled through him.

"I give you my body," she murmured. "A gift, yes, for you help me to France. You keep me safe from men like Jos." *And because I must take everything from you. It is only fair I give you something first.* "I want you, Ruin. Keep me in your bed. Tonight. And tomorrow night." Her hand wandered down his abdomen.

But before it could get very far, his hand clapped over hers.

"I am to marry in France," he said.

"Yes. You will marry a castle." *But not if you're dead.*

"What will you do in France, Zhila Kurian?"

Free Maryam. Beyond that, Zhila had not considered. She shrugged a little. "I will dance again, if I can. Play the *daf.*"

"Then I will find you a minstrel troupe," he declared. "You cannot travel alone."

I will not be alone. I will have my sister and you will be dead. But you will live first. By God, you will live. I will tear down your walls and make you smile. And I will put that expression back on your face—the one you wore when you buried yourself in me. I will begin right now.

She slid her nakedness up against his. Ah, he was so solid, such an intriguing landscape of contours. She wanted this big body. Truly, it was no hardship to do as the Fox commanded.

Was *that* why she hadn't killed him yet? Was she so selfish she could sate her senses on a man who must die?

She stilled. What did that make her?

Worse than any whore. Despicable.

But she had to ensure she had another chance at this.

"Yes, you find me a minstrel troupe," Zhila said. "But you must wait till my leg is better. Wait till you find your castle. I cannot dance yet. Keep me with you a little longer. Keep me in your bed."

She scraped her nails lightly over his abdomen. Then lower. He did not stop her this time.

"This is wrong," he murmured. "I wronged you. No women in the company. You should not... Ah."

Her fingers had encountered crisp hair. Smooth hardness. He closed his eyes, and his expression turned agonized.

"No, this is right," Zhila whispered. "I will not stay with the company long. But before I leave, you will *expiar...reparar...* What is the word?"

"Expiate. I will atone."

That last word was barely comprehensible, so softly was it uttered. Soft, but with infinitely jagged corners.

Zhila smiled and wrapped her fingers around his shaft. Guilt. There was the chink in his walls that allowed her in. *She* had no guilt in using it—it would lead her unerringly to death, to theft, and to Maryam.

She tightened her fingers.

"Yes. Atone. You will make all wrongness right, Ruin." And so would she.

In a flurry, he turned on her. Zhila's breath stopped. She had pushed him too far.

His mouth descended on hers. He was pressing her back against the pillows and kissing her with a ferocity that spoke louder than any words. His hands roamed her body, setting it on fire. She arched beneath them, offering herself to him in a blaze of need…and triumph.

He would keep her in his bed. She would have another chance. Just give her a dark night, a drowsing Ruin, and a leg that was fit to flee upon.

I will kill him soon, Maryam. Not today, but soon. I promise.

"IT IS DECIDED. We must put you in harness, woman."

Garit spoke loudly enough that the men at the table could hear too, not only the woman on his lap. She'd just settled there, panting a little after a bout of *daf* playing. She'd found a stray minstrel—a cittern player—in their current accommodation, and she'd made good use of him. He *had* to play to her shimmering percussion. Zhila hadn't been able to dance for days due to her wound. Tonight she declared she must express herself somehow.

Garit had watched the minstrel blink, blush, and succumb gladly to his lover's demands. And Garit had quashed that twist of jealousy at Zhila's attentions to the dandified fellow, because she was *his* lover. Zhila Kurian inhabited Garit's bed; her lips and hands played wild havoc with his senses nightly. She was his. She only wanted this minstrel fellow for his music.

Now she was back where she felt so right. And wrong. Very publicly on his lap in the midst of his company.

"Harness?" She raised a brow at him, and gave a very credible whinny.

The listening men spluttered their wine or offered the use of their horse leathers. Garit closed his eyes and tried not to think of Zhila dressed only in strips of leather and the odd buckle. Ah, there was a vision that wasn't going away.

Then there were hands cupping his jaw and lips claiming his. Garit kept his eyes closed and let other senses take over... The taste of her, the nip of her teeth, the unbridled *feeling*. Probably best not to see the watching men. He knew she made these demonstrations in order to emphasize that she belonged to one man only. But need she delight in dissolving his control so publicly?

She did. He knew it. Even now, she was snuggling closer to his rocklike groin and kissing him more deeply than ever. And Garit's arms were about her, his mouth opening to hers, his tongue matching hers, stroke for stroke.

A throat cleared. "Harness or horse whip?" the owner of the throat muttered. John the Wreck's dulcet tones.

Garit's eyes opened. He unglued his lips from Zhila's and pushed her away. Only slightly, mind you.

"Yes, harness. Armor." He ran his hands down Zhila's arms, in part to stop them reaching for him again. He attempted not to look at the rise and fall of the bodice between. "You are too vulnerable as you are, woman. One wound is healing. We do not want another."

"Armor? I am not a warrior. No one attacks the company."

"No one has attacked *yet*." He was dwelling upon the steep V of her bodice now, its delicious rise and fall, and beneath that...her heart. One arrow or sword thrust—that was all it would take. "I should have done it sooner," he muttered.

"What? Put me in armor? Yes! I fight too."

"No!" It was bad enough being responsible for the lives of all the men in the company. At least they'd chosen this life of blood and risk. But not Zhila.

"See, we've decided, little dancer. We been talking while you were having your fun."

Praise the Lord that the Wreck saw fit to explain. Garit relaxed his grip and let his engineer continue.

"Oh aye, we were listening to you and your minstrel man. Watching too," the Wreck assured her. "But we gotta decide where we're headed after this, and how. It's not so simple from here on. Our captain wanted to nut it out with us. More heads than one, see?"

It was a fact—John the Wreck was better with explosions than explanations. So Garit took over. "So far, Zhila, we have ridden through territory under English control or in truce to Prince Edward. No longer. Our destination lies north and east. We could reach it the safe way, traveling northwest through English territory, but that is also the long way. We do not have that time."

Time. It was the crux of the matter. The company had left Spain before the bulk of the English forces and even many of the French for precisely this reason. Garit intended to take advantage of a France largely vacant of competing forces. It was time to establish his company properly.

"Ten years ago, companies in France seized castles much as they pleased, but conditions have changed. The French are no longer in tatters. A company without a stronghold is a snail without a shell. The Company of the Ruin must have a castle before the year is old."

He was addressing the men as much as Zhila now. More fundamentally, he was addressing himself. This had been his plan before a certain minstrel. It was his plan still. A company could not continue without a base indefinitely. They had campaigned together, rootless and wandering, for years. They were practically family. And his men needed a stronghold. He owed it to them. This was the best way to get it. Incidentally, it would satisfy a few other troublesome conditions too.

As for Zhila, she was temporary—a temporary pleasure and a

temporary responsibility.

She was looking at him, gazing at him with those brilliant eyes, her head tilted.

"So you find a lady with a castle, you say, *Marry me, lady,* and she says, *Yes please, Sir Ruin.*"

Garit chose to ignore any potential sarcasm or incredulity. Zhila simply didn't understand.

"The lady I have in mind is English. She is a vulnerable widow holding a castle on the contested edge of French territory. I will offer her the protection of a husband and a company. In return, she will offer us a castle."

It did him good to lay out his future in words. His and the company's future. It would be all too easy to lose sight of his goal in the delirium that was Zhila—her body, her spirit, the dark eyes that delved into his soul.

"Nice lady," Zhila commented, wriggling closer on his lap. Closer to his groin, that was. Garit struggled for focus. "So we ride through French lands now, and the not-nice French will attack us? That is why I need armor?"

"Aye. That's it in a nutshell," the Wreck answered for him. Garit's thoughts were somewhat scattered. "Nice, neat little nutshell. We're off to marry a castle, and we gotta ride like the devil's on our tails to get there in one piece. And you've gotta coat yourself in iron if you're coming too."

Of course she was coming. Garit's arms tightened around her. He wasn't ready to let her go quite yet. He would keep her safe a little longer.

Zhila Kurian must be harnessed.

Chapter Nineteen

S HE LIKED HER harness. It was a mismatched affair culled from
the company's supplies. A quilted jacket over her tunic, then
a mail habergeon atop that, and finally a helm with mail coif over
Zhila's head and neck. Garit would have clapped a coat of plates
about her as well, but Zhila declared she already lumbered like an
ox. Hot and heavy it certainly was, but it made her one of them.
The Company of the Ruin. And, God be praised, the dead Jos's
gear had been too large to fit her.

It was nearly a week before she needed it.

They were deep into land held by French lords now, lords
who would naturally object to the presence of an English war
band. Their plan was to move fast, to be gone before those lords
had time to react. The company rode swiftly by day and didn't
halt until the shadows grew long. Then it camped rather than find
a convenient inn. Somewhere forested and lonely. Zhila shared
the Ruin's tent by night. Convenient, really—he got to help her
off with her harness. He was very good at peeling it off, and she
got to return the favor.

No, she hadn't killed him yet. There was no point, for she had
no idea where Edmond Ingram was. Jos the informant was dead,
and the company had probably left Ingram himself far behind. No
need to rid herself of her protector in hostile territory unless the
Fox was there to appreciate it.

She could only pray Ingram would keep her sister safe until he caught up. After all, Maryam was his only means of forcing Zhila to do his bidding.

It was her clear duty to remain in the Ruin's bed until then. To lull him with delirious lovemaking until she knew the moment was right.

Meanwhile, the company avoided towns, saw few people, and found no trouble. Until now.

They had halted for the night in a wooded valley. The company did not travel blindly through hostile territory—the Ruin sent scouts on ahead. Riders also lingered in the rear so nasty surprises did not overtake them from behind. One of the outriders had identified this camp site, equipped with a nice little river for water and pleasantly sheltered by trees. Now the company was spread all over the clearing, looking for dead wood, level tent sites, and any unfortunate pigeons within bowshot.

Zhila was wrestling the canvas that was to shelter her and one nice, warm Ruin for the night when an outrider cantered into the clearing. Walt, his name was. A man-at-arms. The fellow rode right up to where Sir Garit stood consulting with a few others.

"Armed men ahead," he cried.

The Ruin broke off mid-sentence to demand, "How far? Moving our way? How many do you estimate?"

"They're making camp about half a league up the valley. As for numbers, more than us."

"I saw no prints for that number on the road today," the horse-master inserted. "So they're riding toward us."

Zhila paused in her canvas wrestling. What now? Should she bundle the tent back up?

A second rider pelted into the clearing. Another company scout, but this one rode up from the direction they'd come. Zhila stared at the fellow. It was as if she were seeing the whole scene replayed. This man too rode up to the Ruin.

"Force of men behind us, sir."

"How many? Are they moving toward us?"

The answers were identical to the first scout's. She looked at the Ruin, saw him rake his gaze over the clearing and surrounds. Then he issued orders—flat, calm orders that, like a stone lobbed into a pool, sent ripples to the clearing's furthest edge. More men rode out, tents were rolled up again, yet the company did not break camp. Horses continued to be fed and watered, wood collected, and pigeons pursued.

It took some force of will, but Zhila didn't stride up to the Ruin and demand to know what was going on. He was the leader. He must set the wheels in motion before he could inform the company's most temporary member what the hell was happening.

In the meantime, she imitated the others and rolled up her tent. There would be no romps beneath the canvas to offend company ears tonight. Would she just curl up by the Ruin beneath the stars? What about his strange need to sleep separate and sealed off from all others? Except her.

In the end, Garit strode up to her, the Wreck by his side.

"Pack anything you have of value, but pack light. And do it quickly. You leave as soon as you're done."

"No, we leave as soon as *I'm* done," John the Wreck corrected him. "I forget one little thing, and you get no pretty distractions."

"Go then, John. Gather your things. Piers will help load the horses." The Ruin jerked his chin at a Gascon man-at-arms hovering by.

The two hurried toward the baggage beasts, and the Ruin turned back to Zhila.

"Pack. Quickly," he repeated.

His tone was still calm, but there was a flicker of impatience about his mouth.

"I will be quick when you say why," she retorted. "What is happening?"

His lips compressed. She thought for a moment he would simply refuse and order her to obey, but he evidently recognized that would be the longer argument. So he settled for a volley of statements.

"There are two forces of men, one before us and one behind. Both wear the same colors, that of the local lord. Their placement can be no coincidence. They will likely attack simultaneously at first light."

No coincidence. How did this lord know of their presence? Surely it couldn't be…

"What will you do?" she whispered.

"We are trapped." He glanced up at the tree line. "There is but one road through this valley. The valley walls are steep. We do not know the terrain, but we can assume they do. The company is too large to flee through wooded slopes *en masse.*" Then he looked directly at her. "But a small force could do so."

His eyes had iced over again. His meaning was quite plain.

"No. I stay here with you."

She had to. She hadn't completed her task yet. Ingram's despicable orders.

"No, you will ride with John and Piers. If the company is attacked, you are a liability. You will only get yourself or others killed. Go. Ride with John and aid him, and you may live. Perhaps we all may live."

She stared at him. "So I ride away. What about you? You stay here in a trap?"

"It is only a trap if the hunted one steps into it, oblivious. We are forewarned. A clever animal avoids the trap." His face was impassive. A jaw one could break oneself upon. "So avoid it, Zhila. Pack. Now."

This Ruin was good at issuing orders. The impulse to obey was strong, but she resisted.

"This is it? I ride, you stay, and maybe we both die." She stepped closer to him, slipped her hands around his neck. "No more. The end?"

He remained frozen a moment longer, then he crumbled like the Ruin he was. He descended on her lips with all the shock of tumbling masonry. His lips were hard. Zhila melted against him, and her lips took all the ravaging they could get. Her fingers tightened in his hair. As if she could hold him there.

But no, there was no time. It was a kiss to last two heart-beats…and perhaps a lifetime. Her fingers could not hold him.

He wrenched away from her and strode off.

⇶⇷

THEY RODE THROUGH darkening woodland. Piers had been one of the outriders that day. He had ascended this valley slope in daylight. The hope was he could do it again in the dark. Zhila also hoped that no Frenchmen would notice him doing it, for there was more at stake in this escapade than her own life.

If the Ruin died in a French ambush, Zhila would have no means of winning Maryam back. Not on Edmond Ingram's terms. She knew where Garit kept the key to his strongbox now—but what good was that if she were miles away and the box and the Ruin's dead body were in French hands?

And where was Edmond Ingram? Jos, the sneaking go-between, was dead. As far as she knew, Ingram had no other friend in the company. And as for the Fox himself, she had not seen him since Pamplona. He *seemed* to have followed them into Southern France, but she had no way of knowing where he was. Or of handing over any strongbox parchments in return for one sister.

Maryam. Pray God she was still alive, unharmed.

And the Ruin? If things went badly, she might lose him to-night.

But that was the whole point, wasn't it?

Just not like this.

Darkness fell. They stumbled up forested slopes blindly. Thorns tangled in her cloak and raked her hands. They must be silent. No breath to spare for complaints, swearing, or discussion. No Frenchman must hear them.

Except it would have taken a deaf man to overlook the crash of the horses through the undergrowth.

She hadn't met a deaf Frenchman yet.

Finally, the ground leveled, the undergrowth thinned. Stars shivered overhead instead of leaves.

And a voice out of nowhere barked, "Halt! Our arrows are nocked. Give yourself up and you have my word you will not be harmed."

Words snapped out in English. She knew that voice.

The Wreck was within reach. She lashed out at him. She whacked his horse on its haunch and hissed, "Ride! Get away! Go!"

Then Zhila disobeyed her own commands. She clunked her visor down, spurred her horse directly at the disembodied voice, and announced nice and loud, "Don't shoot! I give up."

And Piers and the Wreck pelted away, crashing through sheltering bushes. Yes, praise heaven the Wreck saw fit to do as she said. Meanwhile, Zhila rode at the enemy, her heart pounding as loud as the hoofbeats through the black woodland. She'd said not to shoot, but would they obey? Would she even hear the zip of the arrow before it hit her? Would her mail be any protection at such short range? Had they shot at the Wreck and Piers? Maybe they were already dead. She couldn't hear, couldn't think—she just knew what she had to do.

Ride toward the promise of death.

"Halt!" roared the voice. It was mere feet away now.

This time Zhila obeyed. She let the reins fall and raised her hands against the starlit sky.

"I give up, Edmond Ingram. Where is my sister?"

SHE WAS HAULED off her horse by shadowy hands. She vaguely registered shouts concerning her fleeing friends. Nearer at hand, the familiar voice barked, "Leave them. They're not important. I want the Ruin, not his damned bootlickers."

She was dragged before the owner of the voice. A horn lantern materialized in his hand. He wrenched her visor up and directed the light at her helmeted face, then drew back to survey the rest of her garb. She caught the curl of a foxy lip.

"The whore turns soldier," the lip said.

"Where is my sister?" Zhila cried.

"What are you doing here, doxy?"

"I ride out of a trap. You—do you make this trap?" She jabbed her hand toward the valley she had just scrambled out of, a valley in which the Ruin and his men were caught between two superior forces.

Another twist of the lip. "I may have ensured the ignorant lord who presides over this region knew an English company bearing much silver was passing through."

"Why? What about me? You told *me* to kill him. Where is Maryam? *Tell* me!"

"You, whore, have not delivered," Ingram snapped. "You sleep with him, this I know. Very good. But I grow impatient waiting for you to slit my dear kinsman's throat, not to mention to bring me my parchments. You are out of time, woman. I have taken matters into my own hands—or more properly, let French ones do the work for me."

Then, without waiting for a response, the Fox turned to his men. "Come—there's no further sign of fleeing rats. Bring the woman back to camp."

There was a camp established over the lip of the hill, out of sight of any eyes in the valley. A low fire cast a sick light over sleeping rolls, horses, and one small girl.

"Maryam!" Zhila fought the hands that held her. "Let me go, you son of a pustulant pig!"

The hands held her tight.

Sir Edmond glanced over. "Search her for weapons and be thorough about it. The bitch has a bite."

Zhila barely noticed the grasping hands…the all-too-thorough hands. She was too busy gazing at Maryam. Her little sister was alive, seemingly well, and spittingly angry. She cried out exclamations and accusations in Spanish and broken English. All the while, Zhila was patted and prodded mercilessly. Her habergeon was dragged off, her jacket delved under. The Fox's men needed to know there wasn't so much as a pin lodged in her trousers.

"Where have you been?" shouted Maryam.

"Speak Persian," Zhila said quickly. "They won't understand us then. Tell me, sweet one, are you well? Have they treated you...kindly?"

She tried to ignore the hands on her buttocks, the weapons check of her breasts. She held Maryam's eyes, hoping that she ignored it too.

"They tie me up too much." Maryam tugged at her arms in demonstration. They were bound behind her back and attached to a tree. "I am sore with sitting on the ground and horses. I am bored. I am frightened. You said you'd take me away. Where have you *been*?"

Only one man held Zhila now, but he held her far too close. "No weapons left, Sir Ed. I've stripped the bitch." The man paused. "You called her whore. Does that mean—?"

"No," snapped the Fox. "She is the Ruin's whore. For now. We don't have him yet. Perhaps...yes, when we have him, *if* he still lives, I'll hand her over to your tender ministrations. Ah yes, and I'll make the high and mighty Ruin watch. Be patient, Bart. Your dreams may yet come true."

Zhila froze in the man's grasp. *That* was the plan? The trap in the valley was aimed at seizing the Ruin himself?

And when Edmond Ingram had his ruinous goal, he would have no more use for Zhila and Maryam.

Which should be a good thing, but was not.

For then Sir Edmond Ingram would have no more reason to protect them.

And the Ruin? Zhila did not want to think what would happen to him. Maryam and Zhila might suffer but live, but the Ruin would simply suffer. Ingram could not afford to let him live.

She was released, stripped of her daggers. She ran to Maryam, dropped on her knees, and wrapped her arms around her little sister. Maryam was unable to return the favor, even if she were so inclined. She was bound.

"Where have you been?" was demanded into her shoulder. "I thought you were never coming back! You were having fun and you'd forgotten about me. You should have come back!"

Yes, Maryam was angry. She had a right to be. Zhila *had* been having fun.

Ingram had demanded it.

And now…

Zhila held her sister close. "I never forgot you, ever. Never, do you hear? That Fox knight wanted me to do something. It was…hard."

And all too easy to keep doing it.

The truth of the situation hit her like one of the Wreck's fabled cannonballs.

Zhila had ignored her greater goal in seducing the Ruin. The challenge of melting an icicle was just too delicious—no, *he* was just too delicious.

She had never forgotten her sister, but she hadn't sought Maryam's freedom hard enough. She should have killed the Ruin days ago. Ingram would have known. He was here, after all.

She *should* have done it. She should have slept with her knight, stabbed him, stolen from him, and then run. Well, limped. Her leg still wasn't properly healed.

And now look what was about to happen because of her lack of action.

The Company of the Ruin was pincered between two strong forces in the valley below. With dawn would come inevitable death. Even if Garit survived the encounter, the Fox had evidently made a deal with the French to take him and his parchments captive.

Then Maryam and Zhila would be at the mercy of soldiers who saw them as expendable heathens.

Chapter Twenty

THE FOX LEFT her alone in the dark after that. Some friendly fellow bound Zhila's wrists, then told her if she tried to free her sister or run, he would tie her legs too. Not that it stopped her. Surreptitiously, she had Maryam work at her bonds, and then returned the favor. All they needed now was an opportunity.

In the meantime, Zhila huddled close to her little sister, talking softly. Trying to make Maryam understand why she hadn't come back for her until now. Watching for some chance she might seize.

Sir Edmond and his riffraff company were watching and waiting too. They were obviously expecting something to happen in the valley. They perched like carrion birds on the heights, peered down, and waited for someone else to do the killing.

They also watched her, which wasn't a pleasant feeling. True, they watched that she didn't dart into the bushes or retrieve one of her daggers and plant it in the Fox's nonexistent heart, but they didn't need to eye her cleavage in order to do so.

Time was trickling away. The eastern horizon was not as inky as it ought to be. She had to *do* something. Better to run with Maryam now, risk an arrow in the back or a broken neck in the dark, than remain at a Fox's mercy.

Zhila wriggled her hands free of rope behind her back.

When she looked up, Ingram was watching her.

She had to divert him. "When you have your prisoner, you let us go—yes? I do everything you want, but your man, Jos, he betrays you. You know this? *I* do not betray you. I was about to do your orders, but Jos delayed me—he injured me."

"Yes, I heard my informant got greedy. He paid the price."

"Jos was no knight. He didn't protect women. He tried to—"

Zhila broke off. Maryam likely understood much more English now. No need to mention a dead man's intentions.

Sir Edmond's eyes lingered on her. "Yes, I'm sure he did. You have a certain charm, despite your Saracen appearance."

Zhila resisted the urge to point out his utter lack of charm, despite his foxy appearance.

"*You* are a knight. You protect women. You will not harm Maryam or me. You will let us go when you've got the Ruin."

Her voice cracked on those last words. Her Ruin, in this man's hands.

No, she would not consider Sir Garit. He was a warrior—a killer. She had known he must die all along, only *she* was meant to kill him. Only her. But Zhila could do nothing about the Ruin now. It was Maryam she needed to focus on.

Meanwhile, the east was growing pale. Dawn crept close on icy fingers. Had John the Wreck escaped safely with his precious load? What was the company doing down in the valley? There had been talk of defenses and the strategic use of the river when she left. But wouldn't it be more sensible just to flee? Maybe they had done. Maybe Sir Garit was miles away by now, leaving her far behind.

Better that than dead—or captured by a Fox.

"You're right," Sir Edmond said. "I won't harm you. I am a knight, therefore I have standards. I would not sully myself on a heathen."

"I'm not—!" Zhila began, then snapped her jaw shut.

"Look at you." The knight did just that, his nose crinkling as if he smelled something worse than his foxy self. "You may look like a Spaniard, but your clothing, the way you act, your voice, all betray you. It is no sin in a knight to kill a Saracen, or to give her to his men."

"We are Christian! I tell you before, many times before—Christian!"

His nose wrinkled further, if possible. "Then you are an eastern heretic. Worse than Saracen. You reject the true doctrine. You—"

Whatever further foul nonsense the rusted knight was about to spout was interrupted.

By something quite wonderful.

Dawn burst with a blinding flash of light upon the *western* horizon. A moment later, a thunderclap rattled the leaves. The ground actually trembled—unless that was simply Zhila jumping out of her skin.

Maryam yelped and buried her face into Zhila's shoulder.

"Shh, it's all right, sweet one." Zhila was grinning. She couldn't scrub it off her face, so she hid the evidence by resting her cheek on Maryam's head. "It's a good thing," she whispered in Persian. "It means he's done it."

"Done what? Who? Why's it good?"

That was a sobering thought. Why *was* it good? The Wreck had achieved what he'd set out to do, but that did not help the Kurians now.

Ingram's men were on their feet. They stared at the western horizon and fingered their weapons. Sir Edmond, on the contrary, looked straight at Zhila.

"That was the Ruin's monster, wasn't it? I know his work."

Zhila shrugged. She didn't actually know. Besides, the Wreck was no monster. But it *did* sound like he'd been having fun.

"I should have put an arrow through the ugly bastard while I could," Edmond growled.

There was no answer to that either.

A second flash of light erupted on the horizon. The thunderclap-that-was-not-thunder followed. Zhila managed not to jump out of her skin this time, and Maryam's squeak was less shrill.

And all this came from the ingredients packed onto one unsuspecting horse? John was a talented man.

Zhila grinned again. No wonder horses didn't like the Wreck.

But what now? Her smile drooped. She'd had a vague notion that this was their aim in escaping from the valley, but not why. *She* had been sent off like superfluous baggage, but the Wreck had a mission, and Piers was his guide.

Long moments slipped by. Should she and Maryam escape now? It was still mostly dark, but Ingram's men were alert—moving restlessly, murmuring, throwing lingering looks at her. Then, just as Zhila was whispering instructions into Maryam's ear, one of the sentries burst into the clearing.

"They're moving!"

"What?" barked the Fox. "Who's moving? What are they doing?"

"Your Frenchmen. Lomagne's men—they're on the march."

Sir Edmond got to his feet. He smiled. The glow of the dawn dipped his teeth in blood.

"They advance on the Company of the Ruin, you mean. The rats in a trap. Their teeth tighten upon the Ruin's neck."

THE COMPANY HAD to leave, now. It could not wait for three stray members.

The lure had worked.

At least, that was what Garit hoped when no French forces sauntered up at dawn in their superior and arrogant numbers to demand the Company of the Ruin surrender or be annihilated.

Garit didn't know what the Wreck had blown up, but the evidence was plain—he *had* blown at least two things up, and made a big, flashy noise in the process. Perfect. Even down here in the valley, they'd seen the blaze on the horizon and heard the racket. The horses were still twitchy.

He *hoped* the French forces had hurried away to combat the new threat. But even if they had, it would only be a temporary reprieve—the French lord would soon discover no enemy force besieged his home. If, however, said lord discovered that home was now a collection of smoking stones, he would likely return to express his displeasure in person. At a gallop.

Time to go. Garit could only pray the Wreck, Piers, and Zhila caught up.

If Zhila hadn't already seized the opportunity to leave.

It was entirely likely. After all, she'd taken most of her belongings with her, and she was in France now, just as she wished. A sensible minstrel would deem that keeping company with the company was too great a risk. She was safer without them. Without him.

Time to go.

The company had holed up on the far side of the river. They'd tucked themselves against a small cliff. An admirably defensible spot. From here, they could spray the approaching enemy with arrows, then slow them with a river crossing, and finally pick them off one by one as they stumbled out of the shallows. That was the plan.

A better plan was to avoid fighting at all.

Thank you, John the Wreck, for facilitating Plan B.

If John was still alive to thank.

ZHILA TUGGED MARYAM to her feet. Everyone else was standing by now. It would attract no attention.

"We run, Maryam," she murmured in Persian. "Fast. Down the hill. Stay close to me. If I fall, just *keep on going.* Understand?"

Maryam cast her a terrified look, but nodded all the same.

She should have just said yes. Ingram saw her look and action. He started toward them.

"Now!" Zhila whispered, and sprang into the bushes.

Branches barred their way, clawed their hair, grabbed at their clothing. Zhila held on to her sister's wrist and shoved on, ignoring scratches, gouges, Maryam's squeaks.

Crashing behind them. Cries of "Halt, damn heathens" and other more colorful and less accurate forms of address. The ground began to slope precipitously.

"Nearly there!" Zhila gasped. "Just keep going!"

Maryam's response was a heart-piercing scream.

Zhila whipped about. There was a hand in Maryam's hair. It gripped a fistful of dark curls. In the next instant, her sister was hauled back against a mailed chest and an arm was hooked about her neck.

A moment of frozen indecision. Zhila didn't have her daggers, but she was still free. Fly at the armed, armored attacker, or run?

Without her sister.

Zhila gave an ifrit shriek and launched herself at him. She bit down on the man's ear and reached for his sword simultaneously. A mistake. She did not get the angle right. The sword snagged in its sheath. Her mouth was full of blood. At least it wasn't her own.

"Argh, git her off me! Devil damn you, whore, I'll throttle your sister!"

Zhila loosened her tooth-grip. Just as well, for in the next moment she too was grabbed from behind and hoisted backward. Had her teeth still been clamped, the man's lower ear would have come with her.

They were dragged back to the Fox. Back through the bushes. The first thing Zhila did was hawk blood at the red bastard.

It was probably fortunate it missed. Ingram was already looking distinctly displeased. Rabid might be a better description.

"Where in the devil's arse do you think you think you're going?" he barked.

"You don't need me anymore. No, nor Maryam. You have French to do your killing and stealing for you. You don't need a mere *heathen whore*. So let us go!"

"MOUNT UP! WE ride out on my command!"

Garit shouted the order from the giddy vantage of his war-horse. Crane from its heights as he may, he could see no movement on the other side of the river. But it was still a trial of nerves to abandon their defensible nook.

He glanced about at his men. All mounted. All armed and swathed about with every bit of armor they owned.

They could not linger for one girl, an engineer, and their guide. Who may not be coming back at all.

He drew a harsh breath and cried, "Ride fast, and do not stop unless I order it. We leave this valley *now!*"

Garit snapped his visor shut, motioned sharply forward with one arm, and put his heels to his horse. The beast sprang into the water. His men splashed in behind him, a racket of churning hooves that was over in moments. The water wasn't deep, thank heaven. No horse needed to swim. Even better, no horse lost its footing and gave its rider or luggage a chill bath.

Best of all, no Frenchman stepped out from behind a tree.

They thundered across the clearing where he'd intended to camp. Garit bent low over his horse's neck, offering as small a target as possible. Urging the beast on. If Garit were this French lord, he'd have set an ambush. He'd spring it once the enemy left safety. Any moment now, he would hear the zip of crossbow bolts, the scream of horses and falling men.

You should not be leaving.

Every instinct screamed that what he was doing was wrong. He would get his men killed. He'd likely already got the Wreck killed. And Zhila…

He'd sent her with John for her own safety. Women did not belong in the Company of the Ruin, and the present situation illustrated why. He'd sent her away so if the ruse failed, if the company was attacked, she could flee. She had her belongings, her strange instrument, and her life. She didn't need the company. She'd been with them too long already.

But if she and the Wreck had run into the French after their exploits, she'd be dead already…or worse.

Or she was miles off, riding a stolen horse into the dawn.

Either way, he'd never see her again.

By some miracle, they crossed the clearing without suffering aeration by crossbow. Now they streamed through the trees, heading toward the ultimate ambush location—the winding valley road. It was the fastest way out of here, but it was also the most dangerous. No sensible leader would abandon his beautifully prepared trap just because his home had blown up, surely?

They were about to find out. The horses had slowed though the trees, but now the road was in sight and his stallion's muscles were bunching. The beast wished for nothing more than to pelt down that open path. Garit could sympathize. Speed sounded like a wonderful idea right now.

Then, with a bit of luck, if they galloped into a trap, they'd have enough impetus to simply burst through. Some of them might survive.

How in hell had this happened? The company had offered no violence to any in this region. They'd had no time to—they'd simply ridden fast and inconspicuously so that no lord had the opportunity to raise resistance in time. This shouldn't have happened.

His thoughts flicked to Jos. Did they have another such traitor in their midst? But what on earth would such a traitor gain by getting himself attacked? And how had he engineered it? No, it wasn't possible.

Unless…

His destrier burst out onto the open road, and Garit nudged him northward. The animal accelerated. It was madness, intoxicating insanity. He was galloping into a trap, and Garit was grinning behind his visor. He reminded himself of Zhila. *She* would grin at this danger. She would lean over her horse's neck, gallop beside him, and laugh at the madness of it all.

Unless she was laughing *at* him, even now.

The realization dropped on him right then and there, and Garit nearly fell off his horse.

Zhila had engineered the trap. Then she'd neatly stepped out of it and left them to their fate. He didn't know the details, but it made perfect sense. Someone had leaked information. Jos had accused Zhila before, and not without basis. She had wandered off in Pamplona for some unexplained reason. She'd opened the door to Jos. And how had she escaped Ingram in Nájera? Too many coincidences and oddities.

Garit wasn't grinning any more. The hooves pounded on. They pounded in his head. He had never questioned the woman properly. She was too distracting, too vulnerable, too…

Simply too much.

No women in the company. No women in his damned chamber, either. And certainly no traitorous, tenacious women stirring up sediment from the depths of his being. Fooling him. Plaguing him. Tempting him to feel.

The Ruin galloped on, jaw like a blacksmith's vise. He was not stopping till his horse sagged beneath him. John and Piers could catch up, *if* they were alive. If they hadn't died as a result of a minstrel's treachery. The Wreck knew where they were headed, and the company was only a few days from its destination.

And Zhila?

He wouldn't see her again, of that he was sure. Zhila was no fool. She would know better than to face him after this.

Traitor. Trickster. Consummate performer. If they did meet again, he would see straight through her. And then he would look away in disgust.

Chapter Twenty-One

"THEY'RE HEADING TO La Roque, aren't they?" Edmond Ingram demanded, once he'd stopped frothing at the mouth long enough to pronounce words.

"La rock? What rock?" Zhila asked. "The company passes many rocks. They do not name them."

"Don't play stupid, whore. Vesian la Roque. It's a village. Is the Ruin going there now or not?"

Zhila felt like shrugging. She didn't. She was currently perched before one of Ingram's unsavory excuses for a soldier. The fellow rode with one arm about her, holding her all too firmly against him. Zhila didn't want to move one muscle more than necessary. Ingram's men were all mounted and picking their way along the valley rim. The Fox himself rode beside her.

"If that's where the castle he wants to marry is, then yes. That's where he's going."

"Marry? For God's sake—" Ingram paused to hawk mightily into the bushes.

Just as well his visor was up, really. Whatever did warriors do with their eternal need to spit when fully helmed? Zhila would have laughed another time.

"Yes—marry," she said. "See? I am no use to you. What will the Ruin want with me once he weds his lady? Let us go."

"Devil damn him, I thought this cock-eyed marriage plan was

just a passing fancy. He's already got a cursed castle of his own."

"A ruin," Zhila inserted.

"Aye! A pile of worthless stones. Such a noble knight 'cause he's lord of a quarry. So now the greedy bastard thinks he'll just marry another."

"Will he?" Zhila was genuinely curious. "Is that all it takes? A knight rides up, asks a lady to marry him and give him her castle, and *voilà*, she says yes?"

"Why not? He's a handsome bastard," Ingram said between his teeth.

That was startling. Not that Zhila would contest the handsome charge.

"You think so?"

"Aye, and he's got a company to help convince the lovely lady. Handsome *and* persuasive. Just might do it."

It still sounded strange to Zhila, but who was she, a mere Persian performer, to judge? The Ruin didn't even know this rocky lady, but he seemed set on marrying her. And the lady in question—how could she resist a big, blond knight with a ruinous reputation? Ah, it was the stuff of true romance.

"So, is this La Roque far?" she asked.

"Not far enough," the Fox snapped. "Two days at most."

"Oh."

So soon. Two days and her Ruin would wed. Was that the real reason he had sent her away?

"See?" she whispered. "I am no use. Let me go."

"No, it means you, whore, have one more chance. One *last* chance. Those French worms proved worthless. I set them on a cashed-up company, promise them plenteous silver, and all I ask is that they capture or kill my dear cousin and pass me some parchments they have no use for. It would have worked too, if not for an ape-ugly Englishman playing with powder. Cowardly French curs turned tail at the first bang."

The face in the visor blotched like an ill-conceived sunset. It took Ingram a breath or two to continue.

"You, woman, were always my preferred method, for all you've dithered and delayed. *You* are the truly poetic ending. He chose you over me in Nájera. Let him feel the consequences of that choice. So get back in his bed, get me my parchments, and *make him end*, understand?"

Zhila flicked a look around. The horseman with Maryam was some way back. Ingram had decreed that the sisters remain separated. Just as well right now.

"He will marry. He doesn't want me. Just let us go," Zhila said dully.

Ingram lashed out. He grabbed her by her jacket, the better to snarl at her, "He *does* want you, whore. I saw it in Nájera, and you've since proven it beyond doubt. And he will *not* marry. I will not allow it. You must damn well see that he does not."

He released her, probably only because his horse was objecting to its too-intimate proximity to her mount.

"I will leave you near his camp tonight," Ingram went on. "He's left a trail as wide as a Roman road, and even noble Sir Garit cannot gallop all day. Thus you will return to his loving arms. Kill the Ruin and bring me his parchments, woman. He must *not* marry." It was Ingram's turn to flick a look back at Maryam. "Must I detail what will happen to your sister if you fail?"

"No."

"Perhaps I should. You seem to need an incentive."

"No!" Zhila flung a look over her shoulder. She didn't think Maryam could overhear at that distance. All the same... "Do not say it! I'll do what you want! Do not—"

Edmond Ingram overrode her. He did not shout. He simply enunciated the words with horrible precision. "She will not die. At least, not immediately. I have a very special whorehouse in mind for your sweet sister. In bustling Bordeaux, soon to be home to a host of bored soldiers. Ah yes, they will pay me well for a pretty young thing like her."

SHE REACHED THE camp in the glow of dusk. The lengthening shadows and peach-dust light softened everything—sheltering oaks, cropping horses, a makeshift village of tents and drifting woodsmoke.

Everything except his face.

Ingram's band had ridden all day in the wake of the company. Easy enough to follow a path marked by hundreds of iron-shod hoofs with a scattering of horse excrement. Then Ingram had given Zhila back her daggers, horse, and habergeon as the sun sank. He'd legged her up and whacked the beast's rump before she had her foot in the stirrup. Probably afraid she would knife him before she left.

"Get back to him and do the job properly this time."

Barely time for a shouted exchange in Persian with her sister.

"I'll come back. I'll take you away. Soon!"

Maryam's lips puckered as if she sucked an unripe lemon. "You said that last time."

But this time Zhila was going to make it happen. She'd dwelt on it all day. The Ruin was a killer who might have died at any time in his decade of campaigning. The man was practically living on borrowed time. She, Zhila Kurian, would finish that borrowing and, by way of apology, ensure Sir Garit died deliriously happy.

It was for the best possible cause.

All of these resolutions had hardened to sunbaked clay through the long day of riding after the company. And now...now Sir Garit turned and looked at her.

The blue eyes widened. Then the Ruin's lips narrowed and his lids drooped. A face shuttered, an expression rendered in stone.

As for her own face, Zhila knew her emotions were scrawled clear across it. She had no shutters. Her expression was a blaze of completely unwelcome feeling.

He was alive. He was unharmed. He was big and solid and blonde and ruinous. The need to fling herself off her horse and climb that tower of strength was almost overwhelming, and she was certain her smile was as brilliant as the sinking sun.

The handsome bastard was sweeping all thoughts of Maryam from her mind.

He is a dead man. He just doesn't know it yet. But I will take him to heaven first.

She slipped off her horse. Well, off the Ruin's horse, actually. The poor thing was nearly done in with all its clambering of valley slopes and pursuing the company all day. She would see to it shortly. But first...

Zhila advanced on the Ruin, her whole being alight with purpose. He was her target, her lover, her rock. She would—

Sir Garit raised a palm to ward her off and turned back to his companion.

"You did well, John."

Zhila faltered, but then registered whom he was talking to. "Wreck! Piers! You live! Ah!" She reached out to clasp John's big, burn-scarred hands. "I am glad. I heard your explosions. I *felt* them. You did it, Wreck!"

Her friend's face split into the sort of grin a demon would envy.

"Aye. That we did. Made a nice big bang or two to rattle his Frenchie lordship..." The Wreck cast a meaningful glance toward Garit. There seemed to be a warning in it for Zhila. He squeezed her hands then dropped them. "Just like I was telling Sir Garit when you ambled up." John turned back to said commander. "All worked as planned, I take it, sir?"

"It did." The Ruin's voice was as dispassionate as if he discussed dinner. "I expected the trap to close soon after dawn. We were prepared. It would have been nasty. But then..." The Ruin actually smiled. It was the merest tilt of the lips, and it was directed solely at the Wreck and Piers. "We received a portent of the apocalypse. The French scurried away to combat whoever was creating it, doubtless thinking their homes were ashes and smoke. What did you blow up, by the way?"

John the Wreck shrugged. "Seemed a bit rude to set fire to people in their sleep. Not to mention tricky. So we found a barn in the lord's demesne still half stuffed with hay. Exploded a treat, it did. The hay got tossed in the air, all afire and streaking through the dark. Ah." The Wreck closed his eyes and beamed a beatific smile. "It was a thing of wonder, it was."

"And the other bang?"

The engineer did not open his eyes. The man was off in the realms of honeyed memory, so Piers took up the tale. "I found him a ravine, sir. Not a dwelling in sight, but a fine lot of echoing rock walls. We wanted the most bang for our brimstone, and we got it. Reckon we gave the chamois thereabouts a fright."

"Aye," said the Wreck, stirring himself. "A beautiful great bang it was. Shook the squirrels fair from the trees. It put fire in my nag's hooves and no mistake. Which was all to the good, 'cause we had to get back sharpish and see what we could do about Zhila."

"About Zhila?" the Ruin echoed. The slight smile slipped off his face, and he looked at her. "Yes, pray explain why she has only just appeared, and quite separately from you."

Her stomach tightened. That look—hard and blank. It was not the look of a lover.

"She was taken," Piers said. "There were men at the lip of the valley."

"Aye," the Wreck put in. "She rode straight at 'em so we could make a break for it. Don't reckon we could've got away and made such a lovely great racket if your woman hadn't diverted the hounds."

"Is that so?" Sir Garit said, his cool gaze fixed upon her face. "How noble of you, Zhila." Without shifting his regard, he addressed the Wreck again. "And who were these hounds?"

The engineer shrugged. "It was dark, sir. Couldn't see them.

Only heard 'em shouting at us to surrender or they'd fill us full of holes."

But Zhila barely heard the words. She was too busy holding Sir Garit's gaze, looking as if she hadn't a thing in the world to hide. Praise heaven she had been performing since she could crawl.

"Is that so?" the man she must kill said again.

And then, finally, he touched her. Sir Garit's fingers closed over her forearm.

"Come, Zhila Kurian," he said. "You and I must talk. In private."

HE LED HER into the darkening forest. He wanted no audience for this interview, and he must talk while there was still light enough to examine her face. Garit towed her along until they reached a clearing created by a fallen tree. There he stopped abruptly and turned on her, gripping her shoulders, the better to hold her at arm's length.

"Are you in league with the French?" Garit demanded.

Her lovely face was tilted upward to his, bathed in the dying light. He could scan its expression in minute detail.

It transformed into instant outrage. "No!" she exclaimed. "No, I know nothing of Frenchmen! You think I *want* them to attack? What for?"

Garit did not ease his grip.

"They had warning of our approach. So many men could not have been mobilized without notice. We were moving too fast. Someone told them."

"Maybe so, but not me! If I like the French so much, why do I come back to you now? I help the Wreck. He needs to blow thing up, and Piers must show him where. Me? I help them do it. You put me in harness, so I use it. We were threatened, so I go between the Wreck and them, and pray my armor holds against French arrows."

Garit had been softening. How could he not? He had his wild dancer in his hands, they were alone, and her dark eyes were blazing with feeling. That feeling tugged at him irresistibly, setting fire to his senses, urging him to—

"Arrows? The French threatened you with bows?" he said.

What he did not clarify was that the bow was seldom used by the French. Crossbows, maybe, but crossbows used bolts, not arrows.

She shrugged against his pinning hands. "It was dark. I do not see. They shout for us to halt or they will shoot. I not know *what* they will shoot. I just act. I ride at them so the others could ride away."

Noble...too noble. Why on earth would she risk herself in such a way? Surely she knew the risks of falling into soldiers' hands by now? Yet he still hadn't discovered what had happened in Nájera. Whatever is was, it evidently hadn't been rape. So what *had* Edmond done to her and her sister? That little girl. Dear God. No, surely he wouldn't—

Garit interrupted his own thoughts. "They seized you? They...they took you?"

His hands were not so steady now. The shoulders beneath his palms stilled.

"So. Is that why you act so strange, Ruin?" Her eyes were not smiling anymore. "You think I betray you with more than words. They *take* me? I see. You think I spend all night riding Frenchmen. Other men have had me—*lots* of other men. Now I am dirt to you."

He released her abruptly. "No! I am concerned for the safety of the company. Did you bring a horde of French down upon us? Did you... Christ, did they mistreat you, Zhila?"

She stood quite still before him, practically incandescent in the sunset glow. So very beautiful. And furious.

"And if they did? If every last one of them hump me till it is a miracle I can ride my horse—what then?"

He was rooted to the forest floor. He had sent her away for safety. He sent her with two men to guard her, and she instead had guarded them—and the whole company too. But with what hideous consequences?

"I would kill them." It was the snarl of a ravening wolf. Sir Garit of the Ruin never spoke thus. "I would track down every last one of them and render him a eunuch. Then I would shove his balls so far down his throat he choked."

"And me?" she said. "I am truly a *puta*, then, not fit for your bed? Why, you cannot even touch me now."

Was it true? Garit couldn't think straight. He had done this. He'd tried to protect her in Nájera, and the result? She'd lost her sister. Again, she'd been under his protection when Jos abducted and tried to kill her. And now the pattern had repeated again. The pain he'd caused her didn't bear thinking of. He *couldn't* picture it without losing all semblance of control. Sir Garit brought ruin upon any woman he came to care for. Death, rape, loss of family and home.

"Look at me, Ruin," came that rich, foreign-tinged voice. Garit found he'd shut his eyes and turned his hands into collections of bunched bones. "Look at me and see me for what I am."

Slowly, reluctantly, he obeyed. What did he see? A traitor? Or a woman horribly betrayed, abused, and ruined? One thing was certain—he did not see any echo of his mother or Marie. Only Zhila, dark, intense, and reaching for him.

Garit stepped back instinctively, self-protectively. And cursed himself at the flicker of pain in her eyes.

"I am not, how you say, *in league* with the French," she snapped. "What are Frenchmen to me? And they did not *mistreat* me, as you say. No, not one. When the Wreck made his bangs, my captors all leap up and shout and point. I escape in the confusion. You see, I am not every man's *puta*, Sir Ruin. Only yours."

She had stepped closer again. Now her mismatched harness

bumped up against his. The scent of her stole over him, all heady spices. The relief that no one had abused her was headier still. He had not failed her. Somehow she had survived.

He was in the very act of reaching for her when a flurry of realizations assaulted him.

Impossibilities.

That Zhila should be captured by soldiers and *not* be treated as sexual booty was startling enough, but perhaps chivalry was not dead yet. But that she should escape *and* manage to take her horse with him was more improbable still.

She was his, she'd declared. His what, though—his whore? *Puta* was an ugly word. It should never be applied to Zhila, but he had made her one. She had been a maiden, but now she was a camp follower. She shared his bed. Likewise, she shared his danger.

And Sir Garit of the Ruin would shortly be married. To a château and an incidental wife.

His hands dropped by his sides.

"You are unharmed. I…I am pleased. But you are no whore, Zhila. Not mine, not anybody's. You are a minstrel. Once I have acquired this château, I will take you to Bordeaux. I'll find you a minstrel troupe. Doubtless, they will accept a woman of your talent."

A woman of your vibrancy and beauty. They would be blind fools not to.

"Bordeaux," she murmured, gazing up at him with midnight eyes. "You want to get rid of me. You cannot keep a wife and *puta* in the same castle, yes?"

At the same time, her arms wound about his neck. She was lifting her lips to his. The need to dip down and claim them was almost irresistible.

He jerked back.

"No. I have done you a heinous wrong in taking you to my bed. I will do it no more. In a few days I will marry, then I will go to Bordeaux to gather what is mine. To bring all under the safety of Château la Roque, and to take *you* to safety."

"I see. You go to Bordeaux to gather what is yours and to discard me."

"No. Yes! You wanted this, Zhila. France. Safety. A minstrel life."

She regarded him steadily. The lowering light turned her face more darkly alluring than ever.

"Perhaps I have discovered something I want even more," she murmured. "You and I, we come close to death this day. Now we should celebrate life. You are not married yet, Ruin. Take me to Bordeaux if you must. I will leave you there, if you insist. But first, let us *live*."

She slipped her arms about his nape and tugged him down. She gave him no time to resist. Her lips touched his, a beckoning paradise, and Garit's will crumbled.

He'd thought she was dead. He'd thought she was horribly abused, or riding far away, but here she was in his arms. It wouldn't last. He *must* put her aside—he still didn't trust her—but right now…

Garit dragged her against him, clunky armor against armor, and devoured her with all the pent-up feeling of the day. She did not hold back, but then, Zhila never did. That was her intoxicating power. Her mouth was greedy on his, their tongues twined, and Zhila's hands roamed over his defenses.

Dear God, armor was not designed to accommodate how Garit was feeling right now. His lower regions were distinctly cramped. He wanted to bury himself into her right now, to pin her against the nearest tree trunk and reclaim what he thought he'd lost forever. Selfish bastard that he was.

Zhila was delving beneath his coat of plates with one hand as she kissed him wildly, frantically. Unfortunately, beneath the coat of plates lay his mail shirt. She was almost as heavily attired. All the same, he had actually backed her up against a tree before the realization blew an icy breath of sanity over his nape. Pity it didn't breathe likewise over his yard. That item was too well covered to admit of any cooling.

Zhila wrenched her mouth from his. She stared up at him, breath coming fast from parted lips.

"Not here," she said. "Take me into your bed tonight. Love me one more time."

Chapter Twenty-Two

THE RUIN TURNED to stone. Oh, Zhila appreciated the solidity beneath her fingers, but his expression had just petrified as well. Not such a welcome development.

Worse was what came out of his mouth when that part of his body unpetrified.

"No," he said. "This ends, now. Within days, I woo a bride. Your continued presence in my bed will undermine my suit. Do you think my lady-wife-to-be wants to share her husband with…"

He did not finish the sentence.

So Zhila did it for him. "With a heathen whore."

"No. With a beautiful and talented minstrel, Zhila. With a woman who would cast any other into the shade."

His voice was soft. His body was still cast in stone.

Damn this eternal armor. If they were both in ordinary clothes, she would override all verbal objections with actions far more persuasive than words. She wanted him. He most certainly wanted her.

And yet he was pushing her away. He straightened his coat of plates and stepped back.

"*Ahh!*"

Zhila shrieked. The sound echoed in the wood like some nocturnal bird cry. She *must* establish herself in his bed again. She *had* to access his papers, his heart, his jugular. And, damn it all to hell, she simply wanted him.

But Zhila would not beg. Not that she had any pride where Maryam was concerned, but she *would* find a way.

"Come," he said. "It grows dark. Let us return to the camp. With luck, it will be the last time we sleep in the open for many months."

He was already striding away. Zhila narrowed her eyes at his retreating form. She hoped that walking with a veritable pole between his legs pained him. With any luck, said pole would chafe against the layers of his armor and rub itself raw.

Maybe then he would let her kiss it better.

VESIAN LA ROQUE. The company had reached its target. They'd abandoned war-ravaged Spain, plodded over the Pyrenees, and scuttled through enemy territory to reach the Ruin's destination of choice. It turned out to be a poky little village nestled at the base of an almighty cliff. Zhila stared up at the precipice as they approached. The place was horribly like Nájera in its situation—a settlement sheltering at the base of protective cliffs beside a winding river. Only this river did not run with the blood. Not yet. And Zhila's parents could not die a second time.

She set her teeth and glanced at the man who rode at the head of the column. No, Garit of the Ruin would die here instead.

The company clattered into the village square, all fifty-plus men and double that in horses. And one lonely woman. Locals paused in whatever they were doing to eye the newcomers grimly, then hurry away. Zhila paid them little heed. The Company of the Ruin received a similar welcome in every settlement it entered.

She was more interested in the place itself. Why had the Ruin chosen this location above all others? It had been his goal since he left Nájera, she knew. Possibly long before that. Why? Surely there were other widows and other castles?

But now she was here, Zhila understood, for whoever had named La Roque had suffered from a blinding lack of imagination.

Rock. That was what the place was all about. The village itself was a jumble of limestone buildings. And then there was the château perched above, wedged into the crevices of the cliff, a towering stone stronghold built into the bones of the earth. No wonder the Ruin fancied it. He'd finally found something more rocklike than himself. The man had fallen in love with a cliff, not a woman.

Said Ruin dismounted, left his stallion in Donal's care, and strode toward the largest building on the square. The barrels flanking its doors declared that it served wine. Zhila slipped off her horse and hurried in his wake.

She entered the inn just in time to hear Garit announce to a buxom, be-aproned woman, "My company stays in La Roque, madam. Pray, do what you can to accommodate us. We will not loot. But we *will* stay, whether you like it or not."

Normally Dickon saw to the company's sleeping and eating arrangements. He was an older fellow with a friendly manner and facility with languages. A good negotiator. Today, he simply stood by his leader's side and listened to what was evidently not a negotiation.

The woman thus addressed was silent some moments, but her bosom rose and fell eloquently.

Finally she said in French: "You will pay?"

"Yes."

"How many?"

"Fifty men, over one hundred horses."

"*Mon Dieu, c'est impossible,*" she muttered. Then louder, "There is not room. So many men and horses. Men can sleep on the floor, yes, but the horses…"

"Of course," Garit returned. "Dickon, go. Inform the villagers that we require stabling. Some of us will also billet ourselves in their homes. Assure them no violence will be done. We will pay. But the horses must be accommodated."

"How long do you stay, monsieur?" The woman's hands were on her hips now. There was plenty of substance to prop them up.

The Ruin turned back to his hostess, expressionless. "That is up to the Lady of La Roque," he said. No further explanation was offered. "Do you have a private room I may use? One that may be bolted or locked. I sleep alone."

Garit did not look in Zhila's direction, but those last words were for her, she was sure. They let her know where she stood, or, more properly, lay.

Far from him.

Last night she'd slept by John the Wreck's side. She had done so for safety, and not because she enjoyed the tune of the engineer's snores. As a result of his mangled face, the man's breath emanated as if through a leaky bagpipe. It *was* kind of comforting, hearing him so obviously near, but Zhila would have preferred the quieter comfort of the Ruin's warmth.

Warmth? No, Sir Garit of the Ruin had frozen over again. Zhila was superfluous to his plans. She could not compete with a castle.

Zhila didn't register what the Frenchwoman answered, but she heard the words Garit addressed to Piers all too clearly.

"Walk up to the château," said the Ruin. "You and one other. Request an audience with Lady Eglantine of La Roque on my behalf. I will see her today."

Chapter Twenty-Three

G ARIT SAT IN a corner of the taproom, in the company of a sizable cup of mine hostess's best wine. Mine hostess also had orders to see that said cup never suffered a drought. Sir Garit of the Ruin was in the mood to celebrate, or at least to subject himself to a thorough soaking. After all these years of rootless fighting, his goal was finally in sight—or it would be if he stepped out in the square and gazed upward in the evening light.

This afternoon he had seen the woman who would help him achieve that goal. Eglantine of La Roque. Up close, the woman was surprisingly comely.

Which was good, wasn't it?

Garit stood abruptly—too abruptly. He made a valiant attempt at braining himself on one of the beams arching out from the wall. Heads turned. Garit grabbed his cup of wine and raised it.

"Men, we are here," he declared to the room at large. "Vesian la Roque, our destination!"

A rumble of assent and some thumping of fists or drinking vessels on wooden boards. Now he had their attention, Garit expanded on his theme.

"Today I spoke to the Lady of La Roque. I pointed out that she is an English widow in a hostile land, eminently in need of male protectors. She has but a handful of men-at-arms. Her son is many years from manhood. In light of these deficiencies, I offered the lady an alliance to her great benefit—and ours. I will marry and protect her until her son can inherit. In return, she will provide the company with an admirable fortress. Château la Roque." Garit waved in the direction of the cliff. "Men, we are home."

The roar that followed was reminiscent of the Wreck's precious cannon. Which was, incidentally, now useless for want of gunpowder. The arcane stuff had all been expended on the night of the trap. But, right now, powder was unnecessary. Trestles were abused with fists, and more than one beaker sloshed over the boards.

A grin took possession of Garit's lips. The Company of the Ruin had been too long without a base. A company needed a fortress. Even warriors required protection, and the company had been roofless for far too long. His men were family. They had fought for him and occasionally died for him for years—it was about time he rewarded them with a secure home.

"When's the wedding?" came a bellow. Garit couldn't identify which mouth it came from.

"Aye! Here's to the nuptials of the Roque and the Ruin!"

Garit's smile decamped.

"I meet the lady to discuss the details on the morrow," he announced, and paused, cup still raised. Ah well, he'd better mention it. They'd know soon enough. "The lady has shown some reluctance," he said. "My proposal has caught her by surprise. She has not leapt into my arms. Thus, I have given her till tomorrow to consider."

He looked around at the listeners. Practically all the company. Every bench was full. Fifty flame-lit faces studied Garit's, questions scrawled over all of them. The leader of such a company could show no doubt or hesitation.

"Make no mistake—Vesian la Roque is ours," Garit declared. "If Lady Eglantine continues reluctant, why, we shall give her all the time she needs to come to the right decision. Weeks, if need be."

He watched as comprehension dawned. A few sharp-toothed grins followed, but there was the odd flash of concern too.

So Garit clarified. "Should the lady continue to refuse, we will blockade her château. Eglantine of La Roque has no military force, so we will lose no lives. On the contrary, the Company of the Ruin will occupy this charming village and frequent this even more charming inn until the lady above sees reason. It is time we ceased galivanting over all Christendom."

Garit raised his beaker high.

"To the future Company of the Roque!"

Garit drank to a gunpowder roar of approbation, then sank to his seat. His men knew as much as he did now. So did the villagers, incidentally—any that remained in the vicinity. No matter. The usual sentries were set, but Garit knew there'd be no attack tonight. Various informants had assured him the lady retained but three men-at-arms, and simple villagers knew better than to attack an armed company. Garit's men deserved a rest and a chance to sample the local produce.

On which thought, he raised his cup and did so. He got a proper taste of the stuff this time. It was a full-bodied, fragrant red wine, produced of Vesian la Roque's own grapes. Truly, this was a château worth possessing.

And its mistress?

He'd seen the Lady Eglantine but once before. At her husband's funeral, incidentally. He'd been in the vicinity and helped hunt down the brigands who'd ended the lord's life. He'd only seen her at a distance then, wan and sad, clutching her small boy to her. A youngish, noble English widow with a son. And a château in the heart of Southern France. With her heart in the grave.

Garit had stowed that perfect conjunction of circumstances away in his memory. Now he was back.

All that was wanting now was for the lady to see reason.

Garit lifted the cup again, found it empty, then glanced round for the serving woman.

That glance fell upon an entirely different and far-less-welcome woman.

Zhila Kurian was sashaying into the center of the taproom. No more harness and practical riding wear for this minstrel. She was attired in her strange split skirts and under-trousers, the beautifully embroidered bodice accentuating the curves of her torso. Her instrument was tucked under her arm.

That was all Garit registered. He averted his gaze immediately. He needed a drink, not trouble.

Thank heaven, he got it. The former, that was. The innkeeper was at his elbow with a jug in a moment.

"You'll keep your men friendly-like, Sieur Garit?" she murmured as she poured. "They'll not smash my benches nor break my cups?"

"No, madam. It is not in their interests. We intend to keep La Roque, not destroy it." He spoke in French, realizing that she may not have understood his earlier announcement. "We will patronize your establishment for a good while to come. We cannot do so without cups to quaff from and benches to sprawl over." He raised his cup to her. "Besides, your wine is passing good."

The woman paused, her jug hovering. "And *that?*" she said, nodding to the center of the room.

Garit sighed. He took a mouthful of wine and then looked.

"That, madam, is our nightly entertainment," he answered, flicking his gaze back upon the safer territory of his hostess, bosom and all.

"Ah, so. One woman for, what, fifty men? *Mon Dieu,* that's a heavy burden for one heathen to bear. Just as well she needn't seek absolution for her sins." The bosom swelled. "*Écoutez,* Sieur Garit. I'll not have my inn turned into a whorehouse. It's not the sin I mind so much as the furniture." Another jab of a nod. "Men *will* fight over that one."

Garit's chest was inclined to swell likewise. *She's not a heathen and she's* not *a whore*, was the obvious retort, but the innkeeper would likely not appreciate the subtleties of his argument.

He settled for: "She's a minstrel. She dances and she plays. That's all. No whoring."

Especially not with me.

Mine hostess made a noise most French and incredulous. She inspected his cup for symptoms of drought, then bustled off to attend to the multitude of other needy cups in her establishment.

Then the drumbeat began.

No, it was a *daf*, as Zhila had repeatedly told him. It was both a drum and a shivering, metallic rattle. The drum tangled itself around the beat of your heart, and the hissing, insistent accompaniment raised every hair on your arms. And, by God, Zhila knew how to use it.

He tried to ignore the siren sound. He focused his thoughts on the woman he'd met this afternoon. His wife-to-be.

Eglantine had appeared before him swathed in a wimple and concealing, dull-dyed gown. Not a jewel to be seen. No hint of a smile. Nevertheless, the Lady of La Roque was lovely. English-pale skin, a delicate, aristocratic face, and an utterly cold manner. Yes, she'd make an appropriate wife. A noble English jewel who felt nothing for him. The feeling was reciprocal, and that was how he'd ensure things remained. They simply had to come to a mutually beneficial agreement.

The drum was infiltrating his thoughts. It permeated his pulse. It slowly increased in tempo. The tug of the magnet that was Zhila grew.

Garit set his jaw. Their hostess was right. Zhila's presence would only ever lead to trouble.

Too late to stop her tonight, though. The hush in the tap-room told him the men were fixated. Enchanted.

The beat sped up. The shiver of the metal crawled under Garit's skin, setting every fiber alight, urging those fibers to action. Movement flickered at the edges of his vision—she was dancing. He must *not* react. Should he pay Zhila any public attention, word would reach Lady Eglantine. True, Garit had not professed any devotion to the lady, only his protection. He was offering a marriage contract, not lovelorn dalliance. The Lady of La Roque understood that noble wedlock was not a matter of the heart.

All the same, his cavorting with a foreign dancer on Eglantine's very doorstep might strike the lady as disrespectful.

But looking was not exactly cavorting.

Garit's gaze was lifting even as the thought occurred. He *must* look.

The minstrel woman dominated the taproom. His men had spread out to make space for her. They were a circle of faces to her swirling, dipping performance. All eyes rested upon her, and she was a whirlwind of drumbeat, flying, dark hair, and sultry movement. Her hands performed an intricate dance of their own upon the *daf*. Her skirts belled out as she whirled, revealing the loose trousers beneath, and Garit couldn't help but think of the long, lovely legs they contained, the way they wrapped about him…

No. Never again.

Garit would shortly marry, and Zhila would join a minstrel troupe. She could not remain. It wasn't just that he wanted her in his bed, he—

Garit raised the cup with a jerk and nearly bathed himself in its contents.

Then he stared at her accusingly. He still couldn't trust her. What the hell had she been up to that night above the valley? What *had* occurred in Nájera? Pamplona? Why hadn't he demanded answers of her?

The reason was all too obvious. Her proximity drove clear thought out of his head. Zhila reduced Garit to mere feeling.

Her gaze snared with his. Her fingers never stilled, but her eyes did. Their expression was all fire. Unshielded intensity. Her lips were slightly ajar, as if her music stirred her as much as it did him.

Garit ripped his gaze away. It took real physical effort. He stared at the contents of his cup, sloshing slightly and gripped by tight hands.

Dear God, he wanted her. More than any other woman he'd ever met. Certainly more than that nun-like being in the château. He'd broken his years-long rule of sleeping alone, and every particle of him demanded he do it again. And keep on doing it. But he didn't want a coolly beautiful and contained Eglantine in his bed. He *needed* Zhila. Not just in bed, but on his lap, or laughing madly at danger and slipping a curved dagger from her belt. By his side.

Garit jerked into a semi-standing position. His half-drunk wine teetered on the trestle. He abandoned it to its fate and strode out of the taproom to the beat of a *daf.*

She watched him go—he could feel it. But the *daf* did not cease, thank Christ. If it had, if she'd twined her arms about him instead, he didn't know what he'd have done. Cast her from him? Or scooped her up and borne her off to his room?

Out in the cool night air, he stopped to anchor his gaze on the château. His château.

It was gone.

The whole structure had been swallowed by darkness. Not a light illuminated its battlements.

Garit steadied himself against the inn wall.

It would reappear come morning. It was no fleeting illusion. This thing he'd planned for so long would rematerialize. Zhila was the illusion. She would—she *must*—vanish.

On that comforting thought, Sir Garit of the Ruin turned his back on the invisible cliff and strode through Vesian la Roque.

To his lone and lockable chamber.

❦

Chapter Twenty-Four

THE COMPANY OF the Ruin marched up the hill in glittering array. That was the idea, anyway. Garit had spent the morning seeing to it that each man polished his harness to a mirror sheen, had a tabard of the Ruined Tower in reasonable repair to pull over it, and generally knew his part. Thus a compact but impressive company advanced up the hill of La Roque, a force fit to strike wisdom into any lady's heart.

At least, that would have been the impression if said hill had not been so damn precipitous. La Roque would be better named La Falaise—the cliff. The track up the hillside to the château seemed designed solely to reduce a disciplined company to a panting, sweating, strung-out caterpillar. Meanwhile, the sun beat down, all breeze was canceled out by layers of canvas and steel, and Garit trudged onward with grim determination.

The gatehouse neared. The gate itself was set at right angles to the excuse for a road. It was barely visible from the path. All the more awkward for bringing to bear a battering ram…or a cannon. He would have to speak to John about that.

But what *was* visible was the bristle of figures at the battlements above and arrow slits at all levels. The entire contents of the castle seemed to line the outer wall, equipped with staves, bows, and baskets of rocks.

That did not bode well. Neither did the firmly closed gates.

"Halt!" Garit flung up a gauntleted hand. "Form up!"

Fifty ironclad men clanked obediently behind him.

Garit did not have to glance back to know this. His men were a coherent force. They obeyed his rules. Their leader would not peel his gaze from Château la Roque for one moment. He judged the company was out of range of hand-hurled rocks here, but it was definitely not out of bowshot. His men needed their iron, and Garit needed to face his prey unblinkingly—to catch any aggression the moment it arose.

The clanking behind him subsided. No arrows shivered from the battlements. No stray rocks dropped from the air like heat-struck birds. So far, so good.

Garit raised his visor and lifted his face to the frowning walls of La Roque. A wisp of breeze caressed his cheeks. A well-aimed arrow could strike him lifeless as he stood, despite his flag of truce.

He stepped a pace nearer.

"Do I address the Lady Eglantine?"

Garit projected his voice at the towering curtain wall. His tone was firm and utterly certain. The lady would be his. The castle would be his. This was his longstanding plan, and no briefly flickering flame would shake him from it.

"You do."

An equally firm feminine voice, emanating from an arrow slit rather than the battlements. Sensible lady.

His bride-to-be spoke on. "My mind has not changed, Sir Garit. I declare you are no longer welcome in the village. If you are a true Englishman and knight, you will not harass an English lady in her home. Leave in peace and with my goodwill. There is nothing for you here."

Garit knew his actions and offer to be strictly honorable. His plan had no drawbacks. Everybody benefited. But apparently the lady needed to be reminded of these facts.

"I am a true knight, Lady Eglantine. In that capacity, I offer you my protection as your husband. You are a woman alone in a land at war. I cannot depart and leave you to the returning armies' mercy, French or English. They will not be so courteous as I."

"You have a strange notion of courtesy, coming to my gate fully armed and with a small army at your back," the arrow slit bit back. "I am *not* a woman alone. I have a loyal household and fine men-at-arms. I need no husband to tell me what to do. Take your courtesy elsewhere. The gates will not be opened to you."

Garit eyed the arrow slit steadily. If he was surprised at all, it was that the Lady of La Roque had some fire in her.

Inconvenient. A large part of Eglantine's charm, besides an admirable collection of rocky walls, was her cool, contained demeanor.

"I shall remove my men from your gate if they so offend you," he said politely.

A knight was ever courteous to a lady, especially if he planned to marry her.

But a knight also remained true to his carefully laid plans for his company's future.

"We will, however, remain in the village of La Roque," he added. "There is but one way in and out of your château, I believe, and that is by the path to the village. We shall guard it for you. No one will traverse it, on pain of death. You and yours will remain safe within your château walls until you change your mind, which I trust you will do before your supplies run out. I do not wish to wed a skeleton."

He spoke clearly and calmly. He was not bullying his wife-to-be. He was simply outlining consequences.

For, while the lady's attitude was indeed inconvenient, it did not alter his plan one whit.

He waited. Snatches of speech drifted from arrow slits and battlements, evidence of furious but muted discussion.

One slightly louder declaration reached his ears. It was cast in a feminine timbre. "We have plenty of supplies… He'll soon get tired of waiting for a mere woman to capitulate."

Garit cast John the Wreck a glance. The lady evidently had great faith in her castle's defenses. Well, it *was* a beautifully situated château—that was why he was here—but Eglantine had not met the Wreck.

The engineer did not return his glance. He was too busy raking his gaze over curtain walls, sturdy gatehouse, and looming cliffs.

John was not admiring the scenery.

Lady Eglantine rudely interrupted his musings. "You are no true knight, Garit of the Ruin," she snapped. "To remain on my son's lands is an act of war. An honorable knight would depart immediately. Go. Restore my good opinion of you. It is not too late."

Garit exhaled. It seemed the lady was determined to ignore reason. She was clearly basing her decision on emotion—on personal preference, not cool common sense. A noble marriage was contracted for property and politics, not on the basis of feelings. Garit was certainly not acting to please himself. If he had been, he might…

No. The security of every man in the company hung upon his choice. Eglantine too ought to consider the future of her people and her son.

Garit stared at the stony walls before him with equal stoniness. Feeling was a flimsy, fleeting basis for decision. Human relationships always disintegrated. Loved ones died. But a castle was permanent. It spelled safety and security. Garit needed La Roque in order to rebuild his ruin, and his men needed a stronghold here in France.

He bowed slightly toward those impregnable walls.

"We stay, Lady Eglantine. I bid you good day. I shall return tomorrow in the expectation that you have reconsidered. In the meantime, think of the benefits to you, your son, and your people. This is no act of war—not yet."

⇛⇚

"WELL? WHAT DID she say? I've performed at weddings before...with my family." Zhila paused. Swallowed. "So? Do I perform at another one?"

John the Wreck gave her a level look—well, as level as possible, given the uneven visage. "Don't reckon you'll be performing at any wedding hereabouts," he said.

No, of course she wouldn't. Sir Garit of the Ruin wouldn't parade his lover before his wife on their wedding night. He'd send Zhila away instead. Far, far away.

"See, the lady doesn't want our Garit," the Wreck went on. "She told him to bugger off, and no mistake. Deficiency of taste, if you ask me. He's not so bad looking, eh, little dancer?"

John was observing her far too kindly.

"She...she doesn't want him?" Zhila echoed, scarcely daring to hope.

All this morning, plans to somehow seduce and stab the Ruin had been tumbling through her brain like mountain melt-water. Edmond had demanded she kill him before he wed, and Garit planned to wed imminently. How was she going to do it? *Could* she do it?

But now...

"Nope. She said he was no true knight and then told him blunt to get out of her village."

"I begin to like this lady," Zhila said. "So, is he heartbroken his castle rejected him? And what happens now—does the Ruin obey?"

"He does not," answered a third voice. "There is no need. The lady will see sense, eventually."

So matter-of-fact. Zhila turned to face the owner of the voice.

The Ruin was still in armor, although he'd removed his helm, a fact that did not lessen the impression of stony impregnability in the least.

"Are you so irresistible, Sir Ruin?" Zhila tried an arch smile.

"No, but my engineer is. John, I must speak with you."

"In private?" Zhila challenged. "You send me away, yes?"

He looked at her. Something flickered in the chilly blue depths. "I do," he said. "But not this instant. Stay. What I have to say to John pertains to you too."

There was no warmth in his tone. It was as if he spoke to a stranger.

But of course she stayed.

Before he continued, the Ruin glanced around. He'd found them in a shaded corner of the Place de Vesian. No one else was within earshot, a fact that seemed to satisfy him.

"John, you heard the Lady of La Roque. She bars her gates against us and believes her castle impregnable. Is she right?"

The Wreck shrugged lopsided shoulders. "Course not. Even Château Galliard was taken eventually. Seen the place myself. Stuck on a hill and fortified to all hell, it was, yet they took it. And that was before cannon, too."

"They starved them out, I believe," the Ruin noted passionlessly. "A long process, and I have no great desire to wed a skeleton. But you have a cannon, John."

"Aye, and a smallish one as they go. We've had this conversation, sir. No heavier than one horse can carry, you specified. Don't give me much scope. The bigger the cannon, the bigger the rock it can fire, the faster and further—"

"Yes, we've had this conversation, John. Often. Big cannon are lumbering, slow things. We'd need a cart and team just to transport the thing. No, the Company of the Ruin is fast and agile, and you can perform wonders with your little gun. I've seen it."

"Well, I can't perform no wonders right now. I'd have to be Albertus Magnus himself to get that thing to go bang. We're all out of gunpowder, recall?"

"Which is precisely my point, should you allow me to make it. You need more powder, do you not, John?"

"Saltpeter is what I need," the Wreck retorted. "Plenty of charcoal in these parts, probably brimstone as well. But saltpeter? That's the magic ingredient. I used it all up a week back, and I don't reckon any friendly Frenchman would be willing to part with some hereabouts. I'll get no bang without saltpeter."

"Then go and find us some bang, John. Ride to Bordeaux. Take baggage horses. We won't be needing them for a while—the company is staying put in Vesian for the moment."

"To guard the one path to the castle," the Wreck said.

"Yes, John. Until my lady wife sees sense."

Zhila had no idea why she was privy to this discussion of tactics, but she could remain mute no longer. "Sense? Maybe she's already seen sense, Sir Ruin. Maybe she wants to keep her castle *and* her bed all to herself. Maybe she doesn't want a man to tell her what to do."

The Ruin regarded her impassively. "Lady Eglantine holds a castle in contested territory. She is a woman alone in a land at war. She needs protection."

"Yes, from men like you," Zhila shot back.

"Much worse than me will cross the Pyrenees in the months to come," the Ruin said, and turned back to John. "Go to Bordeaux. Take pack horses with you and find us some saltpeter."

The Wreck's face was a study in torn emotion. A transparent hunger for powder lit the usually kind brown eyes, but the scarred brow above wrinkled.

"That's adding fire to your wooing, for certain, sir. You'll shoot the lady into submission, eh? Cannon aren't so accurate, mind. Have a care for your castle."

"Yes, I am fully aware of their inaccuracy, even in your capable hands, John. I am also aware of their persuasive power. The thunderous noise, the shuddering of the earth. One would think the gates of hell had opened. I doubt the lady or her people have any prior experience of cannon fire. A warning shot or two should suffice to persuade her, and my château will remain in one piece. Besides, you like to play with fire, do you not, John?"

His brown eyes glowed with unholy light. "Oh aye. A shot or three into those cliffs won't harm a fly, but it'll rouse the echoes something ferocious."

"So, you'll terrify the lady into your bed," Zhila retorted. "You set my heart at ease, Sir Ruin. No one will be hurt, though you'll have a castle's worth of soggy braies. And you'll get your fine way. What a lovely wedding."

Sir Garit looked at her. His face was a wall.

"Yes, you may set your heart at ease, Zhila Kurian, for you will see none of it. I will wed and you will be in Bordeaux with your new minstrel troupe. The company has done all it can for you. You will accompany John to Bordeaux tomorrow, and you will not return."

Chapter Twenty-Five

Z HILA PEERED UP at the shadowy wall. The shutters above looked entirely too solid. Why couldn't they be half rotted and hanging off their frames? And who in hell bothered to secure second-story windows, anyway?

It was probably why the Ruin had chosen this house. It was a sturdy stone building that had once housed a merchant. The fellow had vanished upon the company's arrival, like so many in La Roque. But his home was still a small fortress, designed to keep his goods safe.

Now it kept the Ruin and his eternally locked strongbox safe.

They were sealed away behind stout walls of unshaped limestone, walls that, incidentally, offered plenty of handholds and footholds. Zhila gave the shutters one last scowl, then crept around to the back of the house and began to climb.

The roof was tiled. The rough surface gave off a lingering warmth from a day in the sun. Indeed, it was quite pleasant to perch upon, and not at all slippery. Zhila surveyed its starlit contours. No loose or broken tiles. Damn.

So she wedged her fingers under the lip of a tile and tugged. It didn't budge. She wiggled it, then tugged again. The result? One fingernail half ripped off. Zhila swore under her breath and leveled a dagger at the offending tile.

Ah, that did the trick. And, oh God, the noise of tile grating against tile sounded as loud as a rumbling wagon. Zhila gritted her teeth and laid it aside with care, praying she didn't compound the racket by sending it crashing to the cobbles.

The newly made hole in the roof opened onto blackness and was far too small to climb into, so Zhila stuck her hand in and let her fingers do the seeing instead.

Ugh. Cobwebs. The space within was thick with them. She pulled a face and sank the entirety of her arm in. Zhila lay stomach down on the tiles and groped about. She found wooden beams, sundry dust-shrouded objects, then... Damn it all, her fingertips brushed what had to be floorboards. It was a shallow attic, uninhabited except by eight-legged beings.

She sighed and extracted her arm.

Now what?

He'd posted a guard on the street. No one could enter the house without permission, and permission was definitively *not* granted to Zhila. Furthermore, she knew how he felt about locks. No point in accessing the house via the attic only to encounter a locked chamber door.

Which left her only one option.

Zhila hooked one foot into the hole she'd just made, jiggled it a bit to ensure it would hold, then arrayed herself, stomach-down, upon the tiles. To hang upside down over the lip of the roof.

GARIT WAS DREAMING. He must be, for that was the only time he encountered Marie and his mother in this world. Or was it the next?

Age had not touched his mother. It never did. Her face was unlined; her glorious blonde hair would never fade to gray. As for Marie, his little sister would never grow up. She was doomed to wander his dreams a perpetual child.

As ever, they did not speak to the man who'd killed them. They only stared at Garit accusingly, then turned their backs and did whatever mothers and little girls did. He heard the muted clack of weaving, hands rustling through a chest full of fabrics, and the swishing of skirts through the weeds of a blackened ruin.

Garit's limbs were leaden. He couldn't stretch out and touch them. He couldn't even open his mouth.

He strained against the suffocating weight. He must speak to them. *Come with me. I will protect you this time, I promise. You can't stay here. It's too—*

A louder clack, followed by a word Garit's mother would never have uttered.

Some of the drugging weight lifted. Garit reached out. His hand met…nothing. But a channel of chill air flowed over his bare arm. Shifting the fog.

He sat up and opened his eyes.

The room was dark as a cave, save for the grayness admitted by the open shutter.

Open shutter? Garit didn't have time to dwell on that mystery, for a figure stood silhouetted against its dim gray. It was advancing upon him.

He grabbed his dagger from under the mattress and rolled out of bed, naked. Ready to counter a ghost. It seemed they were tired of haunting his dreams. Now one had slid right through his window.

What use was a dagger against a ghost? It glided toward him, and gooseflesh prickled over Garit's too-naked flesh. He should be clothed. He should not be facing her like this. It was madly indecent. It was—

Hands reached out and touched his shoulders. *Warm* hands. They slid over his arms, then wandered across his chest. Down, slowly down over his tensed abdomen, to—

He let his dagger clatter to the floor. He caught her wrists and held them, manacled tight by his fingers.

"You are not my mother."

A low, rich laugh. "Your mother? Ah, no. Would your mother do this?"

He may have her wrists, but that didn't stop her brushing her hips across his. Fabric feathered over his naked nether regions.

Garit closed his eyes.

No, that was a mistake. Lack of sight only accentuated his other senses. They centered upon her soft breathing, the lingering scent of spices, her tantalizing warmth. He hadn't touched her for eons, and here she was, in his chamber. Trust Zhila to simply barge in, disobeying all rules, bypassing mere locks.

Trust her?

"What are you doing here?" he demanded. "You leave tomorrow."

Or was that today?

"I *told* you—I do not leave. I stay to help. You help me, now I help you. I told you before, I can do things none of the other lumbering man-lumps in your company can. But you do not believe me, so now I prove it. See? I climb up your walls and break into your fortress. Now you, my naked Ruin, are at my mercy."

Her hips brushed over his again, slower.

She was trying to distract him. By heaven, she was doing a good job of it.

"Why would you wish to help me? You do not think I should wed the Lady Eglantine."

"No. I think you are a fool. But you will not listen to me, so I stay. I have suffered in war. I do not want this woman to suffer. No one will die if I can help it. So I will climb—I climb the cliffs, the castle, whatever is necessary. I will find another way. My climbing will bring a peaceful end. Can any of your men do this?"

She had suffered. She wanted to help another woman like her. But the situation was not the same. Garit was not making Eglantine suffer. The illogical lady had chosen to resist. And as for Zhila…

"No. You will only turn yourself into a target. This is a siege. I have promised to shoot at any who venture beyond La Roque's walls. How do you think the inhabitants will respond to someone climbing their castle?"

"Pft. They will not see me. I am not so stupid."

She *had* managed to clamber into his chamber without raising the alarm. Garit glanced at the open shutter. How had she done it, and so silently that he hadn't woken until she was almost standing over him? His nape prickled. She seemed determined to prove his defenses worthless.

But her skills might help to penetrate other defenses. Château defenses, for example.

"No," Garit said. "You are a gifted performer, Zhila. Go to Bordeaux and do what you do best. Do not risk your life for something you don't believe in."

"You do not want me," she whispered. "You send me away."

She stepped closer. His hold on her wrists did not stop her snaking her fully clad frame up against his nakedness.

He shivered. A flood of barely containable longing.

"You should not be here," Garit said, mostly to himself. "The Lady of La Roque will recognize the error in her thinking, but your presence in my chamber will not speed that end. Eglantine will assume..." He didn't finish the sentence. *That Sir Garit flaunted his leman before his wife-to-be.* Hardly the act of a persuasive suitor. "You know we must end, Zhila. You will join a minstrel troupe, and I will have a castle."

"And a noble English wife?"

"Yes. And an heir. I will adopt Constantine of La Roque as my own."

"Ah. Your own instant family, and one you don't particularly care about. How apt."

He didn't respond. What she said was true enough, but when Zhila voiced it, the whole plan seemed...cold.

"You do not have to want me, Sir Ruin." She shifted against him again, setting a flame to his resolutions. "Eglantine will never know I entered your chamber. I only do it to prove my skill. I like climbing. Let me help you. I *want* to."

Want. Sweet heaven, the word was a dim shadow of what he was feeling right now.

"Zhila, you must leave tomorrow. I cannot put you in danger again. But tonight..."

She was right, so wonderfully right. Eglantine would never know what occurred in this locked chamber. Zhila would leave for distant Bordeaux tomorrow. He would never see his minstrel again. But right now, her nearness was an irresistible siren song, wine to a drunkard, nectar to a famished bee.

So Garit gathered her to him, all soft cloth and warm woman against his naked, craving skin.

⇶⫷

WELL, THIS WAS inopportune.

She'd climbed the walls and broken into his locked chamber to prove that she ought to stay.

But the Ruin had not woken when she'd levered open the shutter, or even after she'd slithered through the window. Was that why he slept locked in and alone—because he slept too deeply to be as watchful as a warrior ought to be?

It was the perfect opportunity. Zhila should sink her dagger into his throat, now, just as Ingram demanded.

Sir Garit was sending her away, and she'd never get another chance.

So she'd unsheathed the dagger and stolen forward, heart pounding, eyes straining to see shapes in the dark...and noticed something amazing.

The strongbox was open. The dark lid was propped up against the whitewashed wall.

Hands quivering, Zhila sheathed her weapon and knelt by the chest instead. She delved, seeking out parchment by touch alone. And she found it. Lots of it. She bundled the scrolls into the back of her linen underdress, creating an ad hoc bag with its long skirt. It would allow her to climb back down with her hands free.

Then he stirred.

Curse you, Ruin. Why couldn't you sleep on?

She'd just acquired the means to save his stupid life, and he had to open his eyes. He was advancing upon her, and he was going to grab her, so she'd reached for him first.

And then her thoughts and plans dissolved.

His naked warmth against her, the planes of his torso, the gentle strength of his hands, the tremor of his need—she couldn't help but respond.

He was kissing her, his arms were about her, his hands in her hair, mouth insistent on hers in the dark. Zhila couldn't think. She simply opened to him, kissed him back with abandon, and molded herself his muscle—and his rearing need.

There was no doubt what he wanted, but *it mustn't happen.* Garit must not discover the stash of parchments at the back of her skirts. Much more of his hands roaming her person, and discovery would be inevitable. There'd be no explaining away the theft.

Zhila would have to kill him then, or try to.

She didn't like her chances.

Alternatively, she could take the wild ride he promised to its conclusion. She could wriggle free of him, divest herself of her clothing and heap it over the parchments, and return to the Ruin's hungry arms.

And afterward? She had her daggers. She would do exactly as the Fox demanded.

Kill him. Love him to sated slumber and end his life.

Chapter Twenty-Six

Love him?

The thought stopped Zhila mid-kiss.

Of course she didn't love him. This was simply lust. Delectable madness, desire, a furnace of feeling. It was not enduring love such as she felt for her family. For Maryam.

Doubtless, he felt the same. So far as a Ruin could feel.

"What is it?" he murmured against her unmoving mouth.

She ran her hands down his beautifully naked back, all the way down to his buttocks.

"You have the advantage over me, Ruin. You wear no clothes. Let me take off mine."

For a third possibility for tonight was presenting itself. Quite forcibly.

Her hand trailed around to his fore. It encountered hair…then hardness. Length. She wandered her fingers over his manhood, delighting in its silky solidity. The way it responded to her.

The Ruin gave a strangled groan. "I have no objection."

"One moment, Sir Ruin."

Zhila stepped back, or tried to.

"Let me undress you," he murmured, holding her firm. "This is the last time I will touch you. I will not do this by halves."

"No!"

The word came out sharper than she'd intended. She pushed back against his grip. He released her instantly.

No, he must have as little to do with her clothing as possible. She wanted him. Dear heaven, she wanted him. So she would indulge herself one more time, and then she'd depart out of the window in the dark. With a skirt full of parchments. And leave tomorrow.

She would leave him alive.

She need not kill the Ruin to get his parchments. She had crushed his rules, just as Ingram required. Now she could give the Fox what he wanted without setting her dagger into this beloved flesh.

"It is dark. I will not have my clothing damaged," she hurried to explain. "They are Persian and mean much to me. *I* remove my clothes."

"I'll light a lamp," he countered with horrible logic. "I must see you, Zhila."

A second *no!* was on her lips, but she swallowed it in time. Too much protest would only make him suspicious. Oh, this was a bad, bad idea. He was simply too tempting. She should have stuck to her initial plan.

But now…

Now she heard flint strike iron. Saw a scatter of tiny sparks.

There was no time left.

GARIT WAS AN expert in striking fire from flint in the dark, but his fingers seemed to have forgotten the fact. They were as lumpish as if he were wearing gauntlets. They shivered with need. He jagged the flint against his own knuckles, then, to compound the insult, he singed them with sparks.

In the meantime, Zhila was up to something. Over the click of flint on iron, he heard the rustling of cloth.

His mouth quirked. She really didn't trust him with her Persian garb. He could hear her over by the open window. It seemed she needed starlight to undress.

Garit craved more light than that. He would feast his senses upon her naked skin.

He took a firmer grip on the flint and struck again. Finally, the tow flared and he lifted the fiery wisps to the wick. He sheltered the infant flame by keeping his back to the window and his palm curled round the wick.

Oh, he yearned to turn round, to watch the cloth slipping from Zhila's lovely limbs. To see her shake free of all restraint and step toward him with that look in her eyes that tightened his balls and wrapped a fist around his heart. But there was no point in turning too soon, not before the flame could withstand the draft from the window.

Only when he was sure it would not puff out did Garit turn.

Then he frowned. He turned in a circle, casting a slow arc of light about the chamber.

He was its only occupant.

Garit strode to the window. Both shutters hung open now. The flame guttered in the draft. He peered down into the darkness.

"Zhila!"

He didn't shout. He didn't need to. The shadow in the alley below heard him well enough. It glanced up. Garit discerned a pale oval dominated by two large, dark eyes.

Now what was he to say?

"Are you all right?"

If possible, the eyes grew larger. Then their owner laughed.

She spread her arms. "As you see."

She was still clothed. Of course, the rustling he'd heard was nothing to do with her disrobing.

Garit had another question. This one was more to the point. "Why?"

She gazed up at him, silent a long moment. Then, "I am not

your whore. You push me away for this woman you will marry, a woman you do not even like! I climbed to your chamber tonight to prove I am useful, so you do not send me away. That is all. I will not be used for a farewell fuck."

It was like a dagger between his ribs. A sudden, sharp pain, felt too late. He had hurt her. He'd rejected her in favor of a woman he'd barely met.

She'd tried to stay, but Garit the Ruinous Idiot had simply insisted he would slake his lust one last time before she left.

"You were always going to leave, Zhila," he found himself saying. "The company retains no women. You were only a temporary exception. You knew this."

"Yet you will marry. Is this Eglantine a man beneath her skirts, then?"

"She does not join the company. She is merely a wife."

"And I am merely a whore," she snapped back. "You use me, then you discard me. Well, no more. I will not be used one last time."

Then she turned her back and stalked away down the alley. Garit stared after her. She wasn't limping. She'd thrown herself out a second-story window—she might easily have broken an ankle.

But something else had broken instead.

He wanted to leap out of the window after her, to seize her, wrap his arms about her, assuage the pain and tell her... What? It was impossible. Unlike certain dancers, Garit was no mountain goat. He was also naked. He would definitely damage something if he fell.

And what could he possibly say to mend what had been broken?

It was always going to break. Better now than later.

Better still if it had never been at all.

ZHILA HURRIED OUT of the alleyway on shaky legs.

She wasn't sure where she was going. Just *away*, fast. The Ruin must not catch up with her. So she darted into the next shadowy alley she came across. There would be company sentries about too. Garit always set a watch at night. None of his men must see her, or—

A dark figure stepped in front of her. It blocked the alley.

Before Zhila could whirl and run, the figure spoke.

"Why isn't he dead?"

Zhila's heart thumped in her throat.

"I have what you asked for," she said, scrabbling at her skirt.

"No, you don't," said the shadow. "I saw him only moments ago at the window." The figure shuddered at that, the quiver of a dark outline. "I *saw* him. Sir Garit of the Ruin was naked, on show for all to see. His throat was noticeably whole, as was the rest of him."

A shard of insight pierced Zhila's panic. Strange she'd never thought of it before.

"You pay close attention to a naked Ruin," she said.

"As should you," Sir Edmond Ingram snapped. "He was erect, damn you. He was ripe for the taking. You could have fucked him then and there, and severed his throat as he lay flaccid afterward. That was what you were *told* to do. I heard everything, woman, and by God, I did not hear nearly enough."

"You wanted to hear the Ruin making love," Zhila said slowly. "You would like to watch him at it too, yes? You wanted that back in Nájera. Well, is your cock disappointed, Fox?"

Ingram lashed out. He grabbed a fistful of her hair and yanked. "No, you stupid whore. I came to Vesian for the grand finale. Here I am, risking my hide in this Ruin-ridden village, and what do you give me? A botched job. Not a fuck but a fizzle. Disappointed? Every last bit of me is disappointed. And be assured I will assuage my displeasure just as soon as I get back to camp."

He fairly spat the last sentence at her. Its meaning fell on Zhila like ice.

"I've got what you asked for!" she cried. "The parchments. You wanted the parchments from the Ruin's chest. Remember?"

"I wanted *three* things, whore. Parchments and blood. His goddamned heart's blood, bleeding out on his lover's dagger. And the crumbling of all his ridiculous rules. I wanted his end, and I wanted it done properly."

Ingram still had her hair. He jerked it for emphasis.

A sickening jolt that had nothing to do with hair. This twisted man didn't just want the Ruin's humiliation and his valuables. Death was not a means to an end—the whole elaborate betrayal of a death *was* the end.

Zhila seized her hair and yanked it out of his grasp. Ingram swiped at her again, so she shoved a roll of calf skin in his hand.

"No, idiot Fox. I took the parchments first, for the strongbox was open! Never had I seen it open before. I was going to kill him after, but he woke. The Ruin is strong. Even naked, unarmed, he might fight me off. I only have one chance to kill him, so I tried another way—I tried to ride him in the dark, but no, he wants light. *Voilà*, with light, he'd see I had his parchments. He'd want no riding then. I must leave or lose everything, you see? Just be happy I've got your filthy scrolls." She shoved the rest of them at him in a jumble. "As for the rest, I'll kill him just as soon as I can."

There. Not exactly the truth, but an artful selection woven from what Edmond had probably overheard. Ugh. A sly listener in the dark, hoping to hear an energetic bout of fucking, followed by a choking gurgle.

But the dark figure simply regarded her and said, "Will you, indeed?"

He didn't believe her, and he was right not to. She would likely never get another chance to fulfill his orders. For Garit would send her away tomorrow.

But even if she got another chance—even if she sat astride a naked Ruin with a dagger in her fist—could she do it?

"He wants you gone," Ingram said. "I heard him. You've lost your chance. He's reinstating his damned rules. No women in the company. You captured his cock, but now he's casting you aside for a legitimate piece of quim. These parchments"—Ingram shook the one in his fist at her—"are all but useless if he weds. Even if the Ruin dies the day after he's humped the château woman, she and her brat will likely inherit all these represent."

Perhaps Ingram saw her confusion, for he bent closer and hissed, "The parchments are legal documents, woman. Deeds, contracts, agreements with Italian money merchants, and, above all, a will. They represent all that dastard has achieved. Mostly the French loot he's been raking up for the past decade just so he can rebuild his precious ruin. Ha!" The man spat wetly by her feet. "But they only mean aught if the man is dead and *I* remain his sole heir."

"His heir—you?" Zhila managed.

"His cursed heir, yes! The French killed his family when he was a boy. No one left to inherit there. I'm a distant cousin, aye, but I'm the nearest there is. Not that he's ever treated me like his own blood. He invited me into his company, the only other knight in the piece, and then fobbed me off with equal shares, same as the merest peasant archer."

"So you get all he owns when he dies?"

"I *should*. If he doesn't wed, that is. And there's another thing. Sir Gullible Garit has been known to care overmuch for his swinish company. For all I know, there's a will in here"—a shake of the parchment—"that hands them all his loot if he dies. Reckon any such parchment'll meet with a fiery accident forthwith. The other documents I'll take loving care of, though, for all they contain will come to me."

Edmond paused then. She could feel his gaze on her, even in the near dark. A leaden weight. He probably thought he'd said too much.

He would be right.

Zhila didn't want this detail. She just wanted Maryam. Knowing the Fox's secrets only put them in more danger.

"And I won't inherit if Sir Gallant Garit weds either," Edmond growled. "Especially not if he makes the boy his heir. I need these parchments, true, but I need the cold caitiff dead too."

"Why me?" Zhila burst out. "Coward! If you want him dead so much, kill him yourself!"

If Ingram's arms hadn't been full of parchment, she'd have been dealt a wallop. She saw it by his convulsive movement. He aimed a kick at her instead, easily evaded.

"Reckon the law men'd notice that. Bit obvious, the heir offing his benefactor. Much better to get a heathen whore to do the business—or the French."

"Yes, *coward*," she snapped. "You use me or you use an army of French to kill a man you cannot kill yourself. But you chose me first because you don't just want the Ruin dead. I see it now. You want to make his heart bleed before his throat, because *he does not want you*."

It was suddenly so clear. Zhila had always been safe from Edmond Ingram's intimate attentions. It was Garit this man wanted—his wealth, success, status...and the man himself. And because Edmond couldn't have him, he would ruin his cousin instead.

Parchment crackled as Ingram's fists clenched. Zhila cursed her over-ready tongue. She had to appease the Fox, not expose him for the coward he was. Or grind salt into his wounds.

"Mind your filthy tongue, whore, or I'll tear it out. Only one thing matters to you. Do you want your little sister sold to a brothel in Bordeaux or not? Oh, I reckon my men could teach her a few tricks before she goes, too. Won't lessen her value overmuch."

"No," Zhila gasped. She flung out an arm to the nearest wall, else she would have toppled. "You do that, and I'll never do your bidding."

"Aye, true enough. Might be safer to finish you right now and sell the girl anyway," Ingram muttered. "You know too much for a mouthy whore. And you'll not get another chance with the Ruin."

The figure shifted in the dark. His hand moved to his waist. To the dully glinting hilt of a sword.

"No! How will you kill the Ruin then? You want someone he cares for to kill him." *Because he rejected you, you sad sly Fox,* she did not say. "I *can* do it," Zhila hurried on. "I showed him I can climb. He will not send me away. I am useful. He will change his mind."

"Useful?" Ingram snorted. "Useful as a place to poke his cock."

A murdering whore. That was what Ingram reduced her to. He demanded she betray and kill the man she—

No, the Ruin set her ablaze in bed, that was all. She owed him nothing. She owed Maryam everything.

She would do this, if only Ingram gave her another chance.

Meanwhile, Ingram was standing quite still, but at least his hand had left his pommel. It simply held a much-abused piece of parchment.

Silence stretched. Parchment rustled.

"Do it, then, whore," came the hoarse reply. "Convince him you can be *useful.* Then ride the Ruin and slit the bastard's throat. And one more thing—make sure he's watching when you drive that dagger home. Tell him it's with love from me."

"And Maryam?" Zhila managed. "Promise me she'll be safe."

"You do your doxy duty and she'll be safe. Aye, once I've seen you're still in Vesian when that ape Wreck trots west, I'll take her on a little trip to Bordeaux mysel—"

"*No!*"

"Pipe down, woman," Ingram growled. "All I'm saying is maybe these parchments aren't wholly useless. The Ruin employed a man of law in Bordeaux. It's no good if I turn his will to smoke only to find some inky clerk's got its double. It'd be just like our Ruin to be so infernally foresightful. So I'll take these scribblings and track down whoever scribed them. I've lingered in this company's stink too long. Now it's staying put, someone might stumble over me. So I'm off for fresh air, and I'll not leave your little girl behind. Never you fear—she'll be safe enough, so long as you do what's needful."

The shadow in the alley straightened.

"Well, do we understand each other?" it demanded. "I go to Bordeaux, but mind, I'll leave eyes on you. Jos wasn't my only friend in the company, thank Christ. Worse comes to worst, my man will end the Ruin before he can wed. A sword in the dark, an arrow from afar—easily done. See? One way or another, your lover's a dead man."

Zhila swayed in the dark. She thought she'd saved him. She thought all she had to do was hand some pilfered parchments to a Fox and they would all be free.

She should fly at Ingram here and now. Give him a taste of what he wanted to serve his cousin. She had her daggers. She might even succeed.

But then how would she find Maryam?

Trapped. They were all trapped.

Her tormentor in the shadows was watching her. He had one last thing to say.

"And if I get sent word that a certain whore has failed in her task—aye, even if you die doing so—I reckon I'll just cut my losses and cash in a little girl for gold."

Chapter Twenty-Seven

"WHERE'S YOUR TRAVELING companion?"

John the Wreck was tugging at straps on his pack beasts in the *place de Vesian*. Now he looked up.

"Aye, it'll be lonely plodding all the way to Bordeaux without a friend. Not to mention risky. But you sure you want to send that 'un?"

"Where is she?"

John gave him a long look. Then he said, "Come with me."

Garit followed the Wreck down Vesian's central street. Before long, they ran out of village. Then the engineer was leading Garit down a path that snaked between bushes, under trees, and around tumbled boulders. The ground rose.

This was ridiculous. He should stop John and demand answers immediately. He'd asked a simple question, and the engineer, a man under Garit's command, was being downright evasive. Worse, he was siding with someone else who was disinclined to obey him.

John halted at the foot of the limestone scarp and looked up. Then he chuckled and applauded softly.

Garit followed his gaze—and went cold.

The cliff here was even more precipitous than around Château la Roque. Here, there was no ledge halfway up the scarp to perch a castle upon. There were barely ledges sufficient for a falcon. Or a certain female.

Sir Garit of the Ruin did not shout. The expanse of gray-gold rock stretching above would likely catch the echoes, and he did not wish to broadcast this conversation to the world. Nor did he want to startle her *or* alert the château's inhabitants to her odd habits.

"Get down before you fall down, Zhila," he called. Quietly.

She swung her trouser-coated legs in the air and peered down at him. "Do I look like I'm going to fall?"

No, she didn't. Not that Garit was going to admit it. Zhila Kurian looked entirely at ease seated upon a crumbling alcove about halfway up the damn rockface.

"I will come down when you say I can stay, Sir Ruin," she called down. "Bordeaux can wait. See, I *can* climb. Let me help you."

Garit closed his eyes. It was only in part to shut out the sight of his beautiful dancer perched upon a flimsy flake of stone countless yards above him.

"I was going to tell you anyway," he muttered.

"What?"

He opened his eyes to see her leaning forward on her precarious perch.

"No!" he exclaimed, a little too loudly.

She scowled down at him. "Then I stay here."

Garit had to swallow before he could reply. "Do you propose a siege, my lady? Believe me, it would be the shortest in all the annals of France. You cannot sleep up there, and I am intrigued to discover how you'd relieve yourself." He was keeping his tone impassive with some difficulty. "Come down, Zhila. You don't need to prove yourself. I'd already decided to let you stay."

A squeak of unmerited joy. And then, dear God, he had to watch her climb down. Sir Garit of the Ruin was all cool detachment in the heat of battle. He was an enduring rock under hardship. But this was an ordeal to split a granite boulder.

She slithered over the ledge, belly to the rock, and her bare toes wriggled into a crack below. Then she glanced over her shoulder and sought the next toehold. Meanwhile, Garit the Imperturbable hovered at the base of the cliff like a child waiting to catch a kitten.

And when, by some miracle, she was standing before him in scruffed tunic and trousers, a most unseemly smile upon her face, Garit was sorely tempted to go back on his word.

He wanted to crush her to him and reassure himself with hands and lips that she really was in one piece.

But she didn't want that. She'd jumped out of a second-story window last night to avoid such embraces. She wanted to help him, not kiss him.

And Garit had a wife to woo.

Besides, the Wreck was watching.

"Would it not be wiser to travel to Bordeaux now, Zhila?" he made himself say. "You must leave the company soon enough. You gain nothing by staying."

Her chin rose. "You promised. I will see this thing to the end. Let me stay in your company till you get another woman to replace me."

"Eglantine is not your replacement."

She is merely a wife, a means to an end, he did not add.

"Stay if you wish," he went on. "But if you do so, you will act as one of the company. That is, you obey me. If you climb, you do so on my orders. You do not scale any walls without speaking to me first." *Especially those of my bedchamber.* "Do you understand?"

She laid a palm on his chest and smiled at him. "And you, my stony Ruin, must I ask permission to climb you too?"

Words vacated Garit's brain. Last night she hadn't wanted him. What now?

"You do not have permission," his tongue decreed.

Garit wasn't sure the rest of him concurred. So he turned and began to pick his way back down the path.

"Come," he said over his shoulder. "My engineer must leave

for Bordeaux even if you do not. His saltpeter is far more likely to gain us entry to La Roque than your toes are."

SO ZHILA STAYED—BUT for what?

Days crept by. She climbed, she danced, but she could not do Ingram's bidding. The Ruin's door was barred to her. Zhila herself had helped bar it, for she had declared she was not a whore.

But she *needed* to be. Just one more time.

So she danced every night, no matter how tired she was from climbing. She danced only for him, oblivious to the other men in the room. She poured every last bit of yearning for him into her *daf* beat.

He paid her no heed.

She could not sit on his lap or take his face in her hands. His future bride must not be offended.

Days became a week. One week grew into two. And the Ruin never raised hue and cry over his missing parchments, though Zhila feared it every day. Was he really so careless a guardian?

Zhila climbed, but only as the Ruin permitted. Good, obedient Zhila. She scaled the scarp, then discovered a track that the villagers obviously used to do likewise—if they were feeling in need of the exercise. It would be useful if she needed to usher the company up here for an assault.

She crept along the cliff edge to peer down into the château. Yes, one could lob rocks into it from up here, or even cannonballs if the Wreck ever came back. One could definitely damage Château la Roque, but there was no obvious way to take it peacefully. If Zhila clambered into it by day, they'd see her coming. Even by night, there were always guards on the walls. Even if she managed to slip by them, what would she do— conquer the castle single-handedly?

As her ruinous commander pointed out, she'd only get herself killed by attempting something so stupid.

But she did not climb the Ruin. He was barred to her, and it was sending her mad.

Mad with worry over Maryam.

And tortured with longing, for all intimacy with the Ruin was lost. She couldn't rile him like she used to, couldn't stir his stubborn feelings, couldn't seek comfort in his strength. And he simply didn't care, for he never sought her out.

There was only one mitigating factor—Sir Garit was no closer to acquiring a wife. Zhila's mission was only impossible if he wedded. The Fox would not harm Maryam until then, or so her sister prayed.

But Ingram would not wait forever.

Zhila must find a solution, and soon.

YET ANOTHER OFFENSIVELY sunny morning. Yet another pointless trudge up to the château to shout veiled threats at his wife-to-be. Garit was just tightening the points of his shining armor—(yes, his mail was shining. The Company of the Ruin had little more to do than polish their harness. The blockade had dragged on for weeks now, and still Château la Roque showed no signs of opening its gates and clasping a new master to its bosom)—when an armored figure jingled up to him. It held the requisite white flag, the linen strip tied to a lance that signified a parley.

Garit frowned. He always ascended to toss his unappreciated eloquence at the château walls accompanied by such a lance bearer. His choice of bearer varied from day to day. Yesterday it had been John, stumping up the track to survey his target. Finally, the Wreck was back from Bordeaux. He had brought with him a prodigious quantity of saltpeter, and he was itching like a flea-infested hound to play with the stuff. Now John was busy playing alchemist, blending charcoal and brimstone with saltpeter in his own infernal recipe.

Garit hadn't requested a specific lance bearer today. The collection of mismatched harness before him was incognito, its visor down, yet…

"Shall we go and shout at your lady love?" it asked.

"I do not shout," he said flatly.

"Well, let us coo words of sweet persuasion at the walls of La Roque, then." He could almost see the blank helm grin up at him. "That I *would* like to hear."

"Whatever the mode of my address, I require the company of a different banner bearer."

"Why? I hold a white flag as well as any man. Or do you intend to shoot arrows at your beloved? I am better with daggers than a bow, I admit."

Garit closed his eyes briefly. She'd stayed away from him for the most part, just as he'd demanded. There had only been her nightly performances to resist, and, when the rhythm of her *daf* and the wild light in her eyes threatened to wrest control of his senses, he'd dragged himself out of the taproom and ensconced himself in his secure and lonely chamber. Simple.

"What is your purpose, dancer? You have climbed the cliffs. You did not find a way in."

Nor did you tumble off said cliffs or get peppered with arrows. Praise heaven.

The mailed shoulders lifted. "Maybe there is another way. The Wreck brews powders to shake the earth—or shatter the gates. But I think of another way, Sir Ruin. Show me these château walls."

"No." His answer was immediate and ironclad. "It is broad daylight. You cannot attempt the walls while half the castle gawks from above. They would—"

Drop rocks on you until your head is smashed. Or run you through the moment you achieve a crenelle.

He could not complete the sentence.

"I said *look*, not climb the walls for an audience, Sir Ruin."

"You won't look far with that mangled piece of ironwork on." He flicked a hand at her helm, knowing at the same time he was making excuses.

Entirely reasonable excuses.

"I'll see enough."

His tormentor wrestled her visor up. The mechanism did not move smoothly, doubtless due to the denting it had received under its previous owner, now dead. Probably dead of a good whack to the head, in fact. Just another reason its current owner should not ascend the hill.

Midnight eyes regarded him within a framework of iron. Melting, dark eyes. At least, they were having that effect on Garit's insides.

It had been so long since he'd touched her.

"The Wreck looked at the château from an engineer's point of view yesterday," the owner of the eyes said. "Let one who climbs walls rather than blowing them up see what she can see today."

It was a sensible suggestion. Garit would be foolish to refuse. But—

There was a catlike smile on her face now. It looked incongruous within the shabby helm.

"I have another purpose, too," Zhila added. "I want to see your lady love, the woman who refuses to wed you. Show me my replacement, Sir Ruin. You owe me that at least."

✦

Chapter Twenty-Eight

"*SHOW YOURSELF, MY lady.*"

To hell with it all, he'd let himself be persuaded against his better instincts to bring Zhila up the hill, and now Lady Eglantine was playing coy. Apparently his future wife was up there on the battlements, but Garit caught not the wisp of a wimple.

"I am here, Sir Garit. Say what you will."

The English accent floated down from the battlements. They were almost certainly uttered by the Lady of La Roque, but Garit chose to doubt the matter.

"I tire of talking to minions," he declared. For a week or more, he'd only had the joy of addressing Osbert, captain of the defenders of La Roque and possessed of an overly blunt tongue. "I will speak to my bride. I will see her face."

Then, when no linen-swathed face appeared at a crenelle, some devil of impatience took control of his tongue. "I offer you no violence, Lady Eglantine. Look, I will remove my helm."

It was stupidity, he knew, but this siege had dragged on quite long enough. It was time to stir things up. He yanked his protective headgear off.

Sweet relief. A breeze ran its fingers through his sweat-damp hair. The wide, wonderful view came rushing in. Specifically, Château la Roque, future home of the company.

"There," he called up in the direction of her voice. "You will not shoot me—for that would precipitate a wholesale assault by my men—and I will not shoot you, my bride-to-be."

But that devil had hold of him yet. It had more to say.

"And just to set your mind at ease," Garit went on, "my companion will likewise unhelm."

He looked at the collection of scavenged armor that was Zhila. The dented helm gazed back. If helms had eyebrows, they would have arched.

Then the iron emitted a sound that was surely a chuckle and the helm was tugged off, loosing a waterfall of dark hair.

And Garit had found *his* helm overly constricting and sweaty.

But Zhila did not look hot and bothered. The slight flush to her cheeks only rendered her face the more vivid. It seemed the audience on the parapet thought so too, for even down here Garit heard the gasps and murmurs.

A smile threatened the corners of his mouth. It would have been a smile of pride. In Zhila, his fearless minstrel woman in armor.

But she was not his, and she never would be.

He tore his gaze away and directed it at the battlements, just in time to see Eglantine appear in a crenelle, flanked by two men. One was Osbert. The other was taller, much darker. Garit didn't know him, and it didn't matter. What was important—or quite possibly imbecilic—was that Eglantine and Zhila got to stare each other in the face.

After a suitable interval for staring, Garit offered Eglantine a bow. "Thank you for your courtesy, my lady-wife-to-be. It has been weeks since I saw your face. You understand my anxiety to ensure my intended is still at home and in health."

"You think to provoke me, sir." The cool English accent wafted down. "It is unmannerly in you. It is also useless. I have not changed my mind since I saw you last. You will not starve us into submission. Leave La Roque. Find yourself another castle to occupy and another woman to bed."

Garit noted her eyes flick to Zhila on that last statement. Ah well, Garit's supposed celibacy had not inclined Eglantine's heart toward him up till now. *Well, if one strategy doesn't work, try another…*

"Summer is nearly over," he called back. "I will not subject my men to a winter without a secure roof. Yours will suit me very nicely, as will you. You may be assured I will be a respectful husband, Lady Eglantine. I will permit you to remain here in La Roque, your son's patrimony." A brief pause. "Or you may abide in England if you prefer."

Ah, that hit home. The startlement was clear on Eglantine's face. At last something he'd dredged up on the reclusive lady had made an impact.

Garit had questioned every villager he could find, although many had disappeared the moment the company appeared. Garit hadn't threatened those he'd found; he'd just politely inquired. *I wish to marry the Lady of La Roque. Pray tell me about my bride-to-be.* And then he'd offered coin and promises of protection. After all, these villagers were to be his people too.

Some of those villagers had mentioned the lady's incomprehensible dislike of France.

Garit had found a chink in her armor. Why keep a château in a land one reviled?

But Eglantine had recovered her voice, and it betrayed no chinks.

"Summer is nearly over, knight. Move on while you can. La Roque is not for you."

Zhila was shifting subtly beside him. Garit sensed she was no longer gazing directly upward, but observing the château as a whole. He spoke again to shift attention away from her examination.

"Think, Lady Eglantine. Should you spend the winter sealed up in your fortress, you may have food to eat, but will you have the fuel to cook it or to keep yourself warm? And what will you serve your meals on once you've burned your tables for firewood?"

"I thank you for your concern, sir, but I would worry more about your own men if I were you," she shot back.

A chuckle beside him. "Such sweet lovers' talk," Zhila murmured. "You are well matched, you and the lady of rock."

Garit ignored that interesting observation. It was time to lift the stakes beyond polite insults.

"Ah, my men. Indeed, that is a problem," he called back. "They grow restless, my lady. Some of them wish to try their hands at the cannon we have acquired. You have heard of cannon, have you not? Are you familiar with the damage it can do?"

This time he got a different reaction from the watchers above. The movement was minute, but something made Garit glance toward the dark man beside Eglantine. The fellow was helmeted, but his face was uncovered. It radiated tension.

Someone had heard of cannon.

But it was Eglantine who retorted. "Empty threats, knight. You do not want a damaged fortress. And I have better things to do than bandy words with you." The lady straightened. "I bid you goodbye, Sir Garit. Pray, do not come again."

And she stepped out of sight and arrow shot, behind the nearest merlon.

"You won't win your lady's heart with gunpowder."

They were wending their way back down the rocky path from the château. Zhila had to watch her feet on the loose dust and stones. She'd much prefer to examine the Ruin's face. Not that it was likely to show her much.

"I don't want her heart," he said. "I want her castle. Our marriage simply makes my holding it legitimate. So, did you see any means of entry? Any weakness in the curtain walls?"

"The curtain what?"

"The outer walls. The fortifications."

Zhila shook her head.

Of course, the Ruin was watching his feet too and completely missed the response. Not that her negation was directed at his questions.

He slid to a halt on the slippery path. "Well?"

Now he was looking at her.

Zhila halted too. Neither had bothered to replace their helms. If they were going to be shot at, those in the château would have done it by now. That was the theory.

He was regarding her impassively, but Zhila detected a hint of something else beneath that mask.

She grinned back at whatever it was. "Perhaps," she said.

"Meaning?"

"Meaning you should bring me with you next time you tramp up this hill. Or, no…" She paused, considering. "Perhaps I will make my way up alone when you come next. You can be my diversion, Ruin."

She looked around, at the slopes covered in scrubby woodland and the cliff face framing the whole. She could approach the château unobserved. The stronghold depended on its precipitous site for defense. Its owners hadn't bothered to strip the surrounds of cover for attackers. Even now, the Ruin was taking advantage of this. He'd stationed sentries by sheltering trees and boulders, their weapons and attention trained on the château day and night. No inhabitants were permitted out, on pain of perforation.

"Your diversion?" It was barely a question, his tone was so flat. "What, do you intend to breach the walls while I stand by and talk?"

"Oh, but you do it so well. Your words are a lesson in love, Sir Ruin. Troupes of minstrels should sit by and take notes."

"Such topics are best confined to the ditties they compose. True, the lady is lovely. A minstrel might well croon her praises. I do not. Instead, I offer Lady Eglantine a mutually beneficial dynastic opportunity."

Was that why he'd permitted Zhila up the cliff path, to show her that, however lovely a lady might be, Sir Garit cared not? He did not want love. He wanted a castle.

"Big words to cover emptiness, Sir Ruin," she retorted. "Whatever their meaning, will it make you happy?"

"Happiness is as flimsy as butterfly wings. I seek security, not sensation. The company needs a stronghold, the lady needs a husband and protector, I need an heir. So I ask you again—did you see a weakness in those walls?"

I see a weakness in yours, Sir Ruin. Yes, the stones are strong, as unbreakable as the bones of the earth. But what holds them together? The wind whistles through those empty gaps. I see footholds a woman may exploit.

Zhila regarded him, a half-smile upon her lips.

"Perhaps I do, Sir Ruin. Perhaps I see a way that will save the Wreck his gunpowder and you from wrecking your castle gate. But be warned—I will demand a prize in return. Are you willing to pay the price?"

Chapter Twenty-Nine

H E WAS A pretty child. He had blond hair and green-blue eyes, and he peered down at her from the battlements. He reminded Zhila a little of Maryam with his look of bright curiosity.

He reminded her even more of the Ruin.

Was this what Garit had looked like when he was six or seven? The coloring was right. The castle setting too was perfect. The Ruin had lost his home and his family at about this age, she knew. Strange that he wanted to subject this boy to a similar experience.

Yes, this small boy could well be the key.

"Who are you? You don't look like a soldier," the child said in English.

True enough. Zhila had taken care to dress as a woman for today's trip up the hill. She wore her Persian trousers with the split skirt over the top. All the better for climbing in.

She smiled at the boy and answered in his own language. Evidently, this was no French peasant lad. "I am Zhila. I'm not a soldier. I came up here because I like climbing."

The child looked skeptical. "You were here yesterday. I saw you with that man who wants to marry my mother. Are you his friend?"

It *was* him. Zhila had caught glimpses of a small blond boy clambering in a far corner of the battlements yesterday, looking shifty. Zhila knew that look. She'd worn it herself as a child whenever she was doing something dangerous that adults wouldn't approve of.

But it could have been any boy. A serving maid's bastard son, a stable boy in the making. It was not.

Zhila grinned. "Him? Sir Garit of the Ruin? No, I'm not his friend." It wasn't a lie. One wasn't friends with the man one intended to kill. "I just came for a walk with him yesterday because I wanted a look at your castle walls. And the cliff. So here I am again."

"Why?"

"I told you. I like climbing. But Sir Garit thinks I shouldn't climb, so I sneaked around here while he wasn't watching."

Ah, that worked. The small boy grinned back. "Mother doesn't like me climbing either. *She* doesn't know I'm here. She doesn't want me on the battlements. But I had to see. After all, Sir Garit is *my* enemy too."

But she didn't want to discuss Garit, so Zhila steered the subject in a different direction—she kicked off her shoes and began to climb.

The heir of Vesian la Roque had chosen his lurking place well. He was tucked into the far end of the parapet, just where the curtain wall connected with the cliff face. The location provided Zhila with a mass of rocky opportunities. But rather than scare the boy by climbing directly toward him, she began to scale the cliff face instead.

It was an easier ascent than the castle wall. The pitted limestone offered plenty of handholds and footholds, and it featured an alcove a short way up in which she could perch and continue talking to her audience.

He'd been exclaiming and chattering throughout her climb. Now he was bouncing up and down on the battlements, obviously dying to have a go at the cliff himself.

"What's your name?" she asked, just to make sure.

"Con. Lord Constantine of Vesian la Roque. That's me. Now, can you get down again? Mother says it's all very well to climb up, but climbing down is harder."

"What a wise mother." Yet not so wise to let her son out of her sight. Zhila grinned at Eglantine's only child. "But she hasn't met me. Just you watch."

First, Zhila peered down the way she'd come, taking note of useful nicks in the surface. Then she turned onto her stomach and slipped down. Her toes sought purchase, Con called out suggestions, and Zhila reversed her ascent of the cliff.

Once on flattish ground, she baited her trap some more by approaching the curtain wall not on two feet but two hands.

Just another reason to wear Persian trousers. One never knew when it was necessary to impress a boy with an extended handstand.

And it did impress.

"I can't do that," he squeaked. "Well, I can go upside down, but I fall over straight away. Can you show me how, Zhila?"

Just like that. It was ridiculously simple. Zhila was standing on two feet again, a touch lightheaded from the long handstand.

It was probably the swirl of blood to the head that did it. A cold trickle of doubt. This child wasn't much younger than Maryam. He was Eglantine's only son, the heir to this imposing mass of stone. Was Zhila doing the right thing?

Of course she was. He was the key. He was too valuable to come to any harm. Unlike Maryam.

"You can climb, can't you? Come down here and I'll show you," she called back.

To his credit, the boy hesitated. "Mother wouldn't want me to," he said. "No one's to leave La Roque. Sir Garit's men will shoot them."

"She'll never know." Zhila held up empty hands. "See? I don't have a bow, and all Garit's men are down the hill. Besides, it won't take long, and I just *know* you're a good climber."

Yes, she knew how to talk to children. Con had already inserted himself into the crenelle and had his legs dangling over the edge.

It really wasn't a difficult wall to climb. Wind and water had etched pits in the limestone. There were plenty of toeholds—supposing one had toes available to use them.

But Con did not. He'd been in such a hurry to clamber over that he still had his shoes on.

Zhila opened her mouth to call a warning. *Wait! It's so much easier to climb in bare feet.*

But it was too late. Con was dangling from the crenelle by his small hands, his booted feet scrabbling at the limestone, seeking purchase.

Finding none.

He could not haul himself back to the parapet at this point.

"Move your foot to the left! No, not that foot. Your *left* foot...to the left. A bit more. Nearly there—"

Nearly, but not enough.

One of Con's hands slipped. It flailed a moment in midair, throwing the rest of his small body off balance.

What happened next was inevitable.

Zhila watched as if disembodied, seeing herself leap forward, scrabbling over the tumble of stones at the base of the cliff to catch his fall. She saw the boy descend, twisting in a desperate attempt to catch himself even as he fell. And she felt the searing pain of letting another child down when she, Zhila, had promised they'd be safe.

Because she knew she would not make it in time.

Lord Con of La Roque hit the rocks at the base of his château with a thunk.

SIR GARIT OF the Ruin ascended the track to his château for the second time that day. John plodded just behind, employing the truce lance as a walking stick and emitting periodic grumbles.

The grumbles grew less and less frequent as they gained height, replaced by harsh breaths, amplified by the Wreck's helm.

Garit felt a fleeting sympathy. It was midafternoon on a French summer day. This was not what steel armor was designed for. It was not what the Wreck was designed for.

John was also peeved that his chance at explosive glory had been stymied. Garit grinned inside his hothouse of a helm. He had not the least sympathy for that. The current turn of events was so much better.

With just one possible drawback.

You owe me a prize, Sir Ruin.

That was what she had said when she met him in the village at midday, but she hadn't looked triumphant. Her scheme had worked, but Zhila Kurian looked tight-lipped and pale.

Nevertheless, Garit would grant Zhila her prize. She had more than earned it.

They'd reached the bare, stony patch before the walls where Garit was accustomed to stand when he wooed his bride-to-be. It was possibly foolish to present himself as a target in the same position each day, but today his bride would not rain down arrows to bounce off his breastplate.

Now, more than ever, Eglantine could not afford to kill her intended.

Garit looked up at the battlements. A multitude of faces peered down. He only sought one.

He found it and bowed slightly.

"God's greetings, Lady Eglantine. I am glad I need not summon you from the depths of your château. I come to address you, and only you."

"Speak, Sir Garit," the wimpled one called back. "Say your piece and go. The sooner you are out of my sight, the better I will be pleased."

"Perhaps you would prefer to rest your sight on this, Lady of La Roque." Garit reached for an item tucked into his belt. His gauntlets fumbled to grip the fabric.

Moments later, he held aloft a small green tunic.

Eglantine gasped. He saw it rather than heard it. Her mouth opened and all the blood fled from her face.

Garit inspected the tunic as if this were the first time he'd seen it. It was woven of fine wool and dyed a distinctive green. More distinctive still was the jagged rent in its side, and the fact that it was edged with dark stains.

"Do you recognize this item of clothing, my lady?" he called up politely. "I have its owner in my custody. I thought you would like to know."

His wife-to-be swayed. Her lips moved, but Garit heard no sound. He angled his head inquiringly.

"What do you want?" floated down from the battlements. It was barely more than a whisper.

Finally. Eglantine would give him anything he asked because he held the owner of that tunic. Triumph exploded like one of the Wreck's concoctions in his chest. Scattering debris.

Little shards of…what? Sharp-edged doubt?

He ignored them and delivered his ultimatum. "I want what I have wanted from the very beginning of our acquaintance, Lady Eglantine—your hand in marriage and the guardianship of your son and castle. Nothing has changed. As I mentioned before, I swear I will not deprive your son of his patrimony. In fact, he will become my heir."

The ultimatum did not have the desired effect.

"You swear falsely, knight," Eglantine cried. "My son cannot inherit if you have killed him."

Garit frowned. "That is unmannerly of you, lady. I do not swear falsely. Your son lives. He is well. Surrender La Roque, wed me, and he will inherit. This I swear."

He paused, holding Eglantine's gaze.

"If, on the other hand, you remain obdurate in your castle, perhaps your son's future is not so assured."

Eglantine leaned forward so abruptly that Garit feared she would throw herself off the battlements, probably with the intention of clawing his eyes out.

"No!" she shouted. "I do not believe you! I see nothing but a tunic. Your threats are empty. This is a ruse. You do not have my son."

Garit shrugged. "Perhaps I have the wrong boy, then. He said he was Constantine, Lord of La Roque—but then, boys like to boast. Be at ease. I shall tear out the little pretender's tongue so he can never blacken your name with such a charge again. Doubtless, you have your son safe within La Roque this moment."

Eglantine staggered against the dark man beside her. An inconvenient sliver of conscience pricked at Garit.

Unbidden, unwelcome, the image returned. Another small boy. The destruction of his family and home. The howling, bottomless pain of watching but being able to do nothing. One small survivor who swore to rebuild his home from the bones and gold of those who destroyed it.

He was nearly there.

And no one would die this time, not if Eglantine saw sense.

Movement above. His bride leaned into the crenelle and spoke clearly and slowly.

"You will not harm the boy. You will bring him before the walls tomorrow morning, alive and whole. Whoever he is. You will have your answer then."

She paused. Her fingers were gripping the stonework for support.

"*Swear*, Sir Garit. Swear on whatever you hold most holy that you will not harm this boy."

Garit gazed steadily up at the woman he would wed tomorrow.

"There is nothing I hold more sacred than my word, Lady of La Roque." He clapped a gauntlet to his chest. "I swear that the boy who wore this shirt will remain in as good health as when he came to me. I will bring him before the walls of La Roque tomorrow."

Garit bowed, the abused tunic still in his hand.

"Until tomorrow, my lady-wife-to-be."

Chapter Thirty

Z HILA KURIAN WAS not well adapted to sitting still at the best of times—and this was not the best of times. She *had* to remain in this room, perched on a wooden stool in a shuttered bedchamber. Staring. Even occasionally praying.

The child looked lost in the big bed. He didn't runkle the sheets with restless movement but lay as still as a corpse. Zhila had tended his wound and washed his poor, battered head. Her ministrations must have caused him pain, but still he did not wake.

Holy Mary, let this boy live.

For the hundredth time, she laid her palm on his chest, just to feel its slight rise and fall. The guard in the corner watched, but said nothing. Zhila ignored him. She'd captured the heir of La Roque, and now the Ruin didn't trust her alone with Lord Con? But he trusted her enough to tend the child's wounds.

She stared at the bindings about Con's ribs. No blood seeped through to discolor the linen. The rock-inflicted gash that had ripped his tunic and bled so copiously before the walls wasn't deep. So why didn't he wake?

Because he whacked his head on the rocks when you did not catch him in time.

The sound of skull on stone still reverberated in her ears.

She'd carried him down the hill afterward, staggering from

bush to bush while tears streaked her face and a child's blood reddened her clothes. She'd brought him to the village, to the astonishment and delight and fear of the company and its leader.

And this very moment, the Ruin was likely informing the Lady of La Roque he would swap her son for Eglantine's hand in marriage.

Assuming the child lived.

For Zhila knew wounds to the head were horribly unpredictable. One might wake afterward with merely a headache, or one might never wake at all.

She had done this. She had endangered one child to save another. Maryam's image imposed itself over Con. Maryam in pain. Maryam abused.

Zhila closed her eyes and prayed to Saint Nicolas of Myra, patron saint of children. *Please, let him live. Let her live.*

Noise on the cobbles outside jolted her from prayer. The thump-limp of the Wreck's heavy feet, the tapping of a wooden staff, and, more subtly, the clink of an armored Ruin's tread. She knew their footsteps like she knew her *daf*.

They were back.

The door to the house scraped open. A single set of footsteps approached the chamber.

And Zhila was hit by a whirlwind of emotions, a swirl of triumph, dread, and heart-freezing pain. It propelled her toward the chamber door.

To collide with a rocklike Ruin.

Two gauntlets gripped her shoulders, steadying her. "How is he?"

She stared up into ice-blue eyes and could say nothing. So she shook her head.

Sir Garit glanced toward the bed. "He hasn't woken?"

"No." She directed a meaningful glance out of the door.

"One moment." Garit strode to the bed and looked down. He did not touch the boy—his future stepson—just looked long and intently.

And then he followed her into the outer room and treated her to much the same look.

She couldn't bear it.

"Did you speak to Lady Eglantine?" she demanded. "What did she say? Is the siege over?"

"Yes…and no."

She looked at the dark-beamed ceiling and wanted to scream. Perhaps she should. Perhaps it would waken the child next door.

"She wants to see him. She doesn't believe it's him," the Ruin went on. "Are you sure this is Eglantine's son?"

"Yes! He talked of you as his enemy, as the one who wants to marry *his mother*."

"Ah, I thought she was bluffing."

"Bluffing?"

"Pretending."

Yes, that made sense. So much pretending. Zhila was sick of it.

After tonight, all pretending would be over.

"I will take him up the hill tomorrow morning. He must be awake then," Garit went on. Again, that long, intent gaze. "*Will he wake?*"

"I don't know! You set a guard on me. I haven't had a chance to smother him in his sleep, if that's what you mean."

Garit shook his head. "The guard was set to protect you both. What I mean is, you were there when it happened. How bad was the blow?"

"He'd barely started climbing. I'd told him it was easy, but I was wrong. He fell. I didn't get there in time. He landed on his side first and then he hit his head." Her voice cracked, and she covered her face with her hands.

Then his arms were around her and she was held tight against a steel-plated chest.

"You care about this boy. Why?"

"He reminds me of my sister," she whispered. "I thought I could end this siege without blood. I thought I could get you what you want, but I only bring death to those I care about."

"Death." The body against hers stilled. "He cannot die. He is to be my heir. Eglantine will never wed me if he dies."

That wasn't what she meant.

"No, I pray he won't die. His breathing is strong. The wound in his side is not serious. Why—" She paused a moment, listening.

It had to be wishful thinking, but she thought she'd caught the sound of a small voice.

The Ruin's arms dropped from around her.

"Go to him," he said.

"No! I betrayed him. He'll hate to see me."

"One sight of me, and he'll probably pass out again," the Ruin said dryly. "Not what I need. Go, Zhila."

Still she hesitated. The voice came again, unmistakable this time. A small, wavering "Where am I?"

"He's awake," she whispered.

The Ruin's face was no longer impassive. His mouth curved at the edges. "Yes, and the castle is mine. Now she *will* marry me. Tomorrow."

Zhila stared at him. A man so determined to wed a woman he felt nothing for. He was embracing the ice of a loveless, lifelong union. He was using it to fend closeness away.

Sir Garit of the Ruin didn't want to live, not *really* live and experience the full gamut of tiresome emotions. It should only make what she had to do easier.

"But before you do that, you owe me a reward, Ruin. Remember?"

"Before the castle is mine? A bit premature, don't you think?"

"Yes, before." Zhila stepped closer to her target. She gazed up into his cold face with passion and determination enough to melt all resistance. "Tonight. I will meet you in your chamber and demand my reward—then I'll leave your life forever."

Without waiting for an answer, she turned and entered the bedchamber.

THE COMPANY WAS celebrating. Even in his borrowed house at the other end of the village, Garit could hear the racket in the tavern. Oh, the men always gathered in Vesian's sole drinking establishment of an evening—those who weren't on sentry duty—but tonight they sounded more enthusiastic than usual.

"Anyone would think it was my wedding feast," he murmured, inclining his head toward the shouts and off-key singing.

"Near enough. They saw your woman come down the hill with yon child," John pointed out.

"She's not my woman."

"Hmph. I'd tell any other man he was a fool to prefer that Eglantine over our Zhila."

"Just as well I'm not any other man. You know why I'm doing this, John."

"Aye, I know what you *say* you're doing. Anyway, the lads know who the child is, and that the wee fellow's woken up, hale and hearty. Call it a pre-wedding feast. They drink in your honor, sir."

Before Garit could reply, the door from the street burst open. The woman in question entered. Indeed, she lit up the room like a scarlet flame.

"Come. Let us join them," she announced. "I must dance."

She was dressed in her deep red gown, split at the front in that strange foreign style. She held her *daf* in her hand. Her eyes glowed.

And Garit was staring.

Beside him, the Wreck chuckled. "Reckon you'd better do as the lady says, sir. You'll be a married man tomorrow. I'll stay here and mind the young lord."

Lord Con of La Roque was supposedly sleeping in the next room. The chamber was barred and its window far too small to permit the exit or entry of any human being. Nevertheless, Garit himself intended to stand guard over his precious captive, in company with his trusted engineer.

"You owe me a reward," Zhila added when Garit seemed disinclined to move.

He raised a brow. "This is your prize—I drink and watch you dance?"

Zhila laughed, a throaty chuckle. "No, Ruin. Nothing so tame. Come, your goal is in sight. The castle and the lady are yours. Revel in the moment, you lump of unfeeling stone."

The Wreck snorted and valiantly turned it into a cough. Zhila was looking a challenge at Garit—a vibrant, vivid challenge that transcended mere beauty.

She would leave him tomorrow. She must. But tonight, he would refuse her nothing. She had earned her prize, whatever it was.

Garit stood. "Consider this lump at your disposal." He glanced at the Wreck. The man was trying to swallow a grin. It was having a curious effect on his battered face. "I'll send a second man to join you, John. You'll both be relieved at midnight."

THERE WAS A strange man in the taproom. He was a rather attractive man, if Zhila were forced to consider the matter. Straight black hair, deep, dark eyes, and an air about him that would draw attention from a tree stump. But what attracted the attention of this particular minstrel woman was the instrument he held in his hand.

So Zhila sashayed right up to him. The Ruin stalked behind.

The fellow was flanked by two of the company's larger men-at-arms. They were directing hard stares at the newcomer, so Zhila reached out and trailed a slow hand over the curve of his lute. The wood was beautifully smooth beneath her fingers. This was no inferior instrument. It was almost as beautiful as its owner.

"Ah, my dreams come true, Sir Ruin," she said, never letting her gaze drift from the minstrel, for that was what he surely was. He wore the shoes, curled ridiculously at the tip—he wore the air. "I wish for music, and here is music."

"You dreamed of this fellow?" came the flat reply.

"Yes!" Zhila whirled from the newcomer and looped her hands around her blond knight's neck.

She was taking a very public chance—she had been barred from him so long. She had declared she was no whore. But he didn't push her away, so she took another chance. Just one little leap, and she had her legs wrapped about the Ruin's waist. An instant later, her fingers were sifting through his hair, and Zhila closed his mouth with her own.

Just in case he was inclined to make any objection.

Perhaps he did voice an objection, for his lips opened instantaneously. But Zhila wasn't interested in words. She dipped her tongue into his mouth instead. Garit took the point. He clamped his arms about her and kissed her back with a most satisfactory ferocity. As if every eye in the taproom were not eyeing their performance.

Maybe he had missed her too.

Through the haze of desire, she heard a roar of applause. But she didn't kiss him for them. Every man in the company knew she was the Ruin's. No one bar Jos had ever tried to touch her. No, it was the Ruin himself who had to be convinced of the matter.

And Zhila just wanted to meld her body with his, her spirit with his, and never cease.

But of course she had to.

Eventually, with reluctance, she loosed her legs and slithered down from her prominence.

"Yes," she repeated, her voice husky, her hands still on Garit. "I dream of music, and here it is. Now he will play—and I will dance."

And she did. She instructed the bemused minstrel in the sort of music he was to play, then she picked up her *daf* and gave herself up to the beat. The strange minstrel was quite good—he kept pace with the furious, impassioned rhythm of her *daf*. And then, even when she discarded the *daf* to throw herself wholly into the dance, he kept the wild pace going.

She danced as never before. There was a reckless desperation to her every movement. She expressed in movement what could never be said in words.

This is who I am, Ruin. Immodest and impetuous, sensual and wild. The opposite of your noble Lady Eglantine. I am no fit woman for you, but, by heaven, you want me.

I will make our last night one to remember.

At least, you'd remember it if you ever saw another dawn.

$$\text{\textasteriskcentered}|\text{\textasteriskcentered}$$

Chapter Thirty-One

THE *DAF* BEAT entered his blood. It was his heartbeat, pounding and insistent. She danced, a swirl of red skirts and loose, dark hair, and she was movement and beauty itself. Fire personified. Dear God, he wanted to grasp the flame, let it consume him utterly.

Which was inopportune when the dance ended abruptly and Zhila flew like a homing pigeon to land on his lap.

He stifled a gasp as she nudged up against his entirely too-well-filled braies.

Her heartbeat too was pounding. She was breathing hard and her eyes were brilliant with exertion.

She dipped her mouth to his ear and murmured, "My reward, dear Ruin. I would like it now, if you please."

Then she ran her tongue up the outer whorl of his ear. Garit nearly jumped out of his clothes—at least, one part of him tried to do so.

He retained an outwardly impassive expression by force of habit only.

"Name your price," he managed.

"Not here." Her breath feathered his skin. "In private. In your chamber."

Your wish is my command, cried his mutinous nether regions.

"I marry a wife tomorrow," his mouth countered.

She smiled, wide and wicked, down on him. "You are not married now, Sir Ruin, and I have your knightly word. I *will* have my reward." She rose and tugged at his hand. "Come."

She was right—he had given his word. And Zhila Kurian had more than earned her reward. Thanks to her, he would have a castle and a family before the next sunset.

Sir Garit followed Zhila toward the door. Naturally, this movement was greeted with a taproom full of meaningful grins and the odd cheer, but nothing disrespectful. The company had grown used to Zhila. The men treated her as one of them, Garit realized. Strange—he wouldn't have thought it possible that a woman could be anything but an endless source of discord amongst them. And such a woman, too. But maybe her very strangeness was the key. Zhila had earned their respect with her knives, her armor, and her climbing.

And they all knew she was his.

She'd as good as announced it this evening by climbing him like a maypole, and he was only confirming it now. Eglantine suspected the man who wooed her had another woman. Well, that was hardly going to put her off marrying Garit now. He had a far more persuasive argument locked up at the end of the village.

So he permitted Zhila to tow him from the taproom, and wondered what she would demand as her reward. He could only hope it accorded with his own, rather insistent inclinations.

HIS CHAMBER. THE locked room she hadn't been allowed into for weeks. Now the door was ajar before her. All Zhila had to do was nudge it open.

For absolutely no good reason, Zhila hesitated. She'd told the Ruin to go on ahead, that she had to deposit her *daf* in her quarters and splash a bit of water on her heated face before she joined him.

It was the truth, but only part of it.

Now her reward was upon her. Gooseflesh prickled her arms. True, she had splashed much of her body with icy well water but moments ago, but the shiver that coursed her went deeper than that. Soul deep. So much hung on tonight.

Not long now, little sister.

She gave the wooden barrier a shove. It creaked open reluctantly. Revealed within was a big, canopied bed, a rich rug, and a couple of chests on the floor, all softened by the amber glow of candlelight. And one Ruin, sitting on the mattress. Looking at her.

For one cowardly moment, she couldn't meet his gaze. So she turned and sealed the door. But she didn't bar it. After all, she might need a quick exit.

"Come here, Zhila."

He spoke low. His tone thrummed inside her, edging aside trepidation. Yes, she wanted this.

She turned.

"No, I give the orders tonight, Ruin. My reward, remember? You are no longer the commander. For this night only, you do as I ask."

Blond brows rose infinitesimally. "That sounds like many rewards to me. You are greedy, minstrel woman."

"Yes. I am." She stalked toward him. "I am greedy for you, knight, and I will have you in whatever way I want. For one last night."

Something flared in his eyes. His shoulders rose on a long breath, but he said nothing.

Well, let us see how the rest of you reacts, my invulnerable knight.

She sat herself astride his lap and look his face between her palms. "Well?" she demanded. "Will you keep your knightly word, Sir Garit? I leave tomorrow. I will never see you again. Call me a weak woman, but I ask for no greater reward than to do what I will with you now. Before I go."

She leaned in and put his lips to the test. They opened to hers immediately, ferociously. They took her breath away and sent heat spiraling through her. They answered *yes*.

Her knees gripped his hips. His hands twined in her hair, and his mouth moved on hers with all the passion he refused to show on his face.

Moments—decades—later, he pulled away enough to murmur, "Would you not prefer a more enduring reward, Zhila?"

"What, will you not endure long enough for me?"

"Possibly not." A smile warmed his lips, then faded. "But I speak of money. When you leave, you will be alone in the world. Money can offer you some protection."

Money would make me a whore, she might have retorted.

But she was one already, according to the Fox. Because he had made her one.

"Money does not endure. It is soon spent or stolen. It will not keep me safe. Besides, I can earn more money. Memories endure, Ruin. Give me memories."

And give me my sister back.

"I am inclined to give you want anyway, madwoman. Why not take what is offered freely and ask for more?"

She wriggled a little closer on his lap. "You think you know what I want, Ruin? No, you will not dictate to me. You are not the commander tonight. Keep your word, knight. Obey me now—tonight—within the bounds of this room."

He gave her a long, long look. Traces of thought, feeling, flickered in his eyes, but Zhila could not read them. Oh, he wanted her, but enough to do as she asked? He had no reason not to trust her, given the day's events.

So why the hesitation?

He could not possibly guess her intention.

"You have plans for me, I take it," he said eventually. He glanced toward the small bundle she had brought.

She smiled, a slow smile full of promise. "Indeed."

"Should I shout, you know my men will come running."

"You will not make that kind of shout."

A smile tweaked his so-edible lips. "I confess I am intrigued. A knight does not surrender control of his person lightly."

"But a knight must keep his word," she countered.

"Indeed. May this knight ask what your intentions are for him?"

She leaned forward and traced the contours of his mouth with her tongue tip. Slowly. He kept quite still.

She leaned back. "My intentions? Tonight is my last night with you. You protected me in Nájera; you brought me to safety in France. In return, I give you my body…and my heart. Tonight, I express my feelings to the utmost. Grant me that, Garit of the Ruin."

He stilled. "I never intended to take so much from you, Zhila."

"I know. But I must *feel*, Ruin. I must live. Death waits around every corner. Just look at what happened to my parents. I will not spend my life fearful and stilted. I will *live*…and I will love you while I can."

There. She had said it, and it didn't even feel like a lie. But what was love? A feeling that ran as strong and deep as the tide? Aching tenderness? She'd loved her parents. She loved Maryam. But those feelings were inevitable. They'd always been there.

This was different.

Something flickered in the Ruin's expression. It was quickly shut down.

"Then do what you want with me, Zhila. For one last night."

HER SMILE TOOK Garit's breath away. A blaze of delight and desire…and love? His thoughts shied away from the notion like a skittish horse.

"You agree?"

"I do."

"Then here are my rules. You do what I tell you to. You do not act. You just obey…and feel."

"And speak?"

The woman on his lap hesitated. What, did she require him to be both a statue and a mute?

"Yes, you may speak. Occasionally. Now—" A quick backward wriggle, and she stood before him. His lap was bereft. "Stand," she commanded.

Garit stood. He looked down at the woman to whom he was indebted. She was looking at his clothing, her head to one side.

Then she knelt before him, parted his doublet, and began unbuckling his belt.

Garit's breathing turned shallow. The little tugs she made on the leather transferred themselves to his skin. He gazed down on the woman before him, dark, lustrous hair curtaining her face, her minstrel's fingers coaxing his sword belt from about his hips. She demanded *this* as her reward?

She rose to drape his belt, with sword attached, over the larger chest. Then she turned in a whirl of crimson to strip off his doublet, then dip her hands beneath his tunic and run cool palms up his torso.

Garit tried to suppress the tremor. He had promised simply to obey, not act, but his body wasn't having it. Her nails dug in at his resulting half shudder, which of course only made matters worse. He choked back a groan.

It turned into a hiss when she flicked his tunic up and over his head in one practiced movement.

Of course it was practiced. She'd done this before—to him. But this time was different. He couldn't return the favor.

The shirt fluttered down to join the doublet and sword belt, and Zhila turned her attention back to him. But only her attention, unfortunately. She stood at arm's length and surveyed his bared torso for some moments. Then she padded around and presumably did the same from behind.

Garit felt like a horse led to market.

"Well, is my confirmation at fault? Are my withers withered?"

"Your what?" His prospective buyer took the front view again.

He shook his head, swallowing a smile.

"I feel examined." He paused a moment, his choice of words striking him. "See, woman, I am feeling. You have your way."

"Feeling? Ha!" She reached a hand toward him. It possessed nails. She scraped them down his torso from shoulder to navel. Slowly. Watching him like a cat does a bird.

Impossible not to react. Gooseflesh rose. Other parts of him rose too. He closed his eyes to shut the reaction down.

Soft warmth closed about his right nipple, followed by a flash of bright pain. His lids flew open.

"You bit me."

"Yes," she said, and did it again.

He saw it this time—the curtain of dark hair approach his chest, then her lips about him, and…

"*Ah!*"

His hips jolted. It seemed his left nipple was directly connected to his groin. Bite the one and the other fairly pierced his braies.

"There. Are you feeling now, Ruin?"

"Now I know how it feels when a mother suckles a teething babe," he muttered.

"Really?" She stepped in close, looped her hands around his neck, and tugged his mouth down to hers. And as she kissed him, she snaked her torso up against him. "No mother I know reacts like that to her babe."

She released his neck, ran her palms back down his chest, then slipped them both beneath his braies belt to cup the irrefutable evidence that he was no mother.

Garit clenched his fists and managed to stand quite still. She was watching his face while one hand wrapped itself about his aching length and the other stroked his balls.

She watched him with her generous mouth slightly open.

And wicked promise in her eyes.

"There's not much room in here," she told him—as if he hadn't noticed. "Shall I take them off?"

"If you're talking about my braies, then yes," he managed. "I'd prefer my body parts to remain attached."

A low chuckle. "I left you these, didn't I?" She dipped and licked his right nipple.

A shiver shook him. Then her hands were tugging his braies belt loose and easing it over the threatened body parts. She folded to her knees before him to roll braies and hose down his goosebumped legs.

They were goosebumped because she'd seen fit to blow a long, slow breath over his exposed shaft, the tip of which hovered but a finger's length from her lips.

"Sit," she commanded, and placed a palm on his abdomen to push him backward onto the bed. "I cannot get your boots off while you stand on them."

There was a concealed dagger strapped to his right calf too. He was to be a knight disarmed—but who would attack him tonight? And he *had* promised.

Garit sat. She took her time in rolling off his hose, tugging off his boots, and, yes, relieving him of the dagger. All the while she remained fully dressed, regarding him with those cat-that-got-the-cream eyes.

"Lie down."

"On the bed?"

"Unless you'd prefer the floor."

He lay down on the bed. One part of him refused to lie down, but that was well beyond his control at this point.

His tormentor leaned over him. Garit inhaled sharply, then stated the obvious. "You are still dressed."

"I am, aren't I?" Then her hands were on him, tugging his legs wider, lifting his arms up as if he were Christ on the cross.

Garit blinked. Banish the blasphemous thought. Christ was nailed to wood. He, Sir Garit of the Ruin, was to be…

…tied to it?

What?

Garit sat up abruptly. His head swam.

Zhila held a strip of linen. It was a long strip of strongly woven fabric, more than capable of doubling as a rope. She had more of them in that bundle she'd brought.

She'd planned this.

"What are you doing?"

"I did not ask you to sit up," Zhila said imperiously. "You are mine to do what I like with, remember? I do not believe you will remain still, so I must tie you. You are proving my point this moment. Lie down."

"Tie me? Naked? To my own damn bed?"

She smiled at him. "Yes. You promised to obey. Now lie down."

Chapter Thirty-Two

W OULD HE DO it? She had removed his sword, his daggers, every stitch of his clothes, and now she asked for the ultimate imposition—the loss of his knightly liberty. He would only do it if he valued his word more highly than freedom.

Or if he trusted her completely.

Maybe he needed some encouragement.

She began to unfasten her gown. It was secured by a central row of buttons. The skirts flared out about her hips and the gown ended just below the knee, although the buttons ended sooner, creating a deep split in the skirt.

Her fingers were unsteady on the fastenings. She focused on loosing button after button, unbuckling her belt too, until the outer gown hung loose upon her shoulders.

Then she looked up at him again. He still hadn't moved or spoken.

"Well? Do you keep your word, Sir Knight? You promised to obey. I will make it worth your while."

With a little wriggle of the shoulders, Zhila shrugged the gown off. She was still clad in her underdress and Persian trousers, but the linen of the underdress was quite fine.

But Sir Garit looked only at her face.

"You ask much," he said.

"I gave you much," she retorted. "A prize is worth little if it is easily attained."

Which should make the recovery of her sister worth more than a king's jewels.

Zhila bent, slipped her hands beneath the hem of her shift, and began to loosen her trousers. All the while holding that blank blue gaze.

He might be determined to keep all emotion from his face, but the rest of his body was not so cooperative. An expanse of chest rose and fell in quick, shallow breaths, a pulse fluttered at his throat, and then there was the evidence between his thighs.

The Ruin might retain an impassive stare, but Zhila saw through it. The blankness was a façade he used to protect himself, and tonight it wouldn't work.

Her trousers pooled around her ankles. She kicked them away. The blue gaze flickered.

She clambered onto the bed and knelt astride a pair of nicely muscled and definitely naked legs. She put her hands on his shoulders and smiled into his expressionless face. And pushed.

"Obey, Sir Knight. Keep your word and lie down."

She was a little surprised that he did.

He must be rewarded. Zhila sank down against the landscape of muscle and warmth that was his chest. She kissed him, passionate and deep, and he most certainly didn't resist—then, quickly, she knotted the linen strip about his wrist.

He tensed. The thighs beneath her solidified. Zhila had no complaints on that score, but she did reach for the second tie without delay.

"Take off your shift," he said.

She was half sitting on him now. She prodded him in the chest, all candlelit muscle, breath coming fast.

"You do not give me orders, knight." *Prod.* "I knew you would find it hard to obey."

Then she curled her fingers into claws and dragged them down from chest to abdomen, watching white wheals lift in their wake. Feeling the shudder beneath her.

No blood, though. Not yet.

She bent and traced one wheal with her tongue. "One sacrifice deserves another. I'll tie you, then I'll take off my shift. Yes?"

A moment's delay. Then, "Yes. I keep my word. Mind you keep yours."

SHE TIED HIM.

The linen was firm but not harsh about his wrists and ankles. The posts of the canopied bed provided her convenient mooring points. Yes, Sir Garit of the Ruin was now a boat securely moored. He gave one leg an experimental tug, then a wrist. It was a fact. The good ship Garit was not coming loose anytime soon.

She had disembarked from his thighs in order to tie his ankles. Now she stood by his bed, gazing down at him with a peculiar smile. A not-quite-Zhila smile. Usually her emotions were quite unfiltered, her smile pure and wide, but now…

Now he didn't care, for she had bent, the dark waves of her hair slipping over her shoulders as she grasped her hem. She was drawing her shift up, revealing shapely calves, thighs…

Garit ceased to think. He could do nothing but watch—and feel. He could not touch her, draw her to him, or take any cursed action. He was splayed naked on his own bed, vulnerable and craving, simply watching as his glorious torturer tossed her shift aside and moved slowly, sinuously, toward him. Quite naked.

She cocked her head to one side, surveying her captive.

"Are you comfortable?"

"No," he growled.

She laughed, low and rich, and trailed a single finger over his chest and down to his navel. "Good."

And then she proceeded to make him even less comfortable.

She placed a candle at either side of the bed, thus casting

amber light over his every exposed plane. As a side benefit, said light also bathed his beautiful minstrel in a most appealing manner. Which only added to his discomfort.

For Zhila barely touched him. Instead, she examined him from toes to the tips of his ears. Or she ran curious fingers over him, once even trailing a digit up his shaft to circumnavigate its poor, eager head.

She abandoned the appendage to sift her fingers through the curling hair at its base.

"Such pretty-colored hair," she murmured. Then she released him to run fingers through her own nether curls.

Garit had not though it possible he could harden any more.

"My hair is boring black," she said. And dipped her fingers deeper.

He saw the change in her face—her lips opening, gaze seeming to turn inward—as her fingers slipped between her legs. It brought him to the brink of delirium. Garit jerked at his bonds.

That returned her attention from whatever her fingers were up to.

"No, no." She wagged one finger at him, and then reached to run it along his lip.

The scent of her. Garit closed his eyes and groaned. Her chuckle blended with the sound.

"Woman, how long do you intend this torture to go on—the whole night? I warn you, I will break well before dawn."

Another chuckle. She dipped her finger into his mouth. "Yours is not to question, only obey."

He tasted her. His hips jolted.

"For God's sake woman, have mercy."

"Mercy?" she murmured, a shadow flitting over her face. "*He* will not have mercy."

Then she looked directly at Garit, into his eyes rather than surveying his body like an engineer his terrain.

She took her finger from his mouth and used it to caress his cheek.

"I love you, Sir Garit of the Ruin. It is not enough, I know. You will wed a wife and a castle. You will thrust this heretic foreigner away, for you care only for your ruin and your company. But tonight you have kept your word, and I love you for it. And for so many other things. And so…"

She leant over and kissed him.

Not on the mouth. On the head of his aching shaft.

The damn thing lurched. To control the unruly item, Zhila was forced to take it into her mouth. Just the tip.

Dear God in heaven.

Her words—those burning, white-hot words—fled from his consciousness.

"No more, Zhila. Finish this," he managed between clenched teeth.

She nipped him.

He yelped and bucked. The bonds held.

But at least she withdrew her teeth. Her mouth too, unfortunately.

"No orders, Ruin. No actions."

She wrapped her hand about his shaft, gripping it tight to still the beast.

It nearly had the opposite effect.

Perhaps she read it on his face—the face that could remain blank no longer. Broken by torture?

It didn't matter, for Zhila was climbing onto the bed.

THE LINEN HAD proven surprisingly strong. She didn't need to hurry. The knots would hold.

Or they had so far.

Zhila laid her palms on his chest, feeling his breaths coming sharp and shallow, the heartbeat thudding beneath.

A beat you must stop. Tonight.

She shoved the thought to one side. She straddled his spread legs just below where thigh met hip, so that, as she bent to brush her mouth over his, his shaft prodded her stomach. Rigidly insistent.

She laughed low against his lips, but the chuckle frayed around the edges. So she bit his lower lip. Soaked up the tremor that ran through him.

Then she sat up and surveyed her prize.

His eyes were no longer blue. They were stormy-dark with desire. A light sheen overlaid his golden skin, turning his form impossibly beautiful. Her nails curled into his shoulders. This beautiful man who had tried to save her.

But someone else needed saving more.

"Do you want me?" she whispered. "*Really* want me?"

"I do." A quiet, rough-edged voice.

Liar. You want a castle, not me.

She rose high on her knees. Her nails dug into muscle, broke skin. He did not flinch. She lowered herself until the rounded head of his shaft nudged between her legs. Then she held his gaze and sank down, slowly impaling herself on the rigid, rearing manhood.

Ah, the unbearable fullness. The possession. He was hers. His eyes fairly blazed up at her, concealing nothing. He was hers for the last time.

You will never be anybody else's.

She rose on her knees and sank on his shaft again, in no hurry.

He was, though. A shiver ran through him, a tiny tremor before the quake. His arms tugged at their bonds. The linen held.

"Be still, knight," she ordered him.

She scraped her nails down from his shoulders. This time the white wheals beaded blood. Her beautiful golden man marred.

He would be more marred shortly.

Her fingers reached his nipples. Zhila pinched. She rode the resulting jolt of his hips—more than rode. She sat down on him hard, then reached up to cup her own breasts.

Finger and thumb over each nipple, she rose and thrust down upon him again, simultaneously pinching her own flesh.

Zhila cried out, high and sharp.

A strangled curse beneath her. Her mount turned rigid, straining to rein himself in.

She rose and fell on him again.

"Do you want me?" she demanded.

"Yes."

"Do you love me?"

No answer.

She lifted and drove down hard.

"No, you do not," she told him. "You will not permit yourself to love anything, so you focus on a pile of rocks. *Two* piles of rocks."

His lips opened. He was about to deny the truth, so Zhila thrust again. *Do not lie to me, Ruin. Just love me in the only way you know how.*

She clenched about his thickness, then descended again. And again. Ferociously. Punishing him and herself. Loving him. Hating herself.

Until thought and emotion was blotted out in the tidal wave of tension pervading her frame, turning her vision dark, until there was only him.

She thrust down one last, furious time, and the release took her like never before. It was all tearing pain and pleasure, soul-racking convulsions. Zhila screamed. She must release this feeling somehow.

The Ruin cried out immediately after. It was a shout wrenched from a sealed dungeon of a soul. The hips beneath her juddered. They rose entirely off the bed. All the power of his bound limbs seemed to channel through this sole outlet.

Zhila found tears were streaming down her face as the shudders shook her.

Something had torn apart inside her.

This beautiful man who had submitted himself to her must

now die. No more delay.

The shudders subsided, died.

She sank down on top of him. They were still joined. She did not want to let go. She rose and fell to the heaving of his chest, the thud of his heart, as if floating on a gentle ocean.

Get up. Finish this.

✦

Chapter Thirty-Three

"Y**OU'LL HAVE TO** cut me free, Zhila."

The quiet tones sliced through her languor, a drifting dream in which Zhila Kurian could lie, draped naked, over her Ruin forevermore.

"I've pulled the bonds too tight," he went on. "You'll need to use a knife. Unless you have further plans for me in this state, that is."

She did not want to get up.

"Perhaps I do," she murmured.

"Do they require me to be tied? Zhila…" His voice turned deeper than ever. "I need to touch you."

She shifted a little on top of him, skin sliding over naked, damp skin. "Is this not touch enough?"

"What you said earlier, about…"

"About what? About you marrying a castle?" She sat up, hands on his chest, and stared down at him.

"I do not wish to marry the woman."

"And she doesn't wish to marry you," Zhila retorted.

"It will legitimize my holding La Roque."

"So you say."

"I need La Roque for my men. I must provide them a secure base, because…"

"Because?" Zhila prompted when he did not speak on.

"I will leave them for long periods to rebuild the Ruin soon."

"Rebuild…yourself?"

"It is the whole point of my being here, in France, at war," he said. "The French made war on me first. They destroyed my family while I watched. They turned my home into a ruin—*the ruin*—with their incompetent cannon. Now I have taken sufficient from them to remake what I lost. I will return to raise my home from its ashes, but I must provide my men security in my absence."

All uttered by a naked man, spread-eagled and bound upon a borrowed bed with his assassin sitting on top of him. Ironic, really.

Her knees gripped his flanks. "You don't need a castle and a wife for that. The company can look after itself. Just go home. Rebuild." She held his eyes, trying to tell him in more than words. "Cease to be the Ruin. Go now."

Why was she saying this? It would only delay the Fox's plans, and it certainly wouldn't help her sister.

"I lost my family to the French, Zhila. I was there when they died. I should have helped them, but I did not. It will not happen again. The company is my family now."

"Not this woman you will wed?"

"No. I care nothing for her. She will give me a castle and an heir. In return, I will give her protection."

Still so immovably stuck on his plan. Nothing she could do would shift him from it—not love, not lust, not even reason. Well, Zhila had a plan too.

She slipped off him. She padded to the jug of water and bowl in the corner. She soaked a washcloth in the chill liquid, then turned to her captive. Saying nothing, she lifted the cloth to her own skin. She wiped it over herself. Washing him off her, passing the rough, cold cloth over arms, breasts, and finally between her legs.

The Ruin watched her, likewise silent. There was nothing left to be said. This was the end. She just had to end it.

She picked up her clothes. Began to dress.

The man on the bed stirred at that. Certain parts of him had stirred as she had washed herself, but now he tugged at his arms and ankles.

"Cut me free."

Her fingers fumbled her buttons. "I will. Be patient, my Ruin. Not long now."

In the end, she only managed about half of the buttons. Her fingers were quivering too much. Well, so be it. She could flee like this. No more delay.

She picked up the bundle she'd brought with her. It contained just a few essentials—like strips of strong linen and her little curved blades. She reached within and brought out a dagger.

The thing felt alien in her hand. Awkward…cold.

Maryam. Think of Maryam.

Zhila padded to the bed, dagger in hand. She had followed the Fox's accursed recipe all the way to the end. Her prize was in sight. Her sister was all that mattered. Her parents would demand this of her. It was her clear duty.

She laid a hand on his chest, his beautiful golden body, this body she had just loved. Yes, loved. The ribs rose and fell. Blue eyes held hers. She lifted the dagger.

"You are nowhere near my wrists, Zhila."

His tone was quiet. Her hand was shaking.

Even if you let him live, you will never see him again. He does not want you. What does it matter if he lives or dies?

"Zhila, you are crying. Come to me. Free me." Another tug at his bonds.

Where would be faster, less painful—throat or heart? She couldn't even see him clearly now. The tears were blinding her.

Heart. He was her heart. Yes, she would slip her dagger in just below his armpit, so nicely exposed in his current splayed condition.

She bent over him. Tears spattered his bare chest. She lowered her mouth to his.

Just before she kissed him, she whispered, "Forgive me. I love you."

And aimed her dagger.

⇒⇒⇒⇐⇐⇐

OATH BE DAMNED, something was wrong. Sorrow was streaking her face like rain and her mouth was descending on his.

Garit heaved. He wrenched his arms and legs inward in one great, desperation-driven contortion. The bedposts groaned. The skin about his wrists and ankles shredded. Zhila was flung off him in the process.

She bounced right back and came at him with dagger raised. She wasn't going to cut his bonds.

He recalled her actions in Nájera, how deadly she could be with those knives.

She said she loved him, and Garit believed it.

He couldn't let her do this.

A second, even mightier heave, and a wrist bond gave up the fight. Then both of those securing his legs. He was only tethered by one strip now.

And Zhila's dagger descended, swift and sure. Just as well Garit's legs were free. He lashed out with one naked leg and knocked her arm aside.

"Put it down, Zhila. This is not going to work." The battle calmness had descended upon him—cool clarity, compartmentalized emotion.

"Don't you understand, Ruin? I *must!*"

Another stab. This one sank hilt-deep into the mattress, in the dent where Garit's naked body had just lain.

The only reason it wasn't hilt-deep in him was that he'd wrenched his final hand free and rolled just in time.

Then he rolled right off the bed and into Zhila, knocking her backward onto the floor, Garit on top. Unfortunately, he had also knocked her dagger free of its feathery bed.

Blade free, she tried to perforate him again.

Then again.

Garit sprawled inelegantly on top of her, fending off blows and attempting to grab her arms.

"Stop, Zhila. No more."

"I must!" she panted. "This is my last chance. Damn you! You were meant to die happy, not like this. Not… Ah!"

He had her. His hands about her wrists, at least. Her body still writhed beneath his like a dying snake. Her hand still clutched its curved dagger.

He shook the offending hand. "Let it go, Zhila. I have no plans to die tonight."

Her fingers did not loosen. "Get off me, you great man-beast! I can't breathe!"

"Wasn't that the essence of your plan for me? Perhaps I should return the favor," he said.

That stilled her. The dagger fell from her hand. Her breath came in gasps.

"You wouldn't."

He leaned back to look at her face, retaining his grip on her wrists and hips. "You just tried to kill me, Zhila. What else do you propose I do with you?"

Without warning, she writhed. She flicked her hips and lashed out her legs. Dear God, she was strong and supple. She nearly tossed him right off her, although there was no chance in hell he'd release her wrists.

"No more," he growled.

He stood, tugging her upright with him. Of course she then tried to emasculate him with her knee. It was a near thing. So he grabbed her bundle, tipped her onto the bed, and sat on her.

Garit remained motionless a moment, simply breathing hard and considering what a ridiculous sight he must make—a naked knight only able to restrain his lover by sitting on her. And tying her to the same bed she'd tied him to.

Which was what he must now do.

His captive was not inclined to cooperate, so, to expedite matters, he bound both her hands to one bedpost and her ankles to another. Considerately, she'd brought spare linen strips with her in that bundle. Even so, it was a cursedly tricky task to perform by means of sitting on his assassin and peering by the wavering candlelight.

Finally, it was done. A naked knight could sit back and survey his would-be killer.

"So, Zhila. What *should* I do with you?"

SHE HAD FAILED.

She should have been on her way to Bordeaux by now, fleeing through the night in a blood-red gown, but she'd given herself away. She couldn't hide her emotions like the Ruin. They'd streamed down her face and roused him from the sweet web of lust she'd woven about him.

It should have been his death shroud.

Damn her stupid feelings. Maryam was all that mattered.

Now there was only one option left.

She held his gaze and declared, "If you marry that woman up the hill, my sister will meet a fate worse than death."

Blue eyes widened, just slightly. "Your sister? I thought your sister was dead."

Ah, Garit of the Ruin understood sisters and what it meant to lose them. This was her one last, frail chance. "You failed to save your family, but my sister still lives," she told him. "The Fox has her. *Now* do you understand?"

But no, he didn't. She had fed him half-truths too long. So Zhila had to explain all. No holding back any awkward elements now.

The Ruin stared at her throughout the deluge of detail. He

only broke his gaze once to drag a tunic over his head. Perhaps he wanted a barrier between himself and the sordid reality of what she and Edmond Ingram had tried to do. To him.

"Why didn't you tell me before?" he demanded the moment she finished. "I could have helped."

"Helped?" She laughed, but there was no amusement in it. "You, help me, a heretic minstrel woman? I am less than dirt to men like you, Sir Knight. Admit it! You let me travel with you to France. I am grateful. You have no objection to my warming your bed—very well. But that is the extent of my use. Ingram is your heir. He is a knight and an Englishman. I...I am a leaf in the wind."

He stared at her, silent. Well, what did she expect—that he'd deny it? She'd just tried to kill him, for God's sake.

All the same, his lack of reaction twisted a dagger deep within her.

"You should have told me," he said again.

"I couldn't. He *has* her, Ruin. If I don't do exactly what he wants, he'll make Maryam suffer. He'll turn her into a child whore!" Zhila shut her eyes. It didn't make the vision of what that might involve go away. "He wants you dead! You mustn't marry, or he won't inherit a coin! Oh God, I have failed!"

Somewhere in the midst of her anguish, she heard the Ruin say, "Why would he do such a thing? He damns his own soul by treating a woman so. Does he hate me so much?"

"Hate. Love. *Obsesión*. There's no one word for what he feels," Zhila retorted, looking at her captor anew. Sir Garit of the Ruin, the object of Ingram's contorted desires. "Give the man his due—he's got taste."

His brows shot up. "But in Nájera, when we took you, he wanted to..."

"Yes, he'd do it *with* you if he couldn't do it to you. Some men like to watch."

A look of revulsion crossed his face. Oh yes, the Ruin was feeling now.

"Ingram saw," he murmured. "You stirred me, and he wanted that. So when I wouldn't abuse you, when I threw him out of the company for his vile suggestions, he used you to get to me." The Ruin's gaze would have frozen a man at ten paces. "He is my kin, devil damn him!"

Zhila grinned at that. Funny how when you'd lost everything, a sense of mad levity descended. "See, you still have family. You didn't love little Edmond as you should, even though he's your blood and heir."

The Ruin blasphemed under his breath. "I'll disinherit the dastard with my own sword. He's no more family than is a flea."

"And you squash fleas. Good, but—"

She was interrupted by noises below. In the supposedly empty house. The outer door rasped open, voices sounded, and then footsteps were tap-tapping on the stairs. Light, feminine footsteps.

Zhila cast a wild grin at the Ruin. "Is one woman in bed not enough for you?"

Her knight scowled and swung toward the chamber door, but before he could reach it, it was thrown open.

Chapter Thirty-Four

A VISION OF beauty swept unannounced into his bedchamber. It wore a sumptuous dress of green and gold that hugged its slender figure. The lamplight kissed the gold embroidery and set it glinting. So too, the soft light caressed the vision's long, loose hair. Soft brown waves highlighted in gold.

"What in hell is this?" Garit demanded.

He wasn't sure if he demanded it of the vision or the more mundane sight that materialized behind it—Donal, somehow managing to look simultaneously apologetic, startled, and amused.

Damn him.

Garit's answer came not from the doorway but from the bed behind him.

"That is no way to speak to your wife-to-be."

Garit shot Zhila a look. His would-be murderer was reclining on the bed, still tied, and smiling at him.

"Look at her, Garit," his assassin said. "She's put on her finery just for you, while you—" Her gaze caressed the hem of his tunic. "Well, let us say we do not want a stray breeze to toy with your shirt."

"Be silent, Zhila," Garit said, then he cast Eglantine of La Roque the slightest of bows.

He was about to address his unwelcome wife-to-be when a

noise on the street intervened. Some kind of scuffling, a stealthy shiver of metal. Garit tensed. First Eglantine and now this. Was some kind of elaborate ruse underway?

"Go, Donal." Garit jerked his chin street-ward. "See what's amiss."

Donal left.

Garit treated the remaining newcomer to a level look. "To what do I owe this pleasure, Lady Eglantine?"

For it was she. Garit barely recognized the chatelaine of La Roque. He'd never seen her without her severe, constraining wimple, or in any dress remotely flattering. This garment certainly flattered—or it would do if its occupant looked anything but at once terrified and grimly determined.

"I come to offer you my surrender, Sir Garit," she said. "I will marry you. You may use the château as your own. But on two conditions, applicable immediately."

The words came out in a hurry. She'd obviously rehearsed them—now she ejected them in one toneless rush.

But Garit was better at toneless. He demonstrated.

"And what would those conditions be?"

Eglantine shivered. Garit saw it quite plainly. He was the underdressed one, and she shivered. A claw raked over his conscience.

The lady stated her demands. "You will return my son to me, safe and whole. You will swear to keep him safe henceforth. And you will not permit the minstrel Raf to come to any harm."

Before Garit could answer, a shadow appeared in the door. It cried out, "No!"

Eglantine quivered but did not turn.

"Do you agree, Sir Garit?" she said.

Zhila laughed. "Ah, it is better than a play. I would applaud, but sadly I find my hands are tied."

"Do not harm him! Do you promise?" Eglantine cried.

The shadow stepped forward. It became a tall, dark man—the minstrel from the tavern, in fact. Only now, instead of a vielle, said minstrel held a sword. A naked, reddened sword.

"I, harm him?" Garit said. "I rather think it's the other way around, my lady."

The minstrel leaned close to Eglantine and murmured, "Con is alive. I do not know if he is unharmed, but he is alive and conscious."

"Thank you," the lady whispered.

Garit looked from one unwelcome guest to the other, and a few pertinent facts clunked into place. "This, I gather, is the minstrel Raf," he said. "My lady, do you not find it a bit rich to beg favors for your lover as a condition of marriage?"

A peal of laughter from the bed behind.

But it seemed the Lady of La Roque did not like to be laughed at.

"Seize him," Eglantine cried. "Seize the bastard!"

The minstrel fellow raised his sword and leveled it at an unarmed and nearly naked Ruin.

"Surrender, Sir Garit. Give me your bond or I will run you through."

Garit eyed him. "Run me through, minstrel, and you'll still have to deal with the rest of my men."

"And what of your woman?" Eglantine demanded. "Do you care if she is perforated?"

The vision in green and gold strode to the bed and leveled a dagger at Zhila's throat.

Garit stilled.

His dancer chuckled, a sound both macabrely inappropriate and sweeter than any vielle. "You miss your mark there, my lady—just as I did before your arrival," she said. "He'd consider it fair payment. I tried to pierce his heart just an hour past."

Fair payment. Two women wanted him dead in the space of one night. He wanted to sleep with one and marry the other.

A knight was sworn to protect women, not make them wish to murder him.

Garit stared at Eglantine's blade. It hovered but a finger's length from his dancer's lovely, exposed throat. He could not think.

A world empty of Zhila was just that—empty. A great, blank nothingness yawned inside him.

He must act. He must end this dissolution of his plans, his carefully constructed, cold and empty plans.

Then—*praise heaven for the Company of the Ruin*—his men chose that moment to reassert the world's order by bursting in.

In from the street, that was. They barged into the house at ground level—the story below. He heard their thumps and shouts. So did the man with the bloodied sword, who whirled and slammed the chamber door shut, then flung the bolt across. Not that it would hold the company back for long.

But a knight did not dally about his bedchamber, waiting for his men to rescue him. The moment the minstrel's back was turned, Garit snatched up his sword.

SHE WAS TIED up, she had a blade to her throat, and she had failed Maryam. Zhila could do nothing. Only her voice was left to her.

The dark intruder had just challenged Sir Garit to a duel.

So Zhila laughed. "Pity you'd not live to sing the tale, minstrel. Ah, it's the stuff legends are made of—the naked knight and the minstrel."

Madness. Life. This was the end of it. She would laugh in the face of death.

The blade at her throat was quivering.

The Ruin eyed it.

"Your hand is unsteady, Lady Eglantine," he said. "Pray, do not mar my assassin. You will not like the consequences."

"I'll slit her throat if you do not guarantee Raf's safety," the lovely lady snarled.

Zhila believed her.

And the door to the chamber was shuddering under repeated blows. There was shouting on the other side.

"You are honor-bound to fight me," the dark minstrel snapped at Garit. "Else you are no true knight."

Honor. Marriage. Knightly duels. The Company of the Ruin on the verge of bursting in. None of this involved or could ever involve a Persian minstrel and her sister. Zhila was superfluous to requirements. She was a passive pawn in the corner.

She yanked at her bonds, but the one who'd tied them had known what he was doing.

Said knot tier was looking at her. Unreadable blue eyes, but not expressionless. They seemed to hold a question.

Then the Ruin addressed the minstrel Raf. Slowly, as if he had all the time in the world. "You question my honor. That would be reason enough to meet you in combat. But there is no point. I have no wish to win this duel you propose. My honor is engaged elsewhere."

At which the door gave up the fight. The hinges parted company from the wood they secured. Men poured into the room.

"Stop!" Garit barked. "Put up your arms! I will have no bloodshed in my bedchamber. Christ, can none of you wait till I put my clothes on?"

What could Zhila do but laugh?

But, thank heaven, the command was obeyed. There was a prodigious quantity of naked steel in the room, and not an inch of it moved.

"An attempt has been made on my life tonight," the Ruin announced. He did not look at anyone in particular when he said it. "A fresh burden has been placed upon my honor. Our plans have changed."

A knight and his honor. Edmond Ingram's dubious honor had been affronted too. Warped honor got her into this mess. Zhila was not inclined to laugh anymore.

And a dagger still trembled at her throat.

"Leave the lady. Return her son safely, and I give my word I will pay you royally for it." The words were French-accented and emanated from the troublesome minstrel. He was standing by Eglantine now. Two lovers, cornered.

But not as cornered as she was. Or Maryam.

"I have wealth enough, minstrel," the Ruin replied. "What I need is a fortress to keep it and my men safe. I offered the lady honorable marriage. I am no thief. I do not steal castles from unprotected women."

"No, you force them to marry you instead," Eglantine said.

Sir Garit the Honorable regarded the woman he wished to wed.

"Of course. Noblewomen do not choose their husbands, my lady. If they want love, they avail themselves of, say, a handy minstrel…but discreetly, so as not to bring dishonor upon their husband."

"You want a castle? Marry me, then!" the lady cried. "Take La Roque! But you must swear that Raf goes free and unharmed. And my son…my son will inherit. You will keep him safe."

Zhila would prefer Eglantine to pay greater attention to her dagger. Its nastily sharp cutting edge juddered with each word.

The Ruin was paying attention. His gaze rested on Zhila, not on the woman who had just proposed to him.

"No," he said. "My plans have changed. Now, if you will remove your dagger from my prisoner's throat, I will see to it that your son is returned to you." He flicked a glance at a nearby man. "Dickon, fetch the boy."

Dickon departed, but Eglantine did not remove the dagger.

"What do you want?" the lady whispered.

An excellent question, Zhila might have said, but she was disinclined to move her throat, so close had the blade descended.

"I want to put my clothes on without an audience and I want an unmarred assassin—but apart from that, I want nothing from you, my lady."

"What is your intention, knight?" the minstrel man demanded. "Be plain."

Again, the Ruin ignored his visitors. His gaze rested solely on Zhila.

"My intention is to leave La Roque. Tomorrow. Or is that today? And this charming creature will accompany me. I do not believe we will return. We have business elsewhere."

THEY LEFT VESIAN la Roque before dawn.

It was entirely possible, Sir Garit of the Ruin reflected, that he had left his senses behind in that village of rock. If so, he didn't have the time to go back for them. He was in too much of a hurry to get to Bordeaux.

He cast a glance at the rider beside him. "You said Ingram has a second informant in the company. Who?"

"I told you. I don't know. I only found out Jos was Ingram's man after he grabbed me." Zhila flashed him a wide smile. "And the only other man who grabs me is you, Ruin."

His answering smile flickered…and died. He might grab her, but she had only ever slept with him because she had to. He was little better than Jos.

"I thought you might fear to reveal his identity, but now the company is behind us…"

"No, if I knew I would tell," she insisted. "Then *you* would stop him from telling the Fox anything."

Garit's gauntlets tightened on the reins. A traitor, in his tight-knit company. He had spent so long building up his small but formidable force. He had lived with them and relied upon them for years—and then he'd broken his own rules. He'd introduced a woman to the mix.

Cracks had appeared immediately.

"The Fox? You mean Ingram?"

"Yes." Zhila brushed a hand over where her hair would be, if it wasn't tucked away beneath iron. "He has hair like the fox. Eyes, too. And he is cunning and snappy, just like Reynard Fox."

"I take it you don't like foxes."

"Not when they steal my sister."

A girl horribly threatened. The thought of it clamped a fist about his gut. How, then, must Zhila feel?

"She was well when you saw her last? When was it, the night of the trap?"

"Yes."

Garit glanced sideways. Zhila did not do monosyllables. Nor could he gauge her expression. Her visor was open, but the helm still partly obscured her face. They were both riding armed and armored, for they traveled without the protection of the company.

For speed.

And because there was a traitor amongst his men.

Garit would press her no further about her sister. It would do her no good to dwell on Maryam's fate.

Instead he said: "You gave Ingram my deeds and documents. Did you think I hadn't noticed their absence in all this time?"

That startled a look out of her. "You had? You knew it was me?"

"Oddly enough, no one else had climbed into my chamber in the dark to accost my naked person."

"Yet you didn't confront me?"

"You were determined to stay, so my parchments weren't going anywhere." He shrugged. "At least, that was what I assumed. I intended to offer you silver to get them back. A parting gift from me."

One that did not suggest payment for services rendered.

She cocked her helm at him. "Will you give the Fox your silver instead?"

"No, when I find the vermin, I'll offer him honed steel and inquire where he'd like me to shove it."

She grinned at that.

"I will help," Zhila said. "In fact, I am impatient to begin. Let us stop talking and gallop."

Chapter Thirty-Five

"YOU WILL SLEEP in my chamber tonight."

"I… What?"

They had ridden all day. Zhila had seen the first rays of the sun pierce the trees from horseback, and now its last embers were glowing in the west. And the only time she'd laid her head on a pillow last night was when she was tied up. Not a restful experience.

So perhaps her ears were playing games with her scrambled brain. The Ruin slept alone. In his most recent exception to that rule, his bedmate had tried to knife him. He was unlikely to repeat the experiment.

She slithered down from her horse. The Ruin caught her before she could crumple like emptied armor to the ground.

"Yes, you must," he said. "How will I find Ingram without you?"

The words were a stab of cold reality. He had to keep her to find the Fox. She had handed Edmond Ingram all the Ruin's precious parchments. Now the Ruin wanted them back, and he knew Ingram would seek Zhila out.

Ingram would only seek Sir Garit to stick a knife in his back.

"What, you think I will run off in the dark?"

His arms still wrapped around her from behind. "No, I worry that a certain informant will catch up with us and do his master's bidding. On you."

She snaked around in his arms. Armor scraped against armor, but she had to see his face.

"Last time I shared your chamber, I tried to kill you."

Blue eyes regarded her, shadowed by his helm. "Are you inclined to try again?"

"Maybe I should. Then Ingram will give my sister back."

She didn't mean it, but she had to challenge him. She still did not know his full intentions.

"Do you think that was ever his plan, Zhila?" her target countered.

She shifted restlessly. The armor was constraining. She ached to get out of it. In fact, she just ached generally.

"I worry he will not," she said. "But what can I do?"

"Why do you think he chose you, a woman and a minstrel?"

"A lowlife foreign whore, you mean?"

He closed his eyes briefly, as if to blink away dirt.

"Do not apply such words to yourself, Zhila."

"But it is what people think, no?"

"I fear it's what Sir Edmond Ingram thinks. It's why he decided you should kill me."

"Yes, he wants a high and mighty knight toppled by the lowest of the low. He said so."

"Indeed, my cousin bears me a deep and bitter grudge. But there is more to his choice than that, Zhila. He chose you so that no suspicion would fall on him. Even if you revealed all, he thought no one would believe your story over his. He chose you because you have no one to take your side." He paused, gazing down at her. "Zhila, I do not believe he intended to set Maryam free. He will kill you instead. You are an expendable assassin."

His arms were still around her. Despite the layers of armor and padding and linen, Zhila turned to ice.

"Do you see why you must share my chamber tonight?" he said.

"Because I am expendable," she said.

Certainly, she had expended all her energy clinging to the back of a horse all day. Now an inn beckoned. Apparently it possessed a bedchamber in which she might collapse into blessed unconsciousness.

"You are not expendable to me, Zhila." The Ruin's voice was quiet. "Nor will you attempt to kill me again, for you and I will find Sir Edmond Ingram. Together." Something akin to a smile flickered over his face and was gone. "Come. Let us peel ourselves of armor and pour ourselves into bed. The same bed."

IT WAS A big bed. When Garit had climbed into it last night, he'd been careful to keep his distance from its other occupant. She had fallen asleep almost instantaneously, barely bothering to tug the coverlet up over her shift-covered shoulders. Garit had taken somewhat longer. He, after all, was used to long, hard days in the saddle—and far less used to sharing his bed at the end of it.

But he *had* slept. Even better, he was still breathing now. No perforated windpipe or ribs, and he hadn't even divested Zhila of her daggers. As for his would-be assassin, she drowsed on beside him.

Right beside him. One would be hard-pressed to insert a hand between his body and hers. Zhila Kurian had her cheek against his shoulder and a leg draped over his. Garit, perforce, had to remain quite still—and think uncomfortable thoughts.

She had never wanted to sleep with him. She'd only done it because Ingram ordered her to. Now she was only occupying his bed because Garit had decreed it.

Yet here she was, curled up against him as if that was her preferred mode of slumber. Could minstrels act a part in their sleep?

And here he was, feeling more drowsily content than he could ever remember, while the woman who'd tried to murder him lay sleeping in his arms.

Yesterday he'd thrown away a castle, a wife, and a perfectly serviceable heir. He'd been betrayed and stabbed at, and now? He felt somehow larger inside than he had in years. Strangely hopeful.

It just proved that emotions were not to be trusted. Get a good night's sleep beside a lovely woman, and suddenly the dawn's rays dyed everything rosy.

Zhila stirred beside him. Now, along with her leg, her arm was draped over him too. Her breathing altered in rhythm. Garit did not glance down at his bedmate. He had no need to. He knew she was awake.

The first thing Zhila would do when she opened her eyes was move away.

The leg over his tensed. Garit felt himself tensing too, against the inevitable.

"What Ingram made you do was unforgiveable, Zhila," he said.

Damn it. Garit realized a moment too late his words were ambiguous at best.

"*Ingram's* actions are unforgiveable, that is," he corrected himself. "Yours..."

"Mine are merely what you'd expect from a heretic minstrel?"

At least she hadn't used the word *whore*. Garit raised himself on one elbow, the better to gaze down on her.

Her hair swathed the pillow in midnight. Her mouth was soft with sleep, but her eyes were wide awake. And wary.

"He should not have done it, Zhila. He manipulated you, a woman without protection or family, in a way no true knight should ever contemplate."

Something sparked in her eyes. "True. So let us hunt him down. We will make him pay." She began to sit up, but Garit put a hand to her shoulder.

"Wait a moment. I have a question."

She paused. "Well? Speak your question, Ruin. We have a

Fox to hunt."

Ah. Now was evidently the wrong time to ask. His fierce minstrel was all set to leap out of bed and gallop toward Bordeaux.

But he had to know.

"Was it all a performance, Zhila?"

Her hand was still on his chest. She'd been using it to push herself up. Now her fingers softened. They trailed over his tunicked ribs.

"You mean was it a performance when I sit on your lap, when I kiss you, when I tie you up and sit on this?"

Her fingers had brushed significantly lower. Try as he might, Garit could not restrain his jolt of reaction. His cock did not care if it was all an act. It was happy to give a standing ovation.

"I do," he said with creditable calmness.

Zhila looked him full in the face. "I was trained to perform with the *daf*, and to dance in the Persian manner, knight. This is what my parents taught me, and I think of them every time I do so."

Christ, he'd essentially asked her if she performed as a whore upon him. Garit closed his eyes.

The hand wandered on. "I do not think of them when I touch you."

Well, thank heaven for that. Ghosts he was used to, but he didn't need them in his bed. Especially not in some kind of twisted *ménage à quatre*.

"If I had thought of them more—if I had thought of Maryam—you would be dead. You *should* be dead. But I couldn't do it, Ruin. Because it isn't a performance."

Her fingers stopped. They lay across his throat. He opened his eyes, picked her hand up, and brought it to his lips.

"I am pleased to hear that."

She gave him an impish grin. "I noticed."

"Well, then, I've asked my question. I am content. Shall we now arise and gallop Bordeaux-ward in a cloud of dust?"

"One moment. I have a question too."

But first her leg snaked over his. Her bare calf stroked his.

It wasn't a performance.

"I am at your disposal, my lady. Ask your question. If it is within my power to answer, I will do so."

With any luck, her question concerned further bare skin.

"Why do you sleep alone, Ruin?"

Hell.

Was it in his power to answer?

"I did not sleep alone last night," he said. He ran a hand over her shoulder, half proof, half distraction.

"Last night doesn't count. You just wanted to guard me. Answer the question."

"I thought you were eager to get back on the road. We waste time, Zhila."

She shook her head. "The Fox is weeks ahead of us. We will catch him in Bordeaux. Tell me."

"Does it matter? Why rake over the past?"

But even as he said the words, he knew them to be unworthy. A knight did not shy from hard truths.

Zhila knew it too. "It matters, Sir Garit of the Ruin. You would not have lain lonely for so long if it didn't. It is strange to sleep alone. It costs you much silver—"

"It saves my silver too. Perhaps I do it to keep the company valuables safe. Perhaps it keeps me safe too."

"Does it? The Fox thinks there's more to it than that. He could have put an arrow through you from afar. He did not need me in your chamber to kill you."

Her leg stroked his.

"He wanted my parchments too."

"No, Ruin. He wanted *you*, and you locked him out. He wanted to break down your stony walls. I was his lock-picker. His revenge."

It was a thought to turn him cold.

"I sleep alone as punishment," he said flatly.

Still the leg stroked.

"*And* to lock people out," she said. "Not just Ingram. All people."

Punishment and prevention. He preferred to focus on the punishment.

Zhila's hand cupped his cheek. It angled his face to hers. "Tell me why, Ruin."

So he looked at her, expressionless, and told her the truth. "I caused my family's death. My home is a ruin because of me."

Her brow crinkled as the words registered. That was all. No shock or revulsion.

"The French killed your family," she said. "The Wreck told me. *They* destroyed your home."

"Yes, but I let them in. A castle is only impregnable if no one opens the door."

"You were a boy. Your castle is in England. I do not understand. *Tell* me, Ruin."

"My castle, if one can call a pile of rubble such, lies on the south coast of England. On an inlet off a lonely promontory, not a day's sail from France. The French were unhappy about English activity in their lands, so they decided to return the favor. They conducted ship-borne raids on our coast."

He did not wish to look at her any longer. Those shining, dark eyes saw too much. But her hand still cupped his jaw.

"So the French attacked your home, yes? This is not your fault. You did not invite them."

"I opened the door."

"Why? Did they trick you?" Then her brows shot up and he read her next thought clearly before she whispered the words. "Was it like Con at La Roque?"

"No. I was nothing like Eglantine's boy. *He* meant no harm. I..."

It was Garit's turn to shake his head. He'd never spoken of this. No one had ever asked small Garit why he was outside the tumbled castle walls. They'd just assumed he'd run there during the chaos of attack. So he had never revealed his guilt.

Only the ghosts knew.

Her leg stroked his again, whisking him out of England and back to hated France.

"Tell me," she said. "What happened?"

"I was being punished," he said.

"When the French came?"

He nodded, a single, harsh jab.

"Why?"

"I had an evil temper. I had raged at Marie, my sister, that day. I don't remember what she did—or if she did anything at all. I only recall I was uncouth…unbrotherly. My father declared I lacked self-control. I had acted as a lout, an animal not fit to sleep with other human beings. So I was banished to sleep in the stables that night."

He could feel her looking at him. He did not want to consider what she was thinking. The illusion that was the knightly Sir Garit stripped bare.

So he focused on the ruined past, remembered his outrage at being sent where only servants ought to sleep, how strange it had been to lie amongst horses rather than humans, and how none of his family would ever want him in their sleeping quarters again.

"I was angry," he said. "I could not sleep. So, I rose and left the horses. I was not an animal, I told myself. I did not belong with them. So I opened the postern gate and crept out to the estuary instead."

Garit drew a long breath and looked at her. Waiting for the horror to dawn.

"I opened the postern gate," he said, "and I did not shut it. I wanted to sneak back in before anyone noticed I was gone. I could not be seen to be evading my punishment."

"What did you do out there? It was dark, was it not?"

He shrugged awkwardly. "It was nearing sunrise by the time I went out. The estuary in the mist of dawn is a magical place. Animals stir. Birds sing. I imagined myself a hunter—a noble human hunter. I imagined a hawk on my arm. I sidestepped my deserved punishment to pretend I was something I was not, and *I opened the gate.*"

Zhila simply watched him, hand still on his cheek. She said nothing. She waited for him to go on, to tear off the scab and lay bare the rot below.

"I walked by the estuary. The night faded. I began to think I should return. And as I turned back, I saw strange shapes above the mist. Masts. Even then, I did not concern myself. I did not run to slam the gate shut. It never occurred to me they were French ships. Nothing struck me as amiss until I heard the first scream."

Garit lay still, every muscle rigid. The screams returned.

Zhila shifted, and Garit recalled there was a human being lying next to him, in his bed.

"Tell me," she said.

He didn't want to. Zhila would turn her back on him, and he would be left alone with the ghosts.

As it should be. But ghosts always demand the truth.

So Garit gave it to them.

"The French attacked with the dawn. They caught everyone sleeping. My parents. My sister too. I do not know if they killed them immediately. I fear…"

He set his jaw on the unspeakable words. His teeth were in danger of breaking.

The hand on his cheek knew. It caressed.

"You could not see? You were outside. The castle walls hid all?"

"They did. But they did not hide the screams. The sound of steel. Bloody destruction. I saw nothing. I was outside—a witless worm. An arrant coward. I did not run to my family's defense. I cowered in the rushes like the animal I was. I did nothing."

"How old were you?"

"I had seen eight summers. I knew how to hold a sword."

"But I think you did not have one on you, not in the estuary. Would your family have wanted you to die with them?"

"They would wish to sleep secure in their beds."

"But you lived. They would want you to live. So live *for* them."

"I have killed for them. I have destroyed French châteaux, and I will rebuild the ruin with French loot."

"They destroyed your home?"

"It was burning when the French left. But flame alone was not enough for those demons of hell. They sowed gunpowder too. I had never heard of the stuff before, certainly never seen what it could do. I had just mustered cowardly courage enough to crawl back to my ravaged home when it happened."

Garit squeezed his eyes shut. Just as he had done then. A blinding light. A deafening roar. It had knocked him to oblivion then. He had not woken until someone was lifting him, bearing him to undeserved safety.

"They turned my home into a ruin. They killed my parents and my sister. If I had behaved with courtesy and self-control—or if I had taken my punishment as I deserved—it would never have happened."

"Or it might have done anyway, and you would have died too."

"I opened the gate!"

"And so you must punish yourself. Night after night you shut yourself away with your money chest like a guard dog. Because you killed your family and destroyed your home," she said.

He began to incline his head, but her hand caught his jaw.

"No! You lie!"

Garit stopped breathing.

"You lie to yourself," his inexorable judge went on. "You were only a boy. You acted without thought, yes, but without evil too. Children lack self-control. You know this. Control is a learned thing. You *know* the French are to blame, not you. Why did your father not set a guard on the walls of a vulnerable castle? Someone should have closed the open gate."

"I—" he began.

"No, *you* blame the French. You fight them, you loot, you destroy their homes. You have done so for a decade, and I think perhaps they have suffered enough."

Garit's brow did not know what to do—wrinkle, scowl, or shoot his eyebrows hair-ward.

It was spared the choice. Zhila had more to say.

"No, you wanted to marry Eglantine because you don't have to like her. You think she is cold. She already has a son, and you don't have to like him because he's not yours. So you will get yourself a wife and heir and castle and *you don't have to like any of them*. You do the knightly thing—you fight, you act with stonelike control, you protect women—and you lock everyone out. You punish yourself this way, yes, but you also protect yourself. Because you don't want to *feel*."

The words washed over him. She was calling him a coward, afraid of feeling.

If that were not bad enough, she had rolled out of his arms. She stood on the floor in her shift and looked at him. "I say too much. You hate me now, Sir Ruin?"

"No." Uttered in a monotone.

"Good. Show me." And she bent and pulled off her shift.

She tossed the linen aside. She placed her palms on her thighs and slid them slowly up, shaping them over the satin-smooth curves of her belly, waist, and breasts. Quite unabashed. Her gaze never left his.

"I feel," she said. "I do not act—not with you. I think you do not mind this kind of feeling so much. Do you, Ruin?"

It was just as well she didn't seem to require an answer. His thoughts were well and truly scrambled. First the confession, then the accusation, and now this.

His judge and executioner simply continued to slide her palms over her bare form, as if she'd never experienced the silk of her skin before. And Garit could watch her forever—the flit of her expressions, her musician's fingers playing the instrument of her own body.

And then he could not simply watch anymore.

Garit rose in a flurry. He stripped off his shirt and braies with military efficiency. He stepped to her and laid his palms upon her shoulders.

"You are in a hurry to get back on the road, I know," he said. "We have a Fox to catch, and we have delayed long enough. But I need not delay you much more."

She smiled up at him, brilliant as the midday sun, and closed the gap between them. His skin came alive at a hundred points of contact.

Her hands trailed down his back to close upon his buttocks. Tugging him closer.

"I am not in such a hurry as all that, Sir Ruin," Zhila said. "I do not act, but I would have you act on me. With me. *Feel*, my Ruin. And know that a true minstrel does not rush his performance."

SOME DAYS LATER, two cloaked figures entered Bordeaux by the Porte des Salinières. They rode drooping and dusty horses, and bore but modest baggage. The gatemen let them in with minimal inspection. Two ordinary travelers with no merchandise to tax.

Those two travelers found themselves an inn and, with a promptitude that belied their tiredness, immediately called upon a notary. Upon exiting the legal man's quarters, they went straight to a brothel.

A watcher would have admired their energy, for apparently one brothel was insufficient. A second one was essayed, and then a third. More may well have been entered, but by then no one was bothering to watch or wonder at the travelers' stamina.

Or so Zhila hoped.

The last brothel of the day doubled as a bathhouse. So she and her fellow traveler hired a private bath chamber and declined any optional, underdressed attendants. They had days' worth of dust to remove, and the slosh of water would conveniently cover their talk.

Zhila sagged in the wonderfully warm water. She did not want to think of the activities that were conducted in and around this very tub on a daily basis. But at least her sister had not been involved in any of them. The Ruin had offered a large amount of money for the services of a girl of Maryam's precise description, but apparently no such girl plied her wares at this house, or any of those visited earlier.

"How many whorehouses are there in this God-abandoned town?" she demanded of her bath companion.

Two naked and nicely muscled shoulders rose and fell. "It's not something I've had to concern myself with in the past."

Zhila was too tired and disheartened for smiling. She ran a wrinkling toe along his leg instead.

"You mean you always attend the same house, or do you find a woman on the street?"

He slipped an arm around her waist and drew her onto his lap. Wet skin slid against wet skin, and she settled against a wall of man, semi-submerged.

"I like to think I have more discriminating taste than that," he murmured, his arm tucked about her waist.

They sat like that, motionless in the deep tub. Zhila permitted herself to relax against her Ruin, trusting in him, though she had no idea what his real motives in Bordeaux were. Or how this would all end. Right now she could do little more than recline here. They had ridden for half the day and scoured this strange city for the other half. And they hadn't caught so much as a whiff of Maryam.

Zhila had nothing left. No energy. No hope. But at least she had a nice seat.

"Maybe he hasn't put her in a whorehouse yet," she said. "He doesn't know what happened in La Roque. He doesn't know I'm here, and his man hasn't arrived to tell him yet. But he hasn't visited your law man either. Is he even in Bordeaux?"

"Perhaps he hasn't visited the notary because he is content with my will as it stands."

"It gives him everything?"

"Yes, stupidly. I treated him ill as a child." Her seat sighed. "But he is here. He *must* be here. We need to be more obvious, Zhila. Our cloaks will not conceal us forever, and the company will join us soon. The notary was a slim chance. Ingram already has all the documents he needs. What he needs now is my death. And if you do not provide it, he will engage another. There are cutthroats aplenty in Bordeaux. Old soldiers in need of employment."

The water did not seem so warm anymore. The Ruin outlined the probability of his own death with a voice as cool and flat as the Garonne. It was true—Maryam had only ever been a pawn. Garit was the true target. The moment Ingram realized that Zhila would not do his bidding, he would have no more use for her sister.

He might not even bother to sell her. He might deem it safer to simply dispose of her.

And the Ruin? Bordeaux would bristle with potential assassins, all aiming concealed crossbows at her lover's heart.

Maryam. The Ruin. Both teetered on the brink of destruction. And the trail of the Fox had gone cold.

A great shudder shook her. She would never be warm again.

The Ruin's arms wrapped around her.

Sobs rose, shaking her frame.

"Maryam, I'm sorry. *I'm so sorry.*"

Did she speak in Persian or Spanish or English? Who was Zhila Kurian anymore? Minstrel, whore, or failed assassin? It didn't matter. Nothing mattered.

The Ruin held her tight and said, "We will lure the Fox out, sweet one. Fear not. You will see your sister again. I know what we must do."

"What?" Zhila sobbed.

"It is simple. You must kill me."

Chapter Thirty-Six

THE COMPANY HAD arrived in Bordeaux, but Garit hadn't laid eyes on them yet. John had brought word the previous evening. The men had lodged near the docks. It was as good a place for Garit to reunite with them as any.

Now he and Zhila threaded through the chaos that was the midmorning Place du Palais. Garit was visibly a knight again, a lord with money, and the hucksters of Bordeaux swarmed about him like bees to a particularly fragrant bloom. No, Garit was not interested in purchasing pies with dubious fillings, indulgence for sins, or even silk sleeves for his lovely lady.

Which made him glance at that lovely lady. She was back in her Persian garb, the V-necked gown that hugged her torso so beautifully. The concealing cloak was gone. Zhila Kurian sashayed down the street, her scarlet skirts flaring, turning heads, setting mouths a-murmuring. It was almost enough to make him smile.

As for Garit, he wore the tabard of the Ruin over a mail habergeon, and his sword hung at his hip for all to see. The pair of nondescript travelers who'd raked Bordeaux for the last two days had vanished. The Lord of the Ruin would conceal himself no more.

They walked through the Porte du Palais. The mud-brown expanse of the Garonne river stretched before them. It bore a multitude of bobbing masts. Nearly there.

He had deliberated long over this matter. There was no need to delay any longer.

So Garit opened his mouth and said the words, clear and strong.

"After today you must leave us, Zhila."

A moment of frozen silence—and then his companion whirled on him. She grabbed his arm and stalled his progress toward the docks and his company.

"What do you mean, *leave* you? Why? You do not marry your castle anymore."

He extricated his arm and stated the obvious. "That is immaterial. You, Zhila, are in the capital of English France. I have done as you asked and brought you to safety. I can do no more for you. I will have no women in the Company of the Ruin. It is time you found your own kind."

Then Garit walked on. He ignored the outraged cry behind him and instead surveyed his destination—Bordeaux's waterfront, occupying the Garonne's northern bank just outside the city walls. Small watercraft lined the pebbled water's edge. Larger ships were anchored further out. A tributary river exited Bordeaux near the gate, carving a lane of deeper water in its flow. It was spanned by a footbridge. And there were people everywhere. Garit registered sailors, wine merchants, carters, beggars—and a collection of military types, all garbed in matching tabards.

Feeling washed over him at the sight. Yes, genuine emotion. But, like the Garonne itself, it was composed of a number of elements. Amidst the pure water bobbed decaying butcher's waste and the odd turd. These men were his companions, his means of making money, his instruments of revenge against all of France. And more than one of them had plotted to kill him.

A surrogate family? Ah well, every family had its problems.

"No, you will not discard me!"

Zhila had grabbed his arm again. He'd reached the tributary

where it swirled into its great mother, the Garonne. He stared into its murky depths.

Better than looking at her.

"I thought…" she began, but whatever she thought trailed off. "Why didn't you marry Eglantine of La Roque? You said you want a castle and an heir, then you throw them away! So I thought…"

"What?" He looked up from the refuse-dotted water to eye the flotsam who'd bobbed along with him to France. "You thought I'd refused a noblewoman's hand in marriage in favor of a landless minstrel? Zhila, be reasonable. I am a knight. I have appreciated your company in bed, but there can be nothing more between us. I am about to rejoin my company, and I am reinstating its rules. Here in Bordeaux, our association must end."

Zhila dropped his arm. She stepped back. Her dark eyes were huge, her cheeks colorless.

"Why?" she demanded. "You throw Eglantine away. Now you throw me away. *Why?* Because you cannot bear to share your chamber with another human soul? Ah, you *are* a Ruin. You are a pile of unfeeling rock. I lose all my family, but still I *live*. You may be a noble English knight, but inside you are nothing. You feel nothing; you love nothing."

Her voice had risen. It had admirable carrying qualities. Garit, too, had not been overly quiet about his assertions. Porters, sailors, dockside entrepreneurs of all stamps paused for a moment's free entertainment.

She was right, he thought, as the knife of her words twisted inside him. Inside, where nothing but rocks should reside. She was right and quite wrong at the same time.

Garit reached out. He ran a finger over her cheek. Smooth skin. Vibrant warmth. It was an apology, of sorts. Words cut too much. He would simply feel.

It was at that moment, his moment of reaching, that she moved.

"You push everyone away," she cried. "Well, no more. It is

my turn."

And she shoved him. Hard.

Garit teetered. He was right at the edge of the smaller river, and the pebbles were slippery and slimed. All the same, he would have regained his balance, but Zhila wasn't having it. She raised one trousered leg and kicked him in the gut.

Garit fell.

HE TOPPLED LIKE a tree in the forest, majestically crashing to earth. Save this particular forest giant fell off solid earth and into the brown embrace of a river.

There was an almighty splash. There was another noise too, and it cracked Zhila's heart open like an egg. For it was exactly that—a crack. The sound of bone on wood. On the wooden piling of the bridge.

That had *not* been the plan.

She sprang to the water's edge. Saw spreading ripples, bobbing refuse, the darkness of the bridge—but no hint of a ruinous knight.

Zhila threw herself on hands and knees, regardless of the slime and her scarlet skirts.

"Sir Garit! Sir!"

It wasn't her voice, but she recognized it. It belonged to John the Wreck. It was soon echoed by Donal and Dickon and others she had come to know over the weeks. Then it was followed by another splash. A man in a tabard plunged into the water. He thrashed around in the stuff, an approximation of swimming. No, he was doing more than swimming—he was looking for his captain.

Zhila couldn't swim.

Nevertheless, she scrabbled to her feet. Shucked her shoes. Began to tear at her buttons…

She got no further before the arms clamped about her from behind.

"Murderer," was snarled in her ear.

Zhila froze. She could not disagree.

Men in tabards were lining the tributary's edge. Some were sprawled on their stomachs, reaching into the swirling depths. All eyes were on the water, none on her.

Zhila's captor began to drag her back, away from the water.

"No!" She struggled. "No, let me see!"

"See what? You've killed him. That's all you need to know."

Zhila *had* to see. She fought like a polecat, all teeth and claws and squirm. The Ruin was only in the water. He would breach the surface any moment now, spluttering, sopping, and *alive*. He hadn't hit his head on the way down. Even better, she would throw herself in the river and haul him out herself, and somehow learn to swim in the process.

But the unseen man kept on dragging her back. She could not see the water's edge. She could not look for nonexistent air bubbles.

The river was obscured by figures, bending, pointing, shouting, and Zhila—the instigator of it all—was detained by a man she couldn't even identify.

Then a new voice spoke. It too came from behind, but Zhila didn't need to see this speaker. She knew precisely who it was.

"Well done, whore. That wasn't so hard, was it? By the by, I applaud your choice of setting. *And* the size of your audience. Well played indeed, minstrel woman."

"Ruin!" she screamed. "Sir Garit of—"

A hand clapped over her mouth.

"Be quiet, woman. You won't raise the dead."

But he wasn't dead! No, it took much, much more than a knock on the head and a river full of dirty water to end the Ruin.

She kicked. She bit the hand that gagged her. But two men were holding on to her now, and one of them was the Fox.

"What do we do now?" Captor Number One murmured.

"We wait till we know he's dead," Ingram replied. "You'll be the hero of the day for catching their dear captain's killer. Just you hold on tight."

This was all wrong! Zhila squirmed anew. The Ruin had told her to *seem* to kill him before all his men. Then the informant would see and report to his foxy master. With luck, Ingram himself would be lingering nearby. The Fox would be lured into the open. He would be compelled to act, to seize his moment of triumph.

The bait had worked, but the plan had not. For there was no Ruin.

She had screamed for him and he had not come. No dripping man had emerged from the water.

Because he could not.

He had knocked his head as he fell, the stream swept him into the embrace of its mother, and then the great, silt-laden Garonne had closed its monstrous lips about an unconscious Ruin.

Zhila had killed him.

Chapter Thirty-Seven

"IT'S TIME. EVEN a dolphin would be dead by now. Likely the current's washed the corpse away or his men would've fished it out. Look at them, will you? It's a cursed fisherman's guild down there. Dotards. Come, bring the woman. Let's break the happy gathering up."

Thus decreed Sir Edmond Ingram. His accomplice obediently began to tow Zhila back toward the milling Company of the Ruin.

She did not make his job easy. Ingram was obliged to keep his palm across her mouth. Even so, Zhila yelled for John the Wreck, for Donal, Piers, anyone who might decipher a muffled bleat as a shout for aid.

More men stood than crouched at the water's edge now. It had been too long. There was no more hope. You could see it in the slumped shoulders, the downturned, motionless heads.

But no one turned to look at Zhila.

Until Edmond Ingram announced, good and loud, "I have her! The woman who killed your leader."

Oh, they turned at that. Every mercenary man of them.

And Zhila beheld the emotions of a company. Grief, confusion, accusation, anger. Hard to discern which were directed at her, and which at the Fox.

Then Ingram was shouting again. "Sir Garit was my kin! He

was my beloved brother in arms! We had our disagreements, but I came here to reconcile with him. Instead, I find *this*."

Ingram cast a look of infinite scorn at Zhila. Not that she paid it any heed. She was craning to see the rippling water beyond.

"You all saw her," the Fox barked on. "This foreign succubus, this devil-damned whore. She poisoned my cousin's mind against me. And why? So she could twist him to her own vile ends and then, when he wanted her no more, she killed him! You *saw* her push him in."

The water lapped restlessly at slimed boats and rotting posts. It was dotted with the discards of a large city, but the Ruin was not among them.

And Zhila knew with horrible clarity her words and actions today supported the Fox's tale.

The murmurs arising from the company—the nods and gestures—told her they too found Ingram's argument convincing.

"She killed your leader, my friends! She killed my kinsman! If she were one of the baptized, I would drag her before the city authorities this moment, but there is no point. She is a foul heathen—she cannot swear an oath to God. Legal process is not for one such as her."

Zhila was fairly sure she heard the Wreck exclaim at that. Others too, maybe. But now was not the moment for distinctions of theology. She looked like a Saracen, therefore she must be an unbeliever.

And the Fox was building to a foaming conclusion.

"As my cousin's closest kin, I demand justice! You know Sir Garit's mission in France was to wreak revenge. The French slaughtered his family. They turned his home into a ruin. But he took retribution. You all supported him in that. Now this foreign whore puts an end to his noble cause—the cause that enriched you all!"

Oh yes, prod them close to the bone. In their ever-hungry purses, no less.

On one level, Zhila applauded the Fox's craft. On a more

important level, she was still scanning the water. She had even ceased to struggle, so intent was she on the endless ripples.

Edmond Ingram's next words, however, grabbed her attention.

"Yes, I demand justice! And I will take it now. This foul whore of Babylon must die."

Sir Edmond Ingram removed his hand from Zhila's mouth. He wiped it on his thigh. Then he laid it on his sword hilt.

"False knight!" she cried. "Liar! Where is Maryam? You told me you—"

Ingram didn't bother answering. He just drew his sword. And Zhila understood—the Fox could not let her reveal his treachery.

The Ruin had been right. She was the expendable assassin. As for Maryam...

"*Stop!* Kill her and you too will die."

A tidal wave of feeling washed over Zhila at those words. It drenched her in disbelieving joy.

And, thankfully, the sword leveled at her ribs hesitated. But it did not recede.

"Saints be praised, you are alive," the sword's holder declared.

A tall figure emerged from the dock beyond the bridge. It shoved without ceremony through the mass of onlookers, and it was absolutely sodden.

"Sheathe your sword. Let the woman go!" it cried.

Ingram raised rusty brows. "She just tried to kill you, cousin. An attempt on the life of a lord by one so inferior deserves death."

The figure's eyes blazed a burning blue as he advanced. True, the effect was accentuated by his plastered-down hair and the slick of his golden skin, but the evidence was plain.

Sir Garit of the Ruin was allowing himself to feel.

And Zhila cared not that a blade hovered at her ribs. *He was alive.*

"She is in no way inferior, Fox," her knight snapped, shoving ever closer. "And she did not kill me. She did not even *try* to k—"

Garit's words ceased. His gaze flicked to hers.

The forge-bright flare of feeling in his eyes took her breath away.

Then realization dawned—his words were anything but helpful. Her noble knight could not utter the lie. Now the whole dockside was aware that she, Zhila Kurian, had attempted to end the Ruin's life. If not today, then certainly in the past.

"You take my point, cousin. I cannot have her threatening my kinsman's life." Edmond Ingram glanced down at his sword. He eyed his target. Then he adjusted his grip. "It is not murder to kill a heathen whore. It is my Christian duty."

His arm drew back.

"No!" Garit sprang forward, but he was still many paces away. "She is no heathen," he declared. "And she is certainly no whore. She is my wife."

Zhila had been about to make her last, desperate move—one final, frantic writhe—but his words immobilized her.

The Ruin wouldn't lie about her attempt on his life, but he could say that massive untruth? Ah, the strange workings of the noble mind.

"You lie!" Ingram shouted. "She is dirt. She would bring you nothing but disrepute. You would never marry a creature like that. And she just tried to kill you! That, you cannot deny."

"That?" The Ruin quirked a brow at Zhila. "That was but a love tap. A mild disagreement. A discerned need for a bath."

Zhila rolled her eyes at that. Anyone within earshot of their argument would know better.

But Ingram had passed beyond reason. "You are bewitched, cousin. You're thinking cock-first. You've swallowed too much filthy Garonne water and shaken your brains loose."

"Possibly. Nonetheless, you will speak of my wife with respect and you will unhand her. *Now*."

"No! You were to wed Eglantine of La Roque. You wanted a castle that wasn't a pile of rubble, and a ready-made heir. There's no reason on earth you'd marry this creature. You've taken all she has to offer already."

"No reason? Maybe not on earth, but in heaven..." The Ruin's gaze held hers. He moved closer. He addressed the Fox conversationally. "You really don't want me to marry, do you, cousin?" Emphasis on that last word. "Pray, tell me why."

Garit was getting too close. Ingram would feel forced to do something—anything—to remedy the situation.

"Stay back!" Sir Edmond cried. His sword hand quivered.

"Walt, let her go." The Ruin addressed the man who held her this time.

Walt was the Fox's informant? A nondescript, inoffensive man, she'd thought. The only time Zhila had truly noticed him was when the fellow rode in with news of the French in the valley. Not that any of that mattered now.

She couldn't see Walt's reaction. Her captor said nothing, and he certainly didn't release her. Zhila too stayed mute. The moment she spoke, Ingram would delay no longer. He had to silence her. Permanently. But Sir Garit was getting closer, and Ingram could *not* let her go.

He did not know that the Ruin knew everything already.

Maybe Zhila Kurian must stay silent, but she refused to remain the passive hostage any longer.

She looked down at the sword tip, horribly sharp and hovering within a hand's span of her ribs. Wavering most unsteadily. She looked up at the Ruin and tried to tell him everything with her eyes alone.

Then she summoned up every last bit of energy and wrenched herself sideways. Right at the waiting blade.

It worked.

Unfortunately.

The blade pierced cloth, skin, hit the resistance of bone, then slipped down just enough to slide between ribs and delve deep into soft innards.

Zhila felt all this because he still held her tight against him—Walt, the man who'd secured her for the Fox. She'd managed to twist just enough that Ingram's blade struck her captor's ribs rather than her own.

Yet still Walt held her. His body was shuddering, his legs were sagging, and Ingram's sword was being dragged down with the weight of the frame that encased it. Zhila remained a hostage—held by a dying man.

"No!"

Garit couldn't comprehend the horror before him.

Zhila had just thrown herself on Ingram's sword. She was falling. So was the man who held her. It was unfathomable—he didn't *want* to fathom it—so he simply acted. He charged at the trio of maniacs before him and barreled into Edmond Ingram, thus adding a fourth and greatest maniac to the mix.

Ingram pitched backward, yet somehow managed to retain his sword as he did so. The blade exited its victim with an unbearably wet sound. Garit knocked his so-called cousin into the pebbles with lung-emptying force and sprawled over him. Ingram swung the blade at him, again and again. Striking, pounding.

It was a drubbing that Garit completely ignored.

For Edmond was too close, too prone to angle his sword properly. The blade could not pierce his opponent's flesh.

Besides, Garit had his hands about Edmond's neck. Kin be damned, Garit was going to express his inexpressible pain on the Fox's windpipe.

He thumped the knave's head against the earth. Then he squeezed harder. But it was no good. The screaming pain was overwhelming him.

Zhila. His bright dancer. His burning flame. His sweet assassin had assassinated herself. And, by hell and all its demons, Ingram would pay.

"Stop! You mustn't kill him! Don't do it! Stop, Ruin!"

Hands on his shoulders, trying to haul him back, trying to loosen his iron grip about Ingram's throat…but that wasn't what stopped him.

It was the voice of a ghost.

Alive or dead, he would stop for her. He would do anything for her.

Garit let his cousin flop to the earth. The pathetic, purplish fellow was still breathing, admittedly in hoarse gasps. His sword had long since fallen from his hand. Garit grabbed it and sent it whirling away.

Then he looked around, slowly, deathly afraid of what he would see.

It was a minstrel woman garbed in red, and drenched in a darker red. He screwed his eyes shut, then opened them again. She was covered in blood, yet she was kneeling beside him.

"Don't kill him. Please! He must tell me what he's done with Maryam. But if he… If she's…" Those brilliant eyes narrowed to slits. "If anything's happened to her, I will kill him myself."

A vengeful ghost, evidently.

He reached out and touched her. Sticky with blood, but solid.

"Is my wife alive?" he croaked. Anyone would think he'd been the one throttled on hearing him.

"I don't know who you married while my back was turned, but Zhila Kurian lives and breathes."

"And bleeds too?" He frowned at the gore.

She looked down. "He wouldn't let me go. I tried. I asked him. He was the Fox's man, so I stuck the Fox's sword into him. I'm sorry, Ruin."

"Sorry?"

Garit had had enough. Enough of ghosts and traitors and blood and bloody traitorous cousins. He grabbed Zhila. He wrapped his arms about her and drew her to his still-soggy self. He had to feel with his whole body that she was alive and whole.

She wriggled and managed to twine her arms around him too. The soggy and the bloody, too happy to feel the other alive to care.

"Damn me, she killed him." John the Wreck, bending over Walt. "Neat work, little dancer. So what do we do with the other pile of horse turds, sir? Sir Idiot Ingram, I mean. Truss him up?"

Garit reluctantly raised his face from a mass of dark hair.

"Yes, but don't gag him and, for God's sake, don't break his teeth. He has information he *will* impart."

Chapter Thirty-Eight

THEY WERE DOWN at the docks for the second time that day. Only this time, Zhila was keeping different company.

"What will happen to him?" The question was spoken in English, not Persian.

Since when had her sister spoken English so well?

Since she'd kept company with English mercenaries for weeks on end. It was inevitable—now her parents were dead and her homeland just a story, Maryam's Persianness was fading away.

Zhila tossed the question back. "What do you think *should* happen to him?"

Maryam stopped walking. She regarded the men in front of her, head to one side. "He didn't hurt me, you know. Nor you. He didn't even hurt his cousin, though he really wanted to."

Zhila wrapped her arms about her little sister and hugged her tight.

Squeak. "I can't breathe!" All the same, Maryam hugged her back—almost as hard as when they'd reunited a few hours before.

Then Zhila let her breathe.

"He never took you to a…a house full of women?" she asked. "Not once?"

"No. I told you, Zhila. I stayed with the Fox and his men *all* the time. Some of his men are quite nice. When the Fox talked of leaving me somewhere, they argued with him. They wanted to keep me."

Nice. Zhila did not want to contemplate the nature of that niceness. Maybe some of the Fox's mercenary gaggle were fathers themselves. Maybe they had little sisters and notions about how children ought to be treated.

Or maybe not.

But the Ruin had had a sister too. Once.

And Maryam was whole. Nothing hideous had happened to her.

"So you *like* the Fox now?" Zhila said. "You think he's a nice man?"

Maryam giggled. "Course not. He's the Fox. I don't like nasty, bitey foxes. He snaps at everyone, but least he didn't bite me."

Zhila glanced up. There he was, the nasty, snappy animal. His hands were roped, pinned at the small of his back. His neck was very much bruised. But otherwise Sir Edmond Ingram was unharmed.

It was a condition of Maryam's safe return. A life for a life.

Yet the fox-knight had forced Zhila to choose between her sister's life and the Ruin's. He'd plotted to turn her into a whore and pay her in blood. Using Zhila to seduce and slay his cousin had probably seemed, to Ingram, the perfect poetic justice.

For Edmond Ingram had loved his cousin once, and that affection had been rejected. She did not know the how or when, but no one hated so intensely if they hadn't first been hurt. The Fox's every word and action told her so.

"What's going to happen to him?" Maryam repeated.

"He'll go away. A long, long way away."

It was a good solution, but something about the words made her achingly sad. So Zhila hugged her sister a second time. And stared toward the Ruin and his rejected cousin.

The two men were standing by one of the boats that ferried goods and people out to the larger ships. The Ruin was talking to a strange man. He was pointing to a deep-berthed seagoing vessel at anchor in the Garonne. The man nodded. Then the Ruin gestured at the bound man.

"Come!" Zhila stood and wrapped her fingers around Maryam's. She never wanted to let them go. "The Fox will go to sea. The Ruin will put him on a boat and tell its captain to take him far, far away. He will not be hurt, but we will never, ever see him again."

And Zhila turned her back on Sir Garit of the Ruin and his arranging of other people's lives and led Maryam further down the dock.

Far, far away.

She was striding with no particular purpose, her head a whirl of fragmented thoughts, when she heard it.

A most unexpected sound.

Zhila stopped and scanned her surroundings: dozens of small boats pulled up on the pebbles, wine casks by the hundred, hard-done-by donkeys, a river port crawling with activity. Loading and unloading. Men shouting.

Some of them were shouting in Persian.

"What?" Maryam spoke in English and tugged her hand, impatient.

"Come," said Zhila in Persian. "There are people I must talk to."

THE DEAL WAS done. The ship was bound for Constantinople. Its captain was accepting passengers, at a price, and the price Garit was offering was a very good one. It had to be. The captain must give oath that his unwilling passenger did not disembark until journey's end.

The Ruin passed the pouch of coin over. The bewhiskered fellow with skin tanned to old hide tipped the silver into his palm and began to sift through it.

"Weigh it, if you wish," Garit said. "It's good Spanish silver, unclipped."

"Thirty pieces of silver," Sir Edmond Ingram added helpfully.

"Yes, Judas," said Garit.

The captain stared down, confused. There were manifestly more than thirty coins in his cow-hide hand.

"No, *you* betrayed *me*, cousin," Ingram snapped. "You chose her over me, remember? You chose a minstrel leman over your nearest blood kin. You stopped for her when we should have been raking up the rewards of battle. And when I pointed this out—when I pointed out *she* was a rightful spoil of battle—you banished me. You always thought yourself too good for me, ever since we were boys. How fitting that you finally chose heretic street muck over a fellow knight and Englishman."

Garit looked at him—this kinsman he'd lived with in the months after his family died and his home was destroyed. The captain was calling for scales to weigh his not-thirty-pieces of silver, the company were keeping a respectful distance, mostly out of earshot, and Sir Edmond Ingram evidently had some last words to say.

"I treated you ill when we were children," the Ruin said quietly. "I admit it. I arrived at Ingram Manor a broken thing. My family was dead, my home destroyed. I..." He shook his head, dislodging the haunting images. "I was unmannerly. I wanted nothing to do with you or any other living being. I was wrong. I should have shown myself more grateful."

For his kinsmen had taken young Garit in, and he had repaid them with black silence and outbursts of ungovernable fury. Garit was supposed to share Edmond's chamber. His bed. Garit had refused outright. Even so, the younger Edmond had trailed after him, hopeful as a puppy. Garit had either raged at the boy or treated him with stony coldness. Until he realized anger did no one any good, and converted the whole to implacable silence.

He'd known even then he was treating Edmond unfairly. The boy had not killed his family, but Garit had a maelstrom of pain and guilt to deal with, and Edmond got in its way.

Much later, Garit had tried to make amends by taking Edmond into the company. Ingram clearly thought he should receive special treatment in its ranks as a result. He did not get it.

And now there was a war going on behind Edmond Ingram's eyes.

"You should have died," the Fox snarled at last. "I would have killed you myself, weeks ago, only it was sweeter by far to have the scum you drool after do the deed. You wanted her over me; you slavered over her, a filthy minstrel, and I knew full well she could kill. The heathen whore would fuck you and kill you and take the blame."

Ingram stepped back at the look in Garit's eyes.

"Do not call her that."

Garit would not strike a bound man, but the urge was strong. Oddly, he suspected his cousin would welcome the blow.

But Ingram had yet more venom to spit. "She only sat on your cock because I told her to, you dullard. You think she *wants* to keep company with a ruin? A man who never smiles, who locks himself away like a coward, and whose only purpose is to wreak destruction? Pah, no wonder she prefers the company of the Wreck. You should thank me for setting her on you, cousin. She would never have opened her—"

Garit found his hand was raised and Ingram was staring at it. Almost hungrily.

He lowered it. It took some doing. Thank God the captain was approaching again.

"The weight is correct, is it not?" Garit addressed the face of old leather, but he could not wait for a reply. "Then take him. See that he retains his goods and coin, and see him safe to Constantinople. I never wish to lay eyes on him again."

And Sir Garit of the Ruin strode away from his nearest and undearest kinsman before he knocked out a Fox's teeth.

WHEN GARIT FOUND Zhila some way down the beach, she was speaking a strange language. A man with a silver-flecked black beard and eyes nearly as large and dark as Zhila's was listening intently. Worse, he seemed to comprehend every word she said.

Then the fellow smiled at Zhila and her little sister, and the grin was as warm as a southern breeze. It made Garit's jaw ache.

For Zhila was smiling back.

A moment later, she noticed him.

"Ruin!" She whirled around and seized his hand. She treated him to one of her smiles too.

His lips were in the act of mirroring hers when it struck him—only yesterday she would have done far more than take his hand. Garit himself had just held the captain's hand to seal their bargain. Was that what he was to her now—an amicable agreement?

The infant smile died.

A faint frown crossed her brow. It fled before renewed joy. "Ruin, this is Captain Behnam Toma. He is part owner of that ship." She indicated an odd-looking vessel out in the Garonne. "And he is Persian—a Persian Christian, just like us!"

Garit tried not to scowl as he clasped the fellow's proffered hand.

"I thank you for protecting my countrywomen in their hour of need, Sir Knight," Behnam said in heavily accented English. "God knows, it is more than most of your kind would do."

It wasn't usually so hard to retain an impassive expression. Evidently Zhila was a bad influence.

"The lady entertained us well," Garit responded, and then hurried to add, "With her dancing and her *daf*, that is." In case the good captain jumped to unnecessarily correct conclusions.

"Captain Behnam knew our father," Zhila went on. "He is an exile from our homeland, just like us. Most of his crew is too. Ah, you don't know how wonderful it is to hear so many people speak my language!"

"Aye, we Nestorians must look after each other," the captain added. "We're unwelcome in our homeland; we're treated with suspicion abroad. I mourn the fate of Kurian and his wife, but, sad to say, I am not surprised." Then he paused and gave Garit a look most direct and weighty. "Which is why I offer to stand as guardian to these two girls in Kurian's place. It is only right they dwell with my wife and children in Marseille amongst a community of their kind."

A curious immobility spread through Garit. It clamped about his innards, his heart.

This was better, far better than he could have hoped for. He'd promised to take Zhila to Bordeaux and help her find her own people. He'd supposed those people would be minstrels, but here were her countrymen, fellow Christians from the east.

And Zhila sounded overjoyed.

Although, admittedly, she'd made a startled huff at Behnam's latest statement.

Garit steeled himself…

…and looked at her.

Praise heaven for the transparency with which feelings flitted over his dancer's lovely face. It registered surprise, joy, gratitude—and hesitation.

This offer was news to Zhila, and she wasn't immediately grasping it with both hands. Just the one hand for the moment.

But she *should* grasp it with both hands. If the captain was all he claimed to be, that was. After all, Garit had only just got rid of one false fellow countryman. He wasn't about to deliver his dancer into the paws of another.

But how to dredge the truth of this man's offer? Perhaps Behnam Toma simply hoped to acquire two women to slave in his household and dance to his every depraved bidding. Many Eastern lands practiced slavery.

"Zhila, are you sure?" Garit flicked a look at the captain,

hoping she'd read his meaning. "Is he…?"

"Behnam Toma is a good man. My father spoke highly of him," she said immediately.

Ah, that was excellent, was it not? Garit had to admit he discerned honesty in the man's look. But it was not enough. He would check further. Aye, he would interrogate every single merchant and sailor who knew this Behnam.

And if the captain passed the test?

Truly, it was the perfect solution for his minstrel problem. Bordeaux had outdone itself.

Zhila was standing before him, the breeze toying with her hair, eyes dark and sensual as midnight gazing up at him.

Beautiful…and infinitely precious.

A crack in the rock of his heart.

But Behnam would look out for her. He would be the father she had lost. His fellow exiles would be the family and home that had been torn from her.

"I am pleased to hear it," Garit lied.

Yes, Sir Garit of the Ruin lied.

Falsehood ill-befitted a knight. Only a coward hid behind lies.

"I would be more pleased," he forced himself to add, "if you would stay with me."

It was the truth, and possibly the hardest thing he'd ever had to say.

Or tried to say. For the Persian captain was frowning at him. Maryam was peering from one person to the other. As for Zhila, all sorts of expressions jostled for room on her face.

And it struck Garit that he had but half explained what was to him so suddenly, blindingly clear.

"Stay with me," he said. Then he shook his head. What was he saying? "No, you have found your people—countrymen, fellow believers, fellow exiles. I cannot ask this of you."

A moment of silence, then Garit stumbled on.

"But the offer is there, nonetheless. There is a place for you in the company, Zhila. And for Maryam, too, should she wish it."

He raised his hands, then let them drop again by his sides. The words were still not right. He knew what he wanted to say, but somehow it would not shape itself into sounds.

And Zhila still hadn't said anything.

STAY WITH HIM?

Yes! Oh, a hundred thousand times yes!

And no.

Maryam, growing up amid a rough company of men? Forever at war, forever in danger? Had she done everything she could to wrest her sister from the Fox, only to dump her in a situation no better?

What Behnam Toma offered was far preferable.

But there was something naked about the Ruin's eyes. No ice, no stone.

Sir Garit spoke again.

"No," he said. "Not with the company. The Company of the Ruin shall be no more. At least, I will no longer lead it. I realized this in La Roque, Zhila. I realized I was striving to acquire a castle and a family I had not created and did not truly want either. They would be but a tottering façade to hide crumbled walls. I see it now. I must rebuild my own home, *my* ruin. In England."

"Ah. That is why you threw Eglantine away," Zhila said.

Their argument on the dock that morning came back to her. They had needed a public disagreement. Zhila must have a reason to push Garit into the water. But the words that had been uttered…

They contained too much truth.

They had stripped her hopes bare in the process, revealing them for the baseless folly they were. Of course Garit's refusal of Eglantine, her lovely castle, and her sweet son had nothing to do with a minstrel woman of murderous disposition.

And now the Ruin was asking her to stay with him. Why? What did it mean?

"I must rebuild my ruin," he repeated softly. "I do not need a false wife in order to do so. I need you." He was gazing at her, blue eyes vulnerable. "But you must choose. If you choose your own people, I will understand."

The dock disappeared. The captain… What captain? Zhila's hands rested upon a knight's broad shoulders. She sprang. Her legs wrapped about her Ruin's waist, her arms circled his neck, and her mouth descended on his.

An instant of shock, then he surrendered with alacrity. No fortification had ever crumbled so fast.

She kissed him more deeply and openly than ever before, mouth on mouth, heart to heart. Feeling nothing but the Ruin's strength, his warmth, his arms buoying her up, and an all-encompassing rightness.

She would float to heaven. She would combust like the phoenix. His lips were exactly the right combination of hard and soft, ferocious need and aching sweetness.

"Zhila!" A small fist connected with her rump. Then another. "Zhila, stop! Stop now!"

Oh.

Zhila's legs unwrapped and would have descended, save the Ruin's arms were holding her in place.

"Get down!" Maryam ordered her.

A whole company could not censor Zhila's actions, nor a Persian captain, but one small sister just might.

The Ruin permitted her feet to slide to earth, but he still held her.

She gazed up into a face that was anything but ruinous. Sky blue eyes, a future without a cloud.

"Well?" he said.

"Yes!" she declared. "Yes, I will be your leman! I will be your own personal minstrel. I will dance in your bed every night."

The world took a collective gasp.

Zhila frowned. The good captain's inhalation she could understand. Her sister, too, was naturally scandalized. But the Ruin?

"No, you damn well won't," he growled. "You are my wife. Did you not hear me say so earlier?"

"Pah! That was only for the Fox. You only said that because his sword was at my ribs. I understand, Ruin. I am not noble. I am Persian, poor, and very strange besides. English lords do not marry Zhilas."

"Nevertheless," he said. "That is my offer."

Zhila regarded him, trying to pierce the riddle. His arms held her close. His gaze was steady, but not as a rock.

"A knight must keep his oath?" she hazarded. "You said it before everyone, so you must keep it?"

He smiled and shook his head.

"You say it to make Behnam Toma feel better. And Maryam too?"

Still he shook his head.

"Well?"

"I say it because you are my keystone, Zhila. My foundation. You are the queen of my castle, not a lowly minstrel. And because my love for you will never, ever crumble."

Zhila blinked. Words deserted her. The Ruin had stolen them. Sir Garit of the Ruin, her big blond English rock, did not say such things.

"Well?" he echoed. The edge of his thumb traced over her word-bereft lips. "You teach me how to live, Zhila. You set my world alight. You are the sun in my sky, my burning brand at night. But you must choose what is best for you—and your sister."

Zhila flung a wild glance around.

"Maryam?"

Her sister grinned an impish, eight-year-old grin. "Of course, silly. I go where you go. But only if you promise not to kiss him in front of me. Well, only sometimes. Yes! Let us go to England!"

About the Author

Cara Hogarth writes historical romances set in a medieval past full of castles, knights, and damsels who definitely don't need rescuing. Her stories sparkle with passion, adventure, and a touch of humour. Cara studied medieval history at university before realising she much preferred writing fiction to research papers. Now she puts her historical training to good use by underpinning her romances with plenty of research. Her stories are usually set in fourteenth-century England and France.

Cara was born in Salisbury, England. She grew up on a sheep farm, but has since worked as a cake cook, in a fun fair, in a library, and as an academic tutor and editor. She now lives in the wilds of Western Australia with a book-eating ragdoll cat.

Website: www.carahogarth.net
email: cara@carahogarth.net
Facebook: facebook.com/carahogarth